Nightmare Scare

Blue Moon Sacramento

Alex Gates, Steve Higgs

Contents

It's Only a Dream. Monday, October 31st. 2311hrs.

It's Only a Dream. Six months ago...

... comes off the ocean, carrying cold and wet. It breathes over the side of your face, cutting through your clothes, chilling you to the bone. You glance at the shoreline and see the whitecaps breaking. The pale moon reflects off the dark water. You walk in the cool sand...

Alone.

Heather froze. The tide rushed cold and wet over her feet. It drew away, leaving her shivering.

She couldn't remember how she had arrived on the beach.

Glancing over her shoulder, Heather peered back at the endless stretch of sand. To her right roared the unending ocean. To her left stood a thick, dark forest.

Heather remembered taking Halloween shots with Johnny, Chris, and Nick. Nothing after that moment.

She and Johnny had dressed in a slutty couple's costume—corpse bride and corpse groom, in honor of their recent engagement. They had planned the idea for months, ordering their costumes early, hiring a semi-professional make-up artist to apply the artificial wounds.

Now, alone on the cold, windy beach, Heather wore an oversized shirt bearing the cartoonish stamp of SpongeBob and Patrick. Not one of Johnny's shirts, though... nor one of Nick's. Yet, it appeared oddly familiar.

Heather's mind jumped back to the tequila shots, forcing herself to remember the line from A to B. How had she arrived on the beach from the party?

Chris, short for Christina, and her boyfriend, Nick, had also coordinated their costumes for the party—G.I. Joe and G.I. Jane. Slutty, of course.

Johnny and Nick had the lean, hard bodies of twenty-year-old men. Heather and Chris, well, they also enjoyed showing off their youthful accessories.

Shots of tequila with her attractive, half-naked best friends.

What had happened after that, though? How had Heather arrived at the beach, alone?

She hugged herself tighter, cold from the moisture in the frigid air. The Santa Cruz beaches, especially in fall, shared little temperature-related commonalities with the San Diego beaches.

Heather glanced behind her once more. No lights shined in the distance. No fires flickered in the darkness. Nothing revealed to her why she wasn't with her fiancé or friends. Still, before she had stopped walking, Heather had come from that direction. She debated turning around and walking back, though she did not know where she had come from or where she walked toward. Heading back might lead her to her friends, though.

Maybe she had wandered off from the party... which had occurred a mile from the beach. Had that last shot erased her memory? Had they moved to another party on the sandy shore? Had Heather snuck away? Why sneak away, though? To urinate, possibly, or because she and Johnny had one of their patented blowout arguments, and she required fresh air far away from him. Maybe. But Chris would have chased her.

If not Chris, Nick would have slipped away from the group and raced after her.

"Forget it," Heather said, exhausted of running through the scenarios.

If she couldn't remember what had happened, she would walk back to the party and act pouty until Johnny confessed to something and apologized for it. No more walking aimlessly down the beach, though.

Heather would return to the party.

As she strolled back in the direction she had come from, she shivered. Her breath plumed before her—a phenomenon she hadn't ever noticed before on the beach. In fact, now that she could see her breath, Heather realized she couldn't remember ever feeling so cold on the beach. The sand was like walking through icy snow. The wind slashed across her body like frozen steel. Stranger still, the sounds of the night had faded into a deathly, arctic silence. The waves no longer smashed against the shore, and the ocean didn't churn and roar.

Heather, nervous before but now growing fearful, shifted her eyes to the sea. It sat still as bath water, frozen as a winter tundra. The sand no longer felt like snow, but it had turned into snow. A marine layer of fog shrouded the dark water, pitching the night into a deeper silence—like the silence of isolation on an icy wasteland with no one or nothing around. Silence so palpable, it nearly takes on a life of its own. Snow like dandruff flaked from the fog, covering the sand and Heather's body.

Heather noticed something else. From the marine layer, appearing like a demon from the smoking gates of Hell, stepped a dark figure. It stood a little over six-feet tall, broad in the shoulders. The figure dragged a sledgehammer, allowing the head to sink into the slushy water.

"Johnny?" Heather asked, barely forming sound from her lips. "Is that you?"

In response, the silhouette sang along with a ragtime tune she hadn't heard until that moment. Where did the music originate from? It seemed to play from all around her, as if Heaven boomed the song.

The figure in the fog stepped closer, half-singing along, half-speaking the lyrics. "I had a dream last night, that filled me full of fright. I dreamed I was with the Devil below, in his great big fiery hall, where the Devil was giving a Ball. I checked my coat and hat, and started gazing at the merry crowd that came to witness the show." The figure's voice could easily be mistaken for the Devil's own. "And I must confess to you, Heather, there were three there you knew."

Heather backed away, her heels digging too deep into the snowy sand. She tripped, falling hard on her rump. The ground opened beneath her, pulled her downward like quicksand—except it was frigid. So cold it burned her skin. Her hands went numb. Her teeth clattered. She scrambled backward like a retreating crab, turning to her hands and knees, struggling to her feet. Once righted and standing, she sprinted, opting not to continue forward or head back to the party, but escape the wide-open beach and lose herself in the crowded forest.

As she blindly ran, the song played around her, as if from a surround sound system placed amongst the trees.

"I saw the cute Ms. Christina, so pretty and fat, dressed in a beautiful soldier's hat. Nick, the Leader man, who led the band last Fall, he played the music at the Devil's Ball, in the Devil's Hall..."

Heather flew through the trees with reckless abandon. The icy expanse had melted away, shifting into a steaming volcanic landscape. Her bare feet caught on a jutting root or a half-buried stone. She launched forward, arcing through the air, landing hard on her shoulder. Something snapped. A brilliance of pain shot through her right arm. A flurry of stars burned bright pink behind her eyes. She rolled over onto her back and stared through the trees, panting and sobbing.

Standing five yards away, dragging the long sledgehammer behind it, the figure glided toward her, moving as if hovering over the ground. It stepped into the clearing, and the moonlight revealed a face covered in bloody bandages.

The figure spoke, its voice deep and guttural. "I caught a glimpse of my Heather dancing with the Devil. Oh the little Devil, dancing at the Devil's Ball."

"Please." Heather surrendered in her retreat. "Please don't hurt me. Please."

The Devil reached across his body, taking the sledgehammer in both hands and raising it high above its head. The figure chortled—a single hiccupping laugh.

It brought the sledgehammer down on Heather.

A fraction of a second before impact, she gasped, bolting upright in her bed.

Heather breathed quickly and shallowly, nearly hyperventilating. Cold sweat drenched her naked body, and black mascara tears streaked down her corpse-painted face.

Darkness surrounded her, but familiar darkness. The darkness of her room from within her apartment. The bathroom light slipped through the bottom space of the bathroom door across the hallway, and the shower sounded.

Heather's breathing steadied after a handful of seconds. Her heartbeat slowed. She peeled the blankets off her overheated body and creeped out of her bedroom, opening the bathroom door.

Johnny stood naked in the stall, his head pressed against the tile wall. Steam misted over the glass door, fogging up the mirror. Heather, already naked, opened the shower and stepped inside with her fiancé.

"Do you mind?" she asked, hugging him from behind.

"No."

"You okay?"

"A bad dream."

"Me, too," she said.

Johnny turned and held Heather, pulling her tighter to him.

The scalding water reddened her skin, but she didn't mind the heat. The chill from the beach had settled into her bones, and it had remained even after waking.

Bleeding Through. Monday, April 23rd. 0722hrs.

One week ago...

Veins roped along Nick's neck and arms. He screamed, forcing himself through the pain and fatigue to finish his hundredth push-up in less than five minutes. Even on his last one, he refused to allow gravity and exhaustion to defeat him.

When he completed his set, Nick didn't collapse face-first and lay on the ground. He hopped to his feet in a graceful, athletic movement, reached to the kitchen counter, and grabbed his energy drink. Grimacing, he polished off the foul-tasting beverage—at least he considered it foul.

Nick had spent most of his life practicing healthy habits, a curse practiced by pushing away from his slovenly parents. They only cared for immediate pleasure, living second by second off emotions. They consumed energy drinks and soda like water, and the habit had warped their bodies into something obese and amoebic.

Nick ambled to the refrigerator and grabbed a couple of eggs for his breakfast. Unlike the garbage thrown together to concoct energy drinks, at least healthy food provided a natural burst of energy. Eggs, fruit, bacon. Real ingredients. Real nutrition.

In Nick's head, that's where the diet-fads went wrong. They preached this trend or that trend—no carbohydrates, no fat, no sugar, no this, no that. Their forbiddance always missed the mark. Real, natural, authentic food in moderation and an active lifestyle worked better than any dieting fad.

It had always worked for him... at least until it hadn't. Out of desperation, Nick required energy in any form he could gain it.

Over the past week, he had slept eight fragmented hours—twenty minutes here, thirty minutes there.

He, Christina, Heather, and Johnny had concocted a terrible and desperate plan. They agreed to set their alarms fifteen minutes apart, every single hour.

When Nick's alarm sounded, he had to call Christina and check on her, wake her up if needed. Fifteen minutes later, when Christina's alarm sounded, she called Heather, and Heather called Johnny fifteen minutes after that, who called Nick next. They hoped to keep each other awake around the clock. They had done so for three straight days, never allowing for any single person to sleep over forty-five minutes straight.

Johnny and Heather lived together, so they looked out for each other easily enough.

Chris and Nick hadn't taken their relationship to that level, though. Despite their shared nightmares, they were only that—nightmares. Fantasy. Imaginary.

Chris came from an old school, evangelical family. No sex before marriage, though she and Nick had broken that rule a few hundred times over the past few months. However, that was easy to sneak or lie about to Mom and Pop. Moving in with someone, well, that proved more difficult to hide. Chris's parents had her trained, too. She wouldn't even stay the night at Nick's place.

"You're twenty-two," Nick had said to her one night as she pulled on her pants, getting ready to head back to her parents' house.

"They're paying for my college degree. No loans when I graduate. No debt." That's the ground she always stood on—mutual respect. "They don't want me staying over here. Nick, they don't even want me here. You're a convicted felon out on parole. You think they like their baby girl dating a criminal?"

Nick hated that word. Criminal. He wasn't a criminal, despite his history. A felon, sure. Not a criminal.

"Still," Chris had said, "my parents and I have come to an unspoken agreement. I'm home every single night by midnight, and they continue to pay for my college."

Nick had little room for argument, unless he played the pay-for-college-yourself card, a card he dared not to draw. Chris went to nursing school, and she would make an excellent nurse, too. Nick was a convicted felon who had barely skated through high school and worked part-time construction for his uncle's framing business.

Home alone, without Chris to engage him, Nick had to resort to creative and unique ways to stay awake, unless he wished to engage the masked Devil in a nightmare.

Nick had researched military practices. How had soldiers stayed alert for hours on end while on guard? Exercise. Energy drinks. Iced water. Coffee. Constantly snacking. When push came to shove, drinking or eating something so utterly horrendous, it sent a shock of revulsion through their body, providing them with a temporary jolt of energy.

Johnny didn't think staying awake forever would solve their collective problem. In fact, he thought their latest tactic might prove more dangerous to their overall health. Exhaustion not only weakened the body, but the mind. He argued in their fatigued state brought on by unrest, the Devil would grow stronger.

Christina and Nick held their tongues, allowing the engaged couple to duke out their thoughts.

Heather responded. "We're not sleeping, anyway. We dream of him. He nearly kills us with that sledgehammer. We wake up, too afraid to fall back to sleep."

"So, what difference does it make then?" Johnny asked.

"All the difference." Heather stared at her fiancé with crazed, red-rimmed eyes. Staying awake for days on end had been her idea after all, and she meant to defend it.

Nick wasn't sure if the idea was good or bad, but he knew he couldn't continue having the nightmare every single night.

"All the difference? What's that mean?" Johnny asked.

"It means we can prove if it's real or not," Heather tucked a strand of wiry hair behind her ear. In the past six months, she had aged like a veteran smoker—twenty-two going on forty.

"How?"

"If we're awake, and it doesn't show up, it's fake. It's in our dreams. We can go see a dream doctor and she'll fix us. But if we stay awake and it shows, well, guess what? It's real, and it's dangerous, and we need to find help from someone with monster experience."

"Monster experience?" Johnny chuckled. "Like Van Helsing?"

"Yes."

"You're losing your mind."

"We all are." Heather broke into a defeated laugh. "That's the point. I haven't had a full night's sleep in six months. We have to figure this out."

So, the four of them had voted. Three-to-one in favor of staying awake and seeing what happened.

Nothing had happened for five straight days other than absolute misery and living in a waking hell.

Nick's alarm blared.

Beep! Beep! Beep!

He grabbed his phone off the kitchen table and silenced the alert, immediately scrolling through his recent calls and dialing Christina's number.

She didn't answer.

Nick called again, and again, and a fourth time.

"Hello," Christina finally said, her voice groggy and thick with sleep.

"Hey," Nick said.

Christina said nothing at all for a few seconds, then she sobbed into the phone. "I hate this. I want to sleep again. Just for half of a night. That's all. Is that too much to ask for?"

"I know," Nick said, not knowing how else to respond. He wanted to sleep, too. Not for half of or a full night, but for a week or a month straight. He wanted a short-term coma. "Splash some water on your face. Eat something light. Drink some coffee."

"You okay?"

"I'm okay."

"Are you going crazy?"

"Absolutely insane," Nick guffawed—the rare sound of laughter sparked him with a trace amount of energy.

"I'm always sad now," Christina said.

"Me, too."

"When I was little, my mom's best friend used to always say that I was the happiest little girl she ever knew. I was, too. I was so happy all the time, smiling and laughing at everything." She caught her breath from crying. "I'm just... I'm so depressed all the time now. I thought about taking a bath earlier today, or maybe it was yesterday. I don't know. I thought about taking a bath, though, and dropping something electrical into the tub, just so I could sleep."

Nick had also had thoughts of suicide for that exact reason. To experience rest.

"Do you have class today?" he asked, wildly unaware of what day it was. Tuesday? Saturday? Did it matter when every day blurred into one, long, miserable existence?

"No."

"Do you want to hang out? Maybe company would be healthy for the both of us."

"Just us two?"

"Yeah." Nick sat in a chair at his kitchen table. "That okay?"

"I would like that."

They decided Christina would head over to Nick's after readying herself for the day. In the meantime, he had about thirty minutes until Johnny called him.

Why not try to catch a quick nap?

As he considered sleeping, the speaker clicked on in his living room. A song at high volume played throughout his apartment. The ragtime piano cut in first, the beat lively and fast. A few seconds later, the vocals joined in—ragged and gruff, like someone had swallowed a flame before stepping on stage and singing.

"I had a dream last night, that filled me full of fright. I dreamed I was with the Devil below, in his great big fiery hall, where the Devil was giving a Ball..."

A second later, the familiar figure appeared from the living room, stepping into Nick's kitchen. The figure dragged a sledgehammer behind him. He wore a three-piece suit with shiny, light-reflecting shoes. He stood tall and broad shouldered. For a face, he wore a mask—thick eyebrows and a receding hairline and a triangular smirk. The bloody edges curled, as if the Devil had carved it from someone's skull and tied it around its face.

The figure sang along with the song. The mask's thin lips were pinned into a ravenous smirk and never moved.

The Devil inched across the kitchen, moving toward Nick and dragging the sledgehammer's head across the tile floor. The nightmare didn't speak, but it sang every word to the ragtime song.

"I caught a glimpse of Nicholas, dancing with the Devil, Oh! The little Devil, dancing at the Devil's Ball."

Nick attempted to move, to flee, to fight back, but he remained frozen. Paralyzed. His breath came fast and shallow. His heart burned, as if a hot ember had landed on it and sizzled its way straight through the middle of his chest.

The Devil in the Man's mask picked up Nick's limp hand and placed it on the kitchen table. It hoisted up the sledgehammer, high over its head, singing all the while. "Put the pain in champagne wine..." The nightmare trailed off, grunting as he drove the sledgehammer downward, smashing Nick's hand with a sickening crunch. The table snapped, splintering from the impact.

Nick screamed.

Inhaled.

Screamed.

He looked at his mangled, twisted hand and lost consciousness... or rather...

Nick burst awake, still screaming.

The Devil in the Man's mask had vanished. The music had ceased. The table remained cracked. Nick's hand remained pulverized. From sleep to reality, the injury and the pain had bled through.

The Devil wasn't a nightmare. The Devil was real.

Seating Situation. Monday, May 1st. 0807hrs.

"Where are you?" I asked.

Fred Rogers, my assistant-slash-best friend, had a habitual tendency to show up late to everything, including his job. We had scheduled to leave for our business vacation in Santa Cruz from Sacramento at 0800hrs.

"Sorry, Amigo," Fred said on the other end of the phone. He didn't sound apologetic at all. In fact, the big man sounded cheery, humored even. "I did the mental math, and we needed an extra vehicle. Now, I failed algebra in high school and statistics in college, but my basic math is on par."

"What are you talking about?" I asked, twisting my wrist and cracking it.

"Well, there's you. That's one. Maya and Alina. Two and three. I'm four. Daphne makes five." Daphne was Fred's wife—a woman far too good for him, as most wives are to their husbands.

I sucked my lips inward, knowing where Fred steered this ship.

"You went off-script and invited Cambria on our trip. She makes six. Do you know what that means?"

I stood on the sidewalk outside my office building. I had parked my car at the curb. My Honda Civic Hybrid. "Six people won't fit into my car."

"Now, I know Maya and Alina have no trouble breaking laws, but Daphne said no way, no how. Also, you are prudish with things like that."

"Rules exist for a reason," I said.

"Well, there you go. So, to simplify the argument and save us time, Daphne and I—" Fred made a whistling sound, drawing out his inevitable conclusion. "We're driving ourselves to Santa Cruz."

"No," I said, cracking a knuckle and staring across the street at nothing specific. "That can't happen."

"Hi, August," Daphne said, revealing that Fred spoke to me over their car's Bluetooth system.

I clenched my teeth. "Hi, Daphne."

"I'm sorry I kidnapped Fred."

"Me, too."

"Why so glum?" Fred asked, barely disguising his laughter. "It's a car full of women."

"That's the problem."

"Oh. I get it. Your natural incompetency with the better sex has you twitterpated. Twisted up like a wad of panties. Tangled like wet hair in a shower drain."

"What?" I asked.

"Think of it this way, Alina is sixteen, so she's out of the question."

"That goes without saying," Daphne said.

"Well, I'll say this. Maya is so far out of your league, Buddy. She's like a professional athlete, and you're stuck playing Pop Warner. Also, isn't she like your second best friend behind me? That means you have a sixteen-year-old and your best friend in the car. That's easy math. Even I can find the solution to that problem."

I refused to respond and contribute to his amusement. He knew well enough what my seating situation looked like.

"It's Cambria, isn't it?" Fred asked.

"Yes," I said.

"Cambria, who you asked to accompany you on this trip."

"That's right."

"She accepted said invitation, right?"

"That's why she's tagging along."

"Easy, then. Daphne, care to weigh in?"

"Treat Maya like the good friend she is," Daphne said. "As you always do. Treat Alina like an employee."

Fred interrupted his wife, lending his opinion. "Treat Cambria like the woman you want to make her feel like. Easy peasy lemon squeezy."

"It's not that simple."

"Why not? Because you're in love with Maya?"

"No," I said, though with little conviction.

"So, what do you propose?" Fred asked.

"Maya and Alina ride with Daphne and you."

Fred and Daphne shared a patronizing laugh. "That's fine and dandy, my friend. But what happens when we arrive at our vacation rental, and Maya watches you and Cambria sleep in the same room, under the same covers, atop the same mattress?"

"At the house, I won't be stuck in a car with Maya for three hours," I said. "With her and Alina both. You know how they get when they're together."

"When you put it that way, I feel a little bad for you."

"It's question after question, story after story."

"Long-winded stories, too," Fred said. "Someone needs to introduce Alina to a stopwatch."

"Remember, the doctor instructed I take it easy for about a week. Well, a car ride with those three women is the exact opposite of easy. It's literally the most difficult and complicated thing I can imagine. It's a personal Hell." I stood from the curb, grunting as I stretched. My shoulder was stiff from the gunshot wound, my hip achy from the stab.

"Listen, August… it pains me to say this, but you're never getting with Maya."

"That's what you're missing. I'm not trying to get with Maya. I'm trying to get away from her."

"You drive a Honda Civic," Fred said. "Maya wants a man who drives a muscle car, or a motorcycle, or a fighter jet. Something fast and confident and loud, even dangerous. She doesn't care about the environmental effects or the safety features. She cares about the power inside the engine. The sooner you accept that, the easier your life will be."

Maya Adler and Alina Moore turned the corner, coming into my view. They wheeled a single small suitcase each, a number and size which surprised me considering our week-long trip. When traveling with my mom and sister, they usually packed enough clothes to dress a small army.

"I see them," I said.

"Maya and Alina?"

"Yeah."

"How does she look?"

"Like Maya," I said.

"Sexy?"

"Fred!" Daphne scolded.

"I'm asking if August thinks she looks sexy. I don't think that she does."

"Don't lie to me," Daphne said.

"I only think she's a little sexy."

"Fred!"

"I don't know what to say."

"Try nothing," Daphne said.

"What do I do?" I asked.

"You mean, what do you not do?" Fred spoke in a sarcastic, wizened tone.

I said nothing. Rather, I waved at the two women. Maya wore bug-eyed sunglasses and a frumpy outfit. Either she had stayed up late working on her latest assignment for the tabloid, or she had stayed up late drinking too much. Knowing her, it was probably both.

Fred continued speaking in his philosophical voice. "Don't allow Maya or Alina to sit in the front seat."

"He's right," Daphne said.

"I don't care how much they bully you or argue to convince you otherwise. It's your car, and you're in charge. Maya and Alina sit in the backseat. Cambria sits in the front seat. Do you understand that simple logic?"

I bit my lip and nodded.

"August, do you understand?" Fred asked.

"Yes. Maya and Alina sit in the backseat."

"Good."

"I hate you. Do you know that? They could have sat in your backseat."

"Daphne and I may need our backseat."

"Fred!" Daphne said, though she didn't contradict him.

"August," Fred said, lowering his voice.

"Yeah."

"Before I forget, can you do me a favor and remember one thing?"

"What's that?"

"What's up, Dude," Alina asked, grinning at me.

Maya nodded at me with a subtle lift of her chin.

"I'm so excited, I couldn't sleep," Alina said. "I've never been to the ocean before. Never. Honestly, I've never been out of central California. Sacramento is the furthest North, Stockton the furthest south. I'm a caged bird, Gussy. Now, I'm ready to fly."

"How's Maya look?" Fred asked. "Sexy? Gun to your head, who do you pick? Maya or Cambria. Go!"

I raised a finger to Alina and mouthed my apology for ignoring her, turning my back to them. "What do you want me to remember?"

Fred cleared his throat. "Do you remember when I turned thirty?"

"Barely. I was still drunk back in those days."

"I know, because I specifically asked for a Gotham-themed surprise birthday party where I dressed as Batman and all the attendees dressed as someone from Batman's rogue gallery. Except you, I asked for you to dress as Robin."

I rolled my eyes. "I remember."

"What did you do?"

I gnawed on my cheeks, not wanting to answer.

"August?" Fred asked. "What did you do?"

"I forgot."

"You forgot is the correct answer. Remember that you forgot."

"What's that mean?"

Fred hung up the phone.

I scratched my head and sighed, removing the cell phone from my ear and slipping it into my pocket. The warm morning sun baked my face as I peered at the blue sky.

"Howdy," Maya said.

"Howdy." I turned around, facing Maya and Alina.

"You okay?" the far-too observant teenager asked. "You look like you have to poop badly, but there's no bathroom in sight and you don't know what to do. You can't poop your pants, so you're considering pulling those suckers down to your ankles, popping a squat right here in public. Except, boom! The girl of your dreams steps onto the scene. You can't poop in public with her watching. You can't poop your pants." Alina sucked on her teeth. "That's how you look."

"That's about how I feel," I said. "You've never been to the ocean?"

"Nope," Alina said. "Never. Do you think I'll see a shark? I mean, I know I probably won't, but do you think it's a possibility? God, I love sharks. Honestly, I think they're the sexiest of all the predators. I know that's controversial, because most people would say a lion with their drop-dead gorgeous manes, but I have to go with sharks."

"Really?" Maya asked, leaning back at the hips.

"Really what?" Alina glanced at her aunt. "You can disagree, but don't say lion. You're not that basic."

"I don't even think lions are sexy at all."

"No?"

"No."

"What predator then?"

"It's all about the praying mantis."

Alina's eyes went wide as saucers. "See, that's your problem. You're basic in the sense that you're too far out there. A praying mantis? They're not sexy. They're creepy. In fact, they kind of remind me of August."

Maya studied me for a second, then she chuckled. "Oh. My. God. They do, don't they? That's crazy. Is it their eyes, you think?"

I faked a cough, drawing their attention. "I would offer to take your luggage, but I'm currently recovering from a bullet wound." I tapped the button on my key fab, opening the trunk. "You don't mind stowing your own bags, do you?"

"Oh, but Mr. Watson," Maya said, draping her arms around my neck and leaning into me. She smelled like a meadow of wildflowers. "I'm only a weak, helpless woman. You can't use those big, impressive muscles to lift my suitcase? It's so heavy, weighed down by skimpy bikinis and lingerie."

"Gross," Alina said. She hoisted her suitcase and threw it into the truck with no strategic rhyme or reason. She just tossed it in there. "I get why you like the praying mantis, though. Don't the females kill their male mates after sex? Seems like something you would enjoy."

Maya pushed away from me and stuck her tongue out at Alina. "If only that were legal. Anyway, are we going to stand around all morning and insult each other, or we heading to the beach? I told Jonah I would have the doppelgänger story finished by Friday, so I'm fully planning on impersonating Ernest Hemingway. Drinking and writing, all day, every day. Except, instead of lounging in Spain or France, I've settled for Santa Cruz."

As Maya rattled off her diatribe of words, a black Acura pulled up to the curb. A second later, Cambria Parker stepped out of the backseat. Our eyes met, and she smiled at me. She hustled to the back of the Lyft, reached into the trunk, and removed her suitcase. Once situated, she hurried straight to me, hugging me.

"Hi," she said.

Maya frowned, tilting her head with something conveying confusion and surprise. "Who's this?"

"Who are you?" Cambria asked, stepping away from me and pinching her shoulders back.

"Maya, this is Cambria," I said, not enjoying how their meeting had begun. "I asked Cambria to join us on the trip."

"She another ghost hunter?" Maya asked.

"No," I said.

"She's like, what, your girlfriend?" Maya said girlfriend like someone spitting out something nasty.

"Cambria, this is Maya. She's a good friend, and she consults on most of my cases." I nodded at Alina. "That's her niece, Alina, who interns for me."

"Is she?" Maya asked.

"Is she what?"

"Your girlfriend."

"Cambria is a girl who also is a friend. So, in a technical sense, yes, she's my girlfriend."

"Have you two had sex?"

"What do you care?" Cambria asked.

"Have you?"

"Yeah," Cambria said, lying to Maya for no reason other than to make the situation more uncomfortable for me. "It was life changing."

"Okay," I said, clapping my hands together and exhaling. "I think it's time we head out. We're already running twenty minutes late."

"Shotgun," Maya said, reaching for the passenger door.

"Nope," I said, recalling Fred's warning-slash-advice and implementing it. "Throw your suitcase in the trunk, then crawl in the backseat with Alina. Cambria gets to sit shotgun. My car, my rules. I determine the seating situation."

Alina grinned, softly chuckling. "This is going to be a blast. That's not sarcasm, either. I'm sincerely more excited about this drive than I am to see the ocean."

The Longest Drive. Monday, May 1st. 0818hrs.

M AYA M YLENE A DLER'S FATHER had abandoned the family when she was born. He returned a few years later, hanging around until he grew bored and found something shinier and more exciting to chase. To the man's credit, he had remained in touch with his daughters as they grew older. It didn't erase his crimes and make him a good person, but I had come across worse fathers.

Still, he had destroyed his family to chase quick cash and cheap sex. His wife had to work a lot of overtime shifts to keep her and her two girls afloat.

As often happens in single-family households, a mis-balance in parental guidance occurs. Wanda, Maya's sister (Alina's mom), lost her way during those confusing teenage years. She fell into the wrong group of friends, met the wrong man, and never crawled away from her sister's shadow—which prevented light or warmth from gracing her life.

Her sister's shadow, of course, belonged to Maya.

Maya was a prodigy—one of those children who inherited a trait completely disconnected from their family tree, like a generational athlete coming from parents who stumbled when they ran or a musician spawned from humans incapable of carrying a basic tune in a bucket. Maya lacked musical talent, possessed an inkling of athleticism, but she had an IQ off of the charts.

Apparently, a handful of Ivy League universities accepted her application to join their pre-medicine program.

Maya, always marching to the beat of her drum, settled for the University of California: Davis. A strong collegiate program, but not Stanford. She continued medical school at Davis, finding a prestigious residency. However, a day before the residency began, Maya dropped out of the program to pursue investigative journalism.

Her life story, which she had reluctantly shared with me over the four years we knew each other, rattled around in my head for the first five minutes of our drive out of Sacramento.

When we had all piled into my Honda Civic, Maya had positioned herself in the middle seat, directly in line of my rearview mirror. She knew where she sat, because she was intelligent and petty. She wanted to make me uncomfortable by keeping her eyes on me.

It had worked.

The radio played quietly throughout the cab, but I was so mentally far away from the vehicle, I couldn't hear a single note.

I glanced out the corner of my eye at Cambria Parker.

My mom had twisted my arm to attend church last Sunday and meet the young, pretty, single woman. Cambria and I had gone on a date and hit it off. I invited her to the ocean on an impulse. She was a hair stylist in Sacramento. A good kisser. Bluntly honest, which I appreciated. Apart from that, I knew next to nothing about her.

Cambria sat rigidly, back squarely against the passenger seat and feet firmly on the ground, hands folded in her lap. She stared straight ahead, chin titled slightly upward, mouth small and tight.

For a second, I entertained the idea of reaching across the center console and touching her leg or holding her hand. Only for a second, though. A fleeting second.

"Well, I'll say it." After a long five minutes, Alina broke the silence. She stared at her cell phone as she spoke. "This is awkward. The entire world knows that August—"

"I did it," I said, cutting off Alina. I'm not entirely sure what she meant to say, but I had a solid guess, and I didn't care to spend the next three hours arguing why I didn't love Maya.

"Did what?" Maya asked, her voice sour.

Before I could share the news, Cambria broke it for me. Had she hoped to reveal something about August Watson that no one else knew? Boast her privy knowledge of my life? Infuriate Maya further? I couldn't answer any of those questions, but I knew I didn't like the road we headed down.

"He spoke to Raymond and Tammy Brooks." Cambria's voice was icy.

"Did he?" Maya asked.

"He did. We discussed it, and he listened to my advice." Cambria reached across the center console, grabbing my hand.

So much for avoiding that landmine. We were barely outside of Sacramento, still three hours from our arrival in Santa Cruz, and I already couldn't imagine this going any worse.

"Did he not ask you about it?" Cambria glanced back at Maya.

So, I was wrong. It could get worse.

"How did it go?" Alina asked.

"Yeah, how did it go?" Maya stared into the rearview mirror, sending a jolt of chills down my spine.

I glanced at Cambria, half-smiling. "Well."

"That's deep," Maya said.

"What?"

"It's a pun," Cambria said. "A bad one, too."

"What happened?" Alina asked.

Honestly, I thanked all the gods that may or may not exist for that teenage girl right then. She could have stirred the antagonistic pot, pitting Cambria and Maya against each other even more. Instead, she stepped between them and held them at bay.

I owed her one, which meant I should tell her what had happened when I knocked on the Brooks' door.

I twisted my wrists and habitually rolled my shoulders to release tension. A mistake. The gunshot wound to my left shoulder burned brightly at the sudden movement. I grimaced, swallowing the dull pain and hoping to not make a scene. The rolling of my shoulder, like the cracking of my knuckles and wrists, was an unconscious tic I had no control over. I would have to break the practice, though, otherwise I would suffer blinding pain every fifteen minutes.

"What happened?" Maya asked.

My mind jumped back to yesterday afternoon.

I had knocked on Raymond and Tammy Brooks' front door—the parents to the nineteen-year-old young man I had murdered.

Five years ago, I worked for the Galt Police Department. Galt was a small, rural town where not much happened beyond the occasional meth lab getting raided. While on shift, dispatch asked me to respond to a call. Apparently, a young man had a gun at the park.

I responded, obviously terrified of what could happen to me, especially considering what had happened the night before. A Sacramento officer was shot and killed while on duty.

I approached Aaron Brooks with anger and fear ruling my thoughts and actions.

The young man pointed his weapon at me.

I fired mine, taking his life.

Turned out, he only had an airsoft gun. A judge dismissed me of any criminal charges, though, deeming the shooting justified. The Galt Police Department didn't fire or suspend me, but offered me paid leave until I could return to active duty.

I quit instead.

Yesterday, after five years of hiding from his parents, I knocked on the Brooks' door to apologize for what I had done to their son.

"You can't tell me what happened?" Maya asked. "It's a secret?"

I spoke slowly and from far away, as if I had fallen back into the memory and relived it. "Mr. Brooks invited me into his home. Their house smelled like fresh cookies." My eyes burned with tears, and my throat constricted, making it slightly harder to speak.

"Did they know you were coming?" Alina asked. "Did they bake cookies for you?"

A strange question upon reflection. Why would Aaron's parents have baked cookies for me? Unless they poisoned them.

I shook my head. "Tammy baked them for Aaron."

"For Aaron?" Maya asked. "But—"

"Every Sunday, she would bake a batch of his favorite cookies for the week, pack them in his lunch each day for school. After five years without him, she still bakes cookies every Sunday." The tears no longer stung my eyes, but trickled down my cheeks. I sniffled. "I'm sorry."

Maya dropped her gaze and stared into her lap.

Cambria leaned her head against the seatbelt retractor.

"What did you say to them?" Alina asked.

I had stood on their front porch with the smell of roses hot in my nose. The door swung open.

"Nothing at first. I... words eluded me. What could I say? Sorry means nothing. It doesn't bring Aaron back. Anything else seemed insulting or like an excuse."

"You said nothing?" Alina asked, driving the conversation. "What did you do then?"

Raymond Brooks had immediately recognized me. He lunged forward after opening the door, after taking a second to process who stood on his front porch. I thought he might hit me in the face, repeatedly, bouncing my skull of his flatwork. He hadn't, though.

Raymond Brooks had wrapped his arms around me. He hugged me hard and tight, resting his head on my shoulder, sobbing on me, wetting my shirt and my neck. Tammy also joined him, embracing me with her husband.

"They invited me inside their home," I said. "I followed them into the kitchen, sitting at their table, smelling Aaron's cookies. Raymond sat beside me, nearly knee-to-knee with me, and he held my hand." I paused. Tears blurred my vision, and I needed to clear my eyes to see the road.

My mind stepped back into memory, though.

Tammy had busied herself in the kitchen, grabbing a plate and arranging warm cookies onto it, filling a cup with—

"Would you like milk?" she asked. "We also have water and coffee."

"Coffee, please," I said, my voice dry.

Aaron's mother handed me a steaming cup of coffee, and she set the plate of cookies on the table beside me. "Please, help yourself." She sat on the opposite side as her husband and me.

"Did Raymond say anything to you?" Alina asked, drawing me back to the present.

I exhaled. "He told me that... he said... he said that he forgave me." I choked on the last bit. "He said he prayed I would learn to forgive myself, too."

Cambria squeezed my hand.

"We talked about Aaron a lot. I asked them questions."

"They didn't mind that?" Maya asked.

"They said they enjoyed remembering their son, talking about him. It allowed him to continuing living in a way. I don't know. Tammy said it much better than I can. Anyway, they encouraged me to ask questions, so I did, and they answered them. They asked about me, and I... I shared with them what they wanted to know." I ran my tongue across my teeth. "Three hours I sat at their table and snacked on cookies and drank coffee, discussing Aaron Brooks with his parents. Tammy asked me to stay for dinner, but I declined. I had eaten my weight in her cookies by then."

"Was it good?" Alina asked. "Was it good for you?"

I nodded. "I think so."

"Will you see them again?"

I continued to nod. "I don't know. They encouraged me to see a therapist."

I thought of Glacia, the criminal psychiatrist I had a brief affair with. She had, while concussed in a hospital bed after a traumatic experience, gifted me her Nana's haunted house. So far, even throughout her recovery, she hadn't reversed her decision.

"I've been telling you to see a therapist for years," Maya said.

"For years, you've also told me to join your movie club, knowing full well it will never happen."

"A movie club?" Cambria frowned.

Alina answered. "Instead of a book club where you read books, it's a movie club where you watch movies. I'm actually the founder and president of Groovy Movies."

"Is that the name?" I asked. "I never knew that."

"What's wrong with the name?" Alina asked.

"I mean, nothing. You're showing the familial resemblance with your titling, and it's quite amazing."

"What's that mean?"

"Have you ever heard Maya come up with a title for anything?"

"What's that mean?" Maya asked.

"What genre of movies?" Cambria glanced over her shoulder, braving to look into the eyes of the beasts.

"All the movies," Alina said. "Old. New. Good. Bad. Serious. Funny. Romantic. Scary. All of them."

"Unfortunately, a lot of horror movies," Maya said.

"Well, I'm a horror-movie junkie," Alina agreed. "Elevated horror is my jam, but I also enjoy horror comedy. Have you ever watched *Tucker and Dale vs Evil*?"

"No," Cambria said. "Is it good?"

"Incredible."

"It's dumb," Maya said.

"Do you have a favorite movie?" Cambria asked.

"Who, me?" Alina asked.

"Either of you."

"*The Hangover*," Maya said. "It's hilarious. A classic. Or *Deadpool*. Both Deadpool movies. Don't make me choose one or the other."

"Don't listen to her," Alina said. "She watches movies like a simpleton—for entertainment-exclusive purposes."

"That's literally what movies are for," Maya said. "They're not part of the snobbery business. They're part of the entertainment business, with books and music and video games."

"What movie do you like best?" Cambria asked.

Alina clicked her tongue. "My favorite genre is horror, so my favorite movie would have to be a horror movie. It's tough, though. Gun to my head... I'm stuck only watching one movie for the rest of my life... *Let the Right One In*. No. I take it back. Can I do that?"

"Sure."

"*The Exorcist* or *Jaws*."

"You like older movies?"

"They're the best."

"My favorite movie is *The Shining*," Cambria said. "I'm probably cheating with an answer like that. It's also my favorite book, coincidentally written by my favorite author."

I glanced in the rearview to see Alina's reaction. The young girl, for the first time since I had known her, was stunned speechless, though her mouth dropped, opened wide with shock.

"Shut the front door," Alina said.

"Seriously," Cambria said.

"Stephen King is your favorite author?"

"By a mile. Maybe two."

"Mine, too. I also really enjoy Clive Barker, Thomas Ligotti, Dean Koontz, and H. P. Lovecraft. Now, I know what you're thinking. Lovecraft was a massive racist. Sure. Yes, that's true. But he wrote phenomenal horror stories that still define the genre today."

"Hate the player, not the game," Maya said.

"What about Poe?" Cambria asked. "I love Edgar Allan Poe."

"Oh, God." Maya rolled her eyes. "Here we go."

"What?" Cambria glanced from Alina to Maya to me. "What?"

I chuckled. "He's the basis for my name. August, after August Dupin. August Allan, after, well, isn't it obvious?"

Cambria settled back into her seat, slouching a little, kicking her foot up on the dashboard, and playing with her hair.

Maya had also adjusted her posture, no longer glaring at me through the rearview mirror. She scooted to the side seat, lounging so her head rested against the window and her legs sprawled over Alina's lap. No seatbelt, of course. Why would Maya ever fully comply with laws or guidelines?

The three hours zipped away as the women discussed their favorite movies and books and directors and authors.

I enjoyed the feel of Cambria's fingers interlaced with mine. Unfortunately, over the course of the next five days, few other moments would taste so sweet.

Arrival. Monday, May 1st. 1112hrs.

I slowed the Honda Civic as we neared the vacation rental, searching for the correct address amongst the other homes on the street.

"1428," I muttered.

"There!" Cambria had returned to the center seat. She leaned forward, over the console, and pointed across the street.

Block numbers showed along a mailbox's wooden pole. I hit my blinker and turned into the driveway, stomping on my brakes and stopping halfway on the road, halfway on the driveway. I narrowed my eyes, studying the two vehicles parked in front of the garage. Two, as in plural, vehicles. Not just one Lexus sedan belonging to a Daphne Rogers.

"Maya, do you care to explain this?" I turned around, looking over my shoulder at her.

"I don't know what you're talking about."

"Cambria?" I shifted to the woman sitting in the passenger seat. "Do you know anything?"

She stuffed out her lower lip and shook her head. "I don't even know what I'm looking at."

I didn't either. Daphne had parked on the left side of the driveway. Beside her car was an old Ford truck. It was the same forest-green color as my father's, with the same tinted windows and the same decal on the bottom corner of the rear window—Herky the Hornet, the Sacramento State mascot.

"Does anyone in this vehicle know why dad's truck is here?"

"I do," Alina said.

"You do?"

"I do."

"Do you care to elaborate?"

"I feel like that's more of a Fred thing."

I removed a stick of gum from my pocket and folded it into my mouth. In my moment of pause, Fred's warning tickled my memory. *You forgot is the correct answer. Remember that you forgot.*

"He forgot to tell me." I cracked a knuckle. "He purposefully forgot to mention that my parents were attending this vacation." I readjusted my body forward, staring at my father's truck.

"You okay?" Cambria touched my arm.

"The doctor said to relax and take it easy. That's why I agreed on this vacation. Solve a simple case. Relax by the ocean. Except, nobody mentioned my parents would tag along on the said vacation." My jaw twitched.

I'm not the most social person in the world. Agreeing to attend this trip with Fred, Daphne, Maya, Alina, and Cambria felt like a giant, uncomfortable step. However, in the recent past, I had learned uncomfortable steps forward, though sometimes dangerous, weren't always bad. In fact, to continue moving toward a destination, uncomfortable steps were often necessary. So, I had reluctantly agreed to the crowded vacation.

No one had informed me my mom and dad would bolster those numbers, turning the already crammed home into tight, claustrophobic confines. Not only that, but I could barely tolerate my mom on the phone. I know how that sounds. And it's not that I didn't love her, but she loved to ask questions—incessant questions about anything and everything. I didn't really love speaking, especially about unnecessary things, like my love life or my future children or finding a legitimate career. With my mom steering the conversation, all those topics rose to the surface—all those topics and so many more.

My body flushed with heat. I remained parked halfway in the driveway, halfway on the street, staring at my father's truck and wanting to turn around and drive back to Sacramento.

"August," Alina said. "Are you okay?"

"You knew about this?"

"Only for like a day, though."

"You didn't think to tell me?"

"Fred told me not to tell you."

"You listen to Fred now, not me?"

"You never told me one way or another about it." Alina grinned. "Also, you should know, while we're discussing things, that it's not only your mom and dad who hopped in that truck."

"What's that mean?"

"It's also your sister and her husband. And your brother."

"Alina has a crush on Adam," Maya said. "She told me."

"Did not. I never said that."

"You said he was cute."

"I told you not to say anything."

"Sorry. I figured August would want to know if you're shacking up with his little brother."

They continued bickering, but I drowned out their voices, mentally counting the people now attending this vacation. Four in my car. Two in Daphne's vehicle. Five in my dad's truck. Eleven people staying under one roof.

I was wrong before, about things not getting worse.

"So, you... what?" I asked, turning to face Alina. The dull aches exploded in my hip and shoulder, forcing me to scrunch my face, but my attention remained glued to the young girl. "You lie to me now? You keep secrets from me?"

"What? No. What are you talking about? Fred asked me not to tell you. He said you wouldn't come on the trip if you knew, and, well, he said you needed to come on the trip."

"Fred doesn't know what I need. Besides, that's not what I'm talking about."

Alina curled her lip. "What's that mean? What are you talking about?"

"You're lying to me about school."

"What?"

It was a cheap shot, especially in front of Maya and Cambria, but I felt blindsided by my parents, and I reacted rather than responded to the unpredicted situation.

"Your work permit," I said.

"What about it?"

"I know you forged all the signatures. I know you're absent from school every day. I know you're working the system to turn this into a legal matter, hoping law enforcement will go look for your mom. Right?"

Maya's mouth fell open. She faced her niece. "Is that true? You're not attending school?"

"You're an asshole." Alina said, glaring at me with pure disgust. She opened the back door, stepping onto the sidewalk, marching up the driveway, and disappearing around the garage through an arched gate likely leading to the front door.

"Smooth move, ex-lax," Maya said, opening her door. She hopped out of the car and chased her niece into the house.

I stared at the empty backseat, nervous of adjusting my position forward and experiencing another bout of pain. After a few seconds, I braved the inevitable, turning my body and facing the windshield.

"What's going on?" Cambria asked.

I pushed my tongue against my bottom teeth.

"You hate your family that much?"

"No," I said.

"Why are you so upset they're here?"

"I don't know." It really didn't have a logical explanation, other than I didn't want them there. As terrible as that sounds, I didn't want the added stress of my family at a work getaway.

"Care to attempt an explanation? Why do you feel upset that they're here?"

"Because I couldn't mentally prepare for them."

"Why would you need to prepare mentally for your family?"

"There's eleven people here. I'm not sure if you've noticed or not, but I'm not great with others. The more there are, the more... anxious I get, I guess. Did you know I've seen my brother three times in the past three years? He lived in San Diego, so I had an excuse to avoid him, at least. I've seen my parents about three times in the past five years."

"Why?"

I shook my head.

"Be honest. Not with me, but with yourself. Why?"

"I'm embarrassed." Tears pressed against my eyes, stinging them again. I silently wished the rest of the trip wouldn't have me crying every two hours. "I barely enjoy talking to them on the phone, afraid they might express how disappointed they are in me. Cambria, I murdered someone. You think I want to show my face around anyone, let alone my family?"

"You showed it to Raymond and Tammy Brooks, and they forgave you. You don't think your family, your parents, will do that same thing?"

"It's not whether they forgive me, it's how they look at me. It's what they say to me. My mom always asks questions I don't enjoy answering. She's persistent and pestering, and... and I don't know." I sighed. "I came here to relax, not to feel like a disappointment."

"First off, you came here to work."

"That's relaxing to me."

"Well, that's depressing. Second, stop believing others see you like you see yourself."

"With my parents here, the trip becomes exhausting. It's hard to explain, and I'm making them sound terrible. They're not. They're great. It's just... they're not the people for me to be around if I want to decompress." I exhaled and looked at Cambria. In the late morning, the sunlight crossed her features, causing her to glow. She looked stunning. "Also, did I mention there's eleven people here?"

Cambria leaned forward and kissed the side of my mouth. "What if I lay by the pool in my little, teeny-weeny bikini? Would that help you relax?"

I shook my head. "Probably not."

Cambria slapped my shoulder—thoughtfully, though. She slapped my good shoulder. "The answer is yes. No is also an appropriate answer, but only if you justify it by saying, 'Because your body would have me too worked up to relax.'"

"What about, no, because I'm afraid my mom will insist on joining you by the pool, and I'm terrified about what questions she might ask, especially if you're wearing a little, teeny-weeny bikini." I cleared my throat. "Which reminds me... what do we do for sleeping arrangements now?"

"Now? Did you assume I would sleep with you before we knew about your parents?"

I licked my lips, feeling warm in the face. "I didn't know."

Cambria smirked. "Well, considering that you're a grown man in his thirties, and I'm a grown woman, we can sleep wherever we wish."

"True, but only if you desire—"

Cambria put a finger to my lips. "No more. You're here to solve a case and to relax. Family or no family, I'll see that you do just that. However, the first thing you're going to do, even before you unload Maya's, Alina's, and my luggage, is to find that poor girl and apologize for embarrassing her and calling her out like that. Not cool. I don't care how frustrated you were."

"You're right."

"I know."

"Thank you."

"Thank me later." Cambria winked, opened the passenger door, and followed the path Maya and Alina had taken to the front door.

I sat in the Honda Civic alone, gathering my wits and catching my breath, thanking the stars I had blurted an invitation to Cambria. How else would I have survived the chaos?

Crossing the Threshold.
Monday, May 1st.
1119hrs.

THE VACATION HOME STOOD like a barrier before the ocean. On the other side of the stucco walls, the waves purred. Seagulls chirped. From within the house, music seeped through the cracks, catching the saltwater air and riding the breeze. Elton John.

I lowered my head and stared at my feet, disappointed with how I had acted. Alina hadn't ever left the thirty-mile radius of her hometown. She had never seen the ocean in person—felt the mist on her skin or heard the tide sing its lullaby. My immature reaction to my family's unexpected presence had tarnished her initial impression.

I pulled fully into the driveway and parked behind Daphne's Lexus. Once out of the car, I collected Alina's bag from the trunk. After sitting for over three hours, my wounds had stiffened in my hip and shoulder. I could only handle a piece of luggage at a time.

I followed the walkway around a corner, which carried me through a tall rusted archway leading to the front door. The narrow driveway and the wrap-around stucco fence, along with a clustering of soaring trees standing around the property like lazy giants, played a Hogwarts tricks on my mind. The house appeared much smaller than it actually was. Once through the archway, though, and around the corner, I experienced its enormity in honest.

For a terrible second, I wondered how much of the Blue Moon company funds Fred had dipped in to reserve this place. Had he cleared the expenses with Tempest Michaels? Had the famed investigator from across the pond approved of this trip, helped fund it?

The moment passed quickly with a worse and an inevitable conclusion settling. My parents would have paid for everything. Even if Fred stood before a projection screen and presented a PowerPoint to enlighten my mom and dad on how we could deduct the cost of the trip from our taxes, my parents would have paid.

I'm not sure if I mentioned it before, but my family was highly successful, and they were abundantly generous with their money, especially toward their kids.

Someone had left the front door open. Elton John called to me.

I entered a massive entryway. It immediately transitioned—no walls or foyer to break apart the open-concept—into a massive living room and kitchen.

Daphne and Cambria busied themselves in the kitchen, preparing sandwiches for a small army—most likely for Fred. My mom and sister also accompanied them in the kitchen, but they leaned over the island's matte-black counter, not doing much beyond moving their jaws.

My dad, my brother, Fred, and my brother-in-law sat in the living room on the L-shaped couch, probably discussing sports. I couldn't imagine what else they had in common.

I didn't notice Maya or Alina in the area.

"Hey, everyone," I said, raising my voice to catch their attention.

"Gussy!" My mom beamed at me, moving from the kitchen to the front door like getting shot from a cannon. She slammed into me, bear-hugging me.

I grimaced as she pushed her weight into my wounded shoulder. "Hi."

"Thank you for inviting us. I can't tell you how excited I am! Also," she leaned nearer to me, "I knew you and Cambria would hit it off. Isn't she wonderful?"

"She's great. Thank you," I said, keeping the conversation curt. One of Cambria's wonderful qualities was always encouraging me to do the difficult but right thing. In this situation, that meant finding Alina and apologizing to her right away. "I'll go through my round of hugs and greetings in a minute, but I wanted to drop this bag off in Alina's room. Do you know where that is?"

"Upstairs, Robin," Fred said, pointing to ceiling and smirking at me. His reference didn't go over my head. *Except you, I asked for you to dress as Robin.*

I glanced to the side of the room, noticing the metallic stairwell. "Thanks."

After limping up the steps, I peeked into the various bedrooms until I found Maya's and Alina's room at the end of the hall. They sat on a king-sized bed in a room with a window overlooking the ocean. My stomach hurt knowing I had momentarily robbed Alina of her view.

"Hey," I said, pushing her luggage into the bedroom, but not crossing the doorway's threshold. "Care if I come in?"

"Sure," Alina said.

Apology.
Monday, May 1st.
1126hrs.

ALINA SAT CROSS-LEGGED ON the bed. She had her head down, staring at the dark-green mattress and pinching loose threads. Maya slouched against the headrest, scrolling through her phone with a bored expression. Elton John climbed the stairs, too, quietly settling in the room and filling the initial silence.

I shuffled to the open window, basking in the warm sunshine and the cool ocean breeze. Leaning against the sill, I faced the two women, reached into my pocket for a stick of cinnamon-flavored gum, and popped it into my mouth.

"You like Sir Elton John?" Maya asked.

"Me?" I asked.

"Yeah."

"I never really listened to him."

"You recognize his music, though."

"Everyone recognizes his music." I cracked a knuckle. "Alina."

She glanced up at me.

"I'm sorry for calling you out like that. No excuses, other than I'm a childish idiot."

"You're not wrong, you know?"

"About what?"

"About being an idiot. You are an idiot." Alina's face brightened. She spared a small, lips-only smile—one of those smiles that melt away all previous offenses.

"Well, even a broken clock shows the correct time twice a day," I said.

"Gross." Maya stuck out her tongue and gagged. "My old biology teacher in high school used to say that. He's now in jail for taking advantage of young girls who needed a better grade in his class. So congratulations for finding yourself in the same sentence as him."

I didn't know how to respond to Maya, so I opted to wait for someone else to speak.

Alina jumped on that grenade. "You're also right about me avoiding school, hoping that my absences might stack up and help find my mom." She laid back, rested her head on Maya's lap, and stared at the ceiling. "I know the risk of skipping school. The cops might arrest her and send me into foster care. I've weighed that risk, though. It's worth it. If they arrest her, at least I'll know where she is. At least she will have readily available help. At least I can visit her, you know?"

"Yeah," I said, agreeing out of habit because I did not know.

"It makes me so angry when I hear you complain about your mom and dad coming on this trip." Alina scratched her cheek. "I'm losing my education in a desperate hope that my mom might get arrested so I can visit her in jail. You're complaining that your mom cares enough about you to worry about your well-being. That's what makes you an idiot. Just be happy for what and who you have."

I clenched my jaw. "I know. You're right. That was selfish of me."

"It was."

"Can I do anything to make it better? I'll even watch a movie with you. Any movie. You get to choose."

"You won't fire me for lying to you?"

I shook my head. "I wouldn't fire you. You're too valuable to the company."

Alina's lip-only smile stretched into a full grin. "Well, don't show you're entire hand. I might threaten quitting unless you pay me."

"You need a legal work permit if you want to get paid," I said.

Alina chuckled. "I'm sorry, too... for not telling you the truth."

"Can we make a deal?" I asked. "Let's not lie to each other, okay? No matter what."

"Deal." Alina bolted upright, sitting cross-legged again and staring at me like an inquisitive student. "Since we can't lie to each other anymore, what's going on with you and Cambria?"

"Yeah." Maya dropped her phone in her lap, suddenly interested in the conversation. "What's going on with you and Cambria?"

"I saw you two holding hands," Alina said. "Are you trying to make Maya jealous? Or is this something serious, outside of Maya?"

Maya, the Maya in question, stared at me with wide, curious eyes. "You can't lie, remember?"

"What do you care? I thought you were seeing Nick."

"Who?"

"Nick, the burly bartender at the dive bar."

At the mention of the dive bar, I thought of Patricia—the older woman I had danced with a few nights ago. According to local news, the Vampire of Sacramento, a serial killer, had claimed her as his latest victim.

"Oh, him," Maya said. "He's my burly bartender, nothing more. Are you jealous of Nick?"

"Are you jealous of Cambria?"

"No, though she is quite snobby, don't you think?"

"Snobby? She's downstairs making everyone lunch."

"She's a try-hard," Maya said. "Is that better?"

"Are you going to be like this all week?"

Alina elbowed her aunt in the leg. "No, she won't. She's only doing this for the same reason I'm doing it."

"Why's that?"

"To watch you squirm. We both like Cambria fine."

"In fact, I enjoyed her company so much in the car, that I forgot to ask about the pressing details of our vacation mystery." Maya adjusted his position, sitting a little straighter against the padded headrest. "What's the mystery this time?"

"I'm not entirely sure." I glanced over my shoulder at the ocean. "I only know what details Fred shared yesterday at the pub with everyone else. Some Devil is haunting the nightmares of a group of young adults."

"I think we're meeting with them later this afternoon," Alina said.

"Fred didn't tell me that."

"Doctor ordered you to take it easy. To relax. I don't think Fred wants you worrying about things he can take care of, like our schedule."

"I find it more relaxing to know my schedule."

"That's fair," Alina said.

I clapped my hands and stepped away from the windowsill. "I'm headed back downstairs, if my hip will allow it, to say hello to everyone and collect the rest of the luggage in my trunk. Cambria insisted I carry in everyone's luggage."

"I knew she was the worst," Maya said.

"Would you two lovely ladies care to join me?"

Alina looked at Maya. "We did just barge into the house without saying hi to anyone."

"And I feel bad August carried your bags up here. We should, at the very least, carry his and..." Maya trailed off, making a disgusted face. "Hers."

I rolled my eyes, now knowing she spoke disdainfully of Cambria to annoy me. Even with that knowledge, it still annoyed me. "One more thing." I crossed the room and leaned on the doorframe for support. My hip really sang a hard-metal song, and my shoulder carried the aggressive percussion. "This will be the last time I bring it up."

Alina fell backward on the bed in a dramatic display. "I already know what you're going to say."

"Well, it needs saying. I have the school's calendar copied into my phone."

Alina yelped, as if punched.

"I know you don't have the week off, as you said."

"Okay, but here's the—"

I raised a finger, cutting her off. "Here's the thing," I said, completing her sentence. "With me, Maya, your dad, and your mom out of town, I felt more obligated to have you attend this trip than stay home alone and hope you attend school. When we're back in Sacramento, you will attend your scheduled classes, and you'll sign up for summer school to make up any credits you failed during the semester."

Maya stared at her niece, grinning. "Loser. You're going to enroll in summer school."

"Do we have a deal?" I asked.

"Whatever," Alina said.

I considered that a confirmation.

Family Reunion.
Monday, May 1st.
1137hrs.

I HOBBLED DOWN THE stairs and greeted the crowd of people.

"Were you surprised?" Rachel, my sister, asked.

I glared at Fred, though I answered her question. "Very much. Apparently, Fred forgot to mention you guys were joining us."

"It must have slipped my mind," he said, rubbing his head.

"And you brought Cambria, I see," Mom said, smiling with enthusiastic pride. She had arranged for Cambria and me to meet. "I guess my little date idea wasn't so terrible after all, now was it? And to think how much you fought against it."

"Your mother is always right," Dad said. "Whether she's right or wrong, she's always right. You should know that."

"Cambria said you two had a lovely time together." My mom grabbed my arms and squeezed just above my biceps.

I grimaced, grunting from the pain in my shoulder. "Careful."

"What?"

I hesitated, debating whether I should tell her that someone had shot and stabbed me a few days ago. Alina walked down the stairs right then. I could have used her as an excuse to change the subject, instead I wondered how she would feel if she learned I lied to my mom to avoid a few questions.

"Gun shot."

My mom gasped and stepped back, covering her mouth with both hands. "What? Who shot you?"

My dad stepped forward, wrapping an arm around my mother's shoulders. "Are you okay?"

Mom caught her breath and continued with her tirade of questioning. "Did you go to the hospital? Can you even travel? Should you even be here? You didn't shoot them, did you? What happened?"

The rest of my family gathered around me, asking questions all at once.

"Who shot you?" Rachel asked.

"Did you shoot them?" Adam, my younger brother by twelve years, asked, biting his lip after the question popped from his tongue. Excitement probably drove him to speaking before thinking.

I pulled down my pants a modest amount, diving fully in and showing everyone my knife wound, as well. "Stabbed, too."

"Shot and stabbed?" Jake asked. "You auditioning for the next Bruce Willis role?"

"Bruce Willis?" Alina asked.

"He's an old action-movie star. He played in—"

Alina raised a finger, cutting Jake off. "Don't you dare lecture me on movies. I know who Bruce Willis is, what he starred in, the character he's typecast as. It's just a dated observation. His action-hero role has already filled with the new wave. Keanu Reeves with the John Wick movies. The Rock in every jungle movie he plays in. Chris Pratt. Tom Holland."

"No one cares," Maya said. "Literally, read the room. Eyes more glazed than a delicious donut."

"What happened to the other person?" my mom asked, her face long with worry.

I tried to focus on what mattered—spending time with family and not disappearing. "Other people," I said. "Two separate incidents. They're both in jail now. Well, no, that's not quite right. The woman who shot me was shot in the head. Not by me, though. Also, she somehow survived. She's in the hospital, heavily guarded by law enforcement until she recovers. Then they'll transfer her to the jail. The woman who stabbed me sits in a cell, awaiting her trial."

"Both were women?" Jake asked, scoffing.

"What's so funny?" Maya asked. "You don't think women can shoot a gun, stab someone with a knife?" She laughed, manically, like a cartoonish villain. Then she fell deadly silent and glared at my sister's husband. "If you want to know how terrifyingly dangerous a woman can be, ask for a demonstration. I'll gladly show you."

"Her favorite predator is a praying mantis," Alina said.

Everyone looked at the teenager with utter confusion, rendered speechless for a second.

Alina rushed into explaining herself. "Praying mantis cannibalize their sexual partners. It's kind of cool. Well, Maya thinks it's cool... or sexy. I don't remember."

"Sexy," Maya said.

Fred cleared his throat. "Alright. Well, August, tell them about my role in saving your scrawny butt from the scary woman with a knife. Everybody seems to forget I played professional football. They all think I'm terrified of everything."

"You are," nearly everyone in the room said at once.

"You once had me kill a spider on the wall behind your desk," Alina said. "Then you refused to sit there for the entire day because you thought it might have friends avenging its death."

"You never know," Fred said. "August, tell them the story. I think everyone should hear how brave I really am."

"I've heard it a thousand times already," Daphne said. "I don't need to hear it again."

"Fred, in all his bulk," I said, accommodating the big man's wishes, "bulldozed the small, petite woman who stabbed me in the hip."

"Serves her right," my mom said. "Hope he broke her neck, too."

"What? Mom, no. I'm glad he didn't break her neck, or any other bone in her body, though he probably could have killed her."

"I held back." Fred lifted his chin with confidence. "I definitely could have killed her."

"Dude, I watched some of your old highlights on YouTube," Jake said, slapping Fred on the shoulder. "When you smacked Tyronne Gross on that crossing route. Holy smokes. How did he live through that?"

Fred laughed off the compliment. "He's a pastor now, so he had Jesus on his side. But I didn't go half as hard on that woman as I did on Tyronne. I held my punch."

"I'm glad you're okay," Mom said, touching my arm and surprising me with her nonchalance. She smiled, the way only a mother smiles at her baby, erasing all my fears and worries, drawing them toward her like moths drawn to the flame that was her.

Rachel hugged me, careful not to aggravate my hip or shoulder. "I'm glad you're not dead."

"Me, too," I said.

"Also, I'm sorry." She whispered her apology in my ear.

"For what?" I whispered back.

As everyone broke into side conversations, Rachel led me a few feet away from the crowd, keeping her voice low as she spoke. "This was all my idea."

"What was your idea?"

"This vacation."

"What do you mean?"

"I planned it."

"I know. You said that. Why?"

"Well, Friday night, when that woman shot you, Fred and Daphne came over for a game night. He was telling us about how he received an email from a potential client in Santa Cruz. I recommended you should accept the case, we would join you and make a vacation out of it. A getaway in disguise."

"Why would you suggest that?" I asked. "You know I don't enjoy people or relaxing."

Rachel lowered her voice further, barely emitting the words. "I'm going to make the announcement."

It took me a second to connect the dots. I inhaled when the realization hit me. Rachel was twelve-ish weeks pregnant, and no one knew but me. She had hoped to use this vacation to announce the news.

"You're telling everyone this week?"

Rachel placed a finger over her lips, signaling for me to hush up. "I wanted everyone to be around when I did, including you. So, what better way to guarantee we're all in one place than to plan a vacation where we're trapped together in the same house? I'm sorry Fred and I kept it a secret, but would you have come otherwise?"

"You're the literal Devil," I said.

"Lucifina in the flesh."

I leaned forward and hugged my sister. "Secretly, I'm glad you did this. Outwardly, though—"

"I know, I know. You're going to be grumpy. We all have to keep up appearances."

"Lunch is ready!" Daphne called from the kitchen.

A minute later, the eleven of us wrapped around the oversized island. Everyone stood together in a circle, sharing a moment of buzzing quiet. The anticipation for our vacation to start created an invisible, pure energy. We had a week of nothing but spending time with those we loved most in the world.

Despite my initial reaction, was there anything better than that?

My mom broke the silent spell. "I know not everyone here believes in God, but does anyone object to me praying over this meal and this week?"

In response, as if we had practiced, everyone bowed their heads and held the hand of the person standing beside them. I held Cambria's and Maya's hands.

I was also the last to lower my head in prayer. "Mom," I said, looking across the island at her.

"We don't have to pray," she said. "If you're not comfortable, or you don't want to, we don't—"

"Can I pray?"

Cambria squeezed my hand. A second later, Maya squeezed my other hand.

My mom said nothing for what seemed like forever, then she nodded her head and closed her eyes.

I hadn't believed in God or in any gods for five years, not since murdering Aaron Brooks. I had dedicated my life to finding proof of the supernatural, undeniable truth, so that I could believe in an afterlife—that Aaron's soul still existed somewhere. I hadn't prayed to a god in over five years. Even before the incident I hardly ever prayed or attended church. I loosely believed in a higher power, one strong enough to have created the world. That was the extent of my religious faith, though.

Standing around the island, holding hands with Maya and Cambria, volunteering to pray, I did not know where to begin. Everyone remained patient, allowing me to find my voice.

"God," I finally said. "Thank you for family and for friends. Thank you for life and laughter and love. I pray we may enjoy each other's company this week, that we may laugh and love and live together. Amen."

"And bless the food," Fred said.

We opened our eyes. My mom stared directly at me, looking more proud than I had ever seen her look before.

Unfortunately, I think God interpreted an agnostic praying to Him as ridicule, as mockery. Instead of blessing that vacation, He plagued us with curses.

Gift Basket.
Monday, May 1st.
1202hrs.

Daphne had made sandwiches for the group, along with a side salad if we cared for a healthier option, or a bowl of chips if wanted to indulge our vacation urges.

The rental home had a dining room table that seated ten. We had to drag a barstool over to fit the eleven of us. I elected to sit in the awkward chair, lording over everyone else in my higher seat. I held my plate in my lap so I didn't have to bend over whenever I wanted to grab a chip.

"Fred," I said.

The big man sat directly across the table from me. He looked up, cheeks squirreled with food. "Yeah?"

"What do we know about this nightmare case? You haven't really shared much about it yet, and we're meeting with the client in an hour. I'd at least like to know enough to ask the proper questions."

Fred held up a finger, signaling for me to wait a second. He grabbed a glass of water and washed back the mouthful of food. "Clients."

"What?" I asked.

"Plural. You said client."

I raised an eyebrow, questioning.

"Four of them." Fred removed his phone from his pocket. "Let me check my emails for details."

"Will this be dangerous?" Mom asked.

"Honey, let them work," Dad said.

"I'm only asking questions."

"We're here to spend time with August, not to interfere with his case. He doesn't need you asking questions and distracting him."

"It's fine." I looked at my mom.

As the early afternoon sunshine broke through the nook window, it highlighted her age. Her hair, dyed dark, still possessed stray strands of gray. Despite her Botox and fillers, she carried time on her face like a scar—a scar she despised, but one I admired.

"All the cases have a potential for danger," I said. "Case in point, my gunshot and stab wounds came from separate investigations."

The voodoo doll case crossed my mind. That had also ended violently—a bullet grazing my calf, and a dislocated shoulder. Glacia had also suffered a concussion, and I had shot Maya's boyfriend three times. He had thankfully lived.

"I investigate people who go to extreme lengths to get what they want. Once they've gone that far, violence is very much within the realm of reason and possibility."

"Gussy." My mom deepened her tone. "I don't like that."

"It's safer than when I patrolled Galt."

"Yeah, those cows sure get dangerous," Jake said.

"I don't remember you getting shot or stabbed while working in Galt," my mom added.

"You find it?" I asked, turning to Fred and evicting myself from the previous conversation.

"Yup." Fred read his email, though he mostly paraphrased, flavoring it to fit his style and voice. "We have four victims. Heather Thompson, who's engaged to Johnny Lantz. Johnny emailed me. There's also Christina Wyss, who's dating Nick Lane. Apparently, six months ago, they all experienced the same, or an extremely similar, nightmare. Location varied between the four—one of them maybe dreamed of a beach, while someone else was in a warehouse, and another person was…" Fred trailed off, clicking his tongue and squinting at his screen. "Says Chris, short for Christina, had a dream where she was driving a car into oncoming traffic and couldn't swerve or brake."

"That's horrifying," Cambria said.

"What's similar in their dreams?" Maya asked.

Maya worked for a tabloid, *Here & Now*, where they reported bizarre happenings in the Sacramento Region. Though Santa Cruz fell a little outside their jurisdiction, if the story proved entertaining enough, I'm sure Jonah Daniels, her boss, wouldn't keep her from writing it. Maya and I often cross-collaborated on my investigative cases. I provided her with subject material; she provided me with her genius mind. Also, she plugged my business in her story, providing me with free advertising.

"They share the Devil," Fred said.

"The Devil?" I asked.

"A tall, silhouetted person carrying a sledgehammer. The Devil, as Johnny dubbed the nightmare creature, always raises the sledgehammer to crush their skull. That's when they wake up."

My mother grunted, as if the sledgehammer had struck her in the stomach.

Fred glanced at my mom. "Kimberly, hold on to your precious hat, because that's not the worst of it. Even more terrifying, or so I think, the Devil sings."

"What's it sing?" Alina asked. "Always the same song, or something different every time?"

"Neither Johnny nor any of the other three remember the words. He said they can hum the tune, though. Apparently, the Devil sings the same one when it appears in their dreams." Fred slid his phone back into his pocket and shrugged. "That's it. The four of them want to meet at 1400hrs to discuss it further." He bit into his second sandwich, using his offhand to throw a few chips into his mouth. Once again, Fred's cheeks ballooned with food.

Alina looked at me.

"What?" I asked.

"You promised to watch a movie with me, remember? Any movie of my choosing."

"You're thinking about a movie right now?"

"The case reminded me of a movie, and I think we should watch it."

"What movie?" Jake asked. "Something with Bruce Willis?"

"*A Nightmare on Elm Street.*"

"Great movie," Adam said.

"You've seen that?" my mom asked my little brother, now almost twenty-one. "When?"

"As a kid," Adam said.

"Have you already seen it?" Alina asked, looking at me.

I shrugged. "I don't remember. I never really liked horror movies."

"So, if you have watched it, it was still like a thousand years ago? Do you remember it at all?"

"No."

"You know Freddy Krueger, right?" Adam asked.

"I've heard of the name," I said.

"This is what I have to deal with day in and day out." Alina glanced at my brother. "It's like he crawled out from under a rock. He doesn't even have a Facebook account. What thirty-year-old doesn't have a Facebook account? Facebook defined their generation."

"*A Nightmare on Elm Street*," I said, refocusing the conversation. "Why should I watch it?"

"Should I tell him, or do you want to?" Alina asked Adam.

"You can."

"A demon haunts the dreams of his victims, eventually murdering them through their dreams."

I cracked a knuckle. That premise sounded oddly parallel to what Fred had described. "Lucky for us, our Freddy Krueger can't murder people through their dreams."

Alina shrugged, as if she very much doubted that.

How could someone enter another person's dream and murder them? That seemed more unrealistic than Sasquatch roaming the woods or malevolent spirits hanging around and tormenting the living.

"You think someone could enter another person's dream?" I asked.

Before Alina could share her opinion, the doorbell rang.

My mother startled and yelped, grabbing her chest and breathing hard. "Oh, my."

"I'll get it," I said, placing my plate on the table and stepping off my stool.

Alina popped out of her chair like a rocket and skipped to the front door, unlocking and opening it. She stepped back, sucking in a breath. "Woah. Wow. Sorry." She cleared her throat and looked over her shoulder at me, eyes wide, teeth showing. She was clearly embarrassed. Alina returned her attention to whoever stood at the door. "Hello, Sir. How can I help you?"

I limped across the living room to the front door, standing behind Alina.

A man from a horror movie stood before us. He had long blonde hair tied in a ponytail. His lower jaw and chin weren't quite sunken, but completely underdeveloped, nearly invisible; his cheeks were hollow and his ears rotated the wrong way, so small they nearly weren't there at all. And his eyes... they drooped at a downward angle, missing any trace of eyelids.

He held a plastic-wrapped basket filled with two bottles of wine and boxed chocolate.

"Hi," he said, as if congested.

"Hi," I said.

"Hello," Alina said. "Hi. I'm Alina Moore."

"I'm Maxwell Shaye." The man grinned. I felt nauseous, then guilty for feeling nauseous. "I'm the owner of... of this home." He had a strange cadence, as if he never knew which word he meant to say next, perpetually stuttering and searching for the right choice.

"Mr. Shaye, I'm August Watson. Is everything okay?"

"Yes. Fine." He cleared his throat and pushed the basket forward, nearly shoving it into Alina's arms. "This is for you."

"Thank you." Alina frowned, but accepted the gift.

"Normally the property's caretaker, my brother, prepares and leaves the baskets in... in the kitchen for new guests as a welcome gift. He forgot, though. My apologies."

"Thank you for making the trip out," I said. "I'm sure we can find a few people to enjoy the wine and chocolate."

"I'm glad to hear that." He pulled his narrow, nonexistent lips into his mouth. "Would you like a tour?"

"Of the house?" Alina asked.

"Yeah."

I cracked a knuckle and shook my head. "I think we're settling in fine."

"I'm sorry to intrude." Maxwell reached back and untied his hair, mussed it a little, and allowed it to hang around his shoulders and cover part of his face. "If you have questions, please contact me. You can find my number in the basket, written on the card, as well as local restaurants and wineries and other venues of note."

"Thank you," Alina said. "What happened, by the way?"

"Alina," I said.

"What?" She looked back at me. "You avoiding the topic makes it awkward. He doesn't care. I'm sure he would rather me ask him than someone else. If you broke your arm, I'd ask what happened to your arm. What difference does it make?"

"How do you know he doesn't care? You can't assume how others feel, and speak for them."

"Do you care?" Alina asked, returning her attention to Maxwell.

He grinned and wished he hadn't. "I appreciate her bravery and honesty. Most people shy away from my... appearance." Maxwell looked at her. "It's a genetic disorder known as Treacher Collins syndrome. Very rare. Instead of winning the lottery, though, I was the one in fifty thousand born like this."

"Does it, like, hurt?" Alina asked. "I mean, no, that's a dumb question. I mean, can you eat and stuff?"

"Yes. I can live a relatively normal life. Anyway." Maxwell returned his attention to me. "I'm always curious about my tenants. What brings you here?"

"Work," Alina said. "We're paranormal investigators."

"Interesting," Maxwell said, running his fingers through his hair. "There's a lot of paranormal in this area. Have you heard of the Mystery Spot?"

"No," Alina said. "Should we check it out?"

"It's a tourist attraction," I said. "We won't have time to check it out."

"Well, if you don't mind me asking, what are you looking into? Brookdale Lodge? Pioneer Cemetery? No, no, no. Arian Gulch?"

"We don't dive into urban legends," I said. "Clients contact and pay us to help solve paranormal activity."

"We're here about a demon haunting the dreams of four people," Alina said. "They believe it's trying to kill them."

"In their dreams?" Maxwell asked.

"Yes."

"How?"

"Like Freddy Krueger," Alina said.

"I see," Maxwell said, chuckling. No one said a word for a few seconds. "Well, is there anything else I can do for you while I'm here?"

I vibrated my lips. "I don't think so, Mr. Shaye. Thank you for the basket, though."

"Have a wonderful stay."

"I'm sure we will."

The home owner turned and walked away, taking quick steps on tiptoes with his shoulders slightly hunched over.

"Who was it?"

I lurched around. The sudden, jerky movement incited a white streak of pain through my shoulder and hip. I may have squealed at the voice inches from my ear, but only a little and probably mostly from the slush of pain.

Maya stood behind me, grinning like a demented clown.

"You can't sneak up on me like that." I closed the front door.

"What's in the basket?"

"Wine, chocolate, local suggestions for food and fun," Alina said.

Maya collected the gift basket from her niece and held it high, inspecting the plastic-wrapped contents. "Thank you very much. I'll make sure this finds a suitable home."

"Your belly?" Alina asked.

"Where else?" Maya returned to the kitchen, placed the basket on the island, and crinkled the plastic as she untied it.

Alina looked at me. "What do you think about the case?"

"To avoid making false assumptions, I try to keep my mind blank until I speak to the client."

"Clients."

"Plural," I said.

Alina chuckled and bobbed back to the dining room table.

I trudged after her. Not bothering to sit again, I remained on my feet. So much for taking it easy, huh, Doctor? "I'm leaving to meet with the clients." I spoke to Fred. "You joining me?"

"No way, Jose. I'm sitting poolside. Daphne can cook, we all know that. But do you know what she does better than cooking?"

"Don't really care to know."

"Mixology."

"Aye, aye," Jake said, raising his glass. "I can attest to that."

"Do you know what she does better than mixing cocktails?"

"Don't really care to know," I repeated.

"Looking sexy by a pool."

"I can attest to that," Maya said, prying free a bottle of red wine from the gift basket. "Thank you, Mr. Owner."

Fred popped his lips. "I'm going to enjoy delicious snacks while drinking something refreshing and ice cold, as I wade in the pool and ogle my smoking-hot wife."

"This is a work trip," I said.

"I'll have my phone on me," Fred rebutted. "I already set up any emails or incoming calls to forward straight to my cell. I'm a receptionist, remember? I don't go out in the field."

"Too afraid?" I asked.

"Don't get me started on that."

I glanced at Alina.

"Duh," she said. "I'm definitely going."

"I would go, too," Maya said, searching the kitchen drawers for a wine opener, "but since you're not paying me, and since there is this bottle of wine someone has to drink, I think I should hang back and work on writing my latest article. *Doppelgänger Danger*." She found the corkscrew and twisted it into the cork.

"That's the title I came up with," Fred said, pointing at Maya with excitement.

Maya pointed back at Fred.

"I'm not sure if you care, but your father and I plan to head into town to do a little shopping," my mom said, grabbing my dad's hand. "Santa

Cruz has the cutest little places to browse. Rachel, would you care to join us?"

My sister turned to her husband. "What do you think?"

Jake pouted out his lower lip and shook his head. "It doesn't matter to me."

Rachel turned to our brother. "Adam?"

"I'm going with Mom and Dad. I forgot my flip-flops, so I need to buy some. Once I grab a pair, let's walk to the beach."

"Works for me," Jake said.

"I'll join you at the beach," my dad said. "Rachel can shop with Mom."

I faced Cambria. "That leaves you."

"What are you talking about?" Maya asked, walking over to Cambria with the open bottle of wine and leaning into her. "There's two bottles of wine that need drinking. She's staying here with Fred, Daphne, and me. We're getting drunk, and we're going to talk about you, Mr. Watson."

"Me?" my dad asked, sparking a laugh from everyone around the table.

"Yes, you," Maya said, "but also your oldest son. He has quite the way with stringing us women along just to break our poor, little hearts."

"I've always called him my little heartbreaker," my mom said.

"Well, that's my cue to leave," I said. "Alina, are you ready?"

"Born ready. Like, literally, investigating a Freddy Krueger case is my literal dream job—pun intended, of course. Maybe our next case will occur in Texas, with an inbred giant wielding a chainsaw, or at a summer camp on the lake, looking into a string of machete-related grisly murders."

Cambria hopped out of her chair and hustled over to me, wrapping her arms around me in a hug and kissing me on the lips. "All this talk of horror movies has me a little creeped out. Be safe, yeah?"

"Of course. You have fun."

Maya joined us, hugging both Cambria and me in a group embrace. "Oh, we're going to have fun. Don't you worry a single second about us entertaining ourselves."

"Well, you're probably in more danger hanging out with Maya than I am investigating demons."

"He's not lying," Alina said, already headed for the front door.

Questions.
Monday, May 1st.
1306hrs.

ALINA JABBERED THE ENTIRE twenty-minute drive from Santa Cruz to a little cafe in Aptos, a small town outside of the tourist city. Mostly, she blabbered about horror movies, about the Freddy Krueger franchise, listing her favorite and least favorite films in the series.

I tried my best to tune her out, chewing on a stick of gum and rehashing the email Fred had shared during lunch. Four people experienced similar dreams featuring the same antagonist—a figure carrying a sledgehammer. Brutal. They had also heard the same haunting tune of a strange song they could all hum but not identify.

That information alone informed me of two hard facts. First, the four people dreamed of the same nightmare for a reason. They possessed a connection, and I had to pinpoint that connection to drag this case from the paranormal to the mundane. What connected them? Second, the song. Why did they hear the same song?

"August, hey," Alina said, drawing me from my thoughts. "Hello?" She waved her hand in front of my face.

I shooed it away like batting at a pesty fly. "I'm driving. You can't cover my face."

"Are you even listening to me?"

"No."

"Serious?"

"I was thinking."

"About what... or who? Cambria?" Alina made smooch noises, kissing the air. "Do you love her? Do you want to carry her children in your belly?"

"What's wrong with you? No. I'm thinking about the case."

"That's what I was talking about."

"You were talking about movies."

"Don't you find the case and those movies strangely similar? You think that's a coincidence? I don't, and I think we might find a clue if we watch them."

"How many of them exist?"

"Nine."

"Nine! When will we have time to watch nine movies?"

"We're on vacation." Alina rested her head against the passenger window. "We have all the time in the world. Besides, I don't need you to watch the movies with me. I'll watch them with Adam."

"He's twenty."

"So."

"You're sixteen."

"And? You and Maya are four years apart."

"We're adults. You're a kid. Also, Maya and I aren't romantically involved with each other."

Alina twisted her hair around a finger and grinned. "I can still watch a movie or nine with him."

"In the living room of the rental home. No blankets."

"What if we're cold?"

"Blankets if you're sitting on opposite ends of the couch."

"You're a buzzkill, you know that?" Alina kicked her feet onto the dashboard and slid her body toward the center console, propping herself up on an elbow. "Okay, Sherlock, what were you so busy thinking about you had to ignore me?"

I popped a knuckle. "You brought the notebook, right?"

"Notebook? I'm not a ninety-two-year-old trying to destroy the Earth by wasting paper. I brought my phone, which has a note-taking app on it. It can even transcribe what words I speak into notes so I don't have to type."

"Well, open your little gizmo and take a few notes."

"Right now?"

"Right now."

"Okay." Alina swiped her phone's screen. "Don't say gizmo, either."

"You ready?"

"I'm ready."

"Here are some questions. Write these down." I glanced at the navigation screen in my car, checking when I needed to turn into the cafe's parking lot. In a quarter mile. "Can people experience shared dreams?"

"Obviously," Alina said. "That's why we're here."

"There's no such thing as a stupid question during the brainstorming process. So, no comments from the peanut gallery, only scribing."

"What's wrong with you today? Did you read thesaurus before bed last night? Gizmo? Scribing? You know, you're technically a millennial. You don't have to say things as if you're sixty-seven, because you're not. You went to high school with the world's first iPhone. You were born with the internet. Stop acting like a grumpy old man."

"Can people share dreams? Can people get physically harmed in dreams?" I pondered what to ask next.

"That's it? Two questions? You made me type out notes for two questions?"

I turned into the parking lot, found an empty stall, and turned off the car. Facing Alina, I asked, "Do you have any more questions?"

"Sure."

"Note them, then."

"How did this group of four people meet? What's their history? Where did they go to school? Where do they currently work? Did they share a traumatic experience that might contribute to their shared dreams? Would any of them have motivation to make up this story for personal gain?"

"What's the song have do with any of this?"

"That's a good one." Alina's fingers blurred over the screen as she typed.

The coastal sunshine pierced through the windshield and warmed the car's cab, but not in an overbearing, fatiguing way—more in a pleasant, comforting manner. Alina clicked her tongue, thinking. I tapped the steering wheel.

After a second conjuring no other questions, we agreed to venture inside the cafe and meet with the clients.

Odd Behavior. Monday, May 1st. 1311hrs.

KIMBERLY AND JASON DROVE away with Rachel, Jake, and Adam, who rode in the truck's backseat. They all headed to downtown Santa Cruz to shop and lay on the busy, crowded beach.

Why, though, Maya wondered, collecting her personal bottle of wine and crossing through the sliding-glass door into the backward. Why, when the vacation home had a built-in pool, lounge chairs, umbrellas, and a cooler filled with drinks. What could they possibly need to spend their money on? Or the beach… why drive to the over-populated public beach? The backyard went from pool to tidy lawn to a human-sized chessboard to a little fence about three feet tall. Beyond the fence, a stretch of sand led to the ocean. They had a private beach a hundred yards beyond the home's back door.

"Why leave?" Maya asked, wading into the pool's shallow end.

Fred wore goggles much too small for his block head and arm floaties around his wrists. In one hand, he held Daphne's patented margarita, and in his other, he snacked on a second helping of sandwich.

Country music played around them, issuing from the planters around the pool and the house's exterior walls. Fred had synced his phone with the home theater system, and he played some Top Forty station.

"Why what?" Fred asked.

"Why would they leave? Everything they need is right here."

"Not the stores," Fred said. "Well, that's not entirely true. I guess people do most of their shopping from home these days, anyway."

"Who cares about shopping?"

"Kimberly and Rachel care about shopping."

"To leave a perfectly awesome rental house? Sure, I guess. It just doesn't make any sense to me."

Fred stared at the sky and clicked his tongue. "You know how some people poke pins into a world map to keep track of everywhere they traveled, or collect postcards, or have sex in every new place they visit?"

"You do that?" Maya asked.

Fred drank from the margarita. "Do what now?"

"Have sex in every new place you visit."

He nodded his head up and down. "No. I don't."

"Daphne's idea, or yours?"

"Anyway, Kimberly and Rachel buy a souvenir whenever they visit somewhere new. It's usually the first thing they do."

"How often do you travel with them?"

"Only once or twice."

"Does August know?"

Fred coughed on the margarita. "Heck to the no. Not a chance. And if you tell him, I'll know who told him, and I'll tell him your secret."

"What's my secret?" Maya asked.

"What's your secret, like you didn't tell me?"

"I don't have secrets."

"No?"

"No," Maya said, splashing Fred.

Fred glanced at his wife, who lounged on a pool chair on the deck and soaked in the sun. He raised his voice so she could hear him above the music. "Does Maya have a secret?"

"She has a secret," Daphne said. "Fred shared it with me."

"What is it?" Maya asked, splashing Fred again. "What's my secret?"

He showed his teeth, speaking quietly through them and nodding toward Daphne. Cambria also lay on a lounge chair, enjoying the warmth of the afternoon. She read a book and drank from her personal bottle of wine. "I can't tell you with her there."

"Why?" Maya asked.

"It's about August."

Maya splashed him again, more aggressive.

Fred turned his shoulder to Maya, shielding himself from her assaults. "Don't get my sandwich wet."

"Tell me."

"No."

"It's my secret, I should know."

"I shouldn't have to tell you your secret."

"What about August?" Maya asked.

Fred stuck out his lower lip. "It was like a month ago, when I tried to drink with you."

"That was a good night," Maya said, smiling as she remembered Fred singing Toby Keith karaoke. "Not a good next morning."

"The worst next morning."

"What did I tell you?"

Fred leaned forward and whispered the reveal. "You think August is cute."

Maya narrowed her eyes. "Seriously?"

"Seriously."

"You're not joking? That's the big secret?" Maya chuckled, the noise scratching against her throat. "I don't think August is cute. He is cute." Maya raised her voice and looked over her shoulder. "Daphne."

"Yeah."

"Do you think August is cute?"

"Don't answer that," Fred said.

"Yeah," Daphne said.

Fred splashed Maya. "Why would you ask her that? I don't want to know that about my wife."

"Cambria?" Maya asked. "Do you think August is cute?"

"I wouldn't be here otherwise."

"See," Maya said, grinning. "Girls think August is cute. That's not a secret. It's a fact."

Fred growled. "That's not all you said."

"What else did I say?"

"You said he's cute, and..."

"And... what?"

"You want to bite off his nose."

Maya squished her eyebrows together. "I said I wanted to bite off his nose?"

"You did."

"I don't even know what that means."

"That's what I said to you," Fred hissed. "What's that even mean? You said, and I quote, 'I want to bite his nose off and gobble it all up, and I want it to sit in my belly like a seed and sprout and grow and turn into a little baby.'"

"That makes no sense."

"I also said that to you. I asked if you knew about the process of a making a baby. You said, and I quote, 'I know.' I'm not sure if you do, though."

"I'm still confused to how that's a secret."

Fred lowered his voice and waded closer to Maya. "You want to carry and give birth to August's children. That's what you meant. His nose was a metaphor for his wiener."

"Gross. What's wrong with you?" Maya splashed him again.

"My sandwich! You're going to ruin my sandwich. So, if you tell August my secret, guess what?"

"What?"

"I'll tell August your secret."

"That I want his nose to fertilize me? Tell him."

"Okay."

Maya shook her head, her fingers tingling with nerves. "Don't tell him. That's weird. Why would I say that?"

"Because you love him," Fred said.

"No, I don't."

"You think he's sexy."

"I do."

"You want his body."

"On certain lonely nights, yes."

"You want his nose to put a baby in your belly."

"Nope, I don't," Maya said.

"You said it."

"Whatever. I won't tell August you vacation with his family, if you don't tell him I want his booger children."

"Deal."

"Back to the initial conversation," Maya said. "Rachel and Kimberly went shopping. Sure, makes sense... I guess. Why did the boys head out to a crowded beach? Why not stay here, or use our very private beach?"

"Simple," Fred said, finishing his margarita. He looked at Daphne and shook the remaining ice cubes in the glass. "Babe, when you're available, could I get another one."

"Ten minutes."

"Thank you."

"She always waits on you hand and foot?" Maya asked, wincing from Daphne's eagerness to serve her husband. "I would tell you to get your big boy butt out of the pool, dry off, and make your own margarita."

"Yeah, well, thankfully I'm not married to you. Daphne enjoys making the cocktails, so I allow her to do it."

"You allow her? That's super generous of you to allow your wife to serve you alcohol. Wow. Husband of the year."

"Why did the dudes go with the chicks?" Fred asked, repeating Maya's question.

"Don't change the topic."

"You changed the topic. I'm bringing it back home. Jeff and Jake aren't so much independent halves in their marriage as they are extensions of their wives. Does that make sense? Where Kimberly goes, Jason goes. Where Rachel goes, Jake joins. So, when Kim and Rachel go shopping, Jason and Jake tag along, unless they can find something more entertaining to do within a certain radius. Here, in Santa Cruz, they found the beach."

"What about Adam?"

"He's much like his father and Jake. Introverted. You won't hear them say more than a handful of words at a time, and usually only when spoken to. My guess, Adam didn't want to hang out with strangers."

"Lame."

"I agree."

"Why are you wearing floaties?" Maya asked, gesturing to Fred's wrists. "Can you not swim? Are you afraid of drowning? Also, you're in the shallow end. Actually, this entire pool is probably the shallow end for your big self."

Fred inflated his cheeks with a deep inhale and farted the air from his lips. "I don't enjoy holding up my arms."

"What?" Maya squinted her eyes and scratched the back of her neck. "What does that even mean?"

"The floaties just... they let my arms float. I'm on vacation. I don't want to work that hard."

"Like, you don't want to work so hard you have to hold up your arms? You're something else, Frederick Rogers." Maya drank from the bottle of wine, staring at Fred's limp arms moving with the gentle wake of the pool. "Who even thinks of that?"

"I thought Alina asked a lot of questions. Do you two take classes for it?"

As Maya's mouth moved, speaking before thought even formed in her mind, something flew into the pool. A second later, a black bird emerged to the surface, flapping and thrashing its wings, splashing the water as it struggled.

Fred shoved what remained of the sandwich into his mouth and ran to the bird, lifting it from the water and setting it on the deck. The creature acted crazed, sporadic, pecking its face against the cement and leaving beads of blood. It flew two feet into the air and crashed back to the ground.

Daphne and Cambria stood from their lounge chairs, backing toward the back patio and sliding-glass door, away from the bird's odd behavior. It leaped into the pool again, once more drowning.

Fred repeated his lifeguard duties, rescuing the animal and setting it back on the cement. It darted toward the fence, landing on the sandy beach, twitching and screeching as it hopped and half-flew into the ocean.

Maya eyed Fred, who stared at the beach. He put in the effort to raise his hand and point across the shore. "Look there."

A cluster of birds, maybe six, slammed themselves into the wet sand, attacked each other, and dove into the waves. They screeched with pain until an odd silence ensued, interrupted only by the wind and the tide.

"What the actual f—"

"Did they try to commit suicide?" Fred asked, interrupting Maya.

"I don't know."

"I haven't ever seen anything like that."

Maya tipped back the wine bottle, pulling a quarter of the juice in one go. She would need a better buzz to handle anything else like that.

Fred looked over his shoulder at Daphne. "I don't know if I can wait ten minutes."

"I don't think I can, either," Daphne said. She disappeared into the house.

Maya burped, long and loud. When she finished clearing her system, she looked at Fred. "Why are you wearing goggles if you're just going to stand in the water and drink? You look ridiculous."

A Common Enemy. Monday, May 1st. 1256hrs.

THE CAFE HAD A dimly lit interior, industrial themed like a modern brewery, though much smaller. A few patrons sat at the tables, laptops open, headphones stuck in their ears. They hunched over their box screens, eyes squinted, mouths pursed, oblivious to the world around them.

Alina had mentioned I'm technically a millennial, born into the age of iPhones and the internet. That's true. I'm thirty-two. I'm not sure if it gets any more millennial than that. However, after the incident with Aaron, I found technology was toxic to me. It polluted my mind and poisoned my thoughts. So, I prevented myself from spending idle time in front of a glowing screen, choosing instead to focus on getting drunk.

Even before my incident, my parents had never allowed me to have a video game console. We hadn't owned a television set, and they never bought me an iPhone until I could drive. In my teenage years, I played sports and explored the great outdoors. When inside, I read books.

Technology and August Watson had never gotten along.

I glanced around the cafe for a table occupied by two women and two men. I didn't notice a party larger than three.

"Welcome," said a cheery, female voice from behind the front counter. A young, pimply faced girl about Alina's age smiled at us.

I walked over to her, slightly limping. The twenty extra minutes of sitting in the car after the three-hour drive to Santa Cruz stiffened my hip beyond belief. "How's it going?" I asked.

"Good," she said. "How can I help you?"

I scratched my neck. "I'll have a house coffee."

"Lemonade for me," Alina said.

As the young woman turned her back to pour my coffee and prepare Alina's lemonade, I said, "Have you seen a group of four come in here? We're supposed to meet with them."

The barista glanced over her shoulder. "I did. They arrived a few minutes before you." She snapped the lid over my coffee and placed it on the counter, then she pointed behind her, to the back of the building. "They're sitting on the back patio. Don't worry, it's shaded out there. You don't have to deal with any direct sunlight."

"Thank you," I said, removing the business card from my wallet and paying for the drinks.

The young woman prepared Alina's lemonade, handing her the plastic cup and paper straw. We thanked her and crossed through a dingy hallway toward the back patio.

Four people sat at a picnic table for eight. Two women and two men, all in their early twenties, and all wildly attractive—Hollywood attractive—despite their obvious states of exhaustion. Puffy skin. Red eyes. Unkempt hair. Unshaven faces. Twitchy, crazed demeanors, like meth addicts needing their next fix. All of that, though, hid beneath the surface of obscene beauty.

"They even look like they could star in a horror movie," Alina whispered to me, nudging my ribs with her elbow.

I grunted as her bony elbow bore into me. "I don't know what that means."

"They're as hot as Hades on a summer day in the Sahara."

"Can you get their attention?" I asked.

"Heather Thompson!" Alina nearly shouted. "Christina Wyss. Johnny Lantz. Nick Lane. May I have your attention, please?"

The four young adults tiredly turned their heads and faced Alina. She stood with her feet together, shoulders pinched back. Her arms stretched outward, away from her body, as if she might hug the entire group.

"I present to you the one, and the only, August Allan Watson." Alina whooshed her arms to point at me and stepped aside, a matador stepping away from a charging bull.

Red and hot in the face, I hobbled to the picnic table, moving in the exact opposite fashion as a charging bull. "Good afternoon," I said, cracking a knuckle. "Thank you for the introduction, Alina. I'm August Watson, with Blue Moon Investigation Agency. You're aware of my colleague, Alina Moore."

"Hi," said the woman nearest to me. She had sandy-blonde hair pulled up in a sloppy bun, and she wore a baggy sweatshirt. Dark bags weighed down her bright eyes, and red splotches splashed across her cheeks. "I'm Heather."

I glanced at her friends. They all bore a similar resemblance—naturally gorgeous people, with an emphasis on natural. None of them appeared to have readied themselves for the day, or any other day for quite some time. They all sported black bags and heavy eyelids and hunched postures, as if they didn't have the energy to hold up their heads for too long.

"This is my fiancé, Johnathan Lantz," Heather said, gesturing to the young man sitting beside her. "He's the one who contacted you."

"Call me Johnny," said the James Dean looking gentleman. He wore a white T-shirt, and he had raven-black hair.

"I'm Christina," said the other woman sitting across from Heather. She wore an oversized T-shirt, probably her boyfriend's, and she stared at the wood surfacing picnic table. "You can call me Chris."

"Nick," said the last of them—the other young man who looked like another movie star, though I couldn't quite place who. I'm sure Alina had his appearance noted, though. The girl didn't miss too much.

"You care if I sit?" I asked.

"Please," Heather said, scooting closer to Johnny and allowing me room.

I grimaced as I sat. My hip preferred for me to remain on my feet, but business dictated I joined my clients. I didn't want to stand over them during the initial interview.

Alina sat across from me, next to Chris. She placed her phone on the picnic table. "Do you all care if I record this conversation? August prefers me to scribble notes on a pad of paper, like I'm some Earth-murdering monster. Why kill the trees, though?"

No one objected, so Alina started voice recorder. However, the phone only collected our breaths and the gentle breeze. No one spoke. A few long seconds stretched into nearly a minute. Experience dictated that I waited for the client to spark the conversation. Uncomfortable silence often led to a need to fill the void, which turned into incessant talking, a beneficial way to glean information. From there, I would guide the conversation with questions. Not in that Aptos cafe. I'm not sure if the young adults had the mental energy to conjure an original thought without prompting.

Alina must have recognized their distant gazes, too. She broke the silence. "My mom was... well, she is a drug addict."

I rapidly blinked, confused by her approach. I held my tongue, though, allowing her continue.

"My aunt, who I now live with, enjoys celebrating accomplishments with copious amounts of alcohol. When I say accomplishments, I mean any accomplishment. She's a big believer in rewarding success. One time she was constipated for like a week. When she finally pooped, guess what? Maya drank an entire bottle of wine. It was a Monday night, but she didn't care. Accomplishment equals celebration."

"Where are you going with this?" I asked, utterly confused by her poop story.

"I'm just saying, I've seen people at their worst—withdrawing from drugs, hungover, sleep deprived, you name it. You four," she looked at each of our clients, "you look like you're coming off one of the longest benders in recorded history."

Heather chuckled. "I feel like that."

"I've been on the bad side of a long bender," Nick said, his voice gruff. "I would take that over this any day of the week."

"Do any of you do drugs?" Alina asked.

"Weed," Heather said. "Well, we used to, but not anymore."

"Used to?" I asked.

"It makes us too relaxed," Chris said. "Too sleepy."

"I'll take Modafinil," Johnny said.

"What's that?" Alina asked.

"It reduces extreme sleepiness. People suffering narcolepsy take it."

"Does it work? Do you stay awake?"

Johnny chuckled. "It worked better before. But I haven't had a full night's sleep in, oh, I don't know…" He turned to Heather.

"Two weeks," she said, her tone unsure.

"It keeps us awake," Johnny said. "That much works. But once you're awake for so many hours in a row, you suffer hallucinations."

"You have waking dreams," Alina said.

"Half the time, we can't tell what's real and what's not real," Heather said.

"And our minds think negative, paranoid thoughts when we don't sleep," Chris said, staring at the table. "It's hard to remember simple stuff, to think straight and logically. I can doze off at any second." That last statement wasn't too difficult to believe. She looked like she might drift away at any moment.

"Why don't you sleep?" I asked.

"To avoid it," Nick said.

"Avoid what?"

"The Devil."

"Can you tell me anything more about this Devil?" I asked.

"No," Heather said, hugging herself. "We can't ever remember details, like waking from a dream, you know? Everything sort of fades away."

"I saw the Devil," Nick said, raising his red-rimmed eyes to me. "It was my fifth day without sleep. I hallucinated, and I saw the Devil's face."

"What did it look like?" Alina asked.

Nick coughed into a fist. "I don't know. He wore a mask."

"So you didn't see its face?" Alina sat back on the bench and glanced upward. "You saw someone wearing a mask."

"The nightmare wore a mask of a normal face."

"What's that mean?" I asked.

"A man's face. Like it skinned someone's face off and put over its own. There was blood on the edges of the mask and everything."

"Can you describe anything about the mask? Any details might help," I said.

Nick drank from a large cup of iced coffee and closed his eyes. For a second, I thought he had fallen off, slipping into the land of sleep.

With his eyes shut, he said, "Thick eyebrows atop beady eyes drooping downward. A receding hairline. Thin lips turned upward in a creepy, smirky smile. Tiny, knobbed ears." Nick lifted his hands from his lap and placed them on the table. He wore a cast on his right arm.

"What else?" I asked.

"The Devil carried a sledgehammer. It walked toward me. I couldn't run, though. I couldn't move. I couldn't breathe. It walked so slowly, too. Inches at a time, dragging the head of the sledgehammer on the tile so it scraped an awful noise. When it finally made it to me, it reached out and grabbed my hand and placed it on the kitchen table."

"This happened at your house?"

Nick opened his eyes and stared at me. "In my apartment. In my kitchen. The nightmare placed my palm on the kitchen table, raised the sledgehammer as far as the ceiling allowed, and brought it down. It shattered the bones in my hand."

I glanced at Alina.

She scraped her teeth over her lip. "The figure in your dream," she said, choosing her words carefully, "it hurt you in real life?"

"It hit me in my dream," Nick said. "But I suffered the injury in real life."

Alina faced me, not having to say what charged through her mind. I already knew.

Like Freddy Krueger.

"When I woke up," Nick continued, dropping his head as if it required too much effort to keep upright, "the Devil wasn't there. I had a broken hand, though. And the kitchen table looked like someone had brought a sledgehammer to it."

I removed a stick of gum from my pocket and folded it into my mouth. "Have any of you experienced something like that?" I asked, glancing at the other three. "Something that you thought happened in a dream, but it actually happened in real life?"

They shook their heads.

"That happened last week," Nick said.

"We didn't know what else to do," Johnny said. "I've heard of Tempest Michaels. I know he's on the other side of the world, but we were desperate for help. I looked him up, learned you existed, and were in Sacramento. I reached out, hoping you could help."

Chris reached across the table and grabbed my hands, hers cold and clammy. "Can you help?"

"We'll have to discuss my rates," I said, hating this part of my job. These kids were obviously terrified beyond belief, and for me to step in and save them, I had to ask for their money.

"I can pay anything," Johnny said. "Well, my parents can. Give a number, I'll add a zero to it, and my parents won't bat an eye. Just please, help us."

We spent a few minutes going over my procedures and the cost of my time, and they agreed to the terms. I also shared with them that though their situation appeared abnormal, bordering on the supernatural, it probably had a mundane explanation. They understood, and they still desired to hire me. With that uncomfortable part of the business behind us, I ventured forward with questioning.

"Have you filed a report with the police?"

Johnny shook his head and chuckled. "What are they going to do? Investigate our dreams?"

What am I going to do? I thought. "Nick suffered an injury. His table was splintered. That's enough to get law enforcement involved."

"I called them," Chris said, her voice quiet. "They didn't believe Nick's story. Do you know what they thought?"

I looked at the young woman and nodded. I had an idea what the police thought. "That you did it."

"That I did it," Chris said, scoffing. "The jealous or crazy girlfriend attacked her boyfriend. When Nick refused to press charges against me, the police dismissed our report."

"No other evidence existed," Nick said. "The Devil appeared to me in a dream. How do I convince the police of that?"

He couldn't, and we all knew that. We needed to discover actual evidence based in reality and on logic for the police to bat an eye.

"What about the music?" Alina asked. "In your email, you mentioned something about all of you hearing a song."

"We don't remember it exactly, not the words at least," Heather sighed and looked at me. She hummed, and she sounded pleasant, as if she had an extensive background in music. When Heather finished the brief sample of the song, she said, "I don't recognize the tune, but it's old. I've searched through so many songs to find it, but I can't."

"We don't remember any of the words," Chris said.

Alina suddenly hummed the melody, softly and to herself. When she finished, she hummed it again, tapping her knuckles on the table. "I know that song."

"You've heard it before?" Heather asked, excitement flashing through her. She sat up a little straighter.

"I have... but I don't where." Alina continued to hum, as if doing so might unlock the hidden words.

"How long have you all known each other?" I asked.

"Since middle school," Heather said. "Johnny and I started dating in the eighth grade."

"High school sweethearts," Alina said, pressing her palms against her chest. "So sweet." I couldn't tell if she meant that sincerely or sarcastically.

"Nick and I never dated until this past year, but the four of us always hung out," Chris said. "I was Heather's best friend going to back to grade school. Nick and Johnny have known each other since they were babies. When Heather and Johnny started talking, we all grew close."

"Did any of you share a traumatic experience?" I asked, reciting Alina's questions from the car.

They glanced at each other, shaking their heads. "No," Johnny answered for the group.

"You all struggle with sleep," Alina said. "If you doze off, you risk running into the Devil. If you stay awake, well, you risk what happened to Nick—dreaming while awake. So, you're all in a strange state of not being able to sleep, but also not being able to stay awake. How do you function? How do you live?"

Heather stole a sip from her large coffee.

"We don't," Johnny said. "After what happened with Nick's hand, we all stay in the same apartment."

Chris returned her attention to the picnic table. "My parents stopped paying my tuition to college. They don't believe me about the dreams. They think I'm doing drugs, and I'm shacking up with Nick and having orgies and throwing my life away. We're not, though. This is real, and we're so scared."

"We all lost our jobs," Johnny said. "Those of us in school skip class, so we're probably losing any scholarship we have. We take shifts staying awake."

"Take shifts?" I asked.

"Two of us sleep, the other two watch and make sure nothing happens." Chris rubbed her eyes.

"What do you mean?"

"If someone's breathing changes or they start to move or anything. The two standing guard wake up the two who are sleeping."

I grabbed my coffee and drank, not sure how to continue with the meeting. Creating the paranormal investigative business had come with a lot of cases steeped in mythical and supernatural possibility, except they always boiled down to something rational. Not only that, I could often think of different, logical explanations to help launch and direct the investigation. With this nightmare situation—experiencing the same Devil, getting attacked in a dream but gaining real-life injuries—I did not know where to begin or what to do. Maybe Alina was right. Maybe I should watch the nine Freddy Krueger movies.

"Do you have any other information you can share?" I asked. "It doesn't matter how silly or irrelevant it might seem. If you can think of anything, please, let me know."

The four of them chewed on their tongues for a few seconds.

Johnny spoke. "He's going to kill us if you don't stop him."

Opening Up. Monday, May 1st. 1428hrs.

Alina and I remained seated on the cafe's back patio long after the four fatigued friends left. Returning to our vacation rental home would prove less than productive. Our priority revolved around solving this case and saving those poor kids. That task felt more than impossible with eleven people crammed into one house, drinking and arguing and carrying on. I wouldn't be able to think about the investigation properly while there.

So, we had agreed to remain at the picnic table, listening to the recorded interview from her cell phone.

The part that stuck out to me, that I couldn't logically place, was that the Devil had physically hurt Nick. It had appeared to him in a dream and had injured him in reality.

"Or so he says," Alina pointed out.

"You don't believe him?"

"Do you?"

"Based on how they look, yeah. They haven't slept in months. Also, why lie about having his hand smashed? Unless, like the cops believe, Chris did it? Or someone else, and he's too embarrassed to tell the truth." I spoke my mind, verbalizing whatever thought popped into my head. "I keep going back to all of them experiencing the same nightmare. How do you explain that? And if Nick's story is true, which I believe it is, how do you explain that? How does the Devil attack Nick in his dream? If that never happened, how did the Devil attack Nick in real life, leaving behind no trace of its presence beyond Nick's broken hand and his splintered table? Wouldn't Nick, after having his hand crushed, immediately wake up and see his attacker?"

"Wow," Alina said, whistling.

"What?"

"You okay?"

"Why?"

"I've never heard you say so many words in a row. I thought you were suffering a stroke or something serious. You had me worried." She pulled her soggy paper straw from the empty lemonade cup and tore it apart. "I hate these straws. Did you know they're not even more environmentally friendly than plastic straws? It's a scam. It's all a scam."

"Do you have any theories?"

"About the straws? Yeah. A ton. Capitalism doesn't care to educate, only take advantage of. Though they might cause more harm than plastic straws, businesses push paper straws to take advantage of the left-leaning conspiracy theorists. That's right. I said it. Left-leaning conspiracy theorists. Don't get me started on vaccination and autism. Don't even ask."

"I didn't even ask about the straws."

"You asked about my theories."

"Oh." Alina pressed her tongue to the side of her cheek.

"Can someone attack people in their dreams?"

"Freddy Krueger could."

"He's a fictional character."

"Doesn't feel like that right now, does it?"

I finished my third cup of coffee. "What was he? A demon?"

"A Dream Demon."

"There you go. Demons don't exist."

"No?" Alina asked, furrowing her brow. "They're in the Bible."

"To say demons exist, we would have to admit vampires exist, and changelings and Sasquatch. But, as we know from first-hand experience, the supernatural doesn't exist."

"What if all those things you listed, and all the monsters you didn't list, are only manmade iterations of demons?"

"Demons don't exist."

"Angels?"

"No."

"So you don't believe in God, or any god?"

"No."

"You prayed earlier."

I popped a knuckle and stared at the ivy-laced brick wall wrapping around the patio. At the spur of the moment, immersed in complicated emotions about the vacation, I had prayed.

"Why?" Alina asked when I didn't respond.

"It felt... like the right thing to do."

"Because God called you to pray?"

"Because I felt like I've acted poorly toward my mother for quite a while now. Praying was an intentional step to get closer to her."

Alina tucked a strand of hair behind her ear. "Why did you push her away? What did she do?"

I stood and walked back into the cafe. The barista from earlier had clocked out, and a new teenager stood behind the counter—a lanky boy with raven-black hair and ghostly-pale skin. I asked him for a refill, tipped him for the service, and returned to the picnic table, sitting and grimacing as I did. My hip, more than my shoulder, had grown especially tight and achy.

"I asked you a question," Alina said. "Don't think your temporary absence made me forget."

I waited a moment to consider her question. "It wasn't any one thing. It was the culmination of many things over many years."

As I rolled into my memory, thinking of the many manipulations and slights my mother had enacted over the years, finding a couple of specific examples to share with Alina, my phone buzzed atop the wooden table.

I reached for it, noticing Glacia's name on the caller ID.

My heart plummeted, sitting deep in my stomach like a stone. She and I hadn't spoken since spending the night together nearly a week ago. I had attempted to contact her a few times, but she had always sent me to voicemail. Once she responded with a quick text saying it was for the best, whatever that meant.

"You going to stare at her name all day or answer the phone?" Alina asked.

"Should I answer?"

"I don't think so. I think you should ignore the coolest woman ever to come into your life, other than me, of course. Just ignore her call. Heck, throw your phone away so you never have to worry about her calling again."

"Hello," I answered.

A second of quiet. "Hi," Glacia said, exhaling the quick greeting.

"Hi."

"How are you?"

"You know me, I'm hanging in there. Well, Fred's holding me up."

"Fred?" Alina asked. "That boy does nothing but eat. Tell her the truth. Tell her I'm holding you up by a freaking single strand of hair."

Glacia asked something as Alina spoke, and I missed it.

"Sorry. Can you say that again?" I held a finger to my lips, silencing Alina.

"Did you do it?" Glacia asked.

I popped a knuckle and nodded, knowing exactly what she referred to. The day before, I had called her, despite her asking for me not to reach out, and I had received her voicemail. I left a message, letting her know I stood before the Brooks' door and needed her help to proceed.

Cambria had helped me, though—she had been there for me when I needed her.

"Yeah," I said.

"How did it go?"

"It went well, for all of us, I think." The smell of chocolate-chip cookies filled my memory.

"I'm sorry," Glacia said. "I didn't... I really liked you from the first time we met, which I think I made fairly obvious. But I didn't think long-distance was fair to either of us."

"To you," I said.

"What?"

"You don't get to decide what's fair to me. I do. You didn't think long distance was fair to you."

"You're right. I've done long distance before, and it doesn't work. I wasn't ready for that kind of commitment, anyway. I recently ended a long-term relationship. My Nana died. My mom and uncle haunted the house Nana willed to me. I'm sorry to make excuses, but I had a lot happening at one time, and I used you as an outlet—to recharge and forget about everything but the moment. I tried to tell you I only wanted something fast and fun, but I don't know if I ever said it correctly. So, I'm sorry for misleading you."

I thought of my apology to Raymond and Tammy Brooks. They had accepted it without hesitation. They had forgiven me for taking everything from them. If they could do that, could I not let Glacia off the hook? The lighter, more rational part of my mind chimed in. Off the hook for what? She had gifted me with a house worth a small fortune. She had slept with me, no strings attached. Why did I harbor so much anger toward her?

Then it hit me. She had run from me, or so it felt. That angered and hurt me, because it made me realize how I had ran and hid from those who cared most for me when I needed them the most. I had disappeared from my family and friends, turning to the comfort of booze.

I wasn't really mad at Glacia for leaving. I was angry at myself for running away.

"August?" Glacia asked.

"I understand," I said. "I'm sorry, too." I dropped my head back and stared upward at the latticed overhang, peeking through the slats at the blue sky. "You okay?"

"Mostly, yeah. Still working through everything that happened. But I think that will be a long process."

"Yeah."

"You sleeping in the house yet?" Glacia asked, referring to her Nana's house which fell into her possession. Glacia, wanting to rid herself of its responsibility, as she lived over five-hundred miles away in another state, had gifted it to me.

"My apartment's lease doesn't end until July."

"Sublet it."

"For three months?" I asked, scratching the back of my neck and thinking of the headache subletting would inevitably incur.

"Why not?" Glacia asked. "It's only three months."

"I want to do this properly," I said. "Escrow and title and all that before I move in."

"I guess that makes sense. I've already contacted an agent in Sacramento to draft a contract. You should see it in your inbox by the end of the week."

"I'll keep an eye out for it."

Glacia sighed, blowing static into my ear. "You can call me."

"You won't ignore me?"

Glacia snickered. "If I can, I'll answer. Friends?"

"Friends," I said.

When we ended the call, it felt like someone had removed a wet, weighted blanket from my body. I breathed a little easier and moved a little lighter.

"You're welcome," Alina said, sneering at me.

"For what?"

"I called her yesterday evening."

"Why?"

"I told her to stop being such a stuck-up bi—"

"Alina," I said, cutting her off, "why would you call her?"

The kid stared at the picnic table, rotating her empty lemonade cup and leaving behind dark, crisscrossing rings. "To talk. We talk."

"You talk?"

"We have a lot in common, you know? With our parent situation. She's, like, awesome and sexy and successful. It's nice to talk to someone who understands what I'm feeling, especially right now, with my mom God knows where. I mean Maya..." Alina shook her head. "I don't know. Maya lives in her own little world. She was always the star of the family. My mom lived in her shadow, receiving next to no attention. Maya means well, but she doesn't understand. Same with you."

That comment slapped me across the face. "What's that mean?"

"You're nice enough. You have good intentions. But you don't know what it's like. Fred has a decent understanding, but he's a dude. So, it's different. Glacia knows how to relate because she lived this. I call her or text her most every day since she left for Oregon. Last night, she asked about you. I refused to answer. I said suck it up and call him. That's all."

I scratched my eyebrow and leaned forward, planting my elbows on the table and resting my chin on my fist. "I don't mean for this to sound insensitive, but we all struggle with our own demons. We all struggle uniquely with what we know. My dad never left home. To my knowledge he never cheated on or abused my mom. My mom never left us. She never neglected us. Both of them, always and no matter what, loved us, and they loved each other." I closed my eyes, drawing on my childhood memories. "It's nothing like what you've experienced, but we all experience pain in our own way and in our own time."

For a few seconds, birds chirped, and the ocean breeze rustled leaves and tickled leaves. From the distance, the sound of engines on the freeway droned. I thought of my mother and tried to mold into words how I really felt.

"My mom lost her brother when she was in high school, maybe younger," I said. "He was eighteen or nineteen. Car accident. She watched her parents suffer the loss of their oldest child—a suffering they couldn't escape. My mom experienced neglect and abuse from them, mostly in part to their abuse of alcohol and drugs to cope with their son's death. They, her parents, drifted far off-path, and they never really came back to center. I'm not sure how much that influenced her fear-based parenting, but she feared everything with her kids."

I opened my eyes.

Alina stared at me with a wide, curious gaze, soaking in my words. For a teenager who's supposed to see the world only through her narrow, self-centered vision, she practiced a lot of understanding and patience.

I thought of Maya's off-the-charts intelligence, and I wouldn't have doubted for a second if Alina didn't follow in her aunt's genetic footsteps.

Not really sure what I would say next, but knowing I should speak from the heart, I continued. "My mom never allowed her children to go to friends' houses. Friends always had to come over to our place." I coughed and chuckled, embarrassed. "I don't know. It sounds so frivolous to say out loud, but she stole our childhood. We couldn't leave the house because she feared kidnapping or gangs or anything, really. We stayed at home and played board games, swam in our pool, explored the undeveloped lot behind our house. But always within sight of my mom. I think she saw how her parents responded to their son's death, and my mother knew if anything happened to her children, she might act similarly. It was protection... sure. But more than that, she was selfish. She controlled us so she could feel better about herself. So she could manage her fear."

"You're guessing all this?"

I shrugged. "I spent about three years drunk and lost in thoughts of self-reflection, asking myself how I arrived in a dark room, not bothering with drinking glasses, but pulling whiskey straight from the bottle."

"That's depressing," Alina said.

"Very much so."

"So your mom stole your childhood from you, trying to protect you from harm?"

"From experience and failure."

"Sure. Now you hate her?"

"I don't hate her. I love her very much. It's complicated, though. I'm older now, and more aware of what she's doing, especially when she's doing it. She still tries to manipulate her children, to control their behaviors and actions to placate her fears."

"Her fear of losing you?" Alina asked.

"That. Also, she and my dad have built quite a successful life for themselves, and vanity plays a large role in her life. She has to look good—physically, emotionally, socially. Her family has to look good because they represent her. After I shot Aaron Brooks and disappeared into my grief and regret, she told her friends that the FBI or CIA or something like that had recruited me, and that's why no one saw or heard from me anymore. Everything was top secret. Classified. She told everyone that Aaron had a real gun. The media got it wrong when they reported an airsoft gun. She just... she tried so hard to not become her parents, running so far away, she ended up right where they were, only from an opposite path." I sighed. "I'm doing a poor job of explaining this."

"I get it. She's Muriel Fincher, but not as psychotic."

I snorted, snickering.

Muriel Fincher was Randall Fincher's mother, a woman who had controlled her thirty-year-old son to such an extreme, the man did not know how to continue with his life after his mother died.

"Similar, yes."

"I would rather have no mom than Muriel Fincher," Alina said.

"But my mom's not Muriel Fincher. She's flawed, controlling and manipulative, but she also loves harder than anyone I know. I think that's part of her problem. She loves too much. Still, she would do anything—and I'm not exaggerating either... she would do absolutely anything for her kids."

"Except let them fail."

I slowly nodded.

"Anything for love, but she wouldn't do that."

"Exactly," I said. "It's been a lot of years trying to escape from beneath her thumb, and watching her get away with it with my sister and occasionally my brother. A lot of minor incidents compounded." I smiled, though with no amusement or humor. A sad smile. "Here I am, complaining about my far-too-loving parents, and you're dealing with the absence of your parents."

"We all struggle uniquely. Life is funny, huh?"

"In a twisted, dark way."

"There's no better kind of humor."

"I like fart jokes," I said.

Alina giggled. "Did you just make a joke? Mr. Cynical made a joke?"

"Don't get used to it."

"Never."

I exhaled, feeling relatively calm. I almost believed I could actually find time to relax. As my mind decompressed, the Devil crept back into my thoughts. "Where do we start with the case?"

Alina chewed on her cheeks. "I recognized the song they hummed. I just can't figure out from where, though. Also, why is it important? What does it mean?"

"You think you can try to find it?"

"Yeah."

"I'll dive into the lives of our four clients."

"In most slasher movies, the characters all suck."

"What do you mean?"

"The main characters... they're mostly terrible people, or they're portrayed that way. The audience roots for them to die. At least, in slashers. That's the premise, though. A monster stalks a group of individuals, taking them out one by one in gruesome, creative, hilarious ways. The audience has to be okay with all the characters dying. So, the characters often suck, except for one—who's usually a virgin and shy and sweet."

"Those are the best qualities for someone who doesn't suck."

"Exactly," Alina said, sarcastic and shaking her head. "Anyway, my point, the audience shows up to watch the characters die. People aren't fans of the survivors in slashers, they're fans of the monsters. They show up to watch Jason or Freddy or Michael, not root for Alice. See, Jason died from negligent camp counselors. So, he rises from the dead and seeks his revenge on the new generation of negligent, party-seeking, sex-obsessed camp counselors."

"What's your point?"

"I know Heather, Johnny, Christina, and Nick hired us, but none of them seemed like the most awesome people in the world. I don't even think a shy virgin existed among them."

"This isn't a slasher movie."

"It's literally Freddy Krueger haunting their dreams. They're forcing themselves to stay awake. It's a horror movie. And it's a slasher. The main characters in this case, the four that hired us, they suck in some way."

"Alina," I said, rolling my eyes.

"You mentioned looking into them. Find out how they suck. They're the negligent camp counselors. The Devil is Jason Voorhees. Who did our cast of characters allow to drown? We learn that answer, we find our Devil."

The Beach.
Monday, May 1st.
1515hrs.

ALINA AND I SHUT down the coffee shop, which closed at 1700hrs. We hopped in my car and drove a mile west, parking in a public lot across from the ocean. She didn't say a word during the drive, or as we crossed the street and stood on the sand-covered cement, atop the wood-planked stairs descending to the beach.

"What do you think?" I asked.

Alina's mouth parted, but she remained quiet as she stared at the fluffy, white sand carpeting the beach, as she looked across the ocean. "I've never stepped in sand before. It's scary."

"The sand?"

Alina nodded. "And the ocean. It just ends. It goes so far that it just ends." She faced me, her eyes rimmed red and wet. "Will you walk out there with me? To the waves?"

"Of course."

"Would you think I'm a scaredy-cat if I said I'm nervous?"

"I would call you Fred Jr.," I said.

Alina giggled. "Don't be rude."

I reached out my hand, and she grabbed it. We stepped down the wooden stairs and onto the beach. I paused, leaned against the bottom post of the railing, and removed my shoes. Alina slipped off her sneakers and carefully placed her foot into the sand.

"It's warm," she said, digging her feet a few inches beneath the surface. "I thought it would be cold, but it's warm."

"It'll be cold down there," I said, nodding toward where the tide broke over the sand.

"Are there crabs?"

"Big ones," I said. "Be careful stepping into a nest. They'll pinch your toes right off."

"You're serious?"

I smiled.

"Don't mess around like that," Alina said. "How am I supposed to know? I once watched this horror movie called *The Sand*. Some unseen Lovecraftian monster hunts under the surface and devours the characters. How am I supposed to know that's not based on a real thing?"

"You think that's based on something real?"

"Freddy Krueger seems pretty legit right now."

"Come on," I said, taking a few steps onto the beach.

Alina hesitated, but eventually followed. We walked the fifty yards to the shoreline. She allowed the shallow tide to roll over her feet, and she gasped.

"People are swimming in this. It's so cold."

"People are crazy," I said.

"If I'm stung by a jellyfish," Alina said, "do not pee on me. Under no circumstance does anyone pee on me. I would rather die."

"Fine with me," I said.

The kid braved venturing a little further into the waves. The water sloshed around her knees, and she ran in the wake, splashing and laughing. At one point, a wave larger than the rest rolled in, catching her by surprise and knocking her off balance. She fell sideways, washing up on shore beside me.

I laughed with her at that.

After fifteen minutes, we sat in the warm sand and stared across the horizon, not saying much of anything at all. There wasn't much to say. So we lost ourselves in thought. The ocean filled the gaps of quiet. The sky shifted from bright, cloudless blue, to a hazy gray, to a burning orange, to a deep purple.

As we watched the orange-red orb fall into the darkening water, Alina said, "Thank you."

"For what?"

"Everything. The internship. Allowing me to stay at your apartment for a few days. Trusting me with so much responsibility at the company. Taking me here, to this beach, experiencing this. For, and I'll never admit this again, making me go back to school."

"You haven't gone back yet."

"But I will. You'll see to it, won't you?"

I nodded.

"You've changed my life. You've probably saved my life. Thank you."

"Can I make this more awkward?" I asked.

"You always do."

"I can say the same of you—changing and saving my life. You cleaned me up, straightened me out, forced me to take responsibility. Thank you."

Alina rested her head on my shoulder. "Don't tell Maya or Fred I said any of that."

"Don't tell them I made a fart joke."

Alina shoved me, jumped to her feet, and ran into the waves once more.

On the drive home, she sat in the passenger seat, soaking wet, ruining my leather. But what good is leather if you can't ruin it?

Keeping Up.
Monday, May 1st.
2117hrs.

ALINA AND I ARRIVED at the rental home quarter after nine, starving. We hadn't eaten since lunch. During our beach escape, we hadn't bothered with dinner. Without Fred there to nag us about food constantly, we hadn't even thought about eating. Once in the car, though, our stomachs rumbled and roared, demanding sustenance.

I grabbed the door handle and turned, but it wouldn't budge. Locked. "Do you have a key?" I asked, turning to Alina.

"No. Why would I have a key?"

"I don't have one."

"Why don't you have one? You're the adult."

"I didn't think anyone would lock the door. What time is it?" The question was rhetorical. I glanced at my phone. 2117hrs. My dad had a habit of stealing off around 2000hrs for bed. He rose early, so he went down early. Had he continued that trend on vacation and locked the front door out of habit?

"Should I ring the doorbell?" Alina asked.

"No," I said, scrolling to Fred's number. "If someone's knocked out already, I wouldn't want to wake them up."

Fred picked up immediately. "I thought you ran off to escape this madhouse, kidnapping the kid as a hostage in case we went after you."

"I thought about it," I said.

"Where you at?"

"The front door."

"Oh, yeah. I forgot to tell you."

"You're forgetting to tell me quite a lot today."

"I actually, like actually, forgot about the front door. We don't have any keys to the house. Well, we do. We have the key from the lockbox. When I spoke to Maxwell on the phone a few days back, laying out our situation and the amount of people we had, he said he would copy us a few extra keys. I think he forgot."

"He also forgot the gift basket," I said, glancing down at Alina. "Seems there's something in the water making everyone forget."

"Yeah, it would seem that way."

"What are you doing?" I asked.

"We're playing cards at the dinner table."

"That sounds fun."

"Not really. I lose every hand to Maya."

"Forget how to play?"

Fred chuckled. "You would think so."

"You forgetting something else?"

"I don't think so."

"No?"

"Nope," Fred said.

Through the open window first, then through the phone as an echo, I heard Maya speak in a tone suggesting she might have had a few too many drinks. "Who's that? August? Where is he?"

"Front door," Fred said.

"Our front door?"

"Yeah. He's locked out."

I stared at the ground and shook my head, wondering when someone would realize Alina and I stood at the front door, locked out of the house, and they needed to let us in.

"He doesn't have a key?" Cambria asked, her voice amplified by alcohol as well.

"Oh, shoot!" Fred said. A second later, plodding footsteps approached the entry. The deadbolt released, and Fred opened the door. "Evening, folks."

"You having a good time?" Alina asked.

"The best," Fred said.

"Enjoyed a couple drinks?"

"Just a couple."

Alina rolled her eyes and pushed past him. "I'm going to shower and then start my Freddy marathon." She hustled up the stairs.

I slipped by Fred and limped into the kitchen, leaning against the wall. My hip couldn't handle to sit again.

Maya, Daphne, and Cambria sat around the table. My parents, Rachel and Jake, and Adam were absent.

"Where's my family?"

"Upstairs," Maya said. "They snuck away like thirty minutes ago to watch a movie or something. I don't know."

"How did it go earlier?" Fred asked, plopping into the chair beside Daphne.

"Confusing. I expected clarification on the case, but I'm more lost now than before."

"You think some kind of Devil is haunting their dreams?" Maya asked.

I shared the highlights from the meeting. "Alina recorded the conversation. You can listen to that for more details. She doesn't think they're good people, and some monster—like something from a slasher movie—is plotting to murder them."

"Find why the monster wants to kill them, we find our answer to this mystery," Cambria said.

"That's exactly what Alina thought."

"So who or what's the monster?" Daphne asked.

"We don't know." I cracked a knuckle. "A Devil who wears a three-piece suit and wields a sledgehammer and sings an old song. That's all we know, apart from the fact that it hurt Nick in a dream and that injury bled into real life."

"Wait, what?" Fred asked. "Say that again."

"The Devil shattered Nick's hand in a dream."

"Okay."

"When he woke up from his sleep, he had a broken hand, as if the injury from the dream spilled into real life."

"Is that possible?"

I shrugged.

"What if the Devil hurt Nick in real life, not in the dream?" Cambria asked, slurring her words as she struggled through the thought.

"If someone shattered my hand with a sledgehammer, I think I would wake up immediately," I said. "I would see the person who struck me. Not Nick, though. When he awoke, no one was there."

"I'm bored with talking shop," Maya said, reaching for a half-empty margarita and sipping it through a straw. "Guess what?"

"What?" I asked.

"Cambria told me a secret. Want to hear it?"

"Shut up!" Cambria hissed, punching Maya's shoulder. "That's a secret."

"I was going to tell him you like him," Maya whispered. "You don't want me to?"

"No."

"Why? I think he likes you, too."

"What if he doesn't?"

"They're roasted, toasted," Daphne said, glancing at me.

"Maya," I said.

"Yeah."

"You drunk?"

Maya shrugged, pursing out her lips. "I mean, I'm feeling good. I don't know about drunk."

"Uh oh," I said.

Fred glanced at me, concern drawn across his face.

Daphne must have noticed the unspoken conversation between Fred and me. "What's going on?"

"Maya admitted she feels good," Fred said.

"Yeah, so?"

"That really means she's wasted. She downplays her inebriation by about three degrees."

"Okay... she's a big girl, though. She can handle her alcohol."

"She can," I said. "Can she?" I nodded to Cambria. "Has she kept up with Maya all day?"

"She's had to keep up with me," Cambria said.

"That's my fault," Fred said. "I got carried away, you know? They went drink for drink, and I didn't say a word." He touched Daphne's arm. "Remember that night Maya drank me under a table. I'm halfway to seven feet and almost three-hundred pounds, and that little noodle put me under a table. She felt good that night. If Maya is feeling good now..." Fred trailed off, looking at Cambria.

"Oh," Daphne said. "I see."

"We should get Cambria to bed before she gets any worse," I said.

"Are you talking about me?" Cambria asked, butting into our not-so-secretive conversation. She and Maya had continued their shouting during our conversation, somehow jumping subjects from liking me to arguing about whether snails and slugs were the same thing.

"A cold shower," I said, ignoring Cambria. "I'd prefer not to help with that, at least not while she's this intoxicated."

"You don't want to shower with me?" Cambria asked. "Why won't you shower with me?"

I lowered my voice, hoping only Daphne heard me. "I'll help her up to our room, but you will shower her. Cool water. Once you have her dressed, I can take over from there."

"Definitely," Daphne said.

I lip-smiled at Fred and Maya. "Goodnight. I think it's time I tap out."

"Already?" Maya asked. "Cambria had big plans for you two tonight."

"I did?" Cambria asked.

"Remember the secret? Eek. Eek. Eek."

"That's for Thursday night. We said tonight would be too early in the week. What if everything went wrong? That would make the rest of the week awkward."

"Sex erases awkwardness," Maya said. "I say go for it tonight. Why not?"

I moved to Cambria, helping her stand. "You ready for bed?"

"I feel sick," she said.

"We'll take care of that. Daphne, when you come up, could you grab a glass of water?"

"Of course."

I led Cambria up the stairs and into the hallway bathroom next to our room. I knocked in case Alina hadn't finished in there, but no one responded, so I pushed the door open.

Daphne joined us after a minute, and she sat on the toilet while Cambria showered, making sure the inebriated woman didn't slip and fall and break her neck. I waited in the bedroom, sitting on the edge of the bed.

They exited the bathroom almost thirty minutes later and came into the room.

"How did it go?" I asked.

"She threw up in the shower twice, in the toilet once," Daphne said. "When I tried to dress her, she acted like one of those waving car balloon things. I gave up after five minutes. Her pants are on backward."

I thanked Daphne for her help and led Cambria to our bed, laid her down, and kissed her forehead. Before my lips parted from her smooth skin, she was snoring. After rolling her onto her side and wedging a pillow behind her back so she wouldn't roll over, I went into the bathroom, grabbed the trashcan, and placed it beside the bed... just in case. Once Cambria was safe asleep, I went back downstairs.

Drunken Conversation. Monday, May 1st. 2238hrs.

I VENTURED INTO THE kitchen, finding it dark and empty. Out the back window, a dull, orange light glowed. For a moment, I stood in the kitchen and wondered where everyone had gone. My parents, my siblings, Alina, and Cambria had gone to bed. What of Fred, Daphne, and Maya, though? Had they ventured outside? Was that light on earlier, but I had missed it? Had they all gone to bed?

I hoped they hadn't gone to bed. I wouldn't... I couldn't sleep so early in the night. Without alcohol to help me doze off, my sleeping habits mirrored those of Heather and Johnny rather than my parents. I also had a Devil haunting my dreams.

Whenever I closed my eyes, my mind teleported to the park on that hot summer day. I heard the gunshot and the oomph exhaling from Aaron's body, the airsoft BB bouncing along the asphalt.

For three years after the incident, I had drowned that memory with alcohol, drinking until I crossed into a black, voided sleep where nothing existed but darkness. Now, as I pieced my life back together, I had stopped drinking, but the poignant memories remained. So, I avoided sleep, working and exercising and exhausting myself until fatigue grabbed me by the head and dragged me beneath the surface. On a good night, I slept four hours, supplementing my lack of rest with coffee—copious and unhealthy amounts of coffee.

I followed the burning light to the back patio, holding on to hope that someone else beside me couldn't sleep. The ocean rolled in the distance, and the cold, wet breeze rattled leaves and scraped through branches.

Maya sat alone in a lounge chair beside the pool.

I paused on the deck and stared at her for a moment. I could only see the back of her head from my angle, and her feet crossed one over the top of the other. She described her haircut as a frohawk. She and Cambria went on about it in the car, but I had mostly tuned them out. In effect, she had shorter hair on the side of her head, and she fluffed her naturally curly hair on top to create a voluminous crown—Maya's description to Cambria. It was a unique and noticeable haircut, though. Sexy, as well.

"You going to stare at me all night, or would like to join me?" Maya asked without turning around. "You breathe like a woolly mammoth, in case you're wondering how I noticed you."

I stepped down to the pool deck. "Like a wooly mammoth?"

"Like someone with severe emphysema."

"That's the same?"

"You're so persnickety. You knew what I meant."

"Where is everyone?" I sat on the lounge chair beside her. My hip and shoulder barked, but I dealt with the pain.

"Daphne collected Fred after helping with Cambria. She didn't think he should drink anything more. 'He's getting old,' she said. 'No longer in his twenties.' Apparently, if he drinks one beer too many, he's sick all night now. Both ends." Maya chuckled. "You find Alina?"

I reclined in the lounger and looked at the sky. Burning through the light marine haze, a few stars shined dimly, as did a fingernail moon. Directly before us, about a hundred yards from the fence wrapping around the backyard, a beach ran into the ocean. The never-ending tide crashed over and over and over, like the second hand of a clock counting time. The constant waves shared the secrets of the mysterious sea.

"Where's Alina?" Maya asked again.

"Upstairs. She's watching a movie, I think."

"How's Cambria?"

"Unconscious," I said. "Why did you do that to her?"

"Why did I enjoy my day? Because I'm on vacation. Don't blame me for your girlfriend getting drunk. I never once forced her to drink. She kept up with me on her own volition. Unwise. Foolish." Maya spoke clearly, as if she had consumed nothing more than water all day long.

"She's not my girlfriend."

"No?"

"No."

"Why not?"

I sighed and cracked a knuckle.

"She's pretty. She's funny. She's—" Maya rocked her head back and forth, as if weighing the next attribute. "She's intelligent, in her own way."

"In her own way?"

"She's thoughtful and understanding of others' emotions."

I held my tongue and stared across the dark ocean water.

"Do you like her?" Maya asked.

"I think so."

A heartbeat passed. A half a breath. "Do you like me?"

I didn't look at Maya, but I could feel her eyes bearing at me. My throat constricted, and despite the chilly breeze and the moist, heavy air, heat flushed across my body.

"What?" I asked.

"Do you like me?"

"Of course I like you."

"Not like that."

I bit my tongue, not wanting to have the conversation.

"Everyone always jokes you like me, but I've never seen it. You've never made a move."

"A move?"

"Like asked me on a date or tried to kiss me."

"You're one of my best friends," I said.

"So you like me as a friend?"

"Yes."

"Nothing else?" Maya adjust her posture, dropping her feet on the cement and facing me. She leaned forward, cutting the two feet between us in half. "What if I kissed you right now? Would you kiss me back?"

I didn't know how to respond.

Anger and want and fear all boiled together in the same pot. Did I lash out and tell Maya to stay in her lane? Did I tell her she only acted and spoke like this because I had asked Cambria on the trip? Was she jealous? Did I entertain her questions and tell her the truth—that I didn't know how I felt toward her?

"Would you?" she asked.

I wanted to close the distance and do exactly as she asked, but I refrained. "I don't know."

Maya dropped back into her chair and stared at the sky again. "You like me, though, don't you?"

I sighed. "I don't know. Does it matter? Even if I did like you, everyone tells me you are way out of my league. I'm not your type. That it would never work. Do you know what works? Us as friends. I like that."

"Who said we wouldn't work?"

"Everyone."

"Why do they say that?"

"They say I'm too vanilla."

Maya giggled, rolling onto her side and looking at me with her big, intoxicating eyes. "Basic. That's what they mean. You're basic."

"I'm too boring and predictable. My pace through life is too slow for you."

"I hate the way you walk. Are you ever in a hurry?"

"I think Alina said it best," I said. "Or I remember what she said best."

"Alina has a way of saying things that stick."

I nodded, silently agreeing with Maya.

"What did my niece say?"

"That I'm my car—a Honda Civic. You prefer loud, fast, shiny vehicles. Motorcycles, muscle cars, fighter jets."

"Fighter jets?"

"She used it in another one of her examples... or maybe someone else said that. I don't know. I can't keep it straight."

"What was the example?"

"I'm ground control, and you want to fly."

Maya chuckled. "That girl and her examples. She cracks me up."

"You're not denying it."

"I'm not."

"So she's right?" I asked.

"She's not."

The night moved around us. I'm not sure how much time passed. I didn't dare ruin the moment by glancing at my phone. The cold grew colder, and I wished I had brought a sweatshirt outside with me. Maya had thought ahead, having wrapped herself in a blanket. She must have noticed my discomfort after a minute or two. She stood, pulling her chair arm-to-arm with mine, sat again, and spread the blanket over the both of us.

"Thanks."

"I'm a true gentleman," Maya said. She leaned her head on my shoulder (my good shoulder). She smelled like tequila and salt.

I was so aware of every movement she made against my arm. Of every twitch and spasm within my body. A spring of her hair bunched up and tickled my neck, but I didn't dare move. I dealt with the irritable sensation, enjoying the weight of her head on my body.

"Why now?" I asked.

"What's that?"

"Why start this conversation now, about me liking you. Why not last week? Or last month? Is it because I asked Cambria to join me on this trip?"

"Maybe I am a little jealous."

"So you like me?" I asked.

Nothing. No response. Silence, polluted only with the ocean, the wind, and Maya's breathing.

"Did Fred tell you about the birds?" Maya asked after a minute.

"Don't change the subject."

She sniffled "If I answer your question, you might not like me anymore... even as a friend."

"That's not possible."

Maya chuckled, but without humor—more of a chuckle to replace any more irksome quiet. She shoved a finger into her mouth, bit on the nail, gnawed on it for a second. "Okay."

"Okay?" I asked.

"How many men do you think I've slept with?"

Her question surprised me. "What?"

"How many men do you think I've had sex with?"

"Does that matter?"

"To some people. How many?"

"I never thought about it," I said, confused by her question.

"Be vague then. A lot or a little."

"What's a lot?"

"I don't know," Maya said. "What's a lot to you? Three? Twelve? Fifty? I'm just curious, when you think of me, do you think of me sleeping with a lot of men?"

"No."

"What do you think of then?"

I popped a knuckle, reactively. The conversation had taken a turn I hadn't expected, and I didn't enjoy it.

"When you think of me, what do you think of?" Maya asked.

"Obnoxious."

She snickered.

"Confident." I paused. How far did I take this? Cambria slept in the house behind us. I had asked her on this trip because I had enjoyed my date with her and wanted to know her better. However, hadn't I always, since first meeting her, wanted to know Maya better?

"That's it?" Maya asked. "Obnoxious and confident?"

"Persistent," I said. "Reliable. Sincere. Honest." The words bubbled off my lips now. Held back for years and finally released, they sprinted free. "Funny. Intelligent. Beautiful..." I trailed off at the last word, realizing I had maybe gone too far.

"Slutty?"

"Why do you keep saying that? Sex doesn't define a person, Maya. What people do for the world and for others, that's what defines them."

"I'm not perfect. I've made mistakes—a lot of them."

Again, I did not know where Maya steered this conversation or what she meant to say, but I also wasn't sure if I wanted to follow her to the end. Though she didn't sound it, Maya was drunk, and I didn't care to carry on a drunken conversation with her.

"We've all made mistakes," I said, remaining neutral, hoping to diffuse our progress to detonation.

"I don't know how many." Her voice was nearly a mumble. "I couldn't tell you how many men I've slept with."

"I don't need to know this. It doesn't matter to me."

"We grew up poor. Extremely poor."

"Maya—"

"Shut up, August. Just shut up. Please. I want you to know this about me."

I sighed and nodded. "Okay."

Maya gulped. "My dad actively cheated on my mom while Wanda and I were in the house. Instead of finding a job, he found women. My mom busted her butt to keep our heads above water, working two, three, four jobs. My dad threatened to hurt my sister and me if we ever told Mom how he spent his days. He would hurt us good. That's what he said. Hurt us good. Like that song." Maya trailed off for a moment, not saying a word.

We sat in tense silence, her head still on my shoulder, my eyes stretching across the dark horizon.

"School always came easy for me," Maya said. "I received a scholarship to a few different colleges. UC Davis offered me the most money. Not a full scholarship, but enough for me to entertain leaving home and attending. They offered me enough of a scholarship to think of ways I could earn the extra money each semester to pay off my loans. I had to get out of that house and make a life for myself outside of my parents. Once I had enough money, I would save my sister from him, too. Last, I would reach out and save my mom."

"You don't have to keep going," I said. "Not if you don't want to."

Maya's head moved up and down, nodding along my arm. "My dad didn't like the idea of me living at the dormitory, or anywhere not beneath his roof and his thumb. He refused to pay the remaining tuition—rather, he refused to allow my mom to pay for me to attend. She's the one who supported the family. Well, I refused to live with that man a day longer. So, I signed up for student housing and moved into the dorms. To stay there, to keep away from him, I had to come up with a lot of money really fast to pay for school."

"Don't they have loans to help pay for tuition and board and all that?"

"I had a decent scholarship. But I couldn't secure a full loan without my parents or someone else cosigning, though. I had to come up with the extra money."

I knew where the story went now. I saw the path clearly. I pulled in my lips and listened, wondering how many people Maya had shared this information with.

"I was a sex worker. An escort." Maya snickered. "High-end prostitution, dealing with rich clients who liked to dress me, show me off to their friends, take me back to their hotel rooms. I worked weekends—Friday and Saturday nights. It paid more than anything I've ever made since, and it put me through pre-med and medical school."

I pictured Maya in my mind, not wanting to turn and face her and ruin our positioning. She was gorgeous—different from the Hollywood attractiveness of Heather and Chris. Maya was every man's childhood crush. The girl at the amusement park who they dreamed about when they got home. The neighbor's granddaughter who visited once a year. The girl from the other school's bleachers, always noticed by the traveling team. She was more than Hollywood actress or Victoria Secret model beautiful. She was an elusive, fading dream you prayed to fall back asleep for and dive back into. I had no problem imagining rich old men paying a lot of money for Maya to stand at their side in the evening and lay beneath them at night.

"The money kept me away from my father," Maya said. "However, it didn't save my sister. Wanda lost herself in drugs and a terrible relationship. She had Alina young. I couldn't save my mom, either. She went to work one day and never came home. Brain aneurysm."

Maya snapped her fingers. "Gone like that. Only my dad escaped that house without consequence. He left California after my mom's death, leaving his drug-addicted daughter, his grand-baby, and me behind. I had no reason to attend my medical residency after his departure. I dropped out and pursued my dream career. Investigative journalism." Maya laughed, though I saw nothing funny about her story. "Now, I'm enjoying the ocean night with you, one of the greatest men I've had the pleasure of knowing."

"One of?" I asked playfully.

"Fred inches you out. Pun intended."

I wanted to kiss the crown of her head, but I resisted, instead leaning my cheek atop it. "I didn't know any of that."

"I never thought I would tell you."

"Why?"

"I sold myself for money. I feared if you ever learned that, you wouldn't look at me like you do."

"I look at you a certain way?"

"Like I'm the only person in the world."

I licked my lips. "Maya."

"You don't have to say anything. I know this isn't comfortable for you."

"I want to say something."

"Okay."

"That story doesn't paint you in a poor light. It doesn't make you a lesser person or someone who I would suddenly look down on. If anything... I..." I couldn't find the right word without sounding patronizing. I exhaled, buying time and wanting to say it correctly. "I see you as a stronger woman, and I never thought that possible."

Maya peeled herself off of my arm. It instantly felt cold and void without her there. She stood and turned, looking right at me. "You're a good man, and Cambria is a lucky woman. Before I go to sleep, though, can I tell you one more thing?"

"Sure."

"Muscle cars and motorcycles and fighter jets, they're fast and loud and fun... but that all gets old quick. You can't enjoy the sound of the ocean with loud. You can't sit beneath the stars and enjoy the night with fast. More often than not, Honda Civics aren't only more environmental and safe, they're more comfortable and enticing, especially for long drives."

She turned and walked toward the house, leaving me speechless.

"One more thing," she called back. "I want to gobble up your nose."

I furrowed my brow, scrunching face, utterly confused. "Gobble my nose?" I asked the night. "What does that mean?"

A Late-Night Dive. Tuesday, May 2nd. 0134hrs.

Andrea Menard sat in the passenger seat of the car, eyes half closed as sleep wrestled for control. Her husband, Wyman, had rolled down the windows to allow the cold ocean air into the car and entice them to stay attentive. The gimmick had worked, at least for a few minutes.

"You awake?" Wyman asked, reaching across the console and placing his hand on Andrea's thigh.

"Barely. Why don't we stop and get a hotel? We can wake up slow, eat breakfast, and still get to your brothers' house before lunch."

Wyman and Andrea had left from Los Angeles after work, around 1900hrs, driving toward Half Moon Bay, California, where Dale, Wyman's brother, lived. A day ago, Dale's wife had passed away after a long, hard battle with breast cancer. Wyman and Andrea went into work earlier, staying late, knowing they wouldn't return to their respective jobs for another week. They planned to stay with Dale and support him through the funeral.

A tough affair, but the Menards, despite their often tumultuous relationships, believed in two foundational truths. They showed up to weddings, no matter what. They showed up to funerals, no matter what.

Dale and Wyman hadn't spoken to each other in almost a year—the root issue long forgotten, though the pride and bitterness behind the matter remained raw. Despite their differences and disagreements, though, Wyman dropped his life to make the funeral and support his little brother. That's what Menards did, without question or excuse.

"We're an hour from his place," Wyman said. "It wouldn't make sense to buy a hotel. You can sleep if you need to, but I'm driving through."

"You don't find that foolish?"

"I find it fiscally responsible."

"For who? The foundation where all our money goes to when we die? Because that's what will happen if we don't stop. You'll fall asleep, crash the car, and we'll die."

Wyman had insisted they take Highway 1 from Monterey to Half Moon Bay, driving along the beautiful coastline. He claimed the ocean view and tricky road would inspire them to stay awake, at least more than the monotonous drive through farmlands.

"I'm not falling asleep," Wyman said, reaching for the cupholder and drinking iced water. He refused to drink caffeine after noon. It burned his heart and made him jittery for the rest of the day and into the evening, making it near-impossible to sleep. He had found, though, on those nights when he had to burn the midnight oil, iced water did the trick well enough.

Andrea's fear of Wyman falling asleep and veering off into the ocean spiked her adrenaline and fueled her with temporary energy. She turned up the radio, rested her head on the side panel near the open window, and enjoyed the music and the fresh air.

Despite Wyman's foolishness, he was right on one account. The coastal highway proved captivating. Despite the light fog, the sky held a beach of stars and a bright quarter-moon. To her left, if she glanced out of the driver's window, the dark ocean water reflected the moonlight. They had the ocean in Los Angeles, too, but not like in Monterey, where everything was cooler and darker... and more haunting.

Andrea rolled her head along the seat, staring at her husband, sharing a soft smile. It quickly vanished. She gasped, sucking in air.

Wyman's head lolled to the side, his eyes closed.

"Wyman!"

Her husband startled, jolting awake and pulling on the steering wheel. The vehicle jerked to the left. Wyman over corrected, and their car fishtailed. The tires skidded on asphalt, and the stench of burning rubber filled the air.

After a few seconds, though, Wyman righted the vehicle, continuing up Highway 1 at a leisurely pace.

The two of them breathed hard for a second, allowing their bodies to settle and calm. After the song changed on the radio, and the new one ended, and the station's host previewed the next track, Andrea faced her husband, flames in her eyes.

"Don't say a word," Wyman said. "We're not stopping."

"You fell asleep."

"I'm awake now. I'm definitely awake now. Feel my heart."

"I'm sure you are," Andrea said, laughing, though not amused—frustrated laughter. "I'm sure you're wide awake after nearly killing us."

"Are we dead? No. We're fine."

"Because I woke you up."

"You startled me, which made me pull the wheel. Your reaction could have killed us."

"What? You're kidding me, right? Me reacting to you sleeping at the wheel could have killed us? You're something else. All you Menard men are something else."

"What's that mean?"

"You know exactly what it means. You can't admit you're wrong, no matter what, no matter how wrong you so obviously are. It's always someone else's fault."

"What do you want me to say?" Wyman asked, tightening his grip around the steering wheel.

"How about, 'Hey, Andrea, I'm sorry I feel asleep while driving? You're right. Let's pull to the side of the road and get some sleep. Or how about, better yet, we check into a hotel for the night?'"

"We're an hour away."

Andrea ran her hands through her thick, graying hair, staring straight out the windshield. She no longer enjoyed the cool air or the coastal views—in fact, she barely registered any of it. She only saw the headlights exposing the next hundred yards of the winding road.

"You have nothing to say now?" Wyman asked. "Speaking of the Menard faults, way to default to the Griffin habits. Silence. Swallow it all, right? Don't say what you feel. Just make everyone around you miserable because you're miserable."

Andrea chuckled. "Really? You're going to lecture me on silence, when you haven't spoken to your brother in over a year?"

"Well, he never spoke to me. It was mutual. You will sit there quiet as a mouse, bitter as lemon, ignoring every word I say just to make me feel as bad as you."

Andrea clenched her jaw, but she refused to allow Wyman to draw her into his trap. Nope. He was right. She would sit there and say nothing. If he wanted to keep driving, well, who cared, anyway? Let him drive and crash and kill them.

"No?" Wyman said, turning to her—not glancing at her, but turning his entire face and staring at her. "That's it? You have nothing to say?"

Despite her husband removing his attention from the highway, Andrea stared straight ahead, refusing to acknowledge him. Refusing to speak to him. Sure, it proved him right, but who cared? He would think himself right because Menard men weren't ever wrong.

As she stared out the windshield into the light fog, Andrea saw a thin, ghostly woman standing in the middle of the street—hair and eyes as black as the asphalt.

"Wyman! Watch out!"

Wyman whipped his head back to the road, slamming on the brakes. The car skidded. He jerked on the steering wheel at the last moment to avoid crashing into the woman. The car had handled one incident, but it couldn't withstand two. The sudden, aggressive turn of the wheels shifted the balance of the vehicle.

It bucked and hitched, flipping end over end, bouncing over the guardrails, and careening over the cliff to the sandy beach below.

Spare Keys. Tuesday, May 2nd. 0752hrs.

THE ELEVEN OF US crowded into the living room that next morning. We had all woken and eaten breakfast in a staggered manner.

I, per usual, had gone down late and had woken up early. The sun barely touched the horizon when I roused on the lounge chair, groggy in the head. The fresh ocean air helped to burn off the mental fog. I stood and stretched. My hip and shoulder were tighter than yesterday, so I spent a little extra time massaging them to usefulness.

Once the pain was bearable, I went for a morning walk along our backyard beach to push some fresh blood through my body. I preferred to exercise with weights. However, when near the ocean and while recovering from gunshot and stab wounds, weights seemed a little out of place. So, I opted to walk. Well, hobble like a man three times my age.

When I returned to the rental home around 0730hrs, the lingering pain had worked itself out of my body. I vowed not to sit that entire day, not wanting to grow stiff and re-invite the aches.

Both of my parents and my sister and her husband sat on the back patio, drinking coffee and picking at what remained of their breakfast. A French press sat on the picnic table, along with a few empty mugs. I poured myself a cup and joined them, leaning against the patio railing.

"Daphne made breakfast burritos," Rachel said.

Jake, sitting beside her, had swollen eyes and stared listlessly across the horizon. He must have stolen away last night with his own stash of booze.

"Where are the burritos?" I asked, nearly shouting.

Jake squinted his eyes, grimacing. "Why are you like that?"

"Where did you head off to this morning?" Mom asked.

"I went for a walk. Felt good, too. Is everyone else still sleeping?"

"Your brother will sleep until about ten or eleven. You know how college kids get with their sleeping late."

"Alina will probably do the same," I said, thinking of how late she slept on the weekends when she had nothing to wake up for.

"Teenagers," Jake said, his voice thick with sleep. "What I wouldn't give to sleep past eight again."

"To sleep past six," I said.

My dad, as was his custom, remained an active listener throughout the conversation, not sharing his voice unless absolutely necessary—or if he had a terrible joke to tell. After being married forty years to my mom, he had learned to let her speak, for that's where she excelled.

"I can get you a burrito," Mom said.

"No, stay seated. I'll grab one."

I moseyed into the house and found the foil-wrapped burritos lying in a pile in the refrigerator. Daphne had written on them in black marker. Bacon. Ham. Veggie. How Fred had married that woman would always remain the greatest mystery of all; one I would never solve, either.

As my bacon burrito warmed in the microwave, Adam stumbled down the stairs and plopped onto the recliner in the living room, staring at his phone. The microwave beeped, I collected my breakfast and coffee, and joined Adam on the couch.

"Morning," I said.

"Hey," he said, scrolling through his phone.

I didn't know what to say. For the past four or five years, Adam had maintained a lot of anger toward me. Rightfully so. I had ignored him, ran from him, as I had with everyone else. Except, I was twelve years older than Adam, and he looked up to me. Not only that, he needed me, and I was never there. Sure, we had buried the hatchet a week or two ago, but an uneasiness still existed between us. We didn't suddenly have that casual, brotherly friendship. It felt like work to sit beside him in that awkward silence.

"How was shopping yesterday?" I asked.

"Cool."

"What did you get?"

"Some sandals. Then we headed to the beach and sat around for an hour. After that, Dad and Jake were bored and went to the closest bar."

"Sounds fun."

"Except Dad won't let me drink. I'll be twenty-one tomorrow. I mean, come on."

I glanced at the floor and performed some mental calculations. Adam turned twenty-one tomorrow. Was that right? If so, it finally made sense why my mom and dad had readily agreed to the trip. Like me, my dad preferred to not hang around other people. My mom, despite what she says, had never enjoyed traveling. She always stressed about it and worked herself up and never had fun. They tended not to travel.

With Adam's birthday, though...

"You forgot, huh?" Adam asked.

I nodded. "I'm still working on being a better brother. I guess birthdays are something I should pay attention to."

"Well, tomorrow night, I'm getting wasted. Rachel and Jake are taking me out. You're welcome to join." He looked up from his phone, glancing at me.

"I'll see if I can make that."

"You'll be okay?"

"What do you mean?" I asked.

"With the drinking?"

I shrugged. "Drinking doesn't tempt me anymore. I went toe-to-toe with that Devil. I won. I'm not scared anymore." I sucked on my cheeks. "I think that's a big part of addiction. Fear. When I overcame that fear, I stopped craving booze."

Lugging footfalls cascaded down the stairs. Cambria appeared, pinching her head—I'm sure her throbbing, splitting head. She collapsed beside me, nearly on my lap. She groaned. "I think the sledgehammer demon shattered my skull."

"That specific devil is Maya," I said. "Never try to drink with her again. She will put you through hell." Another pair of footsteps sounded on the stairwell, perkier this time down. "Speaking of the devil."

Maya appeared, wearing baggy sweatpants and a black sports bra. Her frohawk stood every which way, as if she had rolled out of bed without risking a glance in the mirror. She strolled straight into the kitchen, poured herself a cup of coffee, popped the cork off a bottle of whiskey, and returned to the living room with a tired smile.

"Don't look at me that way," Maya said, sitting on the hearth across from the couch. "It's my special coffee. I'm on vacation."

"I thought you had to work?" I asked.

"I do, which is why I need a little hair of the dog to scare away my hangover." She glanced at Cambria and pulled in a sharp inhale. "She might need a lot of hair of the dog. Is she okay?"

"No," Cambria moaned.

Fred and Daphne appeared shortly thereafter, with Alina on their tails. Along with the breakfast burritos, homemade muffins and fruit lay across the island. Everyone pieced together their breakfast, eating at their leisure, or gulping whiskey-infused coffee as they pleased. Why not? We were on vacation, right?

"Adam," I said, catching his attention. "You have plans for the day?"

"Same as every other day while we're here," he said. "Nothing at all... except for tomorrow night."

"What's tomorrow night?" Maya asked. "I want to come... join. Let's not confuse what I mean."

"No one confused what you meant," Alina said. "You don't have to be gross all the time."

"We have a room full of juvenile, immature men. I have to remain crystal clear so they don't get the wrong idea."

"Rachel and Jake are taking me out to celebrate my twenty-first birthday," Adam said.

"What?" Maya asked, her voice rising three octaves.

Cambria grunted and pulled a couch pillow over her face.

"What?" Maya asked again, whispering. "You're twenty-one tomorrow and no one told me? I'm the queen of twenty-first birthdays. You want a good time, don't go to Rachel and Jake. They're old and married and not any fun."

"Watch it," Daphne said.

"Twenty-one, huh?" Maya asked. "I'm tagging along."

"Awesome," Adam said, sounding excited.

"Well, Adam," I said, circling back to my original intention, "you want to come along with me today?"

"What are you doing?"

I shrugged, not sure what I had planned for the day. "I'll probably head out to the boardwalk and wander around while I think about the case. If I'm feeling up to it, I may even interview a few people in connection to my clients, see if I can learn anything about them."

"Yeah, sure. Just us?"

"I was thinking the guys," I said. "A no girls allowed day."

"I'm in," Fred said, slapping his thighs. "A boys' trip. I've always dreamed of going on one of those."

"Have you?" Daphne asked, angling away from her husband. "You played in the NFL. Isn't every weekend a boys' trip."

"That's not the same. I mean, like, boys going out and being boys kind of trip."

"I'm not sure that's what August has in mind," Maya said.

"Well, with you hanging around here," Fred said, staring at Maya, "I'm a little nervous leaving the girls alone with you. Who knows what might happen."

Maya grinned and positioned her fingers atop her head like the devil's horns. "I'll take everyone to Hell's private Heaven. It's a secret place, where bad is oh so good."

"Hm," Fred said, musing. "Maybe I'll stay here after all."

"Nope. Boys can't enter Hell's Heaven," Cambria mumbled from behind the pillow.

"Hell's Heaven would make an amazing band name," Daphne said.

"Or an article about a supernatural mystery," Maya added. "August, can you work a case that allows me to title the write up Hell's Heaven?"

"What would that be, like monster-wise?" I asked. "An angel or a demon, or like a Nephilim kind of deal?"

Before Maya or Alina could dive into the rabbit hole of my hypothetical question, the doorbell rang.

Alina glanced at me, shaking her head. "Not this time. Not me."

Fred grunted, climbing to his feet. "Don't worry. I'm the receptionist. I answer phones, emails, and doorbells." He trudged across the living room and opened the front door.

I turned my head, craning my neck to see who visited us this morning.

Maxwell Shaye had made another appearance. Hopefully, the owner of the house wouldn't make a habit of ringing the doorbell.

Despite meeting him yesterday, his physical appearance still jolted me, and a pang of guilt accompanied my initial shock.

"Good morning," Maxwell said.

The front door was fifteen feet from where I sat, unimpeded by any walls to block the sound, allowing me to see and hear the conversation.

"How was your first night?"

"Slept like a baby with a sound machine set to a loud, ocean setting," Fred said, reaching behind him and scratching his butt.

"Wonderful," Maxwell said. "I'm happy to hear it."

"What can we do for you?" Fred asked, speaking in his faux-cheery tone, as he spoke to most every client on the phone. Though he had his back to me, I could imagine the giant, fake smile etched across his face.

"I'm sorry to intrude yet again. I promise you won't see me further, unless, of course, you call and request my help. In that case, though, you'll probably meet my brother, David. He usually responds to any hiccups customers might encounter." Maxwell cleared his throat and reached into his back pocket, handing over an envelope. "The extra keys you requested we make. I forgot to put them in the lockbox for you. When I returned home after my visit last night, I noticed the keys sitting on the counter. I almost came back over then, but I figured it could wait until this morning. I'm glad I caught you."

Fred chuckled, accepting the envelope of keys and pocketing them. "We almost had an incident last night. Luckily, someone was in the house to open the door."

"Well, I'm glad to hear it. Have a great time in Santa Cruz. And stay safe."

"Safe?" Fred asked. "From what?"

"You didn't hear?"

"Hear what?"

"About the accident last night."

"What kind of accident?"

Maxwell chuckled, shaking his head. "I thought you might have heard, considering your business here and all—looking into the supernatural. A ghost haunting Highway 1 late at night."

"A ghost, huh?" Fred asked.

"What happened last night?" I called from the couch.

"A couple passing through from Los Angeles saw the ghost. They spooked and drove their car off the cliff."

"They okay?" Fred asked.

"I'm not sure. I don't have all the details."

"Any other mention of this ghost?" I asked.

Maxwell scratched his head. "None that I know of."

"So someone must have survived last night to claim they saw a ghost in the road," Alina said.

"Must be," Maxwell said.

"You notice birds acting funny?" Maya asked.

The man slowly shook his head. "I spend most of my time at a computer. My brother, though, he's the caretaker. I'm the brain, he's the brawn of the operation. If you see him around, ask him about birds acting strange. He'll have noticed."

"Will we see him around?" Fred asked.

"I think tomorrow or Thursday he comes to mow. I believe tomorrow morning, though. If you're here, you'll see him then."

"Well, thank you for the warning," Fred said. "I don't plan on driving on any highways while I'm here, though. I'm mostly sticking to the beach and the pool. If I find myself on Highway 1 at night—well," he chuckled, "let's be honest, that will not happen."

"Thought I should warn you, anyway."

"We appreciate the concern, and the spare keys."

"Enjoy the rest of your stay."

"Thank you," Fred said, slowly and gently closing the front door. He returned to his spot in the living room, plopping down beside Daphne. "That man creeps me out. Does that sound shallow? I don't care. He gives me the creeps. The heebie-jeebies."

"You know who he reminds me of?" Alina asked.

"Who?" I knew she had something ridiculous in mind.

"The old man at the gas station," Cambria grumbled, face still beneath the pillow.

"Exactly!" Alina said.

"Who?" I asked.

"The old man at the gas station," Alina said.

"What old man and which gas station? What are you talking about?"

"In every slasher movie ever, there's an old man at a gas station—or a variation of that. The heroes—"

"Who no one likes, right?" I asked.

"You're catching on. The characters have to stop for gas, or food, or to use the bathroom, or anything really, and they meet an old man, or woman, or some strange, obscure individual who gives them the creeps. The person also warns them of something, which often turns out to be a warning of the monster that's going to kill everyone."

"So we should watch out for the ghost on Highway 1?" Fred asked. "Easy enough."

Alina twisted her hair around her finger. "This entire situation feels an awful lot like we're starring in some horror movie. Which begs the question, who's going to die first?"

"No one will die," I said.

"Nick," Alina said.

"What about Nick?" I asked.

"Nicholas Lane. He's the perfect candidate for a first death."

"Why?"

"Not as attractive as Johnny, also not a fiancé. He and Christina have only dated a few months, so it's not as emotional if he dies first. His death will only trigger the audience so far as to alert them to inevitable danger."

"We're not in a movie," I said. "You know that, right?"

"Says who?" Alina asked. "August, open your eyes. Look at what's right in front of you. The entire world, all of existence, it's nothing more than a simulation. How do we know that the simulation isn't a video game, or a book, or a movie? We're all just characters living in someone else's world."

I slipped away from Cambria and stood, rubbing my hip. "That's my cue," I said. "You ladies enjoy Hell's Heaven. Us men will head to the boardwalk, where we'll enjoy Heaven's Hell."

"I like that one, too," Maya said, pointing at me. "But not as much. Hell's Heaven comes off the tongue easier, I think."

I ignored her, heading to the bedroom to change.

The First to Dance. Tuesday, May 2nd. 0833hrs.

CHRIS AND NICK LEFT Johnny and Heather's apartment for a change of scenery. Also, for some alone time. Despite their fatigue, they were never quite tired enough to avoid quality time together.

"Just not in the bed," Chris had said as Nick carried her through the front door, her legs wrapped around his waist.

"What? Why not?"

"I don't want to lie down and accidentally fall asleep."

"You would fall asleep?" He kissed her on the forehead and laughed. "Really?"

"Maybe."

"Standing up then?"

Afterward, breathless, sweaty, and somehow more drained than previously, Chris stepped into the bathroom for a cold shower. She allowed the icy water to crash against her neck and stream down her back. The chill shocked her system with energy, taking off the drowsiness brought on from sex.

Once out of the shower and dried, though not dressed, Chris tiptoed into the kitchen and opened the refrigerator door. She grabbed an energy drink and padded through the open bedroom into Nick's room.

He lay on the bed, snoring.

Chris popped the can, not caring if she woke him. Waking Nick was probably the safer option, anyway. He didn't stir. She leaned on his dresser and watched her boyfriend of a few months sleeping.

Tattoos covered his torso, but not his neck or arms—nowhere anyone could see them unless he removed his shirt. On one pectoral, Nick had commissioned the Celtic cross, on the other, he bore the Othala rune. Just beneath his sternum at the top of his abdomen, Nick had tattooed the number eighteen. Each symbol covertly represented white supremacy.

Chris had asked him what they meant, and he had freely shared with her, unapologetic and not embarrassed.

"The eighteen is for Hitler," he said, holding her hand and tracing her fingers over the numbers. "The number one stands for an A, and the eight for an H."

A shock of chills sputtered up Chris's spine. The defiance, the unruliness, the vitreosity of it all exhilarated her. "And the one that looks like a fish?"

"The Othala rune. Nazis used the symbol as a divisional insignia." He looked at her with his hard eyes—eyes like steel. "What do you think?"

Chris swallowed back a lump of nerves and uncertainty. "About your tattoos?"

"Do you like them?"

Christina had loved them, but that knowledge made her feel dirty.

Heather had known a liberal life throughout her childhood. Her parents taught her about systemic racism and the need for reparations. They convinced her that government handouts and bailouts brought society closer to equality. Except, as Chris learned to think for herself, she didn't believe people were equal. Her father, who worked long hours every single day including weekends, was not equal to the crack addict breaking into cars and sleeping on benches. So, why did her father have to pay taxes from his paycheck for that unemployed leach on society to exist? Why punish her father for another man's crimes? Why couldn't the world see that?

Christine had never spoken her beliefs, though. She barely thought them, considering them vile and wrong. If she spoke her mind, her parents would disown her. Heather would hate her. Everyone would hate her.

Not Nick, though. Nick saw the world as she saw it. He understood how backward America had become—mostly through watching his lazy, hand-out accepting parents. They sucked off the government's teats, growing fat and complacent on the taxpayers dime. Their behavior disgusted Nick, drove him as far away from them as possible.

If only they could sleep to regain enough energy to fight against the tyranny.

Nick slept peacefully, and Christina stood at the end of his bedroom and watched him, ready to wake him if he started thrashing or screaming or anything, really. His left hand hung off the edge of the mattress. His right hand, the one in a cast, rested on his chest.

Chris believed him about the Devil incident, too. The police hadn't. And she could see it in Heather and Johnny's eyes that they hesitated to believe his story, as well. That hurt Chris. To not believe Nick meant they believed Chris had harmed him. Why would Heather think Christina had hurt Nick over the Devil? It made no sense.

A couple days back, Heather had asked Chris in private, "Did you do it?"

"Do what?" Chris asked.

"Break his hand?"

The question had ambushed her. Chris stuttered at first, unsure of what to say or how to respond. "Of course not. No."

"I wouldn't blame you if you did."

"What are you talking about?"

"You really didn't do it?" Heather asked.

"Why would think I did it? The Devil did it."

"It's just... none of us has had a nightmare since Nick's injury."

"What are you saying?"

"You didn't, I don't know, plan this entire ordeal?"

"Heather," Chris said, barely capable of comprehending what her best friend accused her of. "You're serious?"

"I'm desperate."

"So you're looking to blame me? Why would I do it? And if I went through so much trouble to do something like this, why would I settle for breaking his hand? Why wouldn't I kill him? Or Johnny? Or you? Why would I suffer along with everyone by not sleeping? You're not thinking right."

Heather wiped away a tear. "I just want to close my eyes and slip away. That's all I want. I want the world to make sense again."

The police suspected Christina. Heather suspected Christina. Johnny probably suspected her, as well.

Only Nick saw things as she saw them. It was Nick and Chris against the world. Bonnie and Clyde.

She chuckled at the image of them jumping into an old Ford sedan and driving across the country, making everything in the world right again. *Natural Born Killers*, like Mallory and Mickey.

Christina moseyed back into the bathroom to check her reflection, a habitual task she recently despised. Her pale face was splotchy with acne and rashes, bruised and swollen from lack of sleep. The skin beneath her eyes drooped, dark as tea bags. She sighed, closing her eyes and splashing water across her face.

From the living room, the Bluetooth speaker tuned on.

Christina froze, eyes still shut. She wasn't asleep, though. Nick was. Had the Devil come for Nick? If so, Chris had to save him and prove her innocence. She had to stop the Devil.

Christina opened her eyes to run and intervene.

The Devil stood behind her, reflected in the mirror. The nightmare wore the three-piece suit and that awful mask—the Man's mask to cover the Devil's face. It held the sledgehammer, and the head touched the ground.

The ragtime piano played beneath Christina's scream.

The Devil half-sang, half-spoke in its deep, raspy voice. "I had a dream last night that filled me full of fright. I dreamed I was with the Devil below, in his great big fiery hall, where the Devil was giving a ball."

Christina had no conscious thought. She only reacted, like an animal fleeing and scurrying from a predator, with only one instinct controlling her actions—survival. She shoved into the nightmare, pushing it aside and bursting through the bathroom into the kitchen.

The front door stood to her right, closed. She could unlock it, open it, run, run, run as far away as possible and save herself. To her left, through the open bedroom door on the other side of the kitchen, Nick slept in his bed. If Christina ran, the Devil would go for him.

Too late.

Her split second of indecision allowed the nightmare to catch up to her. It grabbed the back of her skull, driving her head into the wall. The kitchen burst into a cluster of bright lights. She tried to scream, to call for help, to wake Nick, but nothing more than a gargle escaped from her constricting throat.

The Devil tossed her onto the kitchen floor and loomed over her. It half-sang, half-spoke, the sledgehammer head scraping against the kitchen tile. "I checked my coat and hat and started gazing at the merry crowd that came to witness the show. And I must confess to you, there were many there I knew at the Devil's Ball."

Christina broke through her paralyzing fear and indecision, through the fog clouding her mind. She scrambled to her feet and grabbed the energy drink she had opened off the counter, chucking the can at the Devil. It smacked into its shoulder, spilled across its jacket, and dripped onto the floor. She lunged for the front door, fumbled with the lock, threw it open, crossed into the hallway, and...

She landed in the kitchen, stumbling forward and nearly bumping into the figure.

The Devil continued to sing, though laughter touched its notes.

Christina shoved the nightmare aside and dove into the bathroom. She slammed the door behind her and leaned against it, sobbing.

When she caught her breath and focused her attention, Christina realized she still stood in the kitchen, leaning against the exterior side of the bathroom door.

"Oh! You little Devil, dancing at the Devil's Ball." The Devil wearing a Man's face lunged forward, drawing his sledgehammer over his shoulder. He slammed it down.

The twenty-pound hammer dusted Chris's kneecap. The pain was so intense it didn't exist. Her entire body went numb. Her mind muted all thought and sensory processing.

She screamed—a scream so extreme that nothing but airy breath escaped.

The Devil rose his sledgehammer again, still singing—the stitched lips of the mask never moving, though they angled upward permanently in a twisted, evil grin.

Christina crossed her arms over her face as a shield. She could have wrapped paper around her body to prevent her from catching fire for all her skinny limbs helped.

The sledgehammer collapsed her forearms and pulverized her face. The next strike cratered her skull. She slumped against the door, bleeding onto the tile, staring wide-eyed through fuzzy, fading vision at Nick, who had somehow slept through everything.

The last thing she heard, after her bones cracked and shattered, was the Devil's voice. "Dancing with the Devil, Oh! Little Devil, dancing at the Devil's Ball."

The music faded, ended, and Christina slept.

Hell's Heaven. Tuesday, May 2nd. 1O43hrs.

ALINA SPRAWLED OUT ON the floor, her back on the rug and her legs bent over the couch. Daphne sat with one leg crossed over the other on a plush chair across from the sofa. Rachel sat beside her mom in a similar position on the couch. Kimberly had her arms crossed, staring at the dark television screen.

Maya paced behind the couch, and before the kitchen island, her hands clasped together behind her back. "Alright, ladies. No boys around. We have a few options. First, and the most boring, we spend it as we individually see fit. I'll work on my article, and you can all suntan or swim or walk the beach, whatever hikes up the hem to your skirt, if you will."

"What's the other option?" Daphne asked, bouncing her suspended foot in the air.

"We slip into our sexiest, skimpiest bikinis and pack up a bag of the strongest alcohol we can find, hike across the backyard to that private beach, play volleyball or football, body surf, tan… do whatever we want in Hell's Heaven. Get drunk. Have fun."

"Tempting for sure," Rachel said. "Except I'm pregnant. Diving in the sand for a loose volleyball and drinking doesn't work for pregnant. "

"I don't drink, either," Kimberly said.

"Really?" Maya asked, thinking back to the previous day. She hadn't really been around Kimberly, but for the few moments they shared the same space, Kim never had a drink in her hand.

"Family history of abuse. I just stayed away from it," Kimberly said. "Besides, I don't enjoy the taste."

"That's fair," Maya said.

"I'm also a little old to frolic or dive in the sand after a ball."

"You're never too old for anything," Alina said, winking at Kimberly from her upside-down position.

"You're definitely never too old to dive for balls," Maya said.

That elicited light laughter from around the room from everyone but Alina. "You're always so gross," she said.

"You're gross," Maya said.

Alina stuck out her tongue at her aunt.

"We can drive into town and get manicures or pedicures, shop, get massages, eat a fancy lunch. For those of us who wish, we can drink too much wine."

"I like that option best," Kimberly said.

"Well, then so do I." Maya smiled.

Daphne, Rachel, and Alina also agreed. Maya, never a woman who spent longer than twenty minutes getting ready, put the other women on a timer. They had forty-five minutes to prepare for their girl's day.

"Why waste a beautiful morning in front of a mirror?"

"To hide this face," Kimberly said.

"Oh my god," Maya said, sitting beside Kimberly. "You're stunning. A bombshell. You know what I would give for your tits? You've had three children, and they're still that perky? Please. When I'm forty-three, I would die to look like you."

"I'm fifty-six," Kimberly said.

"You had me fooled. Well, you look forty-three—like a single, never married, had no kids forty-three."

Kimberly snickered with embarrassment. "Stop."

"I'm serious."

"Well, I appreciate the compliment, but..." Kimberly leaned away from Maya, wrinkling her nose. "You smell like the floor of a dive bar."

"Oh, sorry," Maya said, backing away and sitting on the coffee table. "I haven't brushed my teeth this morning. I'm not sure the whiskey-coffee combination helped matters. I'll keep my distance."

"Thank you."

"Forty-five minutes," Maya said. "You're all beautiful, so let's shoot for thirty minutes, if possible."

The women prepared themselves for the day, all of them readied before the timer expired. Once they were ready—dressed, makeup applied, hair styled—they walked toward Downtown Santa Cruz.

It was only a half mile from where they stayed; the weather was perfect, and exercise would help with those who had enjoyed too much alcohol the previous night.

As they walked along the chipped, uneven sidewalk, carrying casual conversations, something suddenly smacked hard into a windshield.

Maya flinched at the noise, turning in the direction it had come from.

A seagull lay on the asphalt, spasming and screeching. Its jerky movements and barking cries of pain eventually faded. The bird lay still. Dead. It had flew straight into a parked car's windshield. The crack spider-webbed across the entire section of glass.

Maya stared at the scene—at the splattering of blood reflecting sunlight off the windshield, and the dead bird bleeding onto the warm asphalt. She thought of yesterday at the pool; the bird spazzing out. "What in Oliver Dickens is happening?"

Another loud smack, followed by agonized screams from another dying bird. That collision originated from the house across the street. The bird had slammed into the roof and rolled down the slope, landing in the flowerbed with a dull thud.

Suddenly, as if the women actually walked through Hell, the Devil called for a storm.

Birds blotted the morning sun and darkened the sky. A torrential downpour hailed birds. They dive-bombed in a kamikaze sprint to the ground, slamming into houses and vehicles, onto the sidewalks and streets. One of them splattered three feet from Maya, exploding in a gory ball of feathers and blood.

"Run back to the house!" Alina said, turning tail and fleeing back the way they had come.

Daphne took off after the young girl, as did Cambria and Rachel. The four women escaped in a panicked hurry.

Kimberly stood in place, though, frozen with fear as birds splattered all around her.

Maya sprinted to August's mom, grabbing her thin arm. "We have to go," she said, speaking calmly to not further frighten Kimberly. "I have you. You're okay. We have to go, though." Maya gently tugged on the woman, leading her back to the rental house quickly and carefully. Once Kimberly fell in stride, Maya picked up her pace, though she never released her grip from Kimberly's arm.

A dozen seconds after Cambria, Daphne, Rachel, and Alina dove into the safety of the house, Maya and Kimberly fell through the door, slamming it closed behind them.

Above them, the bodies of hundreds of birds crashed into the roof, persisting for the next five minutes. The women huddled in the living room, standing around the coffee table and staring at the ceiling, saying nothing.

Kimberly gasped whenever a bird crashed into the house. Cambria flinched. Alina, Rachel, Maya, and Daphne shifted their eyes to the direction of the latest sound.

When the birds ceased their suicide bombing, the women remained quiet, waiting for the peppering to return.

After five minutes of eerie silence, Alina chuckled.

"What's so funny?" Kimberly asked, her voice tight with anxiety. "I find nothing humorous about what just happened."

"Your son," Alina said.

"My son?" Kimberly grabbed her head and her eyes widened. "Oh! My babies. Jason. Do you think they're okay? Do you think they're hurt? I need to call them." Kimberly frantically searched for her phone, found it in her purse, tapped the screen, and placed the device to her ear. "They're not answering," she said, trying them again.

Alina continued giggling—a hysterical fit in response to the unprecedented stress. "First *A Nightmare on Elm Street*. Now *The Birds*. This life really is a simulation."

"Adam!" Kimberly screeched. "Are you okay? Are you guys okay? What happened?"

Maya couldn't hear the other end of the line, but she watched Kimberly's face lighten as the stress melted away.

"We're okay," the woman said. "We're in the house. Do you know what happened?" A few more minutes of her panicked questioning ensued.

Maya dropped onto the couch and exhaled, digging out her phone and navigating to her Twitter feed. She searched for any mentions of Santa Cruz, hoping to find what other people were saying about birds falling from the sky.

Heaven's Hell. Tuesday, May 2nd. 1103hrs.

WE PARKED AMONGST AN ocean of cars for a much too expensive rate in a private lot across from the boardwalk. Jake, Fred, and my dad walked ahead. Adam and I slugged along behind them.

"You enrolling in school for next year?" I asked.

He nodded, opening a bag of candy and tossing a gummy into his mouth. An edible, I assumed, but didn't care to explore. "Probably follow your footsteps and head to Sac State."

"How's Mom feel about that?"

Adam shrugged, folding up his candy bag after the single treat and stuffing it in his back pocket. "She's fine. You know her. She's like a balloon."

"A balloon?"

"Can only hold in so much before she pops, and when she does, she makes a lot of noise. But then she's deflated."

I couldn't help myself. I laughed at the analogy. The balloon comparison was spot-on.

"She yelled at me. Called me names. You know how it goes. The usual stuff. We woke up the next morning, she's chipper as ever, as if nothing happened. As if she hadn't tried to remove my soul and shred it right before my eyes so I could feel for what happened, as if I didn't already feel bad."

I understood what he implied with perfect clarity. Our mother had a tendency to explode and wield her tongue like the world's sharpest razor. If she felt embarrassed or slighted by her children, she wanted us to know we had failed her.

"How you two getting along?" I asked.

"We're fine now. She wants to hang out and watch movies all the time. We do that once or twice a week. There's not much else to do, other than play basketball at open gyms. All my friends are still in school."

"You thinking about getting a job?"

"You looking to hire?"

I scoffed. "I can barely afford Alina, and she works for free."

"What is she, sixteen?"

"Don't even think about it."

"Never," he said. "I like my women older. At least three years older than me. I'm just curious if she's legally allowed to work for you."

"When are you so interested in following the rules?"

"Touché."

"We're working on a system," I said, eyeing him. "What are you planning to do at Sac State?"

He and I walked beneath the boardwalk's entrance arch. Commotion immediately greeted us. Crowds and lines and music playing over the speakers. Rollercoasters and screaming and the ringing of game booths hoping to attract naïve customers. The smell of fried food and ocean water filled the air.

"When you were twenty," Adam asked, glancing around the board-walk, "what did you think you wanted to do?"

"When I was twenty, I only wanted to get laid as often as possible."

Adam snickered, entertaining me with a half-smile. "No goals?"

"I didn't know other than I wanted to be outside, not sitting behind a desk. I think that's why I gravitated toward law enforcement. Turns out, I sat in a car all day doing that. I guess driving is more fun than staring at a computer screen, though."

"Did you ever like it?"

"Policing?" I asked.

"Yeah."

"No," I said. "I never fit in with the other cops. I don't think I had the right personality. I hated fights and arresting people, and I hated looking at everyone like they were criminals. It felt dirty. I enjoyed helping people, though. I liked that part of the job."

"Didn't you major in psychology at college?"

"Yeah, but only for a second. I switched it to English."

"English? I didn't know that."

"Don't tell Maya this because she will want to see a sample. But I enjoyed creative writing. I also enjoyed reading."

"Not anymore, though?"

I clicked my tongue, thinking back. "I haven't read a novel in at least five years. It's been longer since I've written anything creative—probably since my college courses."

"Why don't you ever try it, at least open a book and read it?"

I popped a knuckle, not sure why I hadn't done just that. I exercised like a man possessed, and I dove into my work like it might save my life, which included reading myths and lore and legends... but always for work, never for pleasure. Maybe I could introduce reading into my routine. A little pleasure never harmed anyone, right?

"Well," Adam said, not waiting for me to answer him. "You should try reading and writing again. I think people should do what they love."

"Maybe I will." I thought I actually might, too.

I had always enjoyed literature more than film. Now with Alina constantly pestering me to catch up on the zeitgeist, to feel the pulse of popular culture because life had far evolved from the five years prior when I had stopped caring, I felt a budding need to catch up. I hesitated to do so through television or movies. But why not read? Who knew, maybe it would spark something more deeply creative within me? Maybe reading would inspire me to try writing again. And maybe writing would prove a cathartic exercise to help me exorcise the demons that haunted and tormented my soul.

"What do you love?" I asked. "And don't say weed."

Adam rolled his eyes. "I don't love weed. I like it because it calms me when I'm stressed. It's a tool that helps me feel halfway normal. What do I love, though? I love music. The piano and singing. I love bodybuilding."

"I noticed you're getting bigger," I said.

"I'm thinking about getting certified to train people."

"Well, if you ever need a gym partner, let me know."

"Definitely."

Adam and I caught up to the other three. They stood beside a carnival game, waiting for us.

"Check it out," Fred said, nodding at the booth.

"What?" I asked.

"For five bucks, the dealer will hand us three balls, and we have to knock over that small stack of milk bottles."

"You're going to play?" I asked.

"Why not? How hard could it be?"

My dad stepped forward and handed the dealer a boardwalk card, which he had preloaded money on. "How many want to play?" he asked, turning to the rest of us.

"I'm in," Fred said.

"In," Jake said.

"Want to join?" Fred asked, looking at my brother. "I would ask August, but, you know? He's not much of an athlete."

I cracked my neck. "My assistant only wishes to egg me into a bet, knowing full well I'm not a fan of carnival games. They're rigged, and a waste of money."

Fred didn't know I hated carnival games, but he knew I had an edge for competition, especially athletic competition against him. Fred was a former professional football player, and I enjoyed defeating him in every athletic event I could just to rub it into his overly large, smug face.

Adam waved his hands before his face, stepping down from any competition.

My dad wouldn't allow Adam's refusal, though. "All of us," he said. "That's how many? Five?"

"Five," the dealer said. He had on baggy jeans and a white, sweat-stained tank top. His hair flowed down his back. "Twenty-five dollars."

"I'll Venmo you back," Fred said, patting my dad on the back.

"You have Venmo?" I asked my dad.

"With Fred always bumming cash off me, I had to set it up."

"Why is Fred always... never mind. Let's play."

"Alright," Jake said, tossing one of his three red balls into the air and catching it on the descent. "We all throw once, assess the results, and throw again in coordination."

"What's the winner get?" I asked.

"All the losers buy the winner a drink. Unless the winner is August, who doesn't drink, then the losers buy the winner..." Jake trailed off, clicking his tongue.

"How about we do the loser—last to knock over all their bottles—has to do something crazy?" Fred asked. "Like, the loser, or losers, plural, have to skinny dip in the pool tonight."

"No way," my dad said.

"No one wants to see any of us naked, anyway," I said.

"Speak for yourself."

"It should be something uncomfortable, though," Jake said. "That's the point. Don't lose."

"Loser has to drive down Highway 1 after midnight," Adam said.

We all glanced at each other, silently accepting the bet.

"Deal," I said.

"It is decided," Jake said in a strange, nasally accent.

"Alright then." Fred stepped up to the booth. "I would normally worry about something like that, but I don't even care right now. I know I won't lose to all you punks."

"You played defense, right?" my dad asked the big man.

"Don't think I can't throw because I played defense," Fred said, rolling his shoulders to loosen them. "I threw further than anyone else on my team, including the quarterback. I have God-given talent."

"We ready?" Jake asked, eyeing his competitors.

I stepped up to my stall and nodded. We stood in a line, staring down our targets.

Jake counted us down. "One. Two. Three. Throw."

I threw the ball, releasing high and throwing it over the stack of pins.

Adam threw wide, missing to the right.

Fred and my father hit the top pin, knocking it off the stack, leaving only two more to drop in their grouping.

Jake threw his ball dead center, toppling all three of his pins. He yelped with excitement and punched the air.

"Serious?" Fred asked, staring at my brother-in-law with a mixture of annoyance and awe. "You're that lucky, huh?"

"Lucky?" Jake asked, excited. "No way. I've told you before, I had offers to play baseball. Pitcher. I turned them down, though."

"I never believed you before, and I don't believe you now," Fred said. "Alright, well, enjoy your stuffed prize and the victory. You're eliminated from having to drive Highway 1 tonight. Congratulations."

"Feeling nervous now?" I asked Fred.

"You won't hit a single bottle. What do I have to be nervous of?"

My dad cleared his throat and nudged Fred to get his attention. "Which one should I go for next?"

"Huh?"

"Which of the remaining two? I went for the top one that round. Should I go for the left or right, now?"

"You're calling your shots?" Fred asked, disbelieving.

I chuckled under my breath, knowing what Fred didn't know. Jake hadn't only received offers to play college baseball, he had received full scholarships to big-time athletic programs across the nation. My dad was also a collegiate athlete—quarterback for Fresno State way back in the day. He had aspirations of going professional, but injuries and life stood in the way. Adam had also taken to sports naturally, though he didn't enjoy the work of playing them in an organized fashion. However, he possessed the same pinpoint accuracy as my dad.

My dad stared at the milk bottles. "How about this? Adam, you go for the left pin. I'll knock out the right. Take any randomness out of the equation."

"Sounds good," Adam said, sounding more engaged with the game now.

"Fred, you and August just worry about hitting the stack." My dad moved the ball around his fingers like a pitcher before a pitch.

Jake counted us down once again, standing a few feet behind us as he no longer took part in the contest. We all threw our rubber baseball simultaneously.

My ball nicked the top bottle, but it didn't topple.

Fred, however, caught enough of the bottom right pin to knock it over.

As predicted, my dad also hit the right bottle. Adam hit the left, dropping it and the top bottle. They each had only one more to capsize.

"There's no way," Fred said, so baffled at my brother's and father's skill set, that he completely neglected to chastise me for missing again. "How did you do that? Why not just... I don't know, do like Jake did and knock them all over?"

"There's a certain amount of fun in knocking them all over at once," my dad said. "But there's a sophisticated type of enjoyment watching your competitor realize they have lost and they can't do anything about it."

"You're psychotic," Fred said. "A cat playing with a mouse. I never knew that about you until now, but you're a looney-toon." Fred turned my way, probably realizing his only chance at not losing in the game was to defeat me. "No excuses for you. I don't want to hear them."

"What's that mean?"

"Bad shoulder, bad hip. You're bad at sleeping and the bet is to check out a paranormal adventure, so you lost on purpose to have a reason to check out the ghost, even though you're not getting paid to do it."

"You really think I would want to lose this game and miss watching you drive that highway later tonight? That will be pure gold. You hate driving. You hate the dark. You hate monsters." I raised my eyebrows. "I'm going to join you on the trip no matter what, but I'm going to enjoy the views from the passenger seat."

Fred cracked his neck, moving his head back and forth. "Jake, count us down."

Jake, once again, counted. "Three. Two. One."

My dad and brother pegged their bottles squarely, clearing their area.

Fred missed the left-most bottle by a hair, leaving it wobbling, steadying, keeping its balance.

The big guy had been correct about one thing—my hip and shoulder hurt, and they especially hurt when I threw the balls. But I swallowed the pain, stepped through it, and made a precision throw.

In high school, I played basketball and sat the bench as a receiver in football. Throwing was never in my wheelhouse, but I was athletic enough to make a throw if I needed to.

The rubber baseball connected with the lower middle bottles, flattening them both. The top pin fell straight down, landing on its butt, upright without the slightest warble.

I laughed, unable to fathom the impossibility. "There's no way," I said, staring at the single-standing bottle. How had the bottle dropped straight down without falling?

"We're tied," Fred said.

"I see that," I said. "Jake."

"Yup?"

"You still have those two extra balls?"

He had knocked his bottles down on the first try, leaving him with two spare rubber baseballs.

"Take them with me everywhere I go, since Rachel always hides mine in her purse."

My dad laughed at the joke, as did Fred. I rolled my eyes and snickered. Jake stepped forward and handed me the two extra red balls.

I tossed one to Fred. "Overtime," I said, turning to the dealer. "Don't worry. It's not for a prize, only to settle a score."

The man nodded as if he understood and stepped aside.

"What if we both miss?" Fred asked.

"We won't," I said. "You're not getting out of this bet."

"Three," Jake counted, "Two. One."

Three instances of collisions occurred simultaneously.

Fred's rubber ball whizzed by the bottle, slamming into the tarp behind the stage with a heavy thunk.

My ball connected with the metallic milk bottle, flying it off the pedestal.

Behind us, like someone slapping a fish across another person's face, was the third smack.

Fred groaned, grabbing his head as he realized defeat. "Not possible."

"Sorry, buddy, but it must feel frustrating," I said. "A former professional athlete like you, one who thrived in the NFL, losing to a bunch of average Joe's in a game of physical abilities."

"It's a fluke," Fred said. "A carnival game. They're all rigged, anyway."

"Make any excuse you want, but I'm telling everyone you lost."

"Hey, hey, hey," Adam said, panic flooding his usually stoic and deep voice.

"August!" My dad called a half-second later.

I turned, facing them, seeing Jake lying on the ground. Blood splattered across his face, stained his shirt, puddled on the ground beside him.

For a flash of a second, I returned to the park and stood on the basketball court, holding my sidearm forward and pointing it at the dead teenager on the ground.

"What's that?" Fred asked, pointing at a feathery lump beside Jake. "A bird?"

Jake grunted, grabbing the back of his head and sitting up. He pulled his hand away, seeing blood. "What happened?"

Before anyone could answer him, the storm broke.

Birds rained from the sky. They dove beak-first toward the Earth like missiles, tucking in their wings and slamming into whatever stood in their way. Hundreds if not thousands of them.

People screamed and ran, tripping over and trampling others. Some people stood in place, turning in circles, screaming out names. Birds slammed into other people as the one had crashed into Jake, driving them to the ground in an explosion of feathers and blood.

"Get into the booth," I said, jumping to Jake and helping him to his feet.

I half-carried him to the game counter. My hip and shoulder screamed, but I did my best to ignore the pain, assisting Jake over the counter and into the booth. I climbed in after him. My dad, brother, and Fred had already found shelter, huddling beside the wiry young man who had handed us the rubber balls.

Outside, the birds smacked into buildings, rollercoasters, and into the ground, pelting anyone who had yet to find cover.

A Brutal Awakening. Tuesday, May 2nd. 1132hrs.

Nick woke up with a headache behind his eyes. His mouth tasted sour. Not a hangover, though. He hadn't touched alcohol in weeks, maybe months. It made him too drowsy, and drowsy led to sleep, which led to the Devil.

So why did he feel so groggy, like he had woken up deep underground, with the pressure of the world crushing him?

Reaching for the nightstand, Nick grabbed his phone to check the time. It was turned off. He held down the side button, turning the phone back on and wondering why it was off to begin with. Who had turned off his phone? Chris?

Where was Chris?

"Chris?" Nick called, his voice cracking.

Where was she? If he had fallen asleep, she should have waited in the room, watched over him, woke him up if he showed any signs of the distress. She wasn't in the room, though.

She hadn't responded to his call either.

Nick bolted upright. The pooled blood sitting in his head trickled down his body, steeping him in a quick spell of dizziness. The room spun around him, fizzing in and out of his vision. After a moment, he oriented.

The phone brightened, showing a half-full battery and the time. Half-past eleven.

Nick had nearly slept for two hours—the most consecutive hours he had slept in three, four months. No wonder he felt like a wool blanket, heavy and furry all over.

That time lapse heightened his fear about Chris. They had agreed to wake each other up after forty-five minutes at the most. Why hadn't she woke him up? Would she have left him alone?

Never. Not unless... no. Chris hadn't learned the truth. Impossible. And if she had, she wouldn't have run. That wasn't Chris. She would have woken Nick up herself, wielding a sledgehammer of her own.

Nick went back to his original question. Why hadn't Chris awoken him? Where was she? Had she dozed off?

Nick threw the blankets off his body and stood. He stretched, feeling his muscles loosen, and he cleared the sleep from his throat. "Chris!" he called with more strength that time. He stepped forward, toward the closed door leading into the kitchen. "Chris!"

No response.

Nick felt like a child left home alone for the first time, hearing strange noises from the other room. He didn't want to investigate. He would rather climb back into his bed and throw the covers over his head and tremble in fear.

Except, doing nothing solved nothing.

Nick bit his lower lip and tiptoed to the closed door, wrapped his hand around the knob, and twisted. The door creaked open, revealing the gruesome tabloid left behind it.

Nick dropped to his knees, choking, unable to swallow what he saw slumping against the bathroom door.

So Much for Vacation. Tuesday, May 2nd. 1201hrs.

When I walked into the rental home, I saw Maya first. She stood in the center of the room, hands pinned behind her head, arms akimbo. I nearly sprinted over and embraced her, showered her in kisses.

Cambria sat on the couch a few feet away from Maya, though. She held a nearly empty glass of white wine.

I hesitated for a split-second, mouth agape and eyes wide, momentarily unsure of where to go, or who to go to. My mind pulled me toward one woman, but my body moved toward another.

I scooted to the back of the couch, standing behind where Cambria sat, and I wrapped my arms around her. I leaned forward and kissed the crown of her head. "Are you okay?"

"Yeah. We're all okay." Cambria dropped her head back and looked up at me. A speckle of blood dotted her forehead. "What happened?"

I pulled back and centered my attention on Maya, who watched me with sharp eyes. "I don't know."

"I'll tell you what happened," Alina said from the kitchen. She sat at the dining room table, snacking on a bag of M&Ms.

"Hey," Fred said, glancing at the kid. "Those are mine. Where did you find those?"

"You're not as sly as you think, Big Guy. I know all your hiding spots."

"What happened?" I was quick to not allow the conversation to spiral.

"Have you ever seen *The Birds*?"

"That's exactly what I thought." Fred glared at me. He looped on arm around Daphne's waist, pulling her into him. "I said that same thing to August."

"You didn't say that. When did you say that?" I asked.

"On the drive back from the boardwalk. You were lost in your own little head, though. Probably didn't hear a word anyone said to you."

"It's obvious, no?" Alina asked.

"It's not obvious," I said. "We're not in a movie, or a simulation, or whatever you said."

"Science Fiction predicts real life advancements all the time. Why couldn't a horror movie, especially one created by the genius of Alfred Hitchcock, predict birds attacking humans."

"Because that's not what this is," I said. "Birds didn't attack humans."

"How would you know that?" Fred asked. "Look at Jake."

"Look at me." Jake sat on the kitchen table, while Rachel attended to his head wound.

"Because not only did I watch the movie, I read the short story, too."

Alina scratched her forehead. "Wait, that's a lot to process. You've seen a movie before?"

"I've seen a handful of movies," I said.

"What other ones?"

"Does it matter?" Daphne asked.

"It does," Alina said. "But you're right. It doesn't matter right now. We'll stay on track. You said you read the short story? There's a short story?"

"By Daphne du Maurier." I puffed out my chest a little, feeling cocky for knowing something about media that Alina didn't. "In both mediums, the storyteller presents a plot where the birds attack humans through calculated assaults."

Alina narrowed her eyes and curled her lip. "Go on."

"The birds perched on wires and waited for humans to appear before attacking them in flocks."

"Okay?" she asked. "Get to your point, though."

"The bird Armageddon that we just witnessed—"

"Birdageddon," Fred said, snapping his fingers. "Maya, there's your title."

"Seems lazy, don't you think?" Maya said. "Tired. Overplayed."

"It's fun to say. Birdageddon. You really don't like it?"

"The birds fell from the sky," I said, forcefully enough to prevent Fred and Maya from sidetracking. "They didn't attack us. They had no organization. They didn't even flock in the air or perch and wait. They dropped from the sky, splattering into whatever they collided with first."

"Sure." Alina's voice was dismissive, as if the differences didn't matter. "Still, why?"

I grinned, having the answer to that question, too. I loved knowing things that know-it-all Maya and Alina didn't know.

"Don't smile like that," Alina said. "You look creepy."

Maya leaned over to see me straight on. "Oh, definitely. She's right. When you smile, you look like how I imagine serial killers smile right before they murder someone. It's terrifying."

"I love your smile. It's sweet and mischievous," my mom said. She sat on the other side of the room, nuzzled to my father. "You always look like you're doing something you shouldn't be doing when you smile. A bad boy look."

"No." Maya shook her head. "Definitely not bad boy, in terms of like the good, bad boy. Maybe a bad, bad boy, like a creepy bad boy."

"Like that weird kid in school who always smiles at you, but never talks to you," Alina said, burring her shoulders.

"I can see that," Fred said. "Not even waving either. Just staring across the room, half-smirking like he's hatching up the greatest idea in the world. Except that great idea doesn't settle right for anyone but him."

Daphne craned her head away from Fred, also staring at me. "I can see that. Like he enjoys dissecting the frogs."

I clapped my hands. "Okay. Enough of that."

"I actually was enjoying it," Rachel said from the kitchen, still inspecting Jake's battle wound. "Can we continue telling August how weird he is for a just a few more minutes?"

"I think you're cute," Cambria said, leaning back her head and glancing up at me.

"Yeah. Me, too," Jake said. "Though I might have a concussion. Also, if I'm honest, you're just a lot cuter when you don't smile."

"Well, this has gone on for far too long," I said. "What I meant to say about an hour ago, was that Daphne du Maurier—"

"Who?" Fred asked.

"The author of *The Birds*."

"That's Alfred Hitchcock."

I almost tore out my hair. "Either way, they derived their inspiration for the story from a real-life event in the '60s that occurred in Capitola. Coincidentally, Capitola is located like five miles from where we're at right now."

"What event?" Maya asked, biting a fingernail.

"Seabirds literally fell from the sky, dive-bombing homes and crashing into cars. Does that sound familiar?"

"Slightly." Adam sat on the hearth and scrolled through his phone.

"Did they find a reason for the incident?" Maya asked.

"Recently they formed a theory. Some toxic algae or something like that. I'm not sure if anyone ever proved it, though."

"Those weren't just seagulls today," Alina said. "I saw crows and pigeons and all kinds of different birds."

"You're a bird expert now?" Maya asked.

Alina scowled at her aunt. "If it's algae, as you say, do the birds all eat the same algae at the same time? Why else would they all act so sporadic simultaneously? Seems, I don't know, strange, don't you think?"

"That part confuses me," I said, cracking a knuckle.

Fred's phone buzzed. He raised a finger and answered the call. "Blue Moon, this is Fred Rogers speaking, how may I help you?" He grunted a few agreeable sounds. "He's here. Would you like to speak with him?" Fred extended his cell phone to me. "It's for you."

"Who is it?"

"Heather Thompson." Fred's face showed no amusement. "You'll want to take it. She sounds... flustered."

I accepted the phone and excused myself from the living room, leaving everyone else to discuss the bird situation. I stepped outside the house and paced the front patio.

"Heather, this is August Watson."

"Christina is dead." Heather hadn't hesitated so much as to inhale. She had the sentence locked and loaded and ready to fire.

Its suddenness took me by surprise. I leaned against a column, steadying myself. "Hold on," I said, mostly to myself to buy time and process. "What happened?"

"Someone murdered Christina."

"Murdered her? Who?"

Heather sucked air for a few seconds. "Police think Nick did it."

"What do you think?" I thought I knew how she would answer, but I thought wrong.

"I don't know."

"You don't know? You don't think the Devil killed her?" A leading question, I know, but I couldn't believe she hadn't defaulted to that answer.

"I don't know," she sobbed. "I want to believe the Devil murdered her, that Nick had nothing to do with it. I don't know, I don't know, I don't know."

"You said the police think Nick did it?" I directed the conversation back to familiar ground, to a question she could answer to build confidence to.

"They're not even looking at other suspects. They arrested Nick."

"Arrested, or brought him in for questioning? There's a difference."

"They're telling him they know he did it."

"Do they know that? Do they have direct evidence? Did they read him his Miranda rights?"

"I don't know."

"If they haven't arrested him, their claims are nothing more than scare tactics."

"What?"

"A scare tactic. That's all. They pretend to know more than they do to scare him, maybe convince him into admitting to something."

"He's not saying anything to them, not until he speaks to his lawyer."

"He said that?" I asked.

"That's what he told me."

"When did you talk to him?"

"Five minutes ago. I didn't know who else to call for help. Johnny said to call you."

I couldn't help them unless I found the Devil. It had committed murder, though, if I believed Nick hadn't murdered Christina. Either way, a homicide had occurred. The case had gone from a paranormal investigation to a criminal investigation, leaving the police in charge now. If I continued to look into the case, I could jeopardize the police work. I couldn't dismiss Heather, Johnny, and Nick, either. What if the Devil existed? What if the nightmare and Nick weren't the same? What if the police looked in all the wrong areas, and only I could save the remaining three kids from death?

"Mr. Watson? Are you still there?"

"I'm here."

"I'm so scared. Nick was in the apartment with her. He was sleeping when it happened."

"What? He was there?"

"How did the Devil kill her without Nick noticing?"

I had a couple theories, and they mostly aligned with how Santa Cruz Police Department felt about Nick.

The group of four had repeatedly shared a nightmare, though. The Devil had shattered Nick's hand. Could he have murdered Christina? If so, why?

"Heather," I said as calmly as possible. "I want you to think for a second. Try to detach any emotion from your thoughts. I know that's difficult, but please, for this question, set emotion aside."

"Okay."

"Is it possible that Nick could have murdered Christina and conveniently blamed her death on the Devil?"

Heather didn't respond at first, hopefully pushing away her fear and confusion to think somewhat rationally. Then she said, her voice less than a whisper, but still audible, "We should meet. Only you and me."

A minute later, I returned to my family and friends in the living room. I handed the phone back to Fred. "What's the plan?" I asked, figuring they would have discussed a variety of bird-related ideas in my absence.

Daphne spoke first. "Well, considering none of this comes anywhere close within my realm of knowledge, the plan for me is relaxation—also known as cooking. With a drink in my hand."

"I'm not messing with anymore birds," Jake said, touching his head. "I'm with Daphne."

"Same," Rachel said.

"Gussy, I don't think you should pursue this case, anyway. It seems dangerous." My mom stared at me with nervous eyes. She knew her feeble argument wouldn't go far, but she couldn't help but try.

"Your mom and I will stay here, out of your way," my dad said.

"And Adam's not going anywhere, either," Mom added.

I knew there was nothing I could do to counter that decision, so I didn't try. Instead, I looked at my brother. "We'll have this bird thing figured out before tomorrow night."

"That's a guarantee," Maya said. "You're not missing twenty-one with Maya Mylene Adler."

"I'm going to hang back, too." Cambria touched my hand, squeezed it and pulled me down toward her. "Do you think we can hang out tonight?" Her breath smelled like white wine, sweet and cold. "Maybe we can have a late dinner, you and me?"

"I'd like that." I looked at Maya, Alina, and Fred. "I need to meet privately with Heather right now. What are you guys doing? You looking into the bird disaster?"

"I am," Maya said. "It's too golden of a story not to pursue, at least for me."

"I'll tag along with her," Alina said. "It's not like I ever work for money, anyway. Besides, it's interesting enough for me to care."

"Fred?" I asked.

"Well, seeing that I'm driving along Highway 1 tonight in search of the ghost—"

"You're doing what tonight?" Daphne asked.

"I lost a bet, but I'll explain that later."

"He lost in a throwing competition to four scrubs," Jake said.

"I'll explain it later," Fred said. "Anyway, seeing as I'm doing that, I'm going to stay here and rest. August, I'll forward any calls straight to your phone."

I cracked a knuckle and nodded. "Well, so much for a nice, easy vacation, huh?"

Guilty Until Proven Innocent. Tuesday, May 2nd. 1401hrs.

Detective Todd Phillips of the Santa Cruz Police Department entered the small, barren interrogation room. A two-way mirror hung on the wall behind the detective's chair.

For nearly two hours, Nicholas Lane had sat straight across from the mirror. He stared at his lap, his greasy long hair veiling most of his face.

After hauling in Nick for questioning at the station, they had allowed him to make whatever calls he needed to make. The detectives encouraged their suspects to make the revered call. The phone was tapped; the conversation recorded.

After Nick had reached out to who he needed to speak to, the detectives went back and listened, searching for admission of guilt, suspicious behavior, or anything they could use against him in the interrogation. They took their time before joining him, too, forcing Nick to sit and wait for them, to think and stress and grow antsy. The more worried and uncomfortable a suspect, the easier they were to break.

The police could hold a suspect for forty-eight hours. In that window of time, they could either charge the suspect with a crime or release them. So, they had a few hours to burn, to turn up the heat and let Nick sweat a little. The time had arrived to interrogate.

"I'm Detective Phillips," Detective Phillips said, leaning against the wall and crossing his arms. He didn't carry a notepad or a folder. He found those tools often intimidated his suspects. Phillips preferred a conversational approach, especially during the first meeting. Casual and friendly, not business. Not initially. Ease your way into it. "You're Nicholas Lane."

The kid, twenty-three based on the file, grunted. "That a question?"

"A statement. You've sat in that chair before, haven't you?"

Another confirming grunt.

"I heard grand theft auto from a colleague. What car did you pick up?"

"Nothing worth it," Nick said.

"Too bad. I find when I cave to temptation, it better be worth it. If I eat cake, for example, I'm going to eat a lot of cake." Phillips clicked his tongue. "Battery, as well."

"They dropped the charges."

"Still, you're familiar with this room, or a room similar to it."

"Yeah."

"Flunked out of high school, did you, Nick?"

"Wasn't learning anything."

"Played in a semi-successful band for a while. Went on a state-wide tour, playing at reputable venues. I looked you guys up on Spotify. It's not my style of music—I prefer the slower, laid-back kind of sound—but you sounded good. Lead singer?"

"Drummer."

"All the girls love a drummer, don't they?"

"Sure, I guess."

"What happened?"

"With the band?"

"Yeah."

"Why do you care?" Nick asked, lifting his head and looking up at Phillips. The kid looked more like a corpse than a living person. He had waxy, bruised skin and glazed eyes—like an addict after a long bender.

The young man didn't fidget or cower, not even after having sat on the hard, metal chair for two hours. A lot of times, especially guilty parties, would constantly move their hands. They tugged at their ears, wiped their palms on their jeans, cracked their knuckles, twisted their wrists, tucked their hair behind their ear. Even handcuffed, they would flex their fingers or tap the table. Also, they had a tendency to guard themselves, turning their shoulder to the interrogator, crossing their arms, never making eye contact.

Apart from Nick staring at his lap when Phillips entered the room, the young man seemed more confident than most suspects who sat in that chair.

"Curiosity," Phillips said, intrigued by Nick. "I hate a puzzled to go unsolved."

"Well, good. Maybe you'll solve who killed Christina then," Nick said, his voice shaky.

"You don't know who did it?"

"No."

"You didn't do it?"

The kid shook his head, staring straight at Phillips. "No."

"What happened to your hand?" The detective nodded at Nick's cast.

"Whoever killed Christina, they broke my hand a week ago. You should know that already. We reported it, but you morons did nothing about it."

"I read about that incident. Someone from your dream attacked you, correct?"

Nick returned his attention to his lap.

"How does that work exactly? A monster attacks you in your sleep, and you suffer the actual injury? I can't quite wrap my head around that."

"I can't either."

Phillips snapped his fingers. "I remember," he said, pushing off the wall, walking to the empty chair, turning it around, and sitting on it backwards. "Your third crime. Aggravated assault with a deadly weapon. You broke someone's jaw with a baseball bat."

A flash of irritation passed through Nick's face. "I want to speak to my lawyer."

"Someone's jaw, of course, being your ex-girlfriend's jaw. Apparently, from the rumors I heard, you two got in a heated argument because she found you talking to another woman, right?"

Nick said nothing. The skin near his cheekbones twitched, pulsing as if they had a heartbeat of their own.

"She slapped you, did she not?"

Silence.

"You shoved her into the wall. Of course, we learned all the messy details once she regained the ability to speak, but according to her, after you shoved her into the wall, she lunged at you, clawed at your face. She bled you pretty good, like a wild animal." Phillips fell quiet for a moment, waiting to see if Nick would take the bait and say something.

He didn't.

"You kicked her off of you, stood, grabbed the baseball bat you kept nearby... just in case, I don't know, someone broke into your home or owed you money or accused you of cheating, and you treated her jaw like a curveball, or a knuckleball. I'm not acquainted with baseball. Either way, the boys in blue arrested you for aggravated assault with a deadly weapon. Your band, exhausted from the constant legal trouble you found yourself in, booted you. Drummers, though, they're easily replaceable, right? All the great rock bands replaced their drummer at some point."

Nick's jaw tensed, and he glared at Phillips.

"Hi," the detective said once he had Nick's attention. "I'm glad you've come back to me. Now, did you murder Christina Wyss?"

"I want to speak to my lawyer."

"I'm painting the picture based on the preliminary evidence. History has a tendency to repeat itself, no?"

"Lawyer."

"Christina learned you were talking to her best friend, Heather, who also is your best friend's fiancé. Am I right?"

"Lawyer."

"When she learned about your and Heather's secret relationship, platonic or not, she confronted you. However that confrontation went, it concluded with your hand broken via a sledgehammer. For whatever reason, earlier this morning, you and Christina had another spat. This time, though, this time you grabbed the sledgehammer. You didn't just break her jaw, but you silenced her for good."

"I didn't kill her!"

"Nick, I'm not your enemy. In fact, I want to help you, but I need you to help me do that. Can you help me? What happened earlier? Why did you kill Christina?"

The young man broke down. His face crunched, and he sobbed, but he didn't say a single word outside, "I want a lawyer."

Detective Phillips saw he had hit bedrock with his digging. To go deeper, he would need better equipment. He stood, regarding Nick for a second. "The latest album was my favorite. I feel like the new drummer really brought the band to the next level."

Evan Richards. Tuesday, May 2nd. 1427hrs.

Evan Richards. Tuesday, May 2nd. 1427hrs.

After regaling their bird-survival stories over another one of Daphne's five-star lunches, Daphne allowed Maya and Alina to borrow her vehicle for their field trip.

"Only on the condition you do nothing—purposeful or accidental—to harm her."

"Her?" Maya had asked.

"Her," Daphne had said. "Unlike men, women are reliable."

"What are you saying?" Fred had asked.

"Exactly what I said," Daphne said, scowling at her husband. "Women are sophisticated, cultured, and responsible. As is my car. If you borrow her, you will treat her like a lady."

"Well, I'm a lady who likes a little mistreatment now and again," Maya said, snickering.

"Oh," Daphne said, smirking, "she likes a little abuse now and then. I'll redline her and allow her to scream, but she's pampered, too. Don't hurt her. If a bird falls from the sky, you better jump in the way and protect my girl."

Maya thought of laughing, but Daphne showed no hint of joking.

"I love my grandma first, my car second, and Fred third."

"That's true," Fred said behind a mouthful of food. "We've discussed at length the hierarchy of her love, and though I'm not okay with it, I've accepted it."

"Do you understand me?" Daphne asked.

Maya, who often skipped the fear emotion, swallowed and nodded her head, slightly terrified of Daphne—which allowed her to respect the woman in ways she never thought she could respect another human. "Not really," Maya said. "But I understand enough to not let anything happen to the car." Maya vowed to Daphne, and to herself, that nothing, not under any circumstance, would harm the vehicle.

"Why are you driving so slow?" Alina asked as they cruised ten miles below the speed limit along a residential road.

"I'm not about to wreck this thing. Besides, where we even going?"

Alina shrugged. They hadn't determined a destination before embarking on their hunch-led journey.

"There's no reason to drive nowhere fast. Might as well take our time and observe, see what we can see. That's the first rule of investigation, Padawan. Ask August, he'll say the same thing. Let the truth speak to you. Don't force it. If you're quiet enough, you will hear it."

"What's that even mean?" Alina stared out the passenger window.

The sidewalks and yards were littered with birds, and the parked cars held fresh, bloody dents and scratches. The windows had shattered. People gathered in small groups, probably debating with their neighbors what could have possibly happened. Why had thousands of birds fallen from the sky like something predicted in the book of Revelation?

"A lot of investigation—journalism, police work, private work, whatever—stems from instinct," Maya said, answering Alina's question. "That's why we often sit down and brainstorm before a case. Who are the players? Where's the setting? What's the story? How do they connect? When you can't answer one or more of those questions, you return to the scene or to those involved, and you hope to gather more information. To tickle your intuition."

"Players, birds," Alina said.

Maya clicked her tongue. "Partly."

"Partly?"

"Think of a homicide. The players come as two parties—the victim and the killer. We have the birds, who I believe fall into the victim category here. So, who or what incited the birds to act so strangely?"

"Toxic algae."

"Maybe."

Alina rolled her head, facing her aunt. "Setting, Santa Cruz."

"Five miles from where it happened sixty years ago in Capitola."

"What's the story? Birds acting strangely, falling from the sky, splattering into the first thing they see."

"How are they connected?" Maya asked. "Why did this happen? We need motive."

Maya pulled off the side of the road, parking along a red-painted curb with white lettering stating NO PARKING. A half-dozen other vehicles parked along the same curb, a handful more had driven up onto the sidewalk, parking there, and others had stopped their trucks and cars in the middle of the road, abandoning them to join a large gathering near the beach.

"Do you know why I stopped here?" Maya asked.

"Because you can't drive any further forward?"

"No, genius. I could turn around if I wanted to. But I don't want to."

Alina stared out the windshield, glancing around the area. Apart from the crowd of vehicles parked at random, in illegal places, police cruisers and firetrucks and ambulances flashed their lights further up the road. News vans had also sneaked their way into the chaos, fitting themselves wherever they could. A crowd of people—much larger than the small gatherings from a mile back—bunched together. A few hundred people, standing shoulder to shoulder, faced the ocean.

"News report?" Alina asked.

"Reporters always find the hottest spots. I think we should check out why everyone stopped right here."

Maya and Alina pushed through the crowd, squeezing as near to the front as they could.

The first responders worked along the sandy beach. Police officers stood guard before a stretch of crime scene tape, while paramedics stretchered bodies to their eagerly waiting ambulances. Where the people had once lay, bloody pools remained.

Animal control scoured the beach with cages, collecting birds that had fallen into the puffy sand but had not died. Instead, they hopped and screeched and jolted as if electrocuted.

Standing in the parking lot overlooking the beach, a handful of local news stations interviewed a man. A gorgeous man. He wore slacks and a button-down shirt with his sleeves rolled up, his tie half-loose. He had a square jaw and dark hair and piercing eyes. He answered the reporters' questions quickly, with a sharp confidence that drew Maya nearer and nearer to him.

Before she knew it, her hand touched the sky.

The man's icy eyes cut to her as he finished answering the previous question. "The woman wearing a Pokémon shirt and sweatpants, what's your question?"

Maya's arm remained high above her head, frozen in place as his gaze fixed on her—as if she had met eyes with Medusa and turned to stone.

Alina's elbow poked Maya in the ribs, sending a bright pain down her torso, but waking Maya up. First, embarrassment rushed from her toes to her ears. After the bird incident, she had changed into a more comfortable outfit, but had neglected to change out of it before heading out to investigate what happened. Second, as embarrassment rushed upward, burning her face, Maya's thoughts drained downward, below her mouth and throat, settling heavily in her stomach. She had no words.

"Do you have a question?" the man asked.

"Yes," Maya said, saying nothing else.

"Go on and ask."

Maya had no issues speaking with anyone, let alone with men or in front of a crowd. In fact, the bigger the audience, the more she excelled. But the book-cover model standing before her had rendered her speechless.

She cleared her throat, buying time to regain her poise. "I'm a writer for the *Here & Now*."

A few chuckles popped around her as a handful of reporters most likely recognized the tabloid.

"I only just arrived here, so I'm missing a lot of key information." Like a needle falling into a record's groove, Maya's words now fell off her tongue like music. "Would you care for a private interview once the cameras leave?"

The man leaned back, biting his lower lip. "With a pretty girl like you? I'm not sure I could brave that kind of private interview."

Maya giggled.

"You're so cringy," Alina said.

The man scanned the crowd of reporters. "Well, you all heard the lady. Interview over. I've shared all I'm at liberty to share, or all I know."

Groans of disappointment filled the ocean air.

"Any further information I share will be repetitive. As soon as I know more, you will also know more. Thank you for your time." The man stepped away from the makeshift podium he stood behind, made eye contact with Maya, and nodded his head as if motioning for her to follow him.

Maya wedged herself through the grumbling crowd, breaking free and nearly bumping into the tall, broad man who seemed much taller and broader up close than he had a few seconds ago.

"Hi," he said.

"Hi."

"I'm Evan." He extended a hand. "Evan Richards."

Maya fit her small hand into his mitt, shaking it. "I'm Maya Adler." Her voice was gentle as it nearly stuck in her throat. She didn't know what was happening. Upon meeting a handsome gentleman who caught her attention, Maya normally poured on the charm with practiced ease. Now, in front of Mr. Evan Richards, she felt like a middle school girl meeting her boy band crush.

"I'm Alina Moore," Alina said, crossing her arms and tilting her head. "Her niece."

"It's my absolute pleasure to meet the both of you," Evan said. "Shall we, as you mentioned, head somewhere a little more private? I know a cafe just down the street." Evan turned toward the reporters still gathered around, snapping pictures of the three of them. "I'm positive they will follow us to the cafe, but they won't come inside and bother us. We'll be able to speak freely."

"I'll call an ace a spade," Alina said.

"You mean a spade a spade," Maya said.

"You know what I mean. Either way, you're only meeting us privately because you think my aunt is cute."

"Beautiful," he corrected. "Not cute. Stunningly beautiful."

Alina rolled her eyes. "This isn't a date, Mr. Richards. Don't expect to get into her pants. For whatever reason, these reporters want to hear what you have to say about the bird incident. That makes you interesting to us. So, in your mind, convince yourself that my aunt is only using you to provide us with information. That's all this is."

"She can use me however she wants to."

"Nope. It's an interview, on the record, about the birds."

"Of course."

"Maya, I'm talking to you, too," Alina said.

"Yeah, I know."

"What do you know?" Alina asked.

"Interview. Birds. Jaw-dropping man."

"Two out of three isn't bad," Evan said.

"No more charm from you," Alina said. "Lead us to the cafe, Mr. Richards."

Nothing but the Truth. Tuesday, May 2nd. 1430hrs.

THE LATE-AFTERNOON SUNSHINE BURNED through the windows, but that didn't deter a healthy gathering of rugged individuals from frequenting the bar. Most had reservations for one. They huddled over their beers and drank alone and held court with their thoughts. They stared at the sticky counter or the grimy mirror behind the bar, which held shelves of cheap to mid-level alcohol.

A few burly men with thick beards shot pool at a tattered table. They shared a couple pitchers of something light, along with club tattoos on their sleeveless arms. Apart from billiard balls colliding and the occasional grunts of disappointment or whelps of excitement from the players, the only sound in the dim-lit bar was the jukebox. A slow country song, something in the realm of Johnny Cash, played over the speakers. I had never developed a taste for country music, so I couldn't say for sure who sang what.

Heather sat by herself in a corner booth. She palmed both hands around a chipped coffee mug. Steam rose off the surface. She wore a baggy hoodie with the words PARTY NAKED scrawled across the front, and she had pulled the hood over her head to shroud her face. I thought of a burned out cigarette when I saw her—there, but used up. Finished.

I ambled across the establishment. My thoughts slipped back to when I had last frequented a dive bar a few nights ago. I had danced with a woman named Patricia. Me, dancing. I chortled at the memory. She had enlivened something long dead inside of me, though. Now she was dead, killed by the Vampire of Sacramento, an emerging serial killer.

I slid into the booth and sat across the table from Heather.

From behind the hood covering her eyes, she looked up at me. "Thanks for meeting me."

"It's a nice place," I said, mentally grimacing at the sarcasm. I had spent too much time with Alina lately, and her snark had rubbed off. I'm not sure I liked it too much. I preferred healthy cynicism.

Heather sniffled and looked at the bar counter. "My mom used to bring me here when I was a little girl—eight-, nine-years old."

"I can see why. Friendly. Inviting. Perfect place for a kid." There I went again, saying words just to say them. What was going on with me?

"Her friend owned the bar. Not anymore, though. He died a while back. Anyway, when he lived and owned this place, as he owned half of Santa Cruz, it seemed, I had a pass to come inside despite my age."

Another witty comment rose to my lips, but I sealed my mouth and let it burn a hole through my tongue. I practiced listening instead of speaking.

"My mom always sat right here, in this booth, and she drank house vodka. Her friend who owned this place was a special friend, I might add. Anyway, my mom drank at the wholesale price. She drank well vodka straight. Sometimes, she added pickle juice. I remember thinking that was the nastiest thing in the world. Her mixing the vodka and pickle juice." Heather trailed off, twisting her hoodie's string around a finger.

"What did you do while she drank?"

"I colored. Darryl, the old owner, supplied me with Crayons and a coloring book, some soda. I colored and drank soda. My mom drank and... well, she drank."

"Your dad?"

"I never knew him. From the stories I heard, he died overseas a hero, fighting in the war." Heather hiccupped a quick laugh. "What do I care about a hero, though? I didn't need a hero. My mom didn't need a hero."

"I'm sorry."

"Me, too." Heather raised the coffee mug to her lips and drank. "Sometimes I still come here. It does nothing for me other than remind me of sad memories. I don't know. Sometimes sad memories are comforting, you know?"

I nodded, painfully aware of what she meant. She used the wrong word, though. They weren't comforting. Sad memories were like failed loves—familiar. Familiarity, I guess, creates comfort, especially when someone might feel lost.

"My mom would get so drunk she couldn't drive us home. She had me drive. Eleven-, nine-years-old, and I'm driving her home as she mumbles half-asleep, lying in the backseat. My mom leaving me alone while she flirted with some stranger, sometimes leaving with him."

"Daryl didn't care?"

"As long as he got his, he didn't care who else got theirs." Heather sighed. "That makes him sound like a bad guy. He wasn't. He would drive me home those nights—to his home. I don't think he cared for me to sleep in my house alone while my mom slept at a stranger's house."

I bit my cheeks.

Heather shook her head. "Daryl was a good man. He wasn't, not once, inappropriate toward me. He had his thing with my mom, but that was it. Anyway, Daryl had two sons. One went with his wife—he had some medical condition, and she fawned over him. Daryl's other son was younger than me by a few years. I called him Davie, though his name was David. He hated that."

"You called him Davie, anyway?"

Heather shrugged, as if her bullying didn't matter. "I was an angry, sad, confused kid. I wanted others, especially those who seemed happy, to feel angry and sad and confused, too. Misery loves company, and hurt people hurt people, right?"

"I've heard something like that." A million questions plagued my mind, but I allowed Heather to tell her story. She had invited me to this private meeting for a reason, and I waited for her to share that reason in her time.

"Daryl never drank—well, except on special occasions he would have a glass of wine. Christmas Eve. Thanksgiving. Baptisms. Those things, celebrating and enjoying time with family. I think he struggled with alcohol early in his life, and he had to quit. Before the new owners took over this bar, Daryl had the place tattooed with alcohol anonymous brochures. He made it his mission to help those who suffered like he had."

"Serving them drinks?" I asked.

"We all rationalize that we're doing the right thing, even if it make no sense to the world."

"I can't argue that," I said, considering my quest to prove the supernatural existed so I could apologize to a ghost. Ridiculous? Sure. It made sense to me, though.

"I guess he figured a drunk would get drunk somewhere, why not at his bar—a safe space where help was available if needed. I don't know. Anyway, Daryl never dragged Davie to the bar. He never forced him to color or do his homework in the corner booth, or listen to Hank Williams Jr. and Waylon Jennings and Merle Haggard." Heather stared into her dark coffee. "I hated Davie with all my heart, but only because I wanted with all my heart everything he had. A mother."

"Daryl was married and having an affair with your mother?"

"They divorced. But they were cordial and considerate toward each other. They saw each other often, because of their other son, the one with the illness. Anyway, Davie also had a living father. He had a sibling. Everything I ached for but couldn't have. I despised Davie for it. I wasn't rebellious or bad. I listened to my mother. I respected my teachers. I earned good grades. Yet, God had punished me. Why didn't I have a dad or a mom? Why did I feel so alone?"

I cracked a knuckle, not having the perspective on the situation to speak. Maya or Alina might have known what to say, maybe even Fred. Not me, though. I had no credibility to lend advice, so I remained silent.

"When I became a little older, middle school, I met Christina. Her parents more or less adopted me. Her parents loved me like their own daughter. I spent all my time at their house rather than in this booth, and they never batted an eye. I remember this one stretch of time, I spent three straight weeks at their house, staying the night, eating their food, wearing Chris's clothes. They never asked me to leave. My mom, during that span, never asked me to come home. I told her I was sleeping at Chris's again, and she said, 'Okay,' and that was that."

"Did you hate Chris like you hated Davie?"

Heather nodded her head and rubbed her face. I couldn't quite see her eyes in the dim bar or behind the shadow of her hood, but I had a decent idea she fought against tears.

"Yes, secretly, though," Heather said. "I outwardly hated Davie. I loved Chris, but I also hated her—a small part of me harbored that hate to this day. I couldn't ever let it go."

I leaned back in the booth and waited for Heather to continue. Her lips moved, as if she had something she meant to say, but she couldn't quite form the words. Not at first.

"I slept with Nick."

I lowered my jaw and raised my eyes. "Excuse me?"

"He came from a beat-up home, too. Johnny..." Heather sucked on her lips. "He doesn't understand any more than Chris understood my childhood. They—Chris and Johnny—experienced what we went through as if watching the news. They knew our pain and suffering was real, and they felt sorry for us, but they couldn't quite grasp the reality of our childhoods. Does that make sense?"

"I think so."

"Nick understood me, though. I understood him. Johnny had proposed to me a month before, and I had said yes. Nick and I found ourselves alone shortly after the engagement. Right here in this booth. Drinking. It's scary how life circles, isn't it?"

"Yeah."

"We understood each other. As I harbored a small hate for Chris, I also harbored that same hate for Johnny. A jealous-born hate. That hate, combined with drunkenness and natural physical attraction to Nick... well, it just happened. We slept together."

Puzzle pieces fell together in my head with absolute clarity. Heather had asked to meet privately with me so Johnny wouldn't have to hear this side of the story. He didn't know about the affair, which meant she and Nick kept it a secret. Except...

"Christine found out?"

"I don't know," Heather said. She twisted her engagement ring in circles around her finger. "If she learned of what happened, and if she threatened to tell Johnny..." She sighed. "Nick has a violent history. He's a convicted felon for a violent crime. Assault with a deadly weapon."

"What?" I asked, surprised. "What did you say? You didn't care to tell me this at our initial meeting? That information opens up multiple avenues of investigation."

Heather sipped from her coffee. "It was Nick's information to share, and he kept quiet."

"What did he do?"

"Assaulted his ex-girlfriend with a deadly weapon."

"Like a sledgehammer?"

"Baseball bat."

My shoulders sagged. I slouched in the booth.

"They paroled him six months back, when—"

"When the Devil started appearing in your dreams."

Heather didn't need to respond for me to know I was right, but she said, "Yes," in the tiniest voice possible.

Anger consumed me for a second. I almost allowed it to lash out and strike Heather, to blame her for Chris's death. If she had only been upfront with me from the beginning, we could have saved her friend. We could have stopped Nick.

I breathed, though, and I swallowed my flash of anger. "Would Nick harm any of you?"

"I don't know," Heather said. "He sometimes has crazy thoughts. Maybe he believed we ratted on him about assaulting his ex-girlfriend. I don't know. I really don't know. But I know that he and I had an affair. If Chris learned of that and threatened to tell Johnny, he might have retaliated."

"Do you think he killed her?" I asked. "Do you think he could be the Devil?"

Heather thought for a long time before answering the question. "Yes."

Birds Don't Exist. Tuesday, May 2nd. 1501hrs.

The Gull Cafe had a time warp feel to it. Maya stepped through the green-painted, gold-trimmed door, and a bell rang. Hardwood floors ran from wall to wall. Wooden tables stood atop hardwood, along with wooden chairs or wooden booths. A bookshelf stood in a nook, between two plush sofas. Someone must have commissioned the felling of a small forest to construct the small cafe. The interior smelled old, like an attic—of dust and time—with the overtones of fresh coffee. Pictures of John Wayne, Charles Bronson, Gary Cooper, and Clint Eastwood, among others, adorned the walls. Maya never would have recognized the old faces, but Alina proudly rattled off each actor as she walked by.

Evan Richards led Maya and Alina to the front counter—a glass display boasted homemade pastries. A handwritten sign set beside a tray of muffins stated the coffee shop only accepted cash payments.

A corpulent young man with long, greasy hair stood behind the front counter. He had dyed half of his hair a blood red, the other half a sky blue. Piercings looped around his lips, looped from his nose, lined his ears and eyebrows. He had a million-dollar smile, though—contagious and warm.

"How can I help you?"

Evan stepped forward. "I'll have a small, decaf iced coffee. Black." He glanced over his shoulder at Alina and Maya. "What would you two like?"

"Oh, no," Maya said, raising her palms and waving them. "That's unnecessary. I'm interviewing you, so I should pay for your drink."

Evan shrugged and stepped aside. "By all means. I'm not a man to bicker with a woman."

Maya ordered a cinnamon roll, and Alina asked for a lemonade. Once they had their order number, they slid into an empty booth. Evan sat on one side, Alina and Maya on the other. The table had a glass encasing which showcased newspaper clippings detailing a portion of Santa Cruz's history.

Maya removed her phone and placed it on the table. "You care if I record our conversation?"

"I have a feeling you don't care how I answer," Evan said.

"Morally, no. Ethically, yes. I need your express permission if I wish to quote you, which I do." She activated the voice recorder.

"You have my express permission to record this conversation." Evan leaned back in his seat and wiggled to a comfortable posture. "Ask me anything. I am an open book."

Maya cleared her throat. "Can you state your name for the record?"

"Evan Richards."

"Mr. Richards, we have orchestrated this meeting to discuss a strange occurrence. Thousands of birds simultaneously fell from the Santa Cruz sky. I came upon you as a frenzy of local media outlets interviewed you for information. You have authority to speak on this incident, I assume?"

He smirked. Maya thought he might make a joke, tell her some quick story about why the reporters had flocked to him beyond his expertise. If he entertained that idea, Evan swept it aside after a second thought. "I do."

"In what capacity?"

"I'm one of the top ornithologists in the country." He held a calm smile. "A professional bird watcher, if you will."

"Exciting," Alina said. She stared at the glass-topped table, reading the newspaper clippings beneath the partition.

"Seems my field of expertise is quite exciting today," Evan said.

The barista appeared with their order. He passed out their drinks and food, then he returned to the kitchen.

"Do you have any insight into what happened today?" Maya asked.

"Varying species of birds dropped from the sky without slowing their descent. If they survived their fall, they acted sporadically—out of character, if you will. We have captured a few of those surviving birds, as well as a few of the dead birds as specimens to study. We won't have a conclusive answer until the end of the week, at the earliest."

"Do you have a theory for what happened?"

"Nothing conclusive."

"Toxic algae?" Alina asked. She didn't remove her gaze from the newspaper articles.

Maya glanced at the article her niece read, curious to see what could hold her attention so rapturously. From her quick glance, she failed to glean anything of excitement or note.

"Toxic algae?" Evan laughed.

"Is she wrong?" Maya returned her attention to the devastatingly handsome man sitting across from her. Why had she allowed Alina to tag along?

"I'm not at liberty to share theories," Evan said, his voice professional again. He glanced at the phone recording their conversation. "Speculation is a public safety concern, so I find it important to take precaution. We wouldn't want to cause a panic, especially if our theories prove incorrect. We will study what we collected. Once we have a decisive solution, we'll provide you with more conclusive answers."

"End of the week?"

Evan frowned. "At the earliest. It can take a month or longer. It's hard to tell."

Maya tapped her phone, ending the recording. "Off the record."

Evan chuckled. "Toxic algae? Where did you hear that?"

"A little birdie educated me on a similar situation that occurred in Capitola sixty years back. Influenced *The Birds* movie."

Evan drank his iced coffee, set it on the table, turned his head, and stared outside the front window. "Off the record?"

Maya nodded, breaking off a chunk of her cinnamon roll.

"Domoic acid is a neurotoxin found in certain algae. We believe that's what caused a similar event back in 1961. However, public health agencies now test for its presence. They would have detected the toxin long before that many birds consumed it." Evan held up a finger, as if to stall Maya from butting in. "Not only that, it's only found in marine animals. Fish. Seagulls. Seals. Crabs. I saw more than only gulls fall from the sky today. I noticed herons, pelicans, grebes, hawks, ducks, among many others. How would they have ingested the toxic algae, unless someone fed it to them? That's why we're testing. I can say, off the record, this is probably from a neurotoxin, similar to the Capitola incident. However, I'm not sure it's Domoic acid."

"Hey, hey, hey," Alina said. "Fred just sent me this video. It's happening right now, as we speak." Alina placed her phone at the center of the table and turned up the volume.

Maya watched a video of another press conference. A young, skinny man—no older than twenty-five—stood before a white van with words stenciled across the side panel. BIRDS DON'T EXIST. Beside the young man, stood a young woman wearing sunglasses and a poorly fitting suit, like some kind of cheap secret service agent. The man, whose name Maya hadn't caught, didn't so much answer questions as he preached to the gathering crowd like a fervent pastor aflame with the Holy Spirit.

"... government drones. The United States government exterminated all the birds between the years of 1959 and 1971. In that time, they replaced the birds with lookalike drones to spy on us, the so-called free people. Have you ever seen a bird perched on a telephone wire without getting shocked? They're recharging." The young man paused, taking a moment to catch his breath. He pointed at the crowd. "This also happened sixty years ago, when the government released a batch of drones into Capitola. Their gull drones went haywire and attacked the citizens and their property. Did the government apologize? No. They buried it. Turned into a movie for entertainment so people would forget about what really happened. The government has hypnotized us all into believing what they want us to believe. Into seeing what they want us to see. They use the media and entertainment industries as forms of propaganda to melt our minds and form them like clay so we can serve them and do their bidding, like sheep or puppets. Don't let them erase what happened today from history, or from your mind.

This wasn't an accident like in 1961. This was intentional. They have attacked you. They attacked your home and your property. They attacked your loved ones. Do you know why? To what end? Guess how many casualties we tallied today. Two. I'll say that again. Two." The man held up two fingers. "Their names being, and remember these names, Walker and Graham Alba. Brothers who had a patent pending which would allow cars to run off of ocean water. Coincidence? Not a chance. The government assassinated those two men today with their drone birds."

Maya handed the phone back to Alina and regarded Evan. "You're an ornithologist, huh? Seems to me that birds don't even really exist."

Evan stretched out his smile once more, laughing. "The jigs up. Birds don't exist. I'm a government agent sent to reprogram the birds to attack all humans."

The three of them shared a laugh at the expense of the conspiracy group. The weight of the day melted and drained away. The cloud covering Maya vanished, and she felt light and clear-headed.

Evan turned to Alina, paying her mind for the first time since sitting. "What do you think?"

"I think Maya has a long and dark history of choosing the wrong man." Alina sat up, ripping her attention from the newspapers, and crossed her arms.

"I don't understand," Evan said.

"History has a funny way of repeating itself, Mr. Richards. Do you agree?"

"I do."

"And Maya has proven that repeatedly. Her last boyfriend was arrested for murder only about a week or two ago."

Evan glanced at Maya, narrowing his eyes.

"She's not lying," Maya admitted. "I have a checkered history with men."

"To call an ace a spade," Alina said, glaring at Maya as if daring her to correct the phrase, "Maya likes you, Mr. Richards."

"Evan, please," Evan said.

"I prefer not," Alina said. "Here's the thing, guys come in four packages. They look bad and they are bad. They look bad, but they're good guys. They look good, but they're bad guys. They look good, and they are good. Unfortunately, Maya falls for the wolf in sheep's clothing every single time. Mr. Richards, you look like a good man. Are you?"

Maya glared at her niece, hot in the face from embarrassment and anger. "Alina, my dating life, no matter the history of it, is none of your concern. Besides, we're here for an interview. Nothing more."

"Nothing more?" Evan asked. His dark eyes settled on Maya like a storm cloud over the sky—heavy and filled with unseen energy. It was enough to drive her wild.

Maya chewed on her lip for a second. "Did you have something more in mind?"

"Maybe a drink later tonight."

"I pay for the coffee to interview someone, Mr. Richards," Maya said. "But I don't pay for my own drinks."

The Reveal. Tuesday, May 2nd. 1857hrs.

I SAT AT THE head of the table for dinner, directly across from my father. Fred insisted he should sit on the stool. My hip still throbbed and my shoulder ached, so I hadn't argued with him. The stool remained empty beside me, though.

Daphne had summoned Fred into the kitchen to help transfer platters of food to the dining room table. Gourmet cheeseburgers made with Kobe beef, oven-baked bacon, caramelized onions, homemade aioli, sweet potato fries. Daphne had us eating like royalty.

To my left was Fred's stool, and next to that was Daphne's empty chair. Rachel, Jake, and my mom filled out the rest of that side of the table. Cambria sat to my right, beside Maya who seemed obnoxiously chirpy. She buzzed with an electric energy I couldn't make sense of, considering all that had happened earlier with the birds and Christina's murder. Alina sat beside Maya, scowling at the empty plate set before her. Adam beside Alina.

We all chitchatted and joked, stuck in a vortex of private conversations. An eeriness settled around us and invaded our minds. We were probably all aware of it, at least felt it, but no one would have been able to identify it then. I think I learned to recognize that unsettling feeling for what it was—the brutality of time. Christine Wyss murdered. Nicholas Lane imprisoned. Graham and Walker Alba dead after birds pelleted them from the sky. Death and destruction had owned the day, yet time moved forward without slowing down. We either kept pace or life continued without us. So, in the wake of devastation, we joked and laughed and carried on. It was all so... unnatural. Yet nothing more natural existed than to move forward and survive.

Fred and Daphne found their seats. The table naturally went quiet as everyone now expected the meal and waited eagerly to eat.

Rachel cleared her throat, drawing all our attention to her.

Rachel wore her hair down and had brushed her face with a little makeup, something she rarely did. Everyone else had fitted themselves in loungewear—vacation garb. Rachel, though, wore a nice blouse meant for going out in public rather than sitting with family around a dinner table. I made the connection rather quickly, knowing exactly what Rachel knew. My mom would demand pictures. Rachel had prepared herself for the camera. Glancing at Jake, I noticed he had also combed his hair, wore a clean shirt and a fresh pair of jeans.

"Since August prayed last night, I thought I would pray tonight... if that's okay with everyone?" Rachel asked. She shyly glanced around the dinner table and settled her attention on our mother. Rachel hadn't offered to pray in years. Unlike me, she still attended church and believed in God and Jesus as our savior. However, she hated the spotlight, and she abstained from speaking in public, if she could help it.

My mom held her breath for a second, most likely shocked Rachel had offered to pray. "We would love that."

Without another word, everyone bowed their heads and closed their eyes. Everyone except for me.

Before Rachel prayed, I caught her attention and frowned at her.

She winked and bowed her head. "God," she said. "Thank you so much for food. For friends. And for family... for our current family... and for our future family as we expand and grow and add one more little, tiny person. We love you. Amen."

"Amen!" Fred shouted above everyone else. He clapped his hands and rubbed his palms together. "Let's eat!"

No one moved to breathe. We all stared wide-eyed at Rachel and Jake, refusing to exhale until she confirmed what she had alluded to.

Fred must not have listened to a single world of Rachel's prayer. As everyone stared at her, Fred stared at everyone else, narrow-eyed and confused. "What's going on? What did I miss? I'm hungry, and when I'm hungry, I zone out. What happened?"

"Are you pregnant?" Alina broke the spell. It didn't surprise me in the least that Alina spoke first.

Rachel giggled and excitedly nodded her head up and down. "We're pregnant."

"What?" Mom asked. "What do you mean you're pregnant?"

"You're pregnant?" Dad asked.

For context, Rachel and Jake had tried to conceive a child for years, with no success. They recently agreed to try their luck with in vitro fertilization. They couldn't afford it, though, and they refused to ask my parents for charity. Jake worked private security, but was currently applying for the police academy to earn more money and better benefits. Rachel worked part time for the hospital as a surgical technician in the delivery room. She had recently asked for a full-time position. With Jake joining the force and Rachel going full time at the hospital, they hoped to have the money for in vitro within the next year or two.

Miraculously, according to Rachel, when she shared the news with me a couple weeks back, she and Jake had naturally become pregnant.

Her announcement at the dinner table stunned the crowd into disbelief.

"We're pregnant," Jake said, speaking through a smile. "Can you believe it?"

"Nope," Fred said. He laughed through joyous tears. "Never thought you had it in you, actually."

From anyone else, Jake might have retaliated to the comment. Rachel's fertility wasn't great, but Jake's impotent sperm contributed the most to their conception struggles. Coming from Fred, though, Jake responded with a half-smirk and throaty laugh.

"Congratulations," Fred said. "Shall we celebrate by eating?"

"Shut up, you oaf," Daphne said. She nudged her husband with her elbow and looked at Rachel. "I'm so excited for you two."

"How far along are you?" Maya asked.

"Twelve weeks."

My mom burst from her chair and lunged at Rachel. She hugged her. "I'm going to be a grandma?"

"You're going to be a grandma."

My dad walked to his daughter and quickly hugged her, then he shook Jake's hand. Adam did likewise. In fact, everyone stood from their seats and embraced the happy parents-to-be. We all congratulated Rachel and Jake on the incredible miracle.

Fred, pushing his appetite aside, hurried to the refrigerator and popped a bottle of champagne. He poured a flute for everyone but Rachel and me.

"Hey!" Rachel said. "A little won't hurt the baby."

"Not a chance," Mom said.

"Kim's the boss," Fred said. "I'm also scared of her, so you get nothing. That's okay, though. More for me." Fred poured my mom a small taster of champagne, and though she never drank, she accepted the flute. He also poured Adam a glass.

"Fredrick," my mom said.

"He can't have champagne, either? I'm so sorry, Kim."

I winced whenever Fred referred to my mom as Kim. It felt strange. Mrs. Watson worked fine.

My mom sighed with defeat. "Oh, what the heck," she said. "We're celebrating. But only that one glass."

"Deal!" Fred shouted, carefully filling Adam's flute to the tippy-top. He moved to Alina's glass and glanced at Maya.

"Fill her up, big boy," Maya said. "As the woman said. We're celebrating!"

Rachel and I clinked our water glasses, and everyone else tapped their champagne flutes together.

Maya, never one to shy away from public attention, provided the toast. "I don't know August's family too well. I'm actually not sure we've ever met before this week. But every single one of you has accepted me into your family without hesitation, as if you've known me for years. I walked through that door and immediately felt loved and accepted. That's rare. And that's powerful." She faced Rachel. "You're baby doesn't know how lucky she or he is to have a family like yours. Cheers."

That moment was the last moment of pure happiness during that vacation. Everything shifted after Maya's toast. It was no longer a work trip, simplified by solving an unexplainable mystery and explaining the crime. The vacation jumped into Alina's area of interest—a horror story. One filled with monsters and violence and death.

Without that foreknowledge, though, we ate and celebrated and enjoyed each other. We experienced true happiness and excitement. Fred and Daphne drank themselves asleep on the living room couch. My mom created an online baby registry and told Rachel what she did and didn't need to put in there. Jake, Adam, and my dad went into the backyard, where Jake ignited a fire. After a while, Alina excused herself from the table and joined them.

"Want to walk down to the beach?" I asked Cambria. She and I remained seated at the dinner table, along with Maya.

Of course, Maya interrupted my proposal to Cambria. "No thanks. I have a date tonight."

Her declaration hooked my face and yanked it toward her. "What?"

"What, what?" Maya asked.

"You have a date?"

"Why do you care?"

"I don't," I said, feeling warm, especially with Cambria seated beside me. Truth be told, I cared quite a lot. Especially after our drunken conversation from the night before. Had Maya accepted a date to spite me? It felt that way, which bugged me. It shouldn't have, considering I had asked Cambria to attend the trip with me, but it did.

"Why are you asking then?" Maya asked.

"I'm shocked, that's all. How did you get a date?"

"Because I'm young and sexy. Men find me attractive, believe it or not."

"Well, awesome. Have fun and be safe with the stranger from Santa Cruz."

"What's that mean?" Cambria asked.

"What's what mean?" I asked, turning to her.

"Why did you say it like that, like you're bitter?"

"I'm not. There are birds falling from the sky. It's just strange she found a date today of all days."

"I think my date is the least strangest thing that has happened all day," Maya said. She pushed back her chair and stood. "You two lovebirds have fun on the beach. I'm not sure where I'll end up tonight, but if it's on the beach, I'll look for you." She smirked and bounced away, heading toward the stairs to ready herself for whatever date she had agreed to.

I shifted my attention to Cambria. "The beach?"

"Sure," Cambria said, not looking too enthused by the idea.

"You okay?"

"I'm fine."

I cracked a knuckle. "I don't know too much about women, but I know enough that when someone says, 'I'm fine,' they're usually not fine."

Cambria stood. "I'm fine. I'll grab a sweatshirt and meet you outside. While I'm upstairs, do you want me to relay any messages to Maya? Ask her questions about whatever hunk asked her out?"

I chuckled. "Hunk?"

"I'm sure he's a hunk. Look at her. She's gorgeous, right?"

"I don't know."

"You don't know?"

"I mean, yeah, she's attractive."

"So, it's only plausible to assume she's going out with a hunk."

"Sure," I said, confused by Cambria's behavior. "It's just a funny word."

Cambria marched toward the stairs, leaving me alone at the table. I remained seated for a second, reflecting on what had just happened, then I stood and headed outside, crossing paths with Alina.

"Hey," I said.

"What's up?"

"What are you doing?"

"Why do you care?" Alina asked.

"I don't really care, just asking to be polite. Why is everyone so accusatory right now?"

"What do you mean?"

I shook my head. "Nothing."

"I'm grabbing dessert. Is that okay with you, Boss?"

"You can do whatever you want."

"Can I drink a beer?"

"No."

"So not whatever I want?"

"What did I do?" I asked. "Why is every woman treating me like a cutting board?"

"A cutting board?"

"Cutting me up…" I trailed off, realizing my metaphor had missed the mark. "First Maya, then Cambria, now you. What's going on? Do I have a target on my back?"

"Maya has a date with a sexy, intelligent scientist. She's probably all jazzed about that. You're jealous, so you're interpreting the situation as a slight against you. Cambria has noted your obvious envy, so she feels insecure now, like she has to compete with Maya. And let's be honest, Gussy—"

"August."

"No woman can compete with Maya, and no woman can compete with Maya in your eyes. Me? I'm an angsty teenager who doesn't respect authority. I'm just acting as I always do."

"I'm not jealous."

Alina coughed on laughter. "Okay."

"I'm not."

"Just ask me what you want to ask while you still have time. I won't tell anyone."

"I really hate you."

"You going to ask?"

"Who is he?" I asked.

Alina smirked, proud of herself. "Evan Richards, a bird scientist."

"Like an ornithologist?"

"Why do you know that word?"

"I know a lot of random things. It's what makes me good at my job."

"Decent at your job. Good is a stretch."

"So you two went looking for the bird story, and you found the bird man?"

"Don't make lame puns around me. It makes me uncomfortable. But yes, that's the gist of it. Also, he's wildly handsome and charismatic and a complete gentleman. So, the complete opposite of you. Also, if it makes you feel any better, he's probably a douchebag who will screw Maya over and break her heart. You'll have your shot once again."

"Did you ask him about the toxic algae?" I asked, suddenly more interested in his opinion on the situation rather than his opinion of Maya.

"Yup. He doesn't buy it. Too many species of birds acting crazy. However, he thinks it's a neurotoxin. So, to give credit where credit is due, you were partly correct. Congratulations." Alina brushed past me, paused, and reversed. "Also," she said, "you ever hear of the group, Birds Don't Exist?"

"No."

"So much for knowing random things. Seems like something you should know."

"Who are they?"

"A group who doesn't believe in the existence of birds." Alina threw up her arms. "Duh."

"You know what I mean."

"According to their founder, birds are government drones meant to spy on the American population. Today's incident wasn't a random, supernatural event, but a carefully planned plot by the United States government to assassinate two people—the two people who actually died today."

"Walker and Graham Alba?" I asked.

"No one's paying you to solve this case," Alina said. "Why are you keeping up with it?"

"I'm interested."

"Yes. Walker and Graham Alba. Brothers. Apparently they had some way for vehicles to run on ocean water. We all know that song, right? Take fossil fuels out of the equation, a lot of really rich people lose money, and politicians lose power. So, we can't have cars running on H2O, can we? What does the government do? Bang. Bang. Dead. Dead."

"You buy the theory?"

"What? That birds are drones?" Alina rolled her eyes. "I believe birds are drones as much as I believe you're not jealous of Maya's date."

"I have a date tonight, too."

Alina smirked. "I know. Have fun, lovebird. Try not to fall from the sky."

A Walk on the Beach. Tuesday, May 2nd. 2220hrs.

THE BACKYARD FADED INTO a sloping, sandy beach. I limped along the uneven ground. Cambria walked a few feet away from me, far enough that if we both stretched out our hands, our fingers wouldn't touch. The distance between us was obvious and cold.

She dragged her feet, toppling the slight dunes with her toes, and she stared straight ahead at the craggy coast—not at the moon-reflected dark water, never at me.

The wind broke off the never-ending tide with wet, cold breath. The waves crashed, though not in a calming manner. They broke on the shoreline like a giant hand reaching out for us, constantly trying to grab us and drag us into its dark mouth.

After walking about fifty yards in stony silence, I veered nearer to Cambria, brushing my fingers against her hand. "What's going on?"

I'm not sure if Cambria heard my question above the whipping wind and crashing waves.

I rotated my wrists, cracking them, and debated whether I should say something more. I wondered why I had invited her on this vacation? With Maya in attendance, everything felt so uncertain. Did I even want Cambria there? Would I rather be walking that beach with Maya? How did I really feel about her date with Evan Richards, the bird man? My mom's presence complicated all of that. The nightmare case complicated things further. It all stacked and compounded and... and my gunshot wound ached, and my stab wound stiffened, making it difficult to walk and think.

I stopped and dropped onto the cold sand.

Cambria continued forward a few feet before halting and turning around. "What are you doing?"

"My hip hurts."

She crossed her arms and stared out at the ocean.

"What's going on?" I asked.

"Why did you invite me here?"

I exhaled to buy time to think of an answer. I had already pondered that question. It had plagued my mind from the very second I watched

Cambria step out of the rideshare in front of my office and walk toward me with her luggage.

After a couple seconds, Cambria asked, "Why did you invite me? You're clearly more interested in solving the case, and sure, that makes sense. You mentioned you were coming out here for work. So, I get that. When we're at the house, though, with everyone there, you're still gone. You're absent. You don't touch me. You hardly look at me. You watch Maya half the time."

"That's not..." I trailed off, not caring to lie to Cambria. She deserved a lot more than me, and at the very least, she deserved the truth.

"Why did you invite me if you don't want me here?"

I stared at the sand and dug a hole with my hands. "I don't know. Impulse."

"Do you like me?"

"Of course."

"You just love her."

I practiced a calming breath. Inhale for five seconds, exhale for five seconds. "I don't know."

"What do you know?"

"With women, not much."

"That's obvious," Cambria said.

I shifted my gaze across the horizon. Tendrils of gray clouds covered the night sky, but they didn't blot out the stars or the moon. The immense ocean stretched as far as I could see, rendered minuscule, though, by the eternity of space surrounding the world. If the universe dwarfed the ocean, where did that place me and my life, my worries, my emotions in the grand scheme of existence?

"I've never had a girlfriend." I spoke from far away. "I've had a few physical relationships that lasted a couple weeks back in college and before... before Aaron." I chewed on my cheeks for a second, measuring his life to the endless cosmos. The vastness of the universe couldn't render our existence pointless. Our lives meant something, despite their perceived insignificance. They had to mean something. "That was it, though. I never had an actual relationship built on something deeper and stronger than sex. It's not that I don't like you. I do like you. I like you a lot. I just don't know how to do this."

"Well, first off, don't invite me somewhere when you're going to drool over another woman the entire time."

I nodded, knowing she was right, and that should have been obvious to me from the start. "Maya and I have a complicated past."

"Really?"

No, I thought. In my mind it felt complicated because I had more or less loved her from the second I saw her. Love at first sight—magic that may or may not exist. Those feelings hadn't faded with time, but they had grown. She always had a boyfriend, though. In those short periods of time when she didn't, I couldn't convince myself to risk our friendship. I think that played a colossal role in my decision not to ask her out. I didn't want to ruin what we had. Maya had become a foundational pillar to my life, and to lose her would mean losing a part of myself, collapsing, possibly.

"We have a complicated relationship. She's my best friend."

"Not Fred?"

"Fred's my oldest friend. I've known him since we were babies."

"In your head, when you picture you and me, what do you see?"

I wanted to play honestly with Cambria. So, I took my time to consider her question. I closed my eyes and pictured her. I saw her by herself. I wasn't in the mental image. I didn't see us together. I changed tactics and pictured myself. Beside me, I saw Maya. She stood on tiptoe, reached up with her nose, kissed me on the side of the mouth, and grinned as she did so. She wore baggy sweats and a frumpy shirt, and her hair was a giant, untamed afro. The image was so lucid that it could have been a memory—the memory of a well-worn fantasy.

"How does this work?" I asked, not wanting to share with Cambria what I saw in my mind's eye.

"What?"

"Giving us a shot? A relationship? How do we know it's worth going after?"

Cambria looked at me and chuckled—a short exhale of amused breath. "If you have to ask, you already have your answer." She sat down five feet away from me and dug her feet into the sand. "I should have declined your invitation."

"I shouldn't have asked. I'm not usually that spontaneous, and now we both know why."

"What did you have in your head when you asked? A week filled with sex?"

I shook my head, though she stared at the ocean and didn't see my dismissal of her question. "Honestly, I saw this. Us sitting on the beach at night, bundled up in blankets, snuggling each other and... and just talking. I really enjoy talking with you. Does that sound lame?"

"It sounds nice."

"I like you," I said, not lying. I did like her. But Maya's presence in Santa Cruz had ruined how I felt. My like for Cambria didn't come close to my like for Maya.

She must have read my mind. "You just like her more?"

"I never realized it before now. I promise you that. I never would have asked if I had known how I truly felt." People had always told me, had constantly mentioned how I loved Maya. I always ignored them, though, brushing off their idle comments because I had never accepted that truth.

"Some men might have asked me to join them just to make Maya jealous. But I know you didn't. You're one of the good ones, August.

Complicated, yes. But you're honest and kind, and those are rare traits, or so it sometimes seems."

"If I can continue to be completely honest, I really appreciate how you look in a bikini."

Cambria snickered, breaking her feet from their sandy blanket. "Do you?"

"Quite a bit."

Cambria popped her lips. "Well." She dropped onto her hands and crawled toward me, her hair falling forward. When she closed the space between us, she rolled over and rested her head in my lap. "What do we do?"

"I think we make the most of it," I said.

"Well, fortunately for you, I'm stuck here until Saturday. I don't know if we have any other choice than to have fun."

"I'm sorry that I'm an idiot."

"But an adult, right? We are both mature adults."

"Some might argue otherwise."

Cambria reached up and touched my face with her icy fingers. "If you want to have fun, Mr. Watson, I'm up for having fun. But only until Saturday. Only until we leave. Then we go our separate ways."

"I think I'm following you, but I'm not sure, and I don't want to presume anything."

"Sex."

"That's what I thought."

"We can have a lot of sex while we're here."

In my more youthful years, I had bounced from one woman to the next, never staying with one long enough to have much of anything beyond meaningless sex. Now in my thirties, the simple act of sex felt increasingly more complicated and fruitless. Glacia and I had folded to our baser desires. That led us to living a state apart and hardly speaking.

"That doesn't sound terrible," I said. "It sounds complicated, though."

"What else will we do? Force conversation and spending time with each other, knowing it's pointless come Saturday? Why waste the trip, you know?"

"I hate wasting things."

"I find you attractive. Do you find me attractive?" Cambria sat up straight and faced me.

I found her wildly attractive. "Yes."

She leaned forward, her face inches from mine. I could smell her wine-sweet breath, feel it warm on my lips. "Only if you want to, of course. No strings attached. No looming relationship on the horizon. You invited me on a week-long vacation to unwind. Well, let's unwind, Mr. Watson." She shoved me in my chest, pushing me backward into the sand.

I stared upward at her, at the stars glowing above her and spotlighting us there on the beach.

Cambria peeled off her sweatshirt. The dim moon illuminated her pale skin. In that moment, she looked like a mythical creature—a nymph or a fairy. Her body glowed, and her skin shocked me when I ran my fingers over her cheek, as if I had touched something forbidden.

We existed in a dream, in a fantasy, in a world separated from Earth.

The Date. Tuesday, May 2nd. 2230hrs.

MAYA MET EVAN AT a bar overlooking the ocean. A thin layer of marine fog had settled over the sea water, but not enough to blind them of the view. The sight was nothing short of stunning, and Maya hadn't even glanced at the horizon yet.

Evan looked like the offspring of Idris Elba and Michael B. Jordan. He had dark, dark eyes that pulled Maya in like an aggressive current. She didn't dare swim against them, though. No. Instead, she allowed herself to drown there, in his gaze. When he smiled, which he often did—he threw smiles around like a piñata tosses candy—his entire face melted into something sincere and tender.

In the back of Maya's mind, she thought of Eddie Denier, the Voodoo Doll Killer. He had only murdered one woman, his ex-girlfriend. Before him, Maya had dated another felon—an abusive drug dealer.

Before him... the list went on and on, the pattern never changing. Felon. Abuser. Cheater. Grade-A jerk.

Staring across the table at Evan, Maya couldn't help but convince herself his dark eyes and soft smile masked his faults. What negative attributes had attracted her to him?

Stop it, she thought. She closed her eyes. *Give him a chance.*

"You're from Sacramento?" Evan asked.

Maya blinked and nodded, sipping from her cocktail—an old fashion with tequila. August always went on and on about the drink, so she figured why not give it a shot? Besides, he was sober and couldn't enjoy his favorite drink. Why not enjoy it for him?

"My family is from Lodi," Evan said, swirling the whiskey in his cup.

"Really? My family lived in Stockton for a second."

"We avoided Stockton." He chuckled.

"I don't blame you."

"You're a journalist?"

"Hold on, hold on," Maya said. "Not so fast. That's not how this works."

"How what works?"

"You already asked me a question. You don't get to ask two in a row. We take turns, Tiger."

"Tiger?"

"They're majestic creatures, beautiful to look at. But dangerous."

"You think I'm dangerous? Beautiful? Both?" Evan smiled, disarming Maya. She had no defense against that smile.

"One question at a time, and it's my turn. Where do you live?" she asked.

"Davis."

Davis was a twenty-minute drive west of Sacramento. Maya's heart fluttered. Not only was Evan charming and handsome—so, so handsome—but he lived within a reasonable distance of her.

"You're a journalist?" Evan asked again.

"Do you only ask questions you know the answers to?"

Evan's face brightened.

"I'm a writer for a tabloid called *Here & Now*. We investigate supernatural phenomena and write about the unexplainable."

"I see." Evan sipped his whiskey. "Unfortunately for you and your story, the birds don't fall under the category of supernatural phenomena. What happened to them has a very basic, mundane explanation."

"There's still a story there. Why did a variety of birds, and not just marine birds, pelt the ground? Doesn't that seem strange to you?

Anyway, that's not my question, so don't answer it, because I don't care about work right now."

Evan laughed with his mouth shut. "Very well."

"How did you get into birds? Did your dad, who you adored, take you bird watching as a boy? You adopted his bird-loving legacy, taking it a step further?"

"I counted three questions, but I'll answer them all." He cleared his throat. "Excuse me. My dad was blue collar. A plumber. My mom was a stay-at-home mom. She raised four boys and two girls." Evan leaned forward and grinned. "I'm the youngest."

"In that case, you'll have to introduce me to your brothers. I like my men a little older."

Evan laughed. "I really like you, Maya."

Maya, she repeated the way he said it her head, breaking apart the two syllables, holding them like a musical note. May-a. She liked that. It sounded nice coming from his mouth.

"I like your honesty and your humor," Evan said. "I especially like the way you look."

"Do you?"

"More, I like the way you look at me. It makes me feel young and nervous. Most women make me feel..." Evan trailed off. He shook his head and smiled as if embarrassed.

"Feel what?"

"Bored."

"Like you would rather spend time with birds?"

"Precisely."

"Which, if you remember correctly, I asked you about."

"You did?"

"How did you get into birds?"

Another chuckle—always the preamble of a chuckle before speaking. "It's a simple story, really."

"Those are often the best," Maya said.

"I was ten, maybe, when I came upon a bird with a broken wing. I found it in the backyard. I cared for it, brought it back to full health, and released it back into the sky." He turned his palms toward the ceiling. "That's my story. The end. I've never looked back."

Could anything ever be that simple? Maya thought.

Evan had found a wounded creature. He healed it. He released it. That three-step process had created a burning passion for birds. For Maya, with everything always so tangled, a straight line from A to B seemed next to impossible.

"Is journalism always what you wanted to do?" Evan asked.

Maya gnawed on her cheeks, wondering how to tell her story in as straight a line as possible, and realizing it wasn't an option. Her life zigged and zagged and circled and looped. Except for one fact. "I always craved the truth. I think that's because everyone, including myself, always lied to me." Maya took a turn to chuckle. Not the infectious, joy-filled laugh of Evan, but a dry, brittle sound to fill the silence. "Funny, though, me speaking about truth in journalism, when I write about the paranormal."

"Do you not believe in ghosts?"

"One question at a time, Tiger." Maya drank her tequila old fashion. It was, admittedly, quite delicious. "Do you believe in the paranormal?"

"I believe in angels and demons. I believe in God and the Devil. Some call that religion. Some call it the supernatural or the paranormal. So, yes, I believe in it. Do you?"

"No."

Evan cocked his head. "But you have a career in it. How can you thrive or enjoy doing something you don't believe in?"

Maya dropped her gaze.

"My apologies," Evan said. "Only one question at a time, right?"

"If you could do anything in the world right now, what would you do?" Maya asked, glancing back up at the scientist sitting across the table from her. In the background, playing like a song on low volume, the ocean purred.

"What would I do?" Evan asked. His dark eyes held her gaze for a second. "This."

"This?"

"Sitting right here, with you, asking a single question at a time."

Maya's heart fluttered. A knot in her stomach—a knot that always seemed to get tighter and tighter—released. A warmth rushed through her gut and radiated outward in every direction, making her entire body hot.

"Actually, no. You asked for honesty," Evan said. He reached into his back pocket and removed his wallet. He peeled off a hundred-dollar bill from a wad of cash and laid it flat across the table. "Do you care to be spontaneous?"

"That's my middle name."

Evan laughed, the sound like bubbles that rose to the sky, carrying Maya with them. She floated atop the world across from Evan, knowing but not caring that the bubble would pop and she would fall.

I'm already falling, she thought.

"If you're with me, there's one thing over any other thing I would like to do right now," Evan said.

"I don't put out on first dates."

For the first time that night, Evan frowned.

"Maybe a kiss," Maya said. She put her lips to her nearly empty glass. "If the kiss is nice, maybe first base. Depending on how that goes, you might hit a double."

Evan returned to his default, chuckling. "No, no, no. Nothing like that, Maya."

Again, the way he said her name sent chills down her spine.

"Nothing sexual," he said. "First, just so we're both clear on the matter, I don't engage in any sexual activities with a woman until after the third date. That includes kissing. It's a personal rule. I prefer to know the person's mind before I know the person's body."

"Okay," Maya said. She wanted nothing more than to tear off his clothes. "What do you want to do then?"

Evan grinned. "Come with me." He stood from his chair, turned his back to her, and marched to the bar's exit.

Maya licked her teeth and stared at him. She enjoyed a lot about the current scene. First, the view of him walking away was quite nice. Second, few men ever up and walked away from her on a first date. Rather, they drooled on their collars and padded after her like a scared puppy. Evan, much like August, she thought, wove Maya into his world rather than making Maya his world. She enjoyed that quite a lot. Sharing a world with someone, not being their goddess or their entire life.

Still, could she trust him? Could she trust the ornithologist enough to follow him to wherever he led her?

Biting her lip, Maya stood and chased after Evan.

Only a Misdemeanor. Tuesday, May 2nd. 2322hrs.

"Do you trust me?" Evan asked. He stood beside his Tesla with a smirk splashed across his gorgeous face. The back window had a bird decal that stood out like snow on the beach. Evan had parked at a Holiday Inn a couple miles inland from the beach. The Birds Don't Exist van, shown on the Twitter video Alina had shared earlier, was a few stalls away from them.

Maya glanced at the van, then looked back at Evan. "Should I trust you?" she asked, more flirty than concerned. She, of course, trusted that beautiful stranger with her heart at that moment.

"This might be dangerous."

"I love danger."

"Illegal."

"I thought you didn't advocate for physical affection until after the third date? Illegal might fast-forward that affection three dates."

Evan chuckled and nodded his head. He stared at Maya, his dark eyes darker in the night. "I'm not much of a criminal," he said. "Neither was Martin Luther King Jr., but he still spent time in prison."

"Are you comparing yourself to M.L.K.?"

"You don't see the resemblance?"

"Not even a little."

"Well, it's our desire to fight for what's right, no matter the cost. Even if that cost means jail."

"What are we fighting for?" Maya glanced out the passenger window at the van. She had an idea.

"Birds do exist."

"You're sure they're real?"

"Very real."

"Well, I never would've guessed."

"I did some research."

"On the existence of birds? I would hope so, bird man."

Evan snickered. "I like Tiger better. Anyway, Bird's Aren't Real is a satirical conspiracy group that... it's an organization making fun of people who see something on social media and believe its true."

"Wait, wait, wait. I thought everything on social media was true?"

"Most things are, don't worry."

"You scared me for a second," Maya said. She wiped imaginary sweat from her brow.

"In the words of the group's creator, Birds Aren't Real 'takes the concept of misinformation and builds a safe space for people to come together and laugh about it, rather than become scared of it.' It's a crazy way to escape from these crazy times. The group built quite a following. However," Evan glanced at the van parked twenty feet away from him, "not everyone joined the group for the sake of fun. Some joined because they believed it. They believed the government actually exterminated the birds and replaced them with drones. Those truthers veered off and created their own group." He pointed at the van. "Bird's Don't Exist."

"And I thought August chasing down Freddy Krueger was crazy."

"I don't understand any of what you just said. Who's August? Why's he chasing Freddy Krueger?"

"Nothing," Maya said. "Continue, please."

"That's it for me, really. Bird's Don't Exist never caught on like Birds Aren't Real, probably because they bred toxicity through their so-called truthful crusade."

"Also, and maybe I'm an optimist here, not too many people are dumb enough to believe that birds are actually drones."

"The number might surprise you," Evan said. "Either way, this conspiracy group harms real, living, innocent birds."

"Such a thing doesn't exist."

"The group actively hunts and kills birds. All birds, including endangered birds. They claim they are protecting the everyday citizen from their government overlords."

"Do they search on Google, shop on Amazon with their iPhones? Because if we're talking control and spying—"

"Idiocy lends to hypocrisy," Evan said.

"That's beautiful. Can I use it?"

"Only if you quote me. I need my name out in the world to sell more books."

"Titled, Birds Are Real?"

"Birds Do Exist."

They shared an easy laugh. Evan opened the driver's door and walked to the front trunk, digging into it. Maya joined him. He removed a half-dozen canisters of spray paint and set them on the Tesla's roof.

"Vandalism?" Maya held a canister with a black cap on it.

"It's only a misdemeanor."

"What would Mr. King say about this?"

"I think he would join in."

"Or is that what you want to think?"

"Do you care to join my efforts in saving the birds?" Evan asked.

"I'm not doing this for the birds." Maya shook the black-capped canister. "I'm doing this for the thrill of vandalism. Only a misdemeanor, right?"

"Only a misdemeanor."

Maya crossed over to the van and sprayed it with the black paint. She drew a large, ejaculating, veiny penis with big, hairy balls. She excelled in many areas, but artistry wasn't one of them. However, despite her lack of skill, even the untrained eye could determine what she had sketched across the van's side panel.

She stepped back and admired her work.

"Very accurate depiction," Evan said. "You have an expert eye for detail."

"I try my hardest to present truth."

Evan laughed and stepped forward. He took his turn at the van. On the panel, where it said BIRDS DON'T EXIST, he crossed out DON'T EXIST and wrote above it in sloppy, wobbly letters, RULE. When he stepped back, he looked on his creation with pride, as if it were good.

"Birds Rule," Evan said absently, reading his work.

"Sure," Maya said, internally smiling. He really was a nerd. "Hey. Do you have white paint?"

Evan handed her a canister with a white lid. Maya stepped to the van and littered the windshield and windows and tires with bursts of white dots. She stepped back and bumped her shoulder into Evan.

"What do you think of that?"

"What is it?" he asked.

"What is it? It's bird poop. Birds pooped all over this van."

He laughed. "That's incredible." He snagged the black canister from the asphalt and carefully sprayed it on the van. After a few minutes, he stepped back. His artwork was much more mature than his barely competent handwriting.

"Feathers," Maya said. "Nice touch." She shook the red-capped canister and thought of what to add next.

"Hey!" called a voice from across the parking lot. "What are you doing?" A group of four men marched toward them with angry purpose.

"That's our van." They wore baseball caps curved over their faces, cowboy boots, jeans, and no shirts.

"Your van is causing harm," Evan said. He stepped forward to intercept the small angry mob. Though a scientist who wasn't great at vandalism, Evan boasted an imposing frame—not as imposing as Fred's physique, but he was broad and muscular.

"You're about to experience some harm yourself," the lead man said. He had a slim goatee and tattoos covering his torso up to his neck.

Maya stepped between Evan and the foursome, still shaking her canister of spray paint. "I'm sorry if we interrupted your love-making session, gentlemen. I see you only got so far as to remove each other's shirts. Maybe some nipple play? Camo-hat looks like he's into a little nipple play." Maya gestured with her spray paint canister at the far right man stalking toward them. Along with his camouflage hat, he also sported nipple piercings.

"What did you say?" he said, making twin fists.

"I said," Maya said, "because you have such a little, tiny wiener, you probably have to get off from nipple play. Did I stutter that time?"

"Let's see if you can talk around how wrong you actually are."

Maya scratched her nose and tilted her head. "I'm not entirely sure what that means, but I'm leaning toward a rape threat. I take that seriously. If you put your little, diseased penis anywhere near my mouth, I will bite it off."

The four men fanned out, surrounding Evan and Maya. They all snickered evil little laughs. Venom foamed from their lips.

"How you feeling, Evan?" Maya asked. "You scared of these hicks?" Maya had experienced a lot of threats and abuse in her life, especially from men. Her adrenaline spiked, but she remained poised. She had found herself in worse situations, and she had slipped away. As long as Evan held it together, she didn't fear any harm coming to her or him.

"Honestly," Evan said.

"I love honesty."

"I know. That's why I'm sharing this. I had secretly hoped they would catch us in the act and confront us."

Maya swelled with confidence. Evan found the potential of a fight exciting, not terrifying. "You can fight, huh?"

Evan responded with a low chuckle, humor still rich in his voice.

Maya gripped the red canister of spray paint a little tighter. She placed her index finger over the trigger. *Let them come*, she thought. *Let them do something silly, something they will regret.*

As the thought crossed her mind, camo-hat lunged forward, directly at her, and he threw a wild punch. Maya wasn't a stranger to a fight. She had suffered many beatings in her life, and she had divvied out many beatings. Camo-hat swung wide and careless, going for the haymaker, making everything about what he did easy to predict and evade.

Maya sidestepped and dodged the blow. Camo-hat rushed by her and spun to face her again. She raised the spray paint canister and unleashed it over his face like pepper spray.

Camo-hat, now wearing a mask of red, dropped to the asphalt. He screamed and clawed at his eyes.

Maya stepped up to him and kicked him square in the stomach. He folded in half. His body curled inward—one arm frantically swiped at his face, wiping away the paint, the other shielded his gut.

With him in place, Maya turned to the three other men. To her amazement, they all lay on the ground in varying states of out-of-commission, groaning and bleeding.

Evan massaged his scraped knuckles and glanced at Maya. "You okay?"

"I'm feeling fantastic." She wished Evan didn't have the stupid three-date rule. She wanted to take the spray paint can, shatter the van's window, crawl inside, and have her way with the scientist. "I haven't had so much fun in years. Committing a crime. Getting in a fight. You really know how to treat a girl."

"Well, before we take our bow and—"

"Skedaddle."

"Scoot." Evan grinned. "I have one more order of business."

"Take your time, Tiger."

Evan grabbed the white-capped spray paint off the ground and ambled toward the goateed, tattooed man kneeling before him. He popped off the top and aimed the nozzle at the man's face. "Unlike you, I'm not an idiot. I've come to a few conclusions, and I would like for you to confirm them for me."

The goateed man spat in Evan's face.

Evan chuckled—always that chuckle in response to everything. He didn't wipe his face, though. The spittle slowly slid down his cheek. "Did you poison the birds?"

"Will you spray my face if I don't answer?" the man asked, his voice hoarse.

"I won't torture you." Evan shook the spray paint canister. "This is for self-defense, in case you try something impulsive. I will make a deal with you. You're part of this little conspiracy club, right? Does the leader pay you to tag along with him? To lie to the public? Or do you do it because you're actually dumb enough to believe this nonsense?"

"You're the dumb ones. You're the sheep who blindly walk wherever the media leads you."

"What's his name? Brayden, right? That's your fearless leader's name? I wish Brayden would have come outside, rather than sending his goons to investigate. I'm sure he possesses an inkling of intelligence to carry on a conversation."

"You're the stupid one."

"Maybe I am, but I don't think that's the case. Either way, I have a proposition for you." Evan raised his voice. "For any of you. If you answer my question, I'll conveniently forget to mention you played a role in this crime."

"What crime?"

"You actively poisoned wildlife, causing property damage, grievous injury to humans, and death. Not only that, thousands of birds died because of your actions. Endangered birds died. Those are serious crimes that carry serious consequences. Now, if you refuse to answer my question right now, I will eventually learn the truth of the matter, and I'll identify the four of you in connection to Brayden's ploy, and you will all suffer the law's judgment. If you cooperate right now, well it's dark tonight. I might forget what you look like when the police ask me questions."

For a moment, no one spoke. Then like a thundercloud bursting, Goatee gushed, probably thinking twice about Evan's threat. "Brayden ordered us to do it. He hired us. He paid us to feed the birds, any bird we saw, some food he provided. I don't know what the food was or what was in it, but he paid us to spread the feed so as many birds as possible would consume it."

"Do have any more of the bird feed?" Evan asked.

Goatee glanced at the three other men, all suffering some state of physical pain. "Yes."

"Where?"

"In the van."

"You have the keys?"

Goatee dug into his jeans and removed a ring of keys, handing them to Evan. Evan accepted them and tossed them to Maya. Maya unlocked the rear doors and opened them.

"I see the food," Maya said. "They're in twenty-pound sacks."

"Can you grab one?" Evan asked.

"I'm way ahead of you." Maya hoisted a feed bag over her shoulder and dropped it in the Tesla's open front trunk.

"Why?" Evan returned his attention to the shirtless man. "Why the stunt?"

"Attention," he said. "Followers."

"What about Graham and Walker Alba? The brothers who died?"

Goatee shrugged. "I don't know."

"What don't you know?"

"That was an accident."

"An accident? You had to know people would get hurt, possibly die from this."

"I didn't know what would happen. I didn't know what the feed did."

"Do you know what it does now?"

"It screws up the internal computer of the drones," Goatee said.

Evan laughed and shook his head. "Yeah, you're right. That's what it does. So the brothers were accidental casualties?"

"Yeah."

"No patent existed."

"Not that I know of. But people don't look up details or confirm facts. They accept a single report as truth, and that's the end."

Evan sighed and faced Maya. Finally he wiped the slug of saliva from his face. "Care for a nightcap? I need one, and I'm buying."

"I'm drinking then," Maya said.

They left goons lying on the ground to lick their wounds, walked to the car, and stepped into the Tesla. Evan burned out of the parking lot, the two of them laughing uncontrollably through the night.

A Midnight Drive. Wednesday, May 3rd. 0012hrs.

EARLIER THAT AFTERNOON, AT the boardwalk, Fred had lost the game of knocking over milk bottles, and thus he had lost the bet. Conveniently for him, Rachel had revealed her pregnancy to the family, and Fred had celebrated the news by drinking copious amounts of alcohol and passing out on the couch.

Well, unfortunately for him, after my midnight frolic with Cambria, I felt chipper. Perky. Spicy. I felt like I could walk straight into the sky and skip along the Earth's atmosphere, like finger-walking over a globe.

Something strange had happened in the sand, something beyond just sex. A universal thing had occurred beneath the stars and the moon, beside the constant grind of the ocean. I had liked Cambria a lot, which contributed to me inviting her on the trip. That feeling had become confused with Maya's presence and the candid conversation from the night before. However, the nightly activity on the beach had straightened out my feelings.

I loved Maya, yes, but I loved her as a friend. As much as I enjoyed the idea of dating her, it was a terrible idea. She was spontaneous and impulsive. She drank like a sheltered home schooler tasting freedom for the first time. She was loud and forthcoming. I was none of those things. If we tested the strength of our relationship through a dating experiment, Maya and I would likely kill each other. We worked best as friends.

Cambria and I had something more than friendship, though. It had taken sex for me to see that, but at least I saw that. Now the tough part—backtracking and apologizing, telling Cambria I was confused and ultimately wrong, that I wanted to give us a shot.

Not at the moment, though. She had crept upstairs to shower and clean off the sand.

"You can join me," she had said.

"I would love to, but Fred lost a bet, and a few drinks won't weasel him out of the deal. Can I, maybe, crawl into bed with you when we're back?"

"Only if you wake me up."

A bear-sized lump rested on the couch. I walked over to it. "Fred." I gripped his arm and shook him awake. "Hey, Fred."

He grunted and rolled over, grabbed a pillow cushion and stuffed it over his face. Sleep and the pillow muffled his voice, but I deciphered what he said. "Not now, Daphne. You know I can't when I drink too much. Then we both feel bad about it. Besides, I might throw up."

I switched gears, following my euphoria into a practical joke. Elation carried me, and I rode the high like an oarless boat rides the waves. Instead of squeezing and shaking Fred's arm, I caressed it with the back of my fingers and spoke in a high-pitched voice that poorly mimicked Daphne.

"We don't have to go all the way," I said. "I know you can't operate where it matters, but you have other digits to get the job done. Could you tend to me? It's been so long since you've made me feel like a proper woman. You're always taking, taking, taking, but never giving back."

"Baby." Fred removed the pillow from his face and scooted up to a half-seated position on the couch. He fluttered his eyes and opened them.

I smiled. "Hey, baby."

Fred, with the pillow still in hand, smacked it across my head. "What is wrong with you?" He scrambled to a full seated position and perched his gigantic body on the couch's backrest. "Why would you do that? What if I had kissed you?"

I smiled. "I wasn't too worried about you doing much of anything. You had too much to drink, remember?"

"I'm going to kill you."

"Nope," I said.

"Bet?"

"You're going to put some pants on and climb into my car. "

"No, I'm not."

"Passenger seat. You're too drunk to drive."

"I'm not going anywhere with you."

"We had a deal, and you already tried to slip out of it by getting drunk. I'm meeting you halfway here. I'll drive, and you'll sit in the passenger seat."

"You're serious?"

"As alcohol is on your libido."

Fred grunted. "You're the worst kind of boss. I should take you to the labor board, sue you for overworking me, or making me work while intoxicated. Or sexual harassment. They'll cancel you."

"Should you?"

"I should." He hopped off the couch and searched the area for his sweatpants, eventually finding them and stepping into them. He cursed as he fit them around his waist. "They're inside-out and back-wards."

"Feel familiar?"

Fred paused and stared at me with one eye wider than the other. His mouth pursed. The sleep- and booze-induced fog must have drifted from his cognition. "You're acting strange."

"Nope."

"Yup."

"How?"

"You're happy and goofy. What happened? Are you okay? You're worrying me."

"I'm happy, right? That's a good thing."

"Not with you." Fred pried off his sweats, flipped them around and inside-right, then stepped back into them. "Happy for you is scary—like a manic-depressive. What happened? Was it your mom? Did she say or do something, and you finally snapped?" Fred covered his mouth, gasping. "It's Maya, isn't it? Her date. You found out."

"It's not like that." I smirked.

Fred's eyes widened. He pointed at me, backed away, and shook his head. "No. Impossible."

"What?"

"Twice in one week, with two different women? That's not possible. How is that possible? August Watson doesn't pull off a trick like that."

"I don't know what you're talking about." I knew very well what he alluded to.

"Cambria? Did you put the final nail in the coffin?"

I grimaced. "What does that mean? Nope, I don't want to know. Don't explain it."

"Did you or did you not pluck that flower?"

"You ready to go?" I asked.

"I'm going to keep asking in hyper-sexualized metaphors if your dragon breathed fire until you respond with a crystal-clear answer."

"Did she peel your banana?" The question came as a quiet voice from behind us.

I wheeled around and noticed Alina sitting on the bottom step of the stairwell.

"Did you pour some milk on her cereal?" Fred asked.

Alina stood, using the railing to pull herself up. "Did she flip your burger patty?"

"You dummies are just saying random things that aren't even clever."

"Think about it," Alina said.

"Think about it," Fred repeated, tapping his neanderthal skull.

"I refuse. And look at my face." I angled forward, pointed at my chin, and frowned. "Do I look happy still? No. Because I'm no longer happy. You two have ruined my happiness."

"Thank God," Fred said, sighing with relief. "I was nervous for a second. I thought you... you fell off the wagon and popped a bottle, you know? I hate seeing you that way, buddy."

"Happy?"

"It is weird," Alina said. "Like when you smiled earlier. It's weird coming from you. You're like Clint Eastwood, right? Stoic. Cynical. Smiling is for sissy-women."

"That's a perfect example," Fred said. "Except, Clint is better looking than you. Even at his age, he's an attractive old man."

"He is," Alina said. "Very attractive. It's the eyes."

"Yeah, but August has similar eyes. Piercing, but gentle."

"Okay," I said. "I don't much enjoy these side notes where you two devolve into a discussion about me, right in front of me, and I'm not sure if you're insulting or complimenting me."

"Would you rather us do it behind your back?" Alina asked.

"Why do you have to talk about me at all?"

Fred and Alina eyed each other and shrugged, not saying a word.

"Well, Alina, go back to whatever you were doing. Fred and I are heading out."

"Where to?"

"Does it matter?"

"Yeah. Maybe I want to join you."

"She can join us, don't you think?" Fred asked.

"Why aren't you sleeping?" I asked.

"You woke me up, acting like Daphne, remember?"

"Not you. Her."

Alina shied her attention to the ground, staring at her shoes. "Couldn't sleep, that's all."

I popped a knuckle and sighed, not happy with myself for caving to the sixteen-year-old's request. "Sure. Why not? We'll take a business trip to investigate the ghost on Highway 1 for free."

We all piled into my sedan after about ten more minutes of bickering. Alina called shotgun when we stepped outside, and Fred disputed her claim. He was too big to sit in the backseat. Besides, he didn't know they were even playing the shotgun game. So on and so forth. In the end, Fred squeezed into the backseat and sat in the center like Mr. Incredible stuffed into his sedan. Yes, that's one of the few movies I actually watched.

I merged onto Highway 1 and drove south toward Monterey. The highway cut inland for twenty miles, curved back toward the coast, before bouncing inland again. After we had driven thirty miles, nearly all the way to Monterey, the highway hugged the coastline once more. We continued through to Carmel, heading toward Big Sur. The highway grew dark beneath the rising cliffs. The moon hid behind a layer of fog, which settled over the ocean and veiled the unending waters.

I slowed my speed through the heavy marine layer, not having anywhere to go, so not needing to hurry. Fred had situated himself across the back seats. He laid on his side with his knees angled to his chest, his left arm pillowed beneath his head. He snored like a bear hibernating.

Alina remained awake and alert. She stared at the white haze enshrouding everything in sight.

"It's like *The Mist*," she said after half an hour of silence.

"What's that?" I asked.

"It's a Stephen King story adapted into a movie, starring Ashton Kutcher. Wait." Alina bit her lip for a second and furrowed her brow in thought. "Nope. I'm thinking of *The Butterfly Effect*. *The Mist* starred the guy from *Dreamcatcher*, another movie adapted from a Stephen King novel. I can't remember the actor's name, though."

"Good movie?"

"Which one? Well, it doesn't matter. None of them were great. *The Mist* was okay, but I had read the story right before watching the movie, and I think that ruined it for me."

"You're one of those people?"

"What people?"

"Books are always better than the movie."

"First off, books *are* always better than the movie. Second off, no. I usually prefer movies to reading."

"Just not *The Mist*?"

"On the occasions when I do read, the books stand higher in my mind. I just prefer to watch." She looked at me. "You like to read, right?"

I chewed on my cheeks and nodded my head. "I do. I used to read a lot more fiction. Fantasy, mostly. Epic fantasy—*Game of Thrones, Wheel of Time, Lord of the Rings*. By the way, the Lord of the Rings movies... they're better than the books."

"Blasphemy."

"I'm serious."

"I believe you. It's blasphemy that you watched a movie and liked it better than the book. I can't believe that."

"Fantasy movies I liked as a kid. Superhero stuff, too. But we didn't have all these Marvel movies ruling the box office. So, I always preferred books and comics. I stopped reading a few years back." I didn't have to say when or why. We understood. "When I created the business this past year, I readopted the practice, mostly reading myths, fairy tales, and religious texts that tie into the paranormal business."

"It's still... fantasy, right?"

I nodded. "I enjoy it, if that's what you're asking."

"Maybe that's why I like it here so much, working with you. It ties into my interests so neatly—horror and monsters. Fantasy does the same, I guess, just with a different tone. Good overcoming evil. Losing innocence."

I stole my eyes from the oppressing fog and glanced at Alina, amazed by the young girl. "You need to attend your classes. That's not coming from a boss as a demand. That's coming from a friend as a concern."

She shrunk in her seat.

"I had a teacher when I was your age... well, first, I hated school at your age. I thought I was too smart for it. It bored me. I preferred reading my books, studying what interested me. Anyway, I had this teacher, Mr. Davis. He pulled me aside one day after I failed his history test. He told me I'm intelligent, but intelligence is like everything else in life. It requires effort and practice and honing. 'You're smart for a fifteen-year-old. But if you keep skipping class, not putting forth any effort, you're going to stay fifteen-year-old smart, and you'll be a dumb eighteen-year-old.'"

Alina side-eyed me.

"He was a teacher, though—a good one, and one I respected. But a teacher. I ignored his advice. I skated through high school, never challenging myself or strengthening my natural intelligence. Junior year proved more difficult than my sophomore year. Senior year was a grind. My first year of college, I became lost. Everyone there was levels smarter than me."

"What are you saying?"

I swallowed. "You know exactly what I'm saying. There's no reason for you to make the same mistakes I made. You're intelligent, Alina, more intelligent than I ever was or currently am, or probably will be. Don't waste it. Don't allow it to whither. Go to school. Challenge yourself. Even if you're bored, challenge yourself by stepping outside of your comfort zone. I don't know. Maybe join—"

A figure appeared from the mist ten yards from the car, illuminated by the headlights. A translucent, pale figure with oily black eyes. I slammed on the brakes, knowing better than to swerve. But I hoped for the best.

The car came to a screeching halt. The smell of burned rubber filled the night. My heart pounded so hard, I don't know how it didn't shatter through my ribcage. Beside me, in the passenger seat, Alina breathed quickly and shallowly.

Fred bolted upright in the backseat, smacking his head on the roof. "What happened?"

"Did you see her?" I stared in the rearview mirror. The car hadn't stopped in time, but I hadn't run the woman over. Had she evaded my vehicle?

"I saw her," Alina said, breathless. "Did you hit her?"

"I don't think so."

"Hit who?" Fred asked. "The ghost?"

I opened the door and stepped out of the car.

"August," Fred said. "August, what are you doing? Get back in here."

Alina opened the passenger door and joined me in the fog.

"You two crazies have fun out there. I'll climb into the front seat. If you need a quick escape, I'll act like the getaway driver."

"You're drunk, you're not driving anywhere," I said.

"Well, I'll wait in the backseat all the same."

I closed the driver's side door, stepped forward, and opened Fred's door. "Let's go. You're coming with us."

"To do what?"

"To ghost hunt."

"Nope. Not happening. You're thinking crazy if you think I'm stepping out of this vehicle to hunt for a ghost."

The other door opened, and Alina's face popped into view. "Fred, if you don't get your oversized butt out of the car, I'm going to throw away all the food and candy you have stashed around the office. Don't think for a second I haven't located every single last one of your little hideaways. Notice how I immediately found your M&M's on this trip? I know how you think. I know where you hid every morsel.

That's right, you'll be eating three meals a day. No more snacking. Not on my watch."

"You know nothing," he said.

"Wall vent over the coffee counter."

Fred's body stiffened.

"The hole in the wall covered by that weird frame poster of Melissa McCarthy. The one where's she's pooping in the sink from that scene in *Bridesmaids*. Why do you even have that?"

"She's a comedic genius," Fred said.

"It's weird."

"I said the same thing when he hung it up," I said. "Super weird."

"That's one of the greatest comedic scenes in cinematic history," Fred said through clenched teeth. "And you wouldn't dare steal my snacks."

"I would dare," Alina said. "Now, remove yourself from this vehicle."

A Magical World. Wednesday, May 3rd. 0041hrs.

CAMBRIA LAY AWAKE IN bed, staring out the window. The moonlight and glass played a trick on the night, making the darkness glow like neon. It came into her room like a glowing navy blue. She couldn't quite see the ocean from her position, and she couldn't find an angle to view the stars. But the dark glow beamed into the room, and that small sliver of beauty was a special spectacle—a window (excuse the pun) that allowed a preview or a glimpse into a magical world.

Or maybe Cambria felt romantic. Everything she noticed had a touch of fairy dust sprinkled across it.

Though she would never admit this to anyone, not even to her journal, which she rarely kept anymore, Cambria felt like a young girl after kissing her first crush—the boy whose last name she attached to her first name to see how it looked and hear how it sounded.

"Cambria Watson," she whispered to the dark room, just for the fun of it. It almost sounded natural. She giggled, staring out the window that could have served as a prop in a movie for a portal into another world.

A magical world with August, she thought.

Stop it! Another internal voice snapped. *Don't even think about looking through that window.*

The more logical voice in her head had it right. If Cambria peered through that moonlit, blue-neon glass, and if she peeked into the magical world of her and August's future, she would lose herself to that possibility. Of a life spent together. Of children. Of taking his last name. Cambria Watson.

She wasn't a young girl anymore. Magic and love once coexisted in her innocent mind, but the years and the experiences had eroded her naivety, like the ocean tides cutting across stone.

Cambria closed her eyes and mentally placed herself back on the beach.

She had gripped a sliver of anger, not bothering to hide from August. She wasn't really mad at him, though. Frustrated, yes. Annoyed, absolutely. Not mad, though. She was mad at herself for putting herself in this situation. Why had she said yes to his invitation? She had canceled and rescheduled appointments to make this trip work. She and August knew each other all of one date. Still, she had said yes.

Not only that, but she had initiated sexual activity with August.

He had looked so delicious beneath the moon, though. Not only that, he hadn't blamed Cambria for his actions. He had accepted the responsibility. He had apologized to her. The men Cambria had known in her past, they would have never swallowed their pride, no matter how in the wrong they stood. August had, though, and his vulnerability paired with her anger had all but ripped Cambria's clothes off.

What now, though? What happens?

Cambria had said no strings attached, but did she mean that?

No.

August had accepted her condition. Had he meant that?

I hope not.

Should Cambria spark another conversation on the topic, after they had settled their situation while on the beach?

No, she thought immediately. *Don't confuse the situation with wishy-washy behavior. You said sex for a week then nothing else. That's what this is. Sex and nothing else.*

Cambria rolled over, staring at the wall opposite the window and hugging the pillow August should have slept on. Did she really like him? Or had August's response to Maya's date awoken a competitive nature in Cambria? Had she found herself angry out of jealousy? She didn't know, but it was possible. If it was true, when they returned to Sacramento and the game of August Watson between her and Maya ended, how would she feel about continuing any relationship with him?

As her thoughts shifted and swirled and tugged at each other, Cambria drifted through the glowing window and into that magical world.

She sat beneath a sunny sky in a backyard. A puppy bounced across the grass, hopping like a bunny. It chased a tow-headed toddler. The little boy, Aaron—Cambria and August had named their first baby Aaron—waddled a few steps before plopping onto his butt. He stood and ran after the dog again. Cambria felt warm, inside and out.

Through the speakers Fred had installed around the backyard—Fred had also installed a television on the back wall; it was an excuse to come over, watch football, barbecue, listen to music, and hang out with Aaron—a song played. It came out as static at first, but scratched and cleared. An old ragtime tune played on a piano.

"I had a dream last night that filled me full of fright," sang a voice disconnected from the speaker system. The voice came from nowhere, and from everywhere. It sounded rough, like a smoke-abused throat growled the words.

Cambria glanced around, but she didn't see anyone or anything.

"I dreamed I was with the Devil below, in his great big fiery hall, where the Devil was giving a Ball."

Ghost Hunt. Wednesday, May 3rd. 0123hrs.

THE CHILLY BREEZE STOLE the stench of burned rubber, replacing it with the smell of the wet, salty ocean air.

Fred grumbled as we walked back in the direction we had skidded from, further away from my parked car, and further into the fog, nearer to where I had spotted the specter. "You know I'm terrified of ghosts. The bet was to drive, not get out and risk our lives."

"We're not risking anything." I squinted into the white fog, barely able to see a few yards in front of me. "Besides, ghosts don't exist."

"What do you expect to find in this mess, anyway?"

"I expect to find a ghost," Alina said. "Or someone pretending to be a ghost, and maybe learn who drove that married couple off the cliff."

"Duh, Sherlock, but how do you plan to do that?" Fred asked. "I mean, I can barely see you from where I'm standing."

"I'm pretty sure—" Alina abruptly stopped speaking. "Hey, I found something."

I bolted to her position and stood beside her. She stared at an object resting on the asphalt. A wooden box six inches square. I kneeled for a closer look at the box, removing my phone and activating the built-in flashlight.

"What the heck?" I stared open-mouthed at the name scrawled across the top of it. I hadn't felt nervous or scared to hunt the ghost, but that box had me feeling like Fred's pants—inside-out.

Scrawled in bold handwriting, was a single, ominous word. WAT-SON.

"It's for you," Alina said, her voice slightly confused, as if asking a question rather than making a statement.

"What's for him?" Fred asked as he caught up to us. "What is that?"

"A box with my name on it."

Fred stepped backward and waved his hands before his face.. "Nope. No way. I quit. I retire. Neither of you can boss me around any longer. Adios. Sayonara. Au revoir. My parting advice, don't open the box."

"What's in the box?" Alina said in a near-perfect Brad Pitt imitation. She glanced up at Fred and smirked. "What's in the box?"

"Stop it," he said, not finding the situation humorous at all. "You stop it. August..." Fred shook his head, back and forth like a dog's tail. "August, leave it be. Don't... just don't. Why would you? What does it matter? Leave it. Have you seen that movie?"

"*Seven*?" I asked.

"Yes."

"I've seen it."

"So you know what was in the box?"

I glanced at the box with my name scribbled across the top in bold Sharpie. Spoiler alert, but Brad Pitt's character, his wife's head was in the box. The serial arranged it to draw rage from the detective.

"Please, don't open it," Fred said.

I thought of Maya on her date with the ornithologist. What did Maya really know of the man? Who was he? Suddenly, I found it strange that after birds had rained from the sky, Maya found herself on a date with a bird scientist. Or maybe it was the night playing tricks on my imagination, the mist and the box with my name on it. Maybe Fred's fear was contagious. Either way, unease seeped into my bones and worry settled into my mind.

"Alina," I said, my voice tight.

"Yeah."

"Call Maya."

"Why?"

I stared at the box. Suddenly, I agreed with Fred. I wanted nothing to do with the box, least of all to open it.

"August, why?" Alina asked.

"Do you trust that man she went out with?"

"I don't trust any man she goes out with."

"Call her."

Alina scrolled through her phone, clicked the screen, and placed it to her ear. "Voicemail." She dropped her attention back to the mysterious box. "There's not a head in there." She didn't sound convinced, though. "It's too small for a head to fit in there."

I jumped on that train of thought. "What if it's not Maya?" I asked. "Maxwell Shaye told us about this ghost. What if he wanted me to come out here late at night and investigate the sighting?"

"Why?" Alina asked. "That makes no sense."

She was right. It made little sense for Maxwell to lure me an hour away from the house in the middle of the night. So, who would? Who would jump through so many hoops to draw me away from my family in the dead of night?

The answer dropped on me like a ton of bricks.

Detective (though, he wasn't really a detective—at least not anymore) Daniel Quinn. As he had coined our brief and obscure relationship as the paranormal Joker to my Batman. The Hannibal Lecter to my Clarice Starling.

Had he left the box for me as a gift? As a warning? Why? To flex his knowledge? To show me he knew where I was, who I was with, and what I was doing?

My heart beat spiked. Had he drawn me out there for a reason?

"We have to go," I said. "Now."

"What?" Alina asked. "Go where?"

"Back home."

"Why?"

They could be in danger, I thought. Everyone we left back at the vacation home could face whatever horror Quinn had dreamed up for them.

"It's a trap," I said. "He drew us out here to isolate everyone else."

"Who drew us out here?" Alina asked.

"Daniel Quinn."

"Who?"

I shook my head. "The man who orchestrated the doppelgänger and the changeling cases. He pointed them at me."

"What? Why?"

"I don't know. He's insane. He thinks we're some real-life iteration of Van Helsing and Dracula."

"That's ridiculous," Alina said. "No one would ever mistake you for Van Helsing."

Fred barked a sharp laugh and raised his hand and high-fiving Alina. Apparently humor overcomes fear every time.

"This isn't a joke." I scrolled through my phone and dialed Cambria's number.

No answer.

I dialed Maya.

No answer.

Adam.

No answer.

Rachel.

Nothing.

Jake.

Nothing.

My mom. I saved her for last because I feared she would handle the news and the situation far worse than anyone else in the house.

"August," she answered on the fourth ring, her voice piercing and anxious. "Are you okay? Is everything okay? What's going on?"

"I'm fine, Mom. Listen to me carefully."

"What wrong?"

"Listen to me, Mom. Listen, okay. Wake everyone up. Everyone in the house. Wake them up and gather them together in the same room. Turn on the lights. As many lights as you can."

"You're scaring me. What's going on?"

"I'll explain later. Can you do what I say?"

"Are you okay?"

"I'm fine. I'm about an hour from the house with Alina and Fred, but we're driving back now. Stay awake and keep the lights on until I get back there. Do you understand?"

"Yes."

"What are you going to do?"

"Wake everyone up. Turn on all the lights."

"And?"

"And sit in the same room together."

"No one leaves the group, not for anything. Okay?"

"Okay."

"Pee your pants for all I care, but do not venture off alone. Understood?"

"Yes."

I bent over, picked up the box, and returned to my car in a hurry. "We'll be home soon."

"I love you."

"Love you, too."

Fred and Alina chased after me.

"Shotgun," Fred yelled. He slid to a stop by the passenger door and threw it open. He spared a second to poke out his tongue at Alina as she crawled into the backseat. As Fred pulled the seatbelt across his chest, I tossed the box to him. He handled it like a live grenade and threw it in the backseat, yelping. "What's wrong with you? Are you trying to kill me?"

I twisted the key, started the car, and turned it northward, hoping another vehicle wasn't careening through the fog to smash into me.

"Open it," I said.

"Not happening," Fred said.

"You're such a whiny baby." Alina picked up the box off the floor and set it in her lap. She peeled off the tape holding it closed—it scraped roughly off the cardboard.

"What's in there?" I asked.

"A phone."

"A phone?" I said, puzzled. "Turn it on."

After another minute, she said, "It's on."

"Go to the contacts."

"There are no contacts."

"Recent calls."

"One," Alina said.

"Hand me the phone."

"You're not calling that number, are you? Have you not seen any movie ever?" Fred pressed himself against the passenger door. "You call that number, the phone explodes, and we blow up. Boom! Game over. End of book. No sequel either."

I tapped the only red number showing on the missed calls.

It rang once. Twice.

Laughter answered.

"Quinn," I said.

"August Allan Watson. To what do I owe this early morning pleasure?" The voice unmistakably belonged to Daniel Quinn, the man who had disguised himself as a detective to speak to me on different occasions, one being in the hospital as I recovered from the wound he indirectly caused.

"What do you want?" I asked.

"What do I want? It seems you have called me. What do you want?"

"For you to leave me and my family alone."

Quinn chuckled lightly. "I'm too infatuated with you to leave you alone. How's Santa Cruz? Is the weather nice? Is it a dream, as some might say?"

His question, is it a dream, didn't go over my head. He knew about the nightmare case I investigated. Had he orchestrated that mystery as he had orchestrated the changeling and doppelgänger?

"I know you're filling in the blanks, Mr. Watson. Allow me to share some answers and save you the mental energy. I'm not responsible for the case which drew you to Santa Cruz. However, I have figured it out already. Would you like a hint?"

Yes, I thought. "No," I said, too stubborn to accept help from the maniac on the other end of the call. Even if it had cost me my life to hear his advice, I wish I had taken it. Stubbornness is a cruel and unforgiving burden to carry.

"Alrighty then," Quinn said. "I understand your competitive nature, of wanting to figure it on your own. I will respect that decision, but it might come with deadly consequences."

"What do you want from me?"

"Only to play and have fun, Mr. Watson. Only to go down in history as the greatest paranormal duo of all time." He cleared his throat. "Speaking of duos, how is it going with Cambria? You two hitting it off nicely in the budding romance department, or have you encountered a few road bumps? I know it's probably tough when vacationing with your entire family, as well as Maya Adler."

"Don't you hurt them."

Quinn bubbled laughter. "Me, hurt someone? Never. It's not in my nature to hurt a fly. I would hurt no one."

"What about the couple last night? You didn't hurt them with your little ghost scare?"

Quinn spoke tightly, as if through clenched teeth, and he spat out each word. "I'm not a criminal. Unlike you, murderer."

Reactively, without hesitation, I hung up, not bothering to waste energy by responding to him. My vision tunneled. I saw the headlights illuminating the bends of the highway, but nothing more. My hands wrang the steering wheel's leather, twisting against it. If someone spoke to me, if Quinn called me back, I didn't notice or hear.

My mind jumped to Aaron Brooks. To the sound of the airsoft BB bouncing along the asphalt as his body slumped to the ground and settled in a pool of blood.

The Second to Dance. Wednesday, May 3rd. 0213hrs.

Nicholas Lane sat alone in his motel room, wide awake and staring at the glowing television. He didn't watch whatever unnamed film or show played. Not really. He stared at the screen and distantly observed the characters doing things, but he didn't listen… didn't really hear anything.

His mind buzzed, droning as if the television was stuck on an unreceptive channel. Nothing but static. It was his exhaustion yelling at him—screaming constantly (AHHHH!) for him to sleep, to rest, to recover. Nick hadn't slept since Christina's brutal murder, since the police brought him in for questioning.

They (the police) hadn't allowed him to return to his apartment, deeming it an active crime scene. So, Nick had to deplete his measly savings account—he hadn't worked in weeks—and booked the cheap, dingy room. The carpet was moist, and it stank. The air was humid, too hot, but with no air conditioning in the room to combat it.

Nick sat cross-legged on the stained bed sheets. An open bottle of Modafinil rested in his lap. He had dry swallowed two tablets an hour ago. They hadn't kicked in yet. He debated popping a couple more, maybe with an energy drink. Something to keep him awake. Anything, really.

As he listlessly sat on his bed, fighting against sleep, a heavy knock—Bang, Bang, Bang—sounded on the flimsy motel room door. The force of the knock vibrated the paper-thin walls.

Nick's heavy eyes shifted to the edge of the room, toward the window overlooking the parking lot, illuminated by a single, low-burning, flickering light.

Who dared bother him at this hour? At two in the morning. Had he told anyone the police had released him? That he had checked into a motel? Nick couldn't remember. Everything existed as if from a dream—far away and indistinguishable.

Dropping his feet to the damp, dirty floor, Nick padded to the bathroom and splashed cool water over his puffy face. He glanced at his reflection in the grimy, cracked mirror, and wavered back and forth like a drunk.

Bang. Bang. Bang. A voice accompanied the knocking. "I know you're in there! Let me in!"

Nick immediately recognized the voice. That voice had spoken to him, yelled at him, advised him for over twenty years.

Johnny.

Yeah, that's who knocked on his door. It came back to him in broken fragments. He had called Johnny after the detectives released him. He had asked his best friend if he could crash at his and Heather's apartment. Johnny said it wasn't a good idea.

Had Johnny sounded upset? Nick thought he had, but he couldn't quite recall. Johnny had kept the conversation brief, hurrying Nick off the phone as if angry. Why would Johnny be upset? Also, had Nick shared with Johnny which motel he stayed at?

"I must have," he muttered, grabbing his phone from the bathroom counter and scrolling through his texts. He had last texted Christina.

Why? he thought. *She's dead. What would I say to a dead person?*

"Upon the door, Nick!" Johnny yelled, hammering the door with his fists.

Nick opened his text to Christina. *I miss you*, was all it said. He backed out of the thread, scrolling to the next text conversation, the one with Johnny. Nick had dropped Johnny a pin, sharing his location with his lifetime best friend.

No wonder Johnny had arrived, frenetic and desperate to get into the room. He wanted to check on his buddy, make sure Nick had settled into the motel room after his release.

"Hey!" Johnny said, his voice clearer somehow. A second later, his fists pounded on the front window. "If you're sleeping, wake up. The Devil doesn't get to kill you. I do!"

What, Nick thought. He slowed his pace across the room. Why would Johnny want to kill him? That made no sense.

Nick shook his foggy, sleep-clouded head, and chalked up Johnny's threat to mishearing him. Sleep exhaustion played funny tricks on the mind. Audio and visual hallucinations weren't outside the realm of possibility.

Nick reached the front door. He dropped his forehead against it and closed his eyes for a second. A second of rest before having to muster the energy to meet with Johnny. He was so weak and tired. Tired as a dog, as some say. Why did they say that? It didn't matter. He was as tired as Benjamin, or Benji, the dog he had owned as a kid. A Rottweiler.

Benji chased after the bright yellow (green, his sister always argued—bright green) tennis ball, yapping a high-pitched bark as he sprinted across the park's expanse of grass. It was a perfect area to run dogs, to run Thanksgiving football games. Nick had never played organized football, but he loved to play on Thanksgiving.

He stood on the field, behind the line of scrimmage and watched the football. His older cousin, Wade, played quarterback. Wade turned his head to Nick and winked. *Go long*, that's what the wink meant. *Go long.* Nick bit his lower lip and waited for the signal.

"Blue. Forty-two. Ready. Ready. Hut, hut. Hut. Hike!"

Nick burst off the line of scrimmage. He flew down the field in his blue jeans and ratted tennis shoes. He looked back over his shoulder and saw the ball spiraling through the air, momentarily invisible in the sun, then growing as a dark dot, falling, falling, falling...

"Open the door, Nick!" Johnny yelled. He smashed his fist against the door, vibrating and rattling Nick's skull as he leaned against it.

Nick jerked away and breathed hard. Cold sweat covered his goose-pimpled skin.

His fingers trembled as he unlatched the chain lock, twisted the deadbolt, and pulled on the door handle. Before he could crack the door an inch, Johnny shouldered his full weight—nearly two-hundred pounds of exercised muscle—into the door, throwing it inward into Nick's face. It connected with a loud crack.

Nick staggered backward and grabbed his nose. It felt like it sat sideways on his face. Hot blood poured into his mouth, down his chin, his neck, onto his chest. Onto the motel floor.

An anxious thought flooded into his mind. *How will I pay for the security deposit?* That spurred him into delirious laughter. He held his face, blood rushing through his fingers, and he howled with laughter.

Johnny, like an over-aggressive cousin at Thanksgiving, speared his shoulder into Nick's ribs and drove him into the bed. "What's so funny?" He mounted Nick, cocked back a fist, and punched him square in his crooked nose.

A flash of white-hot pain exploded across Nick's vision, along with a surge of adrenaline. Of sweet, elusive energy.

With a newfound strength, Nick slipped a hand free from Johnny's grasp and half-blocked his next punch. He grabbed his best friend by the back of the neck and pulled him into a hug—into a position that wouldn't allow Johnny to throw any more punches. Now tangled up with Johnny, Nick rolled sideways, and steered them off the bed.

Johnny's back landed hard on the carpet. He breathed a pained sigh as Nick's body landed and squished his. Blood and hot breath and sweat and straining muscles blended together as the two men struggled on the ground. Eventually, Johnny slipped an arm free of Nick's embrace and shoved his palm directly into Nick's broken face, pressing against his flattened nose.

Nick screamed and shoved himself away from Johnny. He scurried back to gain a little distance. He pressed himself against the half-wall just beneath the window. He panted and stared at his best friend.

Johnny sat up and scooted against the foot of the bed, sitting on the floor. He hugged his knees to his chest and stared at the popcorn ceiling. "I thought we were brothers," he said.

"What?" Nick said, his voice nasally and weak with the broken nose. Then he realized what had happened—maybe it was the newfound energy from the spike of adrenaline that helped clear his mind, but he pieced the puzzle together. "Johnny, I didn't... I didn't kill Chris. You know that."

Johnny spat a wad of blood-soaked saliva onto the carpet. "I don't know anything anymore."

Nick sat against the wall and raised his head, redirecting the blood to flow back down his sinuses. His nose pulsed, like it had its own heartbeat. "What's that mean?"

"You know exactly what that means."

"You think I murdered Chris?"

"Sure seems like something you would do. I mean, you almost beat your ex-girlfriend to death with a baseball bat, right? Once you found yourself out of prison from that felony charge, guess what started happening? The Devil appeared in our dreams. You think that's a coincidence? You think it's a coincidence the same Devil that's been haunting us also murdered Chris in your apartment?"

"Us," Nick said. "Haunting all of us."

Johnny laughed—a desperate, terrified sound more similar to a scream than a burst of humor. "What you've lacked in intelligence, you always made up for in creativity. I can believe you created the Devil. What I don't know, is why? Why do it? Were you mad at us for your stupid decisions?"

"It's not me."

"Were you jealous?"

"Jealous?"

"Of me and Heather?" Johnny asked. He dropped his gaze from the popcorn ceiling to glare at Nick.

"What?"

"You loved... you love her, right?"

"Johnny, I'm not following you."

"You screwed my fiancé. I know you did. She told me. She confessed everything to me. Did Chris find out about you and Heather? Is that why you murdered her?"

"I didn't murder her, Johnny!" The pain in his nose thrashed across face, but his anger muted most of it. "I didn't do a thing to her!" Bloody mist burst from Nick's lips as he pleaded his innocence. He panted, staring at his best friend—glaring at him with hurt and confusion. How did Johnny not believe him? How could Johnny accuse him of murder?

"You're nothing but an ignorant neo-Nazi," Johnny said. "You think I don't know, but I know. I know who you really are. I've always known."

"What's that say about you, then?" Nick asked. He dropped his head against the wall and stared at the ceiling. "You stuck around, called me your brother. What's that say about you?"

Before Johnny could respond, a ragtime tune played from the motel's digital radio, scratchy at first, but gaining clarity with each note. Deep, growling vocals soon joined the up-tempo piano. "I had a dream last night that filled me full of fright."

Nick watched Johnny's lips move as he sang the unremembered song. Nick attempted to back further away from his lifelong friend, but the wall impeded his progress.

Johnny rose to his feet. He no longer wore gym shorts and a sweatshirt, but a three-piece suit and a mask—the mask of a man with a triangular smile and bushy eyebrows. In his left hand, he held a sledgehammer.

"It's you," Nick said, breathless, tears and blood streaking down his face. "You're the Devil. You killed Chris."

"... dancing with the Devil..." Johnny moved slowly toward Nick, dragging the metal head behind him. The carpet muted any scraping and forewarning noise it may have made, but the immutable sense of dread still poured over Nick.

He trembled, curled into a ball, and hoped to slip into a crack or phase into the wall. He squeezed his eyes shut and said, "It's a dream. It's only a dream. You can't hurt me. It's a dream. Wake up. Wake up! Wake up!" Nick gasped, failing to control his breathing. He slapped himself in the face, hoping the starburst of pain would wake him. When he opened his eyes, he hoped to see the motel room empty.

He saw the dead face of the Man wrapped around the Devil's face. Johnny's face. Was Johnny really the Devil? Why? To get back at Nick for his and Heather's affair?

"That's why you killed her, isn't it?" Nick asked, his voice so quiet he barely heard it. "You wanted me to suffer, to hurt like I hurt you. Well, I'm so sorry. I hate myself for what I did. I don't have any excuse either, other than I was drunk and flying with the night. I could have stopped, but I didn't, and I'm so sorry. I'm so, so sorry."

The Devil ceased singing, though the ragtime piano continued to play. He rolled his head and stared down at Nick. After a second of careful consideration, he sang again. "He played the music at the Devil's Ball..."

The sledgehammer kissed the popcorn ceiling, dropping flakes of asbestos over Nick's face. That was the least of his concerns, though. The metal cylinder dropped, all twenty pounds careening downward on a trajectory directly for Nick's skull.

Reunited. Wednesday, May 3rd. 0237hrs.

I STOOD IN THE front entry of the rental home, one hand gripping the top of my head and the other holding the door frame, and I stared at my family with physical relief. They all gathered in the living room, healthy and alive.

Fred rushed past me and embraced Daphne. He lifted her off the ground like something from a movie, spun her around, and gently placed her feet back on the hardwood floor. He examined her like a medic inspecting someone for wounds. "You okay?"

"Yeah." Daphne dove back into him and held him tight. "What's going on?"

"I don't know. I'm not sure." Fred turned his cow-sized head toward me, questions flashing across his narrow eyes, so obvious and apparent I could nearly read his thoughts.

Alina stepped before me and scanned the room. "Where's Maya? Shouldn't she be home from her date by now?"

"Where's Cambria?" I asked, noticing her absence like a giant sore within the room.

"I'm here." Cambria popped up from behind the island and flew across the living room to greet me. She slammed into me with electric force, buried her face into my chest, and cried against me. "I'm here."

I rubbed the back of her neck. "Hey, it's okay. We're okay. What's wrong?"

Cambria rolled her face so her lips no longer pressed against my shirt, so her words formed clearly from her mouth. "I heard it."

"Heard what?"

"A song."

"What do you mean?"

"In my dream. I heard a song. An old, strange song."

"I don't understand."

"It was the Devil, the Nightmare, the whatever you want to call it. It came for me, though."

"What song?" Daphne asked. "Like an old-school sound? Ragtime?"

Cambria turned to Fred's wife and nodded.

"I heard that same song."

"What?" Fred asked. "When?"

"Earlier tonight, when I was sleeping."

"You didn't think to tell me?"

"I hear music in my sleep all the time. I thought nothing of it until now."

Fred rolled his eyes and ran a hand over his face. "We had a full-on conversation about how the Devil appears with music."

"First," Daphne said, holding up a finger, "we never said song accompanied him. Second, the Devil isn't after us, is he? Third, I always hear music in my sleep. How am I supposed to know?"

"Did you see it?"

"No," Cambria and Daphne both answered.

"You only heard the song?" I asked.

"Do you remember it?" Alina asked.

"Something about a dream," Cambria said. "Like having a dream about dancing with the Devil. It's fuzzy, though. I remember little about it."

How had Cambria and Daphne experienced the same nightmare as my clients? Fred had read the email over dinner in front of everyone.

Still, we didn't know the song. How had Daphne and Cambria heard the same, ragtime song that Heather hummed?

"I had a dream last night," Cambria sang. She had a pleasant voice.

"It filled me full of fright," Daphne chimed in, also singing.

"I dreamed I was with the Devil," Alina spoke, mumbling the words beneath her breath. "That's the song. It's from the soundtrack of some B horror movie I enjoy as a guilty pleasure."

"What's it mean?" I asked. "Why is it important?"

No one responded to my questions. My father and mother congregated in a tight powwow with Adam, Rachel, and Jake. I held Cambria, and we stood a few feet from the front door, barely in the living room. Fred and Daphne also stood, only a few feet from me. Alina remained at the front door, one foot inside the house, the other in the night. Everyone wore a blank expression—a classroom filled with students who did not know how to answer the teacher's question.

"Where's Maya?" Alina asked again.

"She's with the bird guy, and they're out having fun," I said, hoping I hadn't sounded as concerned as I felt. "That's all." I swallowed, allowing my hopeful sentiment to settle over Alina, maybe ease her mind a little.

"I'm calling Maya." Alina stepped onto the front porch and placed her phone to ear.

Everyone else remained in place, looking at each other with uncertainty painted across their faces.

"What's going on, August?" my dad asked. "Why are we huddled in this room in the dead of night?" He wasn't usually the face or voice of the marriage, but in stressful circumstances, he often made himself visible. My mom, who often lent her voice, made herself invisible in stressful situations. It's funny how adversity brings out our truest self.

I turned away from my parents without a word, exited the house, and removed the phone gifted to me from Quinn. I stepped onto the lawn, a few yards from where Alina paced on the porch, and I redialed the number.

"All accounted for," he said, humor lacing his voice. "All the chickens lay safe in their hen. Well, all but one." Quinn coughed a chuckle.

"Where's Maya? What did you do with her?"

"I haven't done a single thing to anyone."

"Where is she?"

"Why?"

"Why?" I asked, my voice rising. Heat flushed to my cheeks. "Why? Because I don't trust a word you say. Have you hurt her?"

"Can I be honest with you?"

"Please."

"The only people I have ever hurt in my entire life was that poor couple driving through town late last night. Even that was accidental. August, I only meant to scare them enough to keep them awake on their drive. That's it. Why do you think I'm not sleeping right now? I can't. Not with their blood on my hands, not with their lives weighing so heavily on my mind."

"You killed them?"

"The husband unfortunately passed at the hospital early yesterday morning. The wife showed promising signs of a full recovery, but the internal injuries have reared their ugly heads. The doctors now scramble to save her life."

"You're a psycho."

"I now understand how you must have felt after murdering Aaron Brooks. Tell me, August, should I dive head-first into booze like you did? I need something to help drown my restless thoughts."

I panted into the phone. I only saw red—the blood-soaked face of Quinn as I beat his features to a pulp with my bare knuckles.

"I promise, like you policing Galt and serving the community, I only wanted to help Wyman and Andrea Menard. I never intended for them to die. I only wished to scare them awake and keep them safe on the treacherous road late at night."

"That's it?" I asked, nearly roaring the question. "Your intentions were to scare random drivers on a dangerous highway and keep them awake?"

"More or less. I never expected they would crash. A mistake, I admit. An oversight on my end."

"What did you expect?"

"Honestly, I hoped they would survive and report the incident to the police, or seek other professional help. Either way, I have my ways and my resources. They would have contacted you eventually, and enticed you to investigate the ghost on Highway 1." Quinn sucked in air through his teeth. "I guess it worked in the end. So, their sacrifice wasn't in vain."

I pulled the phone from my ear, tempted to throw it as far as possible into the darkness. Instead, I placed it back to my head. "Why did you need them to contact me?"

"To give you the present, of course. I needed to communicate with you, but on a private line."

I closed my eyes, incapable of understanding Quinn's madness. Why had he painted a target on my back? Why me? Why?

"Where's Maya?" I asked.

"On her date with Mr. Evan Richards. They are having quite a wonderful time together. However, you will enjoy knowing that they both drank way too much alcohol and passed out before acting on their carnal desires. Currently, they sleep on his hotel bed as *The Birds* plays on the tube. Fitting, don't you think?"

My personal cell phone (not the cursed gift from Quinn) buzzed in my pocket. I fished it out and checked the caller—a number I didn't recognize. I debated ignoring it, but I had no further use of Quinn. My family was safe. According to him, Maya was safe. Could I trust him, though? He was insane, but I don't think he lied to me. The psycho had only wished to provide me with a cell phone so we could communicate privately. Not bothering to spare him a goodbye, I disconnected our line and answered the incoming call.

"August Watson."

Rapid, shallow breathing filled the other end of the line. I could hear the sheer terror in the broken gasps. In my years of working for the Galt Police Department, I had heard a similar response from people walking into their homes and finding their loved one's dead.

"I didn't know what to do," a male voice said after a few seconds.

I stiffened, freezing in place. I thought of Maya. Had that maniac lied to me about her, or kept truth from me. Did she lay in a hotel room bed with Evan Richards, as he said? Except, not sleeping.

"Who is this?" I asked.

"I didn't know who else to call."

"Who is this?" My voice rose.

Alina must have heard, must have noticed my tense posture. She drifted nearer to me, stopped five feet away, and stood still.

"I didn't do it," said the voice on the other end of the line. "I swear I didn't do it."

"Nick, is this you?"

In response to my question, the caller broke into incoherent sobs.

I waited a few seconds, allowing him to catch his breath and calm down before I asked him again, "Is this Nick?"

"No."

"Who is this?"

"Johnny."

"Okay, Johnny. What happened? What didn't you do?"

"I didn't want to call the cops," he said. "They would blame me like they blamed Nick. They would arrest me."

My body buzzed with adrenaline and anticipation. Blame him for what? Had he murdered Heather?

"Is Heather okay?" I thought of Nick arrested for murdering Christina.

"Heather?"

"Your fiancé. Is she okay?"

"Yes."

I cracked my neck. "Johnny, what's going on?"

"Nick's dead."

My breath hitched. "What?"

"Nick's dead."

My mind reeled, unable to comprehend Johnny's revelation. The Santa Cruz Police had brought Nick in for questioning twelve hours ago. Had they already allowed him to leave? Why so soon? Why hadn't anyone told me earlier? I should have called the department and introduced myself to the detectives, proposed that we work in conjunction on the case. Instead, I had trusted four sleep deprived young adults to hold it together.

I ran my fingers through my hair and exhaled. "What happened?"

"The Devil murdered Nick."

Nothing made sense anymore. Nothing.

The Devil, according to Cambria and Daphne, had visited her dreams earlier. Could it have jumped into three dreams in one night?

If it really was a sleep demon, then yes, I thought.

It wasn't a sleep demon, though. Like all my other cases, this one had a mundane explanation. This development offered another clue into learning the truth. I just had to find that clue. The devil lives in the details. So, how had the Devil visited two dreams in the same night? How did Cambria and Daphne relate to my clients? My other question...

"Nick's not in jail, Johnny?"

"No. They couldn't secure a confession, and they lacked evidence proving he murdered Chris. The lead detective believed him to be innocent. So, they released him." Johnny spoke through a sludge of sinuses, but more clearly and calmly than a few minutes prior. "Apparently, and this came from Nick, the detective didn't want to compromise their investigation by botching the interrogation. They would release Nick until they gathered more incriminating evidence. His apartment is an active crime scene, too. He had to rent a motel room."

I lowered my eyes and stared at the damp lawn and thought. A lot of different thoughts and emotions crowded my mind—Maya, Cambria, Quinn, the birds, this case, the murders—but I tried to wade through them and focus on the details.

"If the detective released Nick so soon, they would have trailed him."

"What do you mean?"

"I'm sure they followed him to catch him doing something suspicious. Maybe hopping on a bus out of town or heading to a buddy's house to lie low. Criminals, when guilty and feeling pressured by the law, act strangely. Their erratic behavior often creates opportunities during investigations."

Johnny went quiet for a second. "I don't see a cop car in the parking lot."

"They're most likely undercover."

"They would have watched me come into the motel room."

"Yeah."

"They'll think I murdered him."

"At first."

"What do I do?" Johnny made a series of short, staccato breaths as he inhaled. "He called me and asked if he could stay with Heather and me. I knew, though. After meeting with you, she must have felt guilty enough to tell me everything. I knew about her and him. I told Nick he couldn't come by. He rented a motel room, and he told me where."

"Johnny." I closed my eyes. "You went there to confront him?"

"I had to hear it from him. He was my brother. I had to hear him confess."

Johnny had a motive to murder Nick. He showed up at the motel room, where the homicide occurred. The police had an open and shut case.

"I need you to tell me exactly what happened?"

"We fought. I think I knocked him out. Then... then time froze. I blinked, and Nick was dead."

"How?"

"Like Chris had died. Skull completely crushed."

"Did you see anyone else in the room with you?"

"No. Nothing. No one. That's why I'm calling you and not the cops. Believe me. Please, believe me. I didn't kill him. I didn't. I wouldn't ever, even after what he and Heather did. I wouldn't. Please, find out who killed him. Please."

"Johnny," I said. "Johnny, calm down, okay? Breathe. Just answer my questions. Yes or no. Can you do that?"

"Yes."

"You learned of Nick's and Heather's affair?"

"Yes."

"You went to the motel alone?"

A pained squeak escaped from his throat. "Yes."

I wondered about Heather's wellbeing, but stuck to a single line of questioning for now. "You entered his motel room?"

"Yes."

"You two fought?"

"Yes."

"You blacked out, lost consciousness, whatever, and you woke up to find him dead?"

"Yes." His voice broke on that confirmation, a cry he couldn't swallow.

"Did you kill Nick Lane?"

A second of hesitation passed, maybe as he considered how to answer. "No."

"Who did?"

"The Devil in the Man's mask with a sledgehammer."

"The same who killed Chris?"

Again, hesitation. "Yes."

"Did you kill Christina Wyss?"

"No."

"Did Nick kill Christina Wyss?"

"No."

I took a second to gather my thoughts. What did all this information mean? How did I make sense of it? I had privately investigated the paranormal for five months now, and I had cracked a few impossible cases. But this one seemed to take the cake in absurdity. None of it made sense. How did a group of people share dreams? How did people die from someone attacking them in their dreams? How had someone murdered Nick right in front of Johnny without Johnny seeing anything?

"You and Nick fought?" I asked, circling back.

"Yes."

"You said you think you knocked out Nick?"

"I think so."

"Yes or no?"

"Yes."

I cracked a knuckle. "So, he could have fallen unconscious, which allowed the dream demon to enter his mind and murder him? If it happened in his head, this brutalizing murder, you wouldn't have seen the dream demon, right?"

"I don't know."

"You saw Nick unconscious but alive. A second later, he had a collapsed skull, and you saw him dead."

"Does that make sense?" Johnny asked.

"Hold on." I muted the phone and gestured for Alina to come over.

Her face blanched as worry overcame her. "Is it Maya? Is she okay?"

"I'm pretty sure Maya's on her date still, most likely passed-out drunk."

"How do you know that?"

"I can't explain right now, but you have to trust me. She's okay. I need your help, though."

"Okay."

I unmuted the phone and switched the call to the speaker. "Johnny," I said. "I have my assistant with me. She's incredibly intelligent. I'm going to share with her what happened. If I'm wrong at any point, please stop and correct me. I think she can offer us unique insight into what's happening."

"Okay," Johnny said.

I sighed and looked at Alina with a deep frown, my eyebrows lifted high. "Police released Nick Lane. They didn't have enough evidence to arrest him, so they had to let him go for the moment. He rented a motel room. Johnny showed up at the motel room after learning that Heather, his fiancé, and Nick had an affair."

"Not good," Alina said.

"Johnny and Nick fought. Johnny is pretty sure he knocked him out. As Johnny stared at Nick's unconscious body, Nick went from living to having a shattered and flattened skull in a blink."

"Dead?"

"Dead," I said.

"I didn't do it," Johnny said. "I swear. I only wanted to beat him up a little, force him into a confession. That's it."

"The dream demon broke Nick's hand, right?" Alina asked.

"Yeah," Johnny said.

"While Nick slept? The injury occurred in Nick's sleep, but he suffered the injury in real life?"

"Something like that."

Alina clicked her tongue. "Same as *A Nightmare on Elm Street*. Freddy's victims experience the actual physical damage they receive in the dream." She exhaled, vibrating her lips. "Okay. During Chris's murder, Nick claimed he saw no one else in the room with them. Johnny, think very hard about answering this next question, okay?"

"Okay."

"Did you see anyone else in the room with you two?"

"No."

"You didn't think long or hard about that."

"Because I know it. No one else was here."

"Did you kill him?"

"No."

"On accident, when you knocked him out? You didn't mean to do it. You punched him and he fell and hit his head awkwardly on the nightstand. It killed him. Did that happen?"

"No."

"So we have three theories," Alina said. She held up three fingers, dropping one as she counted. "One. Nick killed Christina. You killed Nick."

"I didn't kill him."

"Two." She dropped a second finger. "You killed Christina. You killed Nick."

Johnny moaned with frustration.

I held that theory as the likeliest possibility, which terrified me. What about Heather? Was she okay? Had Johnny, after she confessed, also brutally murdered her?

"Three," Alina said, dropping her last finger. "The dream demon killed Christina in her dream, thus killing her real life, same as he crushed Nick's hand in his dream, thus breaking his hand in real life. When you knocked Nick out, the dream demon pounced on his unconscious mind and murdered him, thus murdering him in real life, right before your eyes, without you even seeing or being able to process the act." Alina caught her breath for a half a second. "Objectively, Johnny, pretending you're a detective, which theory makes the most sense to you."

Johnny spoke through his broken sobs. "One or two."

"Which both paint a clear picture of you killing Nick."

"I didn't kill him!"

"Then what happened?" Alina asked. "Because if you didn't kill him, that means dream demons exist and haunted you and your friends for some unknown reason."

"I heard music!" Johnny screamed, a last-ditch effort to save himself.

"What music?" Alina asked. She glanced at me.

"The same song as always."

"Can you recall the lyrics?"

"No. I blinked. The music stopped. Nick was dead. That's what happened."

"Music?" Alina asked. "The same song you always hear in your dream?"

"Yes."

"Did you get knocked out, too? Did Nick knock you out?"

"I heard the music for a quick second. I blinked, and it ended. That's it."

"What does a dream demon want with you, Heather, Nick, and Chris?" Alina crossed her arms. She had a natural gift at this exercise—for cutting into people, speaking bluntly, getting them to move their tongues and answer her questions.

"What?" Johnny asked.

"This is crucial, Johnny, so answer it like your life depends on it. In *A Nightmare on Elm Street*, Freddy was a child murderer. The parents in the neighborhood burned him to death, so he sought revenge on them by murdering their children in their sleep. What does this Devil want to avenge? Why is it after you and your friends?"

Johnny sniffled. "Nick's the only one who ever hurt anyone. Who really, physically hurt someone. He served his time for that. He went to jail for four years."

Alina shook her head. "Hang up, August. Call the cops. He murdered Nick and Chris. There's no reason to entertain his sob story any longer."

"Stop, stop, stop. I didn't do it. I swear."

"I don't believe you," Alina said. "Do I believe what's obvious, or do I believe in a Devil haunting your dreams?"

"I don't care what you believe!" It took him a few tries, but Johnny eventually stuttered out the words, one more time, "I didn't do it."

"We'll be in touch," I said. "Report Nick's death. Tell the police exactly what happened. If you're innocent, the evidence will show that. But call the cops."

"I can't."

"Johnny," I said, "you can and you will. As you said, Nick was your brother. If you fear dying next, if you want his murderer and Chris's murderer caught, if you want to stop whoever is doing this, call the cops and tell them what happened. If you're lucky, they'll arrest you for murder, and you'll sit safely in a jail cell, away from the Devil. The truth will come to the surface, though, and if you're innocent, you're innocent. It's that simple."

Nothing is ever that simple.

Time to Go Home. Wednesday, May 3rd. 0251hrs.

I STEPPED BACK INTO the house, rubbing the back of my neck and craving a cup of coffee. A stress headache, compounded with fatigue, pulsed behind my eyes. Without a word to anyone, despite their wide, questioning gazes, I crossed the living room and entered the kitchen. I cleaned out the coffee machine and brewed another pot.

As the machine hissed and steamed, I leaned against the counter. I needed a second to breathe and catch my breath, to think and process.

Yesterday, someone had brutally murdered Christina Wyss. Now, Johnny called to report Nick's violent death. This dream demon case had shifted from shared nightmares to a serial killer carefully scheming and executing some violent revenge plot. The killer didn't choose its victims at random. Christine and Nick had dated since middle school, and they both knew Johnny and Heather for at least that long, as well. So, what connection did that group of people share with the killer? I had to learn that answer. If I believed Johnny's word that he hadn't murdered Chris or Nick, then who did? I had to find the connection.

Could I pull that off before anyone else died, though? How much time did I have to figure it out? Until Friday night? Tomorrow night? Now that Cambria and Daphne had experienced the Nightmare, had the Devil penciled them onto its hit list? I didn't have until tomorrow night. I had until the morning. The case was personal now, and I had to stop the Devil as quickly as possible.

The coffee machine beeped. I grabbed a mug and filled it with hot, steaming life, and I drank, hoping to declutter my crammed mind.

What worried me more than anything else was Daniel Quinn's involvement. He played me like a fiddle. He knew where I stayed. He knew who attended the trip with me. He knew about my case. He knew everything. How? Why did he care?

As my thoughts spiraled and grew in force like a hurricane building strength as it charges toward the shore, my mom shyly entered the kitchen. She stood across from me, leaning against the island.

Throughout the years, she had spent a small fortune on artificially making herself look young. I found the unnatural appearance of it all—lips too puffy, skin too tight and smooth, eyebrows too straight—unattractive. I never told her as much, but I know Adam let her know his thoughts on the whole cosmetic surgery front. Simply,

Adam—and I—thought she looked more like a wax sculpture than a living woman. Natural beauty always outperformed artificial beauty. The explosion of a trillion stars was more impressive than overlooking the lights of a city. An animal observed in its natural habitat was more terrifying and incredible than any luxurious car or private plane.

No manmade implementations could outshine nature.

In the dim light burning a soft yellow from beneath the upper cabinets, though, my mom looked beautiful standing before me—like I remembered her looking when I was still a little boy. Young and pretty and vibrant and filled with life.

I wanted to shoot across three feet of space separating us and jump into her arms and bury my face against her chest, as I had as a kid. I needed her hands in my hair, scratching my head, and her breath on my ear, whispering that everything would be okay.

That night had stripped me raw, to my barest emotions. I was nothing more than a kid who needed his mother to protect him from the world.

"Are you okay?" she asked.

I wrinkled my nose and squinted my eyes, swallowing tears and shaking my head.

"What's wrong?"

"I'm scared." I spoke plainly. I never dared lie to my mother.

I didn't have to dive into her embrace. She pushed off the island's counter and stepped to me. She wrapped her arms around me and pulled me into her. She didn't run her fingers through my hair, but she rubbed my back and nuzzled her chin against the top of my head, as I rested my face on her shoulder.

"You're allowed to be scared, Gussy," she said with a soft voice. "It's okay to be scared."

"I don't want to lose you."

"You won't."

"I don't want to lose any of you, but I don't know how to protect you."

"That's not your job."

"It's my job to protect my clients. I've failed to do that. Two of them are dead. I'm scared I won't be able to save the remaining two. What if I can't protect them? What if I don't find the killer in time?"

"You will. I know you will."

"You can't stay here," I said. "It's too dangerous now that Daphne and Cambria have experienced the dreams."

"I know."

I pulled away from her and looked into her eyes. They stared back at me with love and concern.

"I'm thinking we're going to head home tonight," she said after a long silence. "After your panicked call earlier, considering the baby, Rachel and Jake feel its best they head back and sleep in their own house. Jake has a shotgun stashed beneath the bed. I think he feels naked here without it. Your father and I drove them out here, so we'll have to drive them back. I'm going to ask Adam to join us, too."

"We promised to take him out for his twenty-first." I spoke the first thing that popped into my head. It's funny what surfaces in stressful situations, what the mind latches onto and worries about.

"You can celebrate when you've solved your case. Just don't let him drink too much."

I smiled and nodded. "Mom, thank you for coming."

"I had fun. I'm glad we came. But you're here for work, and I think you should focus on working now." She touched my cheek with her wrinkly fingers—something she hadn't bothered to infuse youth back into. "I'm proud of you."

The words sucker punched me. I gasped, breathless.

"I know I'm sometimes harsh and critical of my children. I know I often speak without thinking and in the worst possible way—criticizing and judging when things fall out of my control. I pray about it. I really do. It's hard, though. It's difficult to trust that the world will take care of my babies and not hurt them." She softly smiled. "It's an incredible feeling, though, to see my baby taking care of the world. I'm scared, and I don't like what you do, but I am proud of you for doing it. I'm sorry I couldn't tell you that sooner."

I lowered my eyes, not wanting her to see me cry... failing.

She reached out and wiped the tears off my cheeks with her thumb. "Who knows, maybe I'll start trusting Adam and Rachel, too." My mom snickered, as if that would never happen.

I mirrored her laugh and shook my head. "Mom, it's not about trusting them. It's trusting yourself. It's trusting that you parented the right way and prepared us for what life had in store."

"That's the problem then. I don't trust myself."

"You know I wouldn't lie to you, right?"

"Sometimes I wish you did."

"You had your faults as a mom, but what mom doesn't? In the end, you loved us unconditionally. You loved us with your entire soul. That's the best you could have done. Trust in your love."

"For being such a dummy most of the time, you have a lot of wisdom."

"Do as I say, not as I do," I said, repeating a sentiment my father used to always share with us children.

My mom and I shared a much-needed laugh, and we hugged one more time. We left the kitchen and returned to the living room to confront the rest of the crew.

I pulled Cambria aside and whispered to her, not wanting to put her on the spot in front of everyone. "My family is leaving for home right away. You're welcome to take my car and head back, as well."

Fred stood near us, and he must have heard my proposal. "She can ride with Daphne."

"Ride with me where?" Daphne asked. She crossed her arms and stepped away from Fred, frowning at him. "I'm not going anywhere. Who are you to tell me where to go?"

"Your husband."

"Funny, seems like whenever I tell you to do something, you seem fit to ignore it, though I'm your wife."

"Like what?" Fred asked.

"Like what? Like mowing the yard. When's the last time you mowed the yard? It's looking like a meadow out there."

"I've been busy with work."

"You answer phones at work."

"Why don't we hire someone to do that?"

"We're not hiring someone to mow fifty-square-feet of yard. You're more than capable."

"Well, you're not staying here, especially not after having that dream."

"I'll make you a deal," Daphne said.

"Bet."

"When you listen to me about mowing the lawn, I'll listen to you about where I can or can't stay."

"I'm staying, too," Cambria said. She held both my hands and looked at me with inarguable eyes. She wouldn't budge from her stance; I saw that plain as day on her face. "I refuse to sleep alone after the nightmare. If it happens again, I don't want to be alone. I definitely don't want to be three hours away from you."

I exhaled and surrendered to her demand. "Okay. You're staying." I shifted my attention to Adam. "Happy birthday, Man. Sorry it's starting off like this."

"Most exciting birthday I've ever had."

"We can't make good on our promise later. But we'll take you out once we're back at home."

"I'm holding you to that."

"I hope you do." I sniffled, still a little allergic from the conversation with my mom a few minutes prior. I regarded everyone in the room. "My investigation has shifted into a double homicide. I'll have to contact Santa Cruz Police Department and share with them what little information I have collected on this case. Hopefully, they'll want to collaborate and share any pertinent evidence they have secured. It's my goal to identify the Devil and stop it from hurting anyone else."

As I spoke, Daniel Quinn crossed my mind. It was also my goal to identify him, to find him, and to stop him from interfering with my life. Knowing he existed strained me mentally. At any moment, he could lash out and harm someone I cared for.

"What's the plan?" Fred asked.

"We'll recharge for the rest of the night, try to catch some sleep. In the morning, you'll hang back here with Daphne and Cambria."

"And you?" Cambria asked.

"Alina and I will head out and do some legwork. I need to meet with my clients. I need to speak to the lead detective on the murder investigation. Alina's going to dig through the histories of Chris, Nick, Johnny, and Heather. We're finding the Devil, if we have to go to Hell to stop him."

Skull-Splitting Headache. Wednesday, May 3rd. 0505hrs.

A STRANGE, OLD-TIME SONG woke Maya from her sleep. Fast-paced piano filled the hotel room like sand fills an hour glass—a sprinkle at first, but before long, a pile existed. The song touched Maya's consciousness like a tickle, and it became more and more aggressive until it woke her.

She squeezed her eyelids shut and tried to crush a headache splitting her skull in half. Not only that, but she attempted to suffocate the song from existing—that loud, cacophonous, fast-paced, ragtime song.

As she groaned and rolled onto her side, blindly searching for her phone with her hand to check the time (it couldn't be later than six, and she needed more sleep) a gruff voice spoke along to the merry melody. A voice that existed within the room, not within her dream.

"I had a dream last night that filled me full of fright."

Maya bolted upright and sat in the bed, eyes wide. She scanned the room. "Evan," she said, whispering, her volume muffled by an obstruction inside her mouth.

She reached between her lips and removed a wet, crumpled piece of paper.

A voice spoke-sang around her, disembodied but not coming through the hotel alarm like the music. It came from everywhere and nowhere. "... I was with the Devil below."

Maya flattened the wadded paper out. It was damp with saliva, but not ruined. The ink had smeared some, but not enough to make the handwriting indecipherable.

Tell August Watson to cease his investigation. Otherwise, you're next.

"... merry crowd that came to witness the show."

Maya blinked, and the hotel room subtly shifted, like a shimmer of hot air on a summer day.

No more obnoxious, old time music. No more half-singing, half-speaking from a disembodied voice.

Beside Maya, Evan slept, snoring loudly. Her phone rested on the nightstand, as did an alarm clock that showed the time—a little past five in the morning. Her splitting headache remained, though, as did the crumpled, wet note. Maya held it in her hand, as if she had brought it back from her dream. Had she? How else would she have come into possession of the note?

"Hey," she said, sharply whispering. She shook Evan's shoulder. "Wake up!"

He awoke with a startle, groaning and rubbing his head. His hangover must have slammed into his consciousness like a twenty-pound sledgehammer. "What's going on?" Evan asked, his voice ragged. "What time is it?"

"Five."

"In the morning?"

"Yes."

"Why are we awake? What's wrong?"

"What's this?" Maya shoved the note into his hand.

Evan reluctantly accepted the paper, turned it around, and read the handwriting. "What is it?"

"I'm asking you."

"I don't know. Where did you get it?"

"From my mouth."

Evan grimaced. "In your mouth? I don't... what's that mean?"

"The note was in my mouth. I thought you maybe crumpled it up and shoved in there."

"Why would I do that?"

"I don't know."

"It wasn't me." Evan dropped the note on the comforter and rolled away from Maya. "I'm going back to sleep. Wake me up around eight, if you don't mind."

"You're going to have to set your alarm. I have to go." Maya stepped out of bed. The room whirled around her, as if part of a spinning ride on the boardwalk. She reached for the nightstand and dropped her head, closed her eyes, breathed through the dizziness.

Had she drank that much? She didn't think so. Maybe the alcohol paired with the lack of sleep worked double against her body. Maybe it was that she would turn twenty-nine in October. That was enough to make her want to vomit.

"Where are you going?" Evan asked, his voice groggy and distant, half-asleep again.

"To show August the note."

"Will I see you again?"

"I hope so," Maya said.

"Leave your number?"

"If you're into me, I'm sure you can find me." Maya, after regaining her composure, leaned over the bed, hoping she didn't lose her balance and face plant onto Evan. She kissed the side of his face. "I hope you find me."

Maya grabbed her phone off the nightstand and tapped the screen. It didn't activate. She pressed the side button, holding it, and her phone fired on. When had she turned it off? Maya couldn't recall. She never turned off her phone, unless she needed a software update and a restart was necessary.

When it activated, notification after notification pinged. She switched the volume to silent, hoping she hadn't reawakened Evan, and she crept out of the room into the hotel's hallway.

Alina. Alina. Alina. Missed calls. Voicemails. Texts. August had also called her. Every alert time stamped during the middle of the night. Were they concerned about her, or had something happened to them? A heavy, unsettling feeling landed in the pit of her stomach. Her hands trembled—maybe from the hangover and the lack of sleep, but maybe from the worry.

She dialed Alina's phone.

"Answer the phone. Come on."

Nothing.

Maya called August.

"Maya," he said, awake and alert. Had he slept last night? Probably not. "You okay?"

"I'm okay. I'm fine. Are you okay?"

"Yeah."

"What's going on?"

"You coming to the house?"

"On my way."

"Okay. I'll update you once you're here."

"Hey," Maya said.

"Hey."

"I dreamed of it, I think. Of our Freddy Krueger. He passed me a note in my dream."

Silence. At first, Maya thought the line disconnected. Sometimes hotels are like that with cell phones. She pulled the phone from her ear, saw the seconds still clocking, and returned it. "August?"

"What did you say?"

"I brought the note back with me, from my dream."

"What note?"

Maya shared what the letter had said without having to read it. The words had scarred into her mind.

"Get back here immediately."

"I'm going to need some coffee. Do you have coffee?"

A Second Chance.
Wednesday, May 3rd. 0613hrs.

THE SUN SAT LOW in a brilliantly colored sky. A few clouds hovered across the horizon, aflame in purple and orange and pink.

I sat on the back patio, sipped coffee, and watched the sun slowly raise into the sky. I thought of the case and everything that surrounded it, involved with it. Cambria, Daphne, and Maya had all experienced the song, had all dreamed of the Devil. Why? To scare me away? How had the Nightmare infected those closest to me?

As I pounded my head, thinking of every viable solution, Cambria sat beside me at the table. She palmed her coffee mug and stared across the horizon. After a second, she leaned sideways and kissed me on the side of the mouth.

"I hope that's okay," she said. "Kissing you."

"I see nothing wrong with it."

"Good." She leaned over and touched my chin, pivoted my face toward her, and kissed me full on the mouth. "That okay, too?"

"I like that." I kissed her. She tasted like coffee, which I enjoyed. "About last night. I'm sorry."

"Sorry? For what?"

"How I reacted to Maya having a date. It was immature of me and disrespectful to you. Even if I felt a certain way, I shouldn't have reacted like a child."

"We've moved on from that. It's okay." Except, her, 'It's okay,' sounded less than convincing.

I shook my head. "No, it's not." I sighed. "I was wrong a lot last night. Mostly, I was wrong about my feelings."

"What do you mean?"

"I don't want a purely physical relationship with you. That's not why I invited you on this trip. I don't want to only have sex with you, then not see you again when we're back in Sacramento. If it's okay with you, I want to continue to see you after this trip. I want to see you every day."

Cambria grimaced. "That's a little desperate—a bit much. How about every other day? I enjoy breathing, and every day sounds a little suffocating."

"Well, I really like you. I like you a lot."

"Really liking me and liking me a lot are the same thing. You're repeating yourself now."

"It's because this is hard for me, and you're not making it any easier."

"I don't think you deserve easier after last night."

I couldn't argue over that. "I have complicated feelings toward Maya, but they're also simple."

"That makes no sense."

"I love her, but not like that. I love her as a friend. I've never had a female friend before, though, and I think that confuses me. I want to give us, you and me, a shot, though. A real shot. Can we do that? Can we try that? Not a stop and go thing, either, like we've been doing."

"Just a go thing?"

"A go thing," I said.

"I can get on board with that. But only under one condition."

"What's that?"

"The sex was fun last night, but it came from a place of no-string-attached. Do you know what I mean? If we're really going to give this a shot, I want to move slow."

"You gave and now you're taking sex away from me?"

"Is that a problem?"

I pretended to think about it, but I already knew the answer. "No. Not a problem." I leaned over and kissed her cheek, and we watched the sun rise over the ocean together.

Out and About. Wednesday, May 3rd. 0641hrs.

ALINA AND I SAT in a dingy, dusty, cluttered office. A bookshelf filled with binders vomiting files stood to my right. A desk rested against the left wall, covered in unbound papers and facedown books and half-empty coffee cups.

Detective Todd Phillips of the Santa Cruz Police Department sat on the other side of the desk, slouched in his swivel chair. He pinched a wad of tobacco and placed in his mouth. He sucked on the plug, grabbed one of the many coffee cups, and spit a dark stream in it.

My stomach rolled.

"Disgusting," Alina said. She was more apt to speak her mind. "Chewing is worse than smoking."

"The sound of a child offering her opinion is worse than learning your dog of twelve years has a week to live," Phillips said. "If you talk too much, Miss Little Girl, I might find myself bored with you. When I'm bored, I find something more exciting to spend time on. Life is too short for boredom, and bored hands are the tools of the Devil."

"Idle hands are the Devil's workshop," Alina said.

"Excuse me."

"You quoted it wrong."

"I'm not quoting anything, young lady. Mind your mouth now." Phillips turned his wet eyes to me. They sank into his sallow face like beady eyes on a teddy bear—though he was anything but a teddy bear. "You tell your little bimbo to keep her mouth shut or leave and wait outside. I'm not a man to be corrected in my office."

I had an urge to correct Detective Phillips with a few well-placed fists, but I kept my composure. We had stopped at the police department to speak with the lead detective about Nicholas Lane and Christina Wyss. I couldn't flush his information or possible cooperation down the drain, no matter how irksome and brash he was.

Alina hopped from her chair. "I think I'm thirsty. Where can I find a vending machine?"

"Out in the hall," Phillips said. "Take your time, little lady. You won't be missed."

Without a word—which honestly terrified more than if she had released the fury of thoughts resting on her tongue—Alina marched out of the room, leaving me alone with the man.

Phillips spat into his cup, crossed his arms, and leaned back in his chair. "I see why you keep her around. She's spunky, and not bad to look at."

"She's sixteen," I said.

"An investment." He grinned and sucked air through his teeth and shook his head.

I really wanted to break his nose. My fingers clenched into fists, and my nails dug into my palms. "I'm August Watson, a paranormal investigator from Sacramento."

"I know that name." Phillips wrinkled his nose. "How do I know that name? August Watson." He snapped his fingers and pointed at me. "You shot and killed that kid who pulled a gun on you."

"An airsoft gun."

"Still a gun. How were you supposed to know the difference? You did what you had to do. That's what I call good police work."

I bit my cheeks hard, tasting blood in my mouth.

"What did you say you did? Paranormal investigator? What on God's green Earth does that even mean? You investigate ghosts?"

"Exactly."

"Your department has something like that?"

"I don't work in law enforcement anymore. It's private."

"Money good?"

"Not really."

"Why you do it then?"

"This isn't about me, Detective. Johnny Lantz hired me. That's who this is about. He, Heather Thompson, Christina Wyss, and Nicholas Lane hired me."

At the mention of Christina and Nick, the detective's demeanor changed. His round shoulders stiffened and his jaw clenched. "Hired you for what?"

"They claim a Devil is haunting their dreams."

Phillips spat another stream of black liquid into the cup.

"This Devil appears to them in their sleep. According to Nick, while Christina slept, the Devil killed her, and she died. Johnny said the same about Nick. He said he watched it happen. Nick was alive. Johnny blinked, and Nick's head had caved in."

"Freddy Krueger, huh?" Phillips asked. "That movie terrified me as a kid. I don't think I slept for almost a week after watching it."

"This is serious. Two people have died. Brutally murdered. I would like to find out who did it and why. More than that, I would like to prevent anyone else from dying."

"No one else is dying, Mr. Watson."

I stared at him with a doubtful gaze and waited for him to expand.

"We arrested Johnny... Johnny Lantz. He shared the entire story with me already in a blubbery, messy conversation. People snap, you know that, right? Emotions work like a sledgehammer. Pun intended." The detective smirked, proud of himself.

"Did you find a sledgehammer at Nick's apartment?"

Phillips eyed me.

"At the motel room?"

"Mr. Watson, emotions beat and beat and beat against our mentality, until we snap. The stronger and more negative emotions we feel, the more powerful the strike against our psyche. That's what happened. Johnny snapped. That's it. He learned that his little fiancé ate at another restaurant—his caged bird who he had fed since middle school. So, he retaliated. Christina first. Why not let Nick mentally suffer a little, just like poor Johnny had suffered. When we released Nick, though, Johnny took justice into his hands. That's the story. Case closed, Mr. Watson."

"But you didn't find a sledgehammer at the motel?" I asked.

"We aren't releasing certain details of the investigation."

"Yet, you had tailed Nick from the police station. Some plain-clothes officer, maybe yourself, watched Johnny barge into the motel room. Did you notice anyone else enter? Did you notice Johnny bring a sledgehammer in or take one out? Yet, the murder happened with a sledgehammer? Where is it?"

"Johnny killed him, Mr. Watson."

"What does Johnny say?"

"What every guilty criminal says. 'I'm innocent.'" Phillips showed off teeth stained with tobacco.

"What time did you arrest him?"

"He called last night to report the crime around... oh, I don't know." Phillips moved some papers around on his desk, found a report, and read it. "A little before 0300hrs."

"What do you make of the song?"

"What song?"

I thought of Cambria, Daphne, and Maya. They had experienced the Devil's presence last night and Maya early this morning. Nick in a motel. Maya in a hotel. Cambria and Daphne in the rental home. Had Johnny murdered Nick? If so, how had he pulled that trick off while having to visit Cambria, Daphne, and Maya?

I hoped the detective's hunch proved correct.

"What song, Mr. Watson?" Detective Phillips asked, breaking me from my thoughts.

"The song they all hear before the Devil appears."

"Do you know the song?"

"It's called, *At the Devil's Ball*. It's from 1913. You know of anyone who might have musical knowledge or interest to fit that description?"

Phillips sucked on the tobacco, sucking the juice from it. "Not off the top of my head. There's a lot of strange folk in Santa Cruz, though. I'm sure someone fits that bill."

I cracked my knuckles. "Can you tell me anything more about that group of people? Anything peculiar—their upbringing, juvenile offenses, their reputation in this town... anything at all?"

"Oh, yeah," Phillips said with a grin. "I can tell you two of them are dead, murdered by their good buddy, Johnny Lantz."

This meeting wasn't going anywhere. Detective Phillips was about as helpful as a blind traveler offering directions in a city they had never visited.

"Well, Detective," I said, "thank you for your time and your service to this community." I grunted as my hip fired with a dull ache when I stood.

"Can I tell you something, Mr. Watson?"

"I would prefer not," I said, tired of the detective.

Before he responded to my denial, Alina threw the door wide open. "Hi, Boys. August, we have to leave. Goodbye, Mr. Walrus." She smiled at Phillips, turned away, then looked back over her shoulder. "I would hate to leave you in a state of confusion, though you're probably accustomed to it. But to help you understand the comparison, I said Mr. Walrus because you're old—like long in the tooth. Bald. And well, your body composition isn't too far off. Blubbery and soft. Anyway, August, we should go. I learned a little tidbit of fun information."

"Have a nice day, Detective Phillips," I turned my back to him and exited his office with Alina.

She moved through the police station with expediency, probably expecting for Phillips to chase after us after he processed her insult.

Once outside and breathing ocean air in the cool morning, Alina looked at me and laughed like only a kid can laugh. One of those high-pitched, uncontrollable, folded over laughs with train-like momentum. I don't think she could have stopped if she wanted to. That kind of laughter had long vanished from me, but it was contagious.

I smiled and chuckled from my throat. "You're trying to get us arrested?"

Alina stood and staggered toward my car, wiping tears from her eyes. I unlocked the vehicle, and we loaded inside.

Alina continued to hiccup her amusement. She breathed hard to catch her breath. "Did you see his face? His little tiny eyes on that big, flabby, bald head. He looked more like a walrus than ever." She fell forward, once more possessed with pure amusement.

"Where are we going?" I asked. "We should get out of here before the entire force falls on us."

"Okay," Alina said, employing labor-breathing techniques. "Okay. Gull Cafe."

"Where?"

"Just type it into your navigation. We—me, Evan, and Maya—had coffee there yesterday. They have newspapers chronicling the history of Santa Cruz all over the place. I skimmed a headline while Evan and Maya ogled each other, but I thought little of it then."

I steered the car toward Gull Cafe and trusted Alina's hunch more than Detective Phillips' arrest. Johnny hadn't visited Maya, Cambria, and Nick in one night. I couldn't believe that. How could he break into the rental home? How had he entered Maya's hotel room? It made no sense.

"I'll fast forward a little," Alina said. "First off, were you proud of me?"

"For what?"

"Uh, for what? For not grabbing Detective Walrus' gun and shooting a hole through his ugly face. I separated myself from the situation."

"I'm very proud of you."

"Thank you. Second, while cooling off, I noticed a young officer sitting at the reception desk. She was chatting up a middle-aged lady. That lady was asking frantic questions about—"

"Johnny," I said.

"Bingo."

"His mom?"

"You're on fire. Anyway, I drifted into the waiting room and conveniently placed myself next to the woman biting her nails and staring blankly at the wall."

"You spoke to Johnny's mom?"

"No, I just sat beside her and enjoyed the way she smelled. Like laundry left in the washer for too long, in case you're wondering."

"I wasn't. I'm wondering what you asked her."

"I told her I worked for August Watson, California's top paranormal investigator under the world's foremost authority on all things paranormal: Tempest Michaels and Blue Moon. I informed her that her son hired our services, and we believed him innocent of any crimes. That pried the seal off her lips and got her tongue moving. Oh, boy!"

"What did she say?"

"First, she wouldn't stop mentioning Johnny was innocent. 'He's innocent. He's innocent.' Like a parrot stuck in a cycle of one annoying phrase, over and over. 'He's innocent.' Each time, I said, 'I believe you.'

Finally, she looked at me with wide, desperate eyes. I told her we could help Johnny if she answered a few questions. Eagerly, like a boy about to lose his virginity, she agreed."

I secretly wished I had questioned the woman, but I trusted whole-heartedly Alina's abilities. Remaining silent, I waited for her to continue.

"Johnny and Nick knew each other forever. Johnny's mom, Patricia—"

Like the woman I danced with, the woman who danced with the Sacramento Vampire, I thought.

"... never liked Nick. Apparently, his family was rough around the edges, and she didn't like the idea of their opinions influencing Johnny's young mind. Johnny argued with her, though, claiming Nick was a good kid, just confused. He said he would influence Nick's mind and behaviors, not the other way around. Anyway, Patricia trusted her son enough to allow him to hang out with Nick, but only at school or if Nick went to their house. She didn't want Johnny going to his place."

I thought that sounded awfully familiar to my mom's parenting.

"The boys met the girls in middle school."

"We know all this," I said.

"They formed a clique. Them four versus the world. Apparently, Heather had also suffered an abnormal childhood. Patricia Lantz never liked her. She liked it less when Johnny proposed to her."

I recalled my meeting with Heather in the dive bar. She had a drunk, lonely mom and no father. According to her, Nick understood her pain, because he had endured similar pain. That was their connection, their attraction.

"Anyway, it was Heather and Nick's idea," Alina said.

"What was?"

"The prank."

"The prank?" I asked.

"Contrary to what Mommy wanted to believe, Johnny allowed Nick to influence him that time. Apparently, Heather knew this family somehow, and she hated the son her age. Hated him. He had a younger brother, too, who she also hated. His parents weren't just rich, they were *rich*. Also, he had parents, plural, though divorced, present and active in his life. I guess Heather would occasionally stay over at his house."

Everything grouped in my head. It didn't fit together yet, but it sat on my tongue like a word I couldn't quite come up with.

"Heather hated seeing how good life could be. It was like a tease, you know? I understand that. I hate some kids I know for that same reason—they have it all."

Heather had also shared this story with me. Who had she stayed with? What name had she shared?

"Daryl?" I asked. "Was that the kid's dad?"

"I don't know. Why?"

"Heather shared a similar story with me. Daryl had a son who lived with him, one younger than Heather, I believe. Davie. That's what she called him, and he hated it. Davie had an older brother with some kind of disability who lived with their mom."

Alina pointed at me. "The kid with the disability. That's him. Did Heather tell you what she did to that poor boy with everything... with everything but a normal physical appearance. That was his disability, you know. He looked different."

"What do you mean?"

"He suffered Treacher Collins syndrome."

I narrowed my eyes and thought back. "Why does that sound familiar?"

"Daryl was the dad. Daryl Shaye. Davie, the brother. David Shaye. The kid they bullied, the one who lived with his mom, he was and is Maxwell Shaye."

"Wait, rewind. What?"

"The owner of our vacation rental knows our clients well."

"What do you mean? What happened?" The grouping in my head fell into place. Maxwell had keys to our vacation home. He could have easily entered the house without setting off any alarms. I grabbed my phone from the cupholder and scrolled to Heather's number. "What did they do to him?"

"Max's mom homeschooled him because of the condition. Kids can be harsh, you know? Anyway, Heather knew about him. I don't know why she had the idea or why they all agreed to do it, but they kidnapped him one day after school."

"Kidnapped him?"

"Coaxed him out of the house, asked him to hang out with them. He agreed, not having many friends. I don't know all the details. Patricia said they would always put a brown bag over his head and tell him he was too ugly to be seen in public. I guess that had gone on for a while, them bullying him."

"Middle schoolers?"

"Kids are cruel."

"What happened?"

"A lot of things. Patricia didn't know everything, but she knew enough to break into tears as she relived what her precious boy had done to Maxwell. The culminating incident, though, the one that broke their corrupt relationship, happened near the end of eighth grade. They gave Maxwell a duck mask, for the *Ugly Duckling*. They biked across town to an isolated spot, stripped him of all his clothes, other than the mask, did God knows what else, stole his bike, and pedaled away."

My heart tightened in my chest. It hurt for Maxwell. To what end had those kids tortured him? Why?

"Apparently, he didn't move from the spot they had left him for a day. His dad called the cops and everything. They found him like sixteen hours later, still naked, digging through a dumpster and looking for food. He was too embarrassed to walk back home naked."

I pulled into the cafe parking lot, turned off the car, and stared out the windshield at nothing in particular. "You think he's the Devil?"

"A mask of a Man to cover his face," Alina said. "The mask of a normal face to cover his abnormal face. He has keys to our rental home, so he could have entered Cambria's and Daphne's room. Also, we told him we were here to investigate the Devil. He probably did whatever he does to them to dissuade you from pursuing the case."

I cracked my wrists. "How did he kill them in their dreams, though? That's what I don't understand. How did he get to Maya in her hotel room?"

Alina turned to me and smiled like she knew all the secrets in the world. "I'll show you the answer to that last question." Alina unbuckled and stepped out of the car.

"Wait," I said. "I have one thing to do first."

"I'll meet you inside then. I want a lemonade." Alina crossed the parking lot and entered the Gull Cafe.

I called Heather.

She answered on the third ring, her voice tired and raspy.

"I asked you a very pointed question," I said, not holding back my frustration. "You lied to me."

"What?"

"Do you, Nick, Christina, and Johnny know anyone that would want to harm any of you?"

"No," she said. "Not that we know of."

"What about your childhood buddy, the one you hated so much? Daryl's son."

"Who?" The word sounded more like a question to buy time and think of an answer rather than confusion to what I had asked.

"Davie's brother. Maxwell Shaye. What about him?"

"How do you know about him?"

"It's my job to upturn every stone. Had you shared this information earlier, Christina and Nick could still be alive."

"It's not Max," she said. "It can't be. He couldn't have killed them." It sounded like she was trying to convince herself more than me. "Besides, he's worked so hard to become a pillar in this community. He has money and power and influence. Why throw that away for revenge?"

"People do a lot of crazy things for revenge."

Heather sniffled and gasped. "They arrested Johnny for Nick's murder."

"I know."

"He didn't do it."

"I know."

"Will you help him?"

"If you stop withholding information from me, I'll have a better chance at helping him."

"What do you want to know? I'll tell you anything."

"Who are you with right now?"

"No one."

"Where are you?"

"Mine and Johnny's place."

"Go somewhere public and safe. I'll call you in an hour to check on you."

"You're going to find the Devil?"

I stared across the parking lot, not daring to lie to Heather. "I hope so." I hung up the phone and called Fred.

"We're all alive," he answered, his words mumbled. I guessed he was probably chewing on something.

"Maxwell Shaye is our primary suspect."

"The owner of this place?"

"Yeah," I said. "I don't want to tip him off to our knowledge. If you see him, though, you have my permission to detain him."

"What if he has a sledgehammer?"

"You're three times his size. Figure something out." I hung up the phone, exited my Honda Civic, and headed toward Gull Cafe.

The Third to Dance. Wednesday, May 3rd. 0709hrs.

HEATHER STARED AT HER phone after disconnecting with August. She sighed, knowing he was right. The least safe place at the moment was alone in her apartment. She was beyond exhausted. If she dozed off for even a minute, the Devil could appear in her dreams and murder her, as it had murdered Chris and Nick.

Heather shivered at the thought of her friends brutally killed. Anger sparked and fizzled, like trying to ignite a flame during a storm. Her tiredness wouldn't even permit proper rage to fuel her with energy. Instead, her mind fogged and her thoughts sludged through the thick mud. The Devil had killed her friends, not Johnny. Yet, Johnny sat in a prison cell, wrongly accused of the homicides.

"That's where I should go," she said aloud, her voice sounding strange in the apartment with no one but herself to hear it.

Still, she would listen to August and go somewhere public and safe. What was safer than a police station? Maybe they would allow her to visit Johnny.

Did she want to see him, though? Could she bare to show him her face after what she had confessed?

After sharing her darkest secret with August yesterday, guilt had consumed her like it never had before. The shock of Chris's death combined with her fatigue had convinced her to confess her affair to her fiancé.

Johnny hadn't taken the news well. He had sat stone-faced and silent for a solid minute, staring blankly across the room.

Heather had allowed him his time to process, but each second grew longer and longer. After so long, she couldn't stand the heavy tension. "Johnny," she had said, reaching out and touching his hand.

He pulled away, as if a spider had crawled across his skin. He jumped to his feet. "Don't follow me. Don't call me. Just... leave me alone."

"Johnny, I'm so sorry. It only happened once That was it. I was so scared and vulnerable and confused."

"Then why did you say yes to me?" Johnny waved his hands in the air, as if erasing the question. "Don't answer that. Don't follow me or try to contact me. I need... I need time. Okay? Give me that. I think you owe me that." He turned, opened the door, and gently closed it behind him, leaving Heather alone.

He contacted her hours later from jail, sobbing on the other end of the line that the Devil murdered Nick. Heather believed him, too. She had to believe him, right? She had to stand by him, now more than ever. Johnny hadn't killed Nick, despite what seemed obvious. He definitely hadn't killed Chris.

Right?

Heather grabbed her car keys from the bowl on the kitchen counter. She would head to the jail and visit Johnny. If she could see his face, she would know if he told the truth or not. She would know if he murdered Nick. She just had to sit down with him.

As she walked to the door, Johnny's old record player turned on, scratchy at first, but clearing after a second. It played the ragtime tune—the same one she always heard in her dreams; the same one that always accompanied the Devil's presence.

Heather didn't wait for the Nightmare to step into view. Her heart sprinted, and she followed, racing across the kitchen, to the door, threw it open, and lurched into the apartment's hallway.

She staggered back across the kitchen toward her and Johnny's bedroom.

"What?" she gasped, confused at how she had reappeared inside her apartment after leaving. Heather glanced over her shoulder, seeing the closed door. She ran back to it, opened it again.

The Devil, in its three-piece suit and the masked face of a man, greeted her. It held a sledgehammer downward, leaning on it like a walking stick.

Heather turned away from the Nightmare and darted across the kitchen toward her room. There was a window leading to a fire escape there.

In high school, Heather had ran track. Not well enough to draw college scholarships, but well enough to compete at a high school level. Heather had continued to run, though more cross-country, after high school, competing in 5ks and half-marathons and a few full marathons. Occasionally, she hopped the local high school's fence and sprinted on their track, just to see if she still had it. Mostly, she still had it.

As she dashed across the kitchen, Heather moved faster than she had ever ran in her life. But she didn't go anywhere. The floor moved like a treadmill, and it kept pace with Heather's speed.

She glanced over her shoulder. The door was tightly closed. The Devil gone.

Heather slowed, as did the floor's rotation. She held back sobs.

"I had a dream last night that filled me full of fright." The Nightmare stepped through the front door without opening it, like a ghost phasing through solid matter.

Heather ran again, and the floor fired back up. It glided beneath her feet and kept her from fleeing and escaping.

The Devil walked across the treadmill floor. Walked right across as if the floor didn't move at all. It raised the sledgehammer over its head, laughing and singing.

Heather closed her eyes, and she never opened them again.

Called Away. Wednesday, May 3rd. 0709hrs.

Fred stood in the doorway like a big, dumb, hairless bear. Maya sucked on her teeth and debated how to handle the dilemma. She opted to rationalize before resorting to physical violence. But if she had to, she would resort to physical violence,.

"Move your big, dumb body, or I will hurt you."

"August told me to watch you." Fred lowered his voice, nearly whispering. "Maxwell is our suspect. It's my job to keep you safe."

"It's your job to stop acting like a chauvinistic pig. I don't need a man to save me or protect me or make my decisions for me."

"You're going to play that card? That's going to work with me."

Maya growled. "If I want to leave this house to confront Maxwell by myself, all alone, not even your big-for-nothing self can stop me."

"I'm only trying to help."

"I'm not a little baby."

"You act like one."

"You act like one. And you look like one. An oversized baby with a big, giant, dumb-dumb head."

"What's a dumb-dumb head?"

"You know exactly what it is, because you have one. Now, go help someone who needs it," Maya said. "Watch August's girl toy. Or your wife. Not me, though. It creeps me out when you fix your doughy eyes on me."

Fred sighed and lowered his shoulders. "Think this through."

"I'm going to meet with Evan. He's a good dude with big muscles, and he will protect me from the sleep demon. Besides, I'm working on an article about the bird situation, and he uncovered some information he wanted to share with me."

Maya didn't lie about that. Evan had contacted her fifteen minutes ago. Apparently, he had called *Here & Now*, asked for Maya, claiming he had a lead on a story and would only share the pivotal information with her. Jonah, Maya's boss, who only ever saw dollar signs, shared Maya's personal number with the stranger. So, Maya had to add a boundaries conversation with her boss to her to-do list.

"Brayden wants to meet," Evan had said.

"Who is this?" Maya asked, though she had recognized his smooth, confident voice immediately. But why not give him a little grief?

"Evan."

"Evan who?"

"The bird scientist."

"The bird nerd," Maya said. "Good morning. How did you find my number?"

Evan shared his methods. "Brayden, the Bird's Don't Exist leader, wants to meet with us."

"It's a trap," Maya said. "Retaliation for embarrassing his cronies last night."

"I'll gloss over the fact that you said cronies, and mention that I picked the location where we meet. The boardwalk. You in?"

"Do bears defecate in the woods?"

"I'm a bird nerd, so I wouldn't know."

Maya squared up to Fred, who stood in the doorway and prevented her from leaving. "Okay, Smoky."

"Smoky?"

"The Bear."

"Lazy nickname. You can do better."

"I can go out the back door," Maya said. "I can jump through a window. I can go through the garage. Are you going to chase me around all morning to prevent me from leaving?"

"Sneak out all you want, but I won't let you walk out of here. This way, I can tell August I tried, at least." Fred scratched his chin. "By the way, what vehicle are you taking?"

"A Lyft."

"When will it arrive?"

Maya glanced at her phone. "Three minutes."

"You have plenty of time then. Walk around the back."

"I see how it is, Fredrick. I see whose side you're on."

"He pays my bills."

"Daphne pays your bills."

"Yeah, you're right."

Maya rolled her eyes and about-faced. She walked through the sliding-glass door and around the house to the driveway, and piled into the Lyft when it arrived. The driver listened to AM political radio. Maya stared out the window and watched the world pass her by. After ten minutes, they pulled up to the boardwalk. Maya exited the vehicle and called Evan.

"A little desperate, don't you think?" Evan answered. "Most women wait forty-eight hours before calling me back."

"I'm not most women," Maya said.

"No. You're not."

"Where are you at?"

"Straight through the entrance to the right, sitting at a table overlooking the ocean."

Maya found Evan where he directed her. He stood, hugged her, and kissed her cheek.

"You look gorgeous," he said.

Maya looked down at her outfit—short shorts and an oversized shirt. She hadn't bothered with makeup, and she had slammed a hat over her untamable hair. "I look like a hobo."

"Hobo's can be gorgeous, especially if they look like you."

A couple minutes later, Goatee and Camo-hat appeared. They both carried backpacks, and to Maya's relief, they both wore shirts. Camo-hat also wore a mask of red spray paint. They escorted the young man known as Brayden.

The Birds Don't Exist leader slipped into the table across from Maya and Evan. He sucked on a lollipop for a moment before popping it out of his mouth. "Good morning."

"Howdy," Maya said. She glanced at Camo-hat and winked. "I liked you better without a shirt. However, I do like the hint of paint leftover on your face. It disguises your natural ugliness."

"What do you want?" Evan asked, no amusement or patience present in his voice. "I have some bird feed to analyze, so let's make this quick."

Brayden breathed heavily through his lips, vibrating them. He shoved the lollipop back into his mouth—a big, colorful sucker—and tongued it over to his cheek. "One-hundred thousand dollars. I have the money in cash with me. You take it and you forget about anything you may have learned last night. I run my story without rebuttal from you." He looked at Maya. "Or you."

"Do I get a hundred thousand, too?"

"You two can split the payout as you see fit," Brayden said, moving the sucker to the other side of his mouth. "What do you say?"

"No deal," Evan said. "Not for a million dollars. You harmed and killed birds to perpetuate a false narrative that they don't actually exist."

"They don't," Brayden said, but the corner of lips twitched, as if he fought against a smirk. "They don't exist. You can't actually tell me they exist. You're an ornithologist. You know better than anyone they don't exist. Stop your lies and admit to the world what you know is true."

"Your rhetoric is harmful," Evan said. "I will expose you for your crimes. Once I have the proof, I will hand the evidence over to the proper authorities and point them in your direction."

"Two-hundred thousand dollars," Brayden said, removing the sucker from his mouth again. "You're a supposed scientist, so you should have a semblance of intelligence. Right? Do the smart thing. Take the money."

"Is that a threat?" Evan asked.

Maya hated to sit back and listen, and she had held her tongue far too long. "Listen, Brayden, I would love nothing more than to sit here all day while you hike up your random price and subtlety threaten us, but let's cut to the chase. I'll put this into terms your bird-sized—see what I did there?—brain can understand. Your mommy and daddy had a lot of money because they worked really, really hard, mostly because they didn't want to spend any time with a spoiled, bratty little boy. So, you lashed out for attention. You got in trouble with teachers, with the law, with any kind of authority, hoping Mommy and Daddy would look your way. 'Mom, Dad, watch this.' They didn't look. They refused to watch."

"Shut up," Brayden whispered.

"In order to ignore you continually, they never allowed you to face accountability. They threw money at you to solve any problem you found yourself in. They bailed you out of any punishment you might have had to face—suspension, expulsion, fines, jail time, et cetera."

"I said, shut up," Brayden said.

"So, you found a desperate group of people to give you some attention. 'Look at me.' Right?" Maya snickered. "Now, you find yourself in trouble again, but Mommy and Daddy won't bail you out. So, you stole a trick from their book. Maybe, just maybe, if you offered enough money, you can buy yourself a way off the hook."

Brayden sniffled, threw his lollipop across the walkway, and dropped his hands to his lap. After a second of fidgeting, he said, "Listen carefully. I have a gun pointed directly at the whore."

"Don't call Evan a whore," Maya said. "He doesn't even put out until the third date."

"I meant you."

"Oh, yeah. That makes more sense." Maya's nonchalance visibly frustrated Brayden. For a second, she almost saw steam spurting from his ears, like something from a cartoon.

"If you don't agree to my terms, I will shoot her. What does it matter at this point? If you don't agree to my terms, I'll spend time in jail, anyway. Why not make you two pay for putting me there."

Maya glanced at Evan. She noticed a flicker of doubt pass across his face. To her, he looked scared and uncertain for the first time since they had met.

"If you scream, I shoot. Do you understand?"

"What do you want?" Evan asked.

"Take me to the bird feed you stole last night. Hand it over. Accept my payment of a hundred-thousand dollars. That's all I want."

"You raised the offer to two-hundred thousand, remember?" Maya asked.

"I lowered it again."

"I don't think that's how negotiations work."

"Once you have the money in hand and I have the feed, we go our separate ways. Are we clear?"

Camo-hat marched toward Maya, and Goatee went toward Evan.

"Now," Brayden said, "don't make a scene."

Maya glanced around the boardwalk and frowned. They had met well before operating hours, and they had the place to themselves. Even if they made a scene, no one would have noticed.

"Evan, you'll lead us to your car. If you try anything brave, I'll shoot the whore."

"The whore?" Maya asked. "Can we come up with something more clever? The whore sounds so obtuse and juvenile."

"Are we clear?" Evan asked.

"Mostly confused," Maya said. "If Spray-paint-face-camo-hat escorts me, does that mean he walks behind me or at my side? That's impor-tant to know. If he's behind me, and I try something funny, well... you don't look like you're very adept with a gun. You might just shoot him in the back."

"We're clear then?" Brayden asked.

"I literally just said I'm confused and explained my confusion. We're not clear."

Brayden stood, briefly flashed his sidearm to prove he held one. He covered it with his jacket to hide it from plain view. "Let's go."

The two men grabbed Maya and Evan, roughly dragging them to their feet. Evan led the way across the street, walking straight for his Tesla. Without a word, Evan popped open the trunk, revealing the half-dozen canisters of spray paint and the single sack of bird feed.

Maya glanced at Evan. He glared at Brayden, a spasm twitching in his jaw.

"You know." Brayden glanced over his shoulder. "Come to think of it, I could shoot you both right here, take the feed, and leave. Police will think some desperate drug addict saw you two exiting the Tesla, thought you might have money, and shot you dead." He shrugged. "I guess this spoiled little boy found himself off the hook yet again."

Brayden raised his gun level with Maya's face. "I think I'm going to shut up the whore first."

"I always fantasized about dying by the ocean," Maya said.

Crack!

Brayden flinched at the sudden noise. He shifted to the source. A bird had dove straight into the windshield of a truck parked ten yards away from Evan's Tesla. The glass cracked and smeared with blood. The bird lay on the asphalt.

Maya also reacted to the smack.

She wheeled around and drove her knee straight into Camo-hat's crotch. He exhaled hot air into her face and collapsed into a ball on the ground.

Brayden shifted his attention back to his hostages, and he hesitated to shoot or run or do anything as he processed the most recent development. Camo-hat moaned in the fetal position on the ground. Evan had made quick, easy work of Goatee, and he lay on the asphalt, his nose sitting the wrong direction on his bloodied face.

Maya had learned never to hesitate. She grabbed the hat off her head without thinking, really just reacting, and she chucked it at Brayden.

Somewhere along the line, she had learned (maybe from Eddie) that active shooters will instinctively respond to stimuli. If someone threw something at them, they naturally dodged, which prevented them from shooting, or, at the very least, threw off their aim. If Eddie had informed Maya of that trick, her murderous ex-boyfriend saved her life.

Brayden dodged to the side and avoided the hat, which allowed Maya a window. She stepped forward and performed a series of maneuvers (also learned from Eddie) to disarm the gunman.

As she and Brayden struggled, a shadow crossed over her, followed by a blur of movement and a sickening crunch. Brayden went limp and heavy in her arms. Maya stepped back, and the man sagged to the asphalt where he lay still, bleeding from his ear.

Evan stood next to Maya. He clutched a spray paint canister and grinned. "Nice work."

"We have a lot of fun together, don't we?" Maya asked.

"Too much fun."

"No such thing." Maya's phone buzzed in her pocket. She removed it and answered without checking the caller ID. She hardly ever screened her calls, afraid that if she did, she would miss out on a potential story. "Maya."

Familiar ragtime music played on the other end of the line—the same she had heard a few hours before.

"Hello?" Maya asked again.

"I had a dream last night that filled me full of fright."

Yard Work. Wednesday, May 3rd. 0811hrs.

CAMBRIA SAT AT THE picnic table on the back patio, right where she had sat with August a couple of hours prior. The view overlooked the pool and, beyond that, the ocean. She enjoyed the scenery alone.

Daphne busied herself in the kitchen with breakfast.

After Maya had caused a scene and forced her way out the house, despite Fred's pleading with her not to leave, Cambria had stepped into the kitchen to convince Daphne to relax. "You've cooked all week. Sit down. Kick up your feet. Let me make breakfast."

Daphne glared at her with utter disbelief. "Girl, no. Not a chance. Listen, I work every single day, from the dreaded second I wake up to that blissful second I fall asleep. When I'm not working, I'm dog tired, lounging on the couch, and watching bad television to rest my mind. When I'm extremely exhausted, I drive my baby girl around to clear my head. Let me tell you something, though. My passion, my love, it's not that giant oaf over there."

"I can hear you," Fred said from the living room. He ate cereal from a mixing bowl as an appetizer, and he sat on the couch watching morning cartoons.

"It's cooking. I don't cook at home, because I'm too busy or too tired. When I'm on vacation, though, and I don't have to worry about working, I'm cooking. End of story."

"Just let her do her thing," Fred called through a mouthful of cereal. "She likes it. I like it. Everyone is better off because of it."

"There's coffee in the pot," Daphne said, nodding at the carafe. "Grab some and enjoy this beautiful morning."

So, Cambria had. She poured herself another cup of coffee and slipped into the backyard to enjoy the fresh air and watch the ocean.

Her thoughts drifted to August. Much to her surprise, he wanted to give their relationship a legitimate shot.

Cambria liked the idea of dating him. He was emotionally distant still recovering from his trauma, but cracks showed in his stoic demeanor. Since first meeting him a couple weeks ago, he flashed more humor and joy. He smiled and occasionally laughed. According to Kimberly, August had been a carefree, joyful kid. Over the past couple of days, Cambria had noticed hints of that child trying to break free, and she wanted to be there when it fully emerged.

As her thoughts carried across the ocean and danced the breeze, movement caught her eye. A shadow in the shape of a man. A shock of fear jolted through Cambria. She turned her head.

A strange man stood in the backyard. He had blonde hair styled after Chris Hemsworth from the first Thor movie, and he bore a similar physique—broad, muscular, and handsome. He wore cargo pants, stained with mud and grass, and he wore black boots. He also had on a white T-shirt. His face had freckles of mud (or is that blood, Cambria wondered) splattered across it.

He raised a hand and waved at Cambria.

"Hi." She cocked her head, not sure how to proceed with this encounter. "Can I help you?"

"I'm the caretaker," he said. "Max's brother, David. Did he not tell you I was coming this morning?"

Cambria had not heard that information, but maybe Maxwell had told August.

"I'm sorry if I startled you," he said.

"You surprised me. I wasn't expecting someone to come through the gate." Cambria half-smirked, half-chuckled, feeling more anxious than humored though. Wouldn't a caretaker have tools—a lawnmower or an edger or anything, really?

"Should I come back later?" David asked. "I don't want to bother your morning."

"No, you're fine," Cambria said. She stood from the picnic table. "I think breakfast is about ready, anyway. I'll head inside to eat. You do your thing."

"Thank you. It saves me a trip."

"Yeah, not a problem." Cambria shuffled across the wood-planked porch and grabbed the sliding-glass door. "Fred!" she called into the house.

No response.

The television played cartoons at a low volume, but Fred no longer sat on the couch. His bowl of cereal rested on the coffee table, though.

The kitchen was also vacant, but the stovetop remained on. A pan of eggs smoked and burned.

Where had Daphne and Fred gone?

A quickie, Cambria thought, but she quickly dismissed the idea. After Daphne's reaction to Cambria offering to cook, she doubted the woman would allow her eggs to burn.

"Fred! Daphne!" Cambria closed the sliding door behind her. "Fred!" She slipped her phone from her pocket and scrolled to August's contact. "Daphne!"

Music filled the house. It blared loud enough to vibrate the pictures hanging on the walls. The ragtime tune she had heard last night in her dream played again.

Cambria reached back to lock the sliding door. Her hand touched fabric, and she instinctively turned to inspect.

The Devil wore a three-piece suit. It smelled like salt air mixed with rotting fruit.

Cambria backpedaled, and her feet crossed as she spun around to flee from the kitchen. She tripped, falling hard on her bottom. Her teeth clanked together. A jolt of pain ran up her spine.

The ragtime song played around her so loud, Cambria barely heard her thoughts. She scooted back and bumped into the side of the cabinets. "Fred! Fred!" she screamed, tears and snot pouring down her face. Cambria scrambled to her feet and lunged for the knife rack on the counter. She ripped free a chef's knife and held it shakily before her. "Stand back," she said to the Devil. "Don't come any closer."

"I had a dream last night that filled me full of fright," the raspy, smoke-filled voice half-sang.

As the words tumbled off its lips, Cambria's shaking ceased. She stood statue-still, eyes wide, her breathing shallow. The Devil cocked its head, regarding her with the mask resembling a man.

Cambria shifted her gaze and looked out the sliding-glass door. She hoped against hope that David would sneak up behind the Devil.

She had no such luck.

The Devil stepped forward and pinched the blade of the knife, removed it from her hands, and placed it on the counter. The Nightmare leaned forward. The lips of its mask touched her skin. "Climb into Daphne's Lexus." Keys fell into Cambria's outstretched hand, replacing the knife. "Drive south on Highway 1 at a leisurely pace. You're not in a hurry. In fact, you'll drive almost illegally slow. When you see August's car, pull to the side of the road and stop driving. If you don't see his car after you reach Davenport, drive as fast as the car allows, and don't bother turning the wheel." The Devil moved away from her and circled the island. He leaned against the counter and shooed her away with a flick of his wrist. "Off you go."

The Nightmare. Wednesday, May 3rd. O817hrs.

A BELL DINGED AS I entered the cafe. A small brass bell, one with a clapper that jingled back and forth to announce a new customer. The barista glanced in my direction—a teenager with purple hair and pimples. I headed away from her, toward Alina, who leaned over a corner booth in the back.

The Gull Cafe was the demolition and subsequent construction of a small forest. Hardwood floors. Wood-planked walls. A wooden counter with a glass display. Wooden tables and chairs, a bookshelf filled to the brim with old, faded books.

When I reached Alina, I glanced at the table she hovered over. Like the other tables I had passed on my way over, that table had a collection of newspaper clippings with headlines detailing major events in Santa Cruz history.

"What took you so long?" Alina asked.

"I spoke with Heather. She doesn't believe Max would do something like this. She doesn't believe he would risk whatever status he has built within the community to exact revenge."

Alina hummed, and she pointed at a clipping in the table's corner. The headline read something about a new mayor. The content below the headline, introducing the mayor and his plans for office, filled most of the clipping. Near the bottom of the write-up, was another headline. Someone had cut the bottom half of the text away, though, apparently only caring for the cafe patron to learn about the new mayor.

With enough effort, I pieced together the half-shown letters.

MAXWELL SHAYE PURCHASES HOTEL, ADDS TO HIS REAL ESTATE EMPIRE

I read the heading aloud and scowled at Alina after finishing.

She raised her eyebrows. "When I first read that yesterday, I thought nothing of it. Good for him, you know? He's had his adversity, rose above it all, and now he has a hospitality empire. Vacation homes. Hotels. He's crushing it." Alina glanced back down at the half-showing headline. "Then the Devil visited Maya last night, in her hotel room. The logical question, at least in my head, was how? How did the Devil enter the room? I didn't connect the dots until after speaking with Johnny's mom. She said his name in relation to Johnny and his friends. It all crashed into place."

"He owns our vacation home." I spoke absently, threading the string into a pattern. "He owns the hotel Maya stayed at last night."

"Bingo, Dingo. I bet everything I own—granted, that's not much, but it's still everything—that Maxwell owns the hotel where the Devil murdered Nick. That he owns the apartment where the Devil murdered Christina, too. I bet he also owns Heather and Johnny's place. He could bypass, as he pleases, any locked door in this town."

I stared blankly at the newspaper clipping, thinking rather than reading. "They see him in their dreams."

"They hear that annoying song," Alina said. "They all hear the same song every single time. That's the catalyst. That's his tell. That song."

I slipped my phone from my pocket and clicked on the internet browser. I typed in the name of the newspaper on the table. I navigated to their website and filtered my search by the date shown on the clipped article.

A series of results popped up. I scrolled until I found Maxwell Shaye's name in the headline. I clicked on the link, and it brought me to the full write-up on his purchase of the local hotel. The article also had an image beside it. One of Maxwell Shaye holding a pair of scissors, ready to cut the ceremonial red ribbon. Standing behind him was another man—one I didn't recognize.

The other man leaned against a long sledgehammer; the head weighted down in the dirt.

My breaths came short, and my fingers tingled—they perspired and became clammy. "Who's that?" I handed my phone to Alina.

She zoomed in on the screen and narrowed her eyes. "I don't know."

"The Devil wielded a sledgehammer in every sighting," I said.

"You don't think it's Maxwell? You think it's that guy?"

Heather didn't think Maxwell would do anything like murder. "Give me the phone."

Alina returned it to me without a word. I went to the cafe's front counter. The purple-haired, pimply faced girl smiled at me, showcasing her braces.

"Can I help you, Sir?"

I set my phone on the counter and slid it to her. "Who's the man with the sledgehammer?"

The kid glanced at the screen, pouted out a lip, and shook her head. "No idea."

"Would anyone in here know?" I glanced over my shoulder, instantly realizing there wasn't anyone else in there.

"Maybe Wrench."

"Who?"

The teenager shook her head. "I don't know his real name, but he comes in here every day. Everyone calls him Wrench. I think he's some kind of mechanic or something. Or he used to be. He's old now."

I turned and peered across the cafe to the front door. "What time does he come in?"

"Usually around eight-thirty."

I grabbed my phone and checked the time. 0826hrs. "What's he look like?"

"Old. He wears a military hat. I think he fought in some war. A veteran, you know?"

"Thank you," I said.

"Can I help you with anything else?"

"I'll take a coffee while I'm waiting."

The kid poured me a cup of drip coffee, and as she handed it to me, the front door jingled, signaling another patron.

I turned, holding my breath, and I saw the old man with the United States Marine Corps ball cap. He shambled up behind me with a stooped posture, waiting his turn to order.

"Sir." I extended a hand. "Thank you for your service."

His arthritic hand wrapped around mine. "My pleasure," he said, his voice wheezy.

"Could I buy your drink?"

"I won't say no to that." He chuckled, a dry, grating sound. "Though, I eat breakfast, as well."

"Order whatever you wish."

"That's quite a lot."

"Well, if you feel guilty about it, you can help me with something."

"What's that?"

I showed him my phone and hoped his aged eyes could determine the image. "The man in the back, the one with the sledgehammer, do you know him?"

The old man craned back and scrunched his face. "I know that boy. That's Daryl Shaye's youngest. What's his name? He had Maxwell first. I remember that name because we had a dog—a Labrador at the time—named Max. Anyway, that poor boy had a terrible condition. Sweet kid, though. Hard worker, too. You would think someone like Maxwell would've quit on life after seeing the hand God dealt him. He worked hard, though. Absorbed Daryl's businesses and expanded some more."

"The one with the sledgehammer, though, that's his brother?" I remembered Heather sharing the kid's name. *I called him Davie, though his name was David. He hated that.* "Was his name David?"

"Yeah. I think you're right. I think that was his name. I'm not sure, though. But you would think that boy was the one to launch instead of

Maxwell. Tall, strong, handsome enough." Wrench clicked his tongue and shook his head. "Kid never went much further than his front porch." The old man tapped his skull. "I think he missed a few screws, you know?"

"Where's he at now?"

"I can't say for sure. Last I heard, though, he worked for Maxwell. Caretaker or something like that for those properties. That Maxwell, he works hard."

I glanced at Alina, back to Wrench. "Thank you for your time, and again, for your service." I peeled a twenty from my wallet and placed it on the counter.

"Thank you," Wrench said.

I walked to the door, glanced over my shoulder, and nodded at Alina to follow.

She ran to catch up, meeting me in the parking lot. "What did you learn?"

"David Shaye, Maxwell's brother. Look him up and report any information you find on him. Anything at all."

"Is he the Devil?"

I unlocked my car, stepped inside, and called Fred.

When had Maxwell said his brother would swing by the place to mow the yard? Today or tomorrow or morning.

The call went to Fred's voicemail.

"Did you find anything?" I asked as I backed out of the stall. My heart vibrated in my chest. My head buzzed with worry.

"Nothing yet."

My phone rang. I glanced at the screen, hoping to see a familiar name.

Heather.

"Hello," I answered, nearly out of breath.

"August," Alina said, her voice soft.

I ignored her and listened to the heavy, ragged breathing from the other end of the line. I slammed on the brakes, half-parking in stall, half-parked in the lot.

"Who is this?" I asked.

"The Devil," the raspy voice said, "on your shoulder. It's time for you to make your choice. The choice."

I couldn't have spoken had I tried. My lips had sealed shut, my voice had diminished to nothing. My heartbeat throbbed in my head, drowning out all thoughts, and nearly drowning out the Devil's voice.

"Your dear friend, the love of your life. Or your newest thrill."

Alina spoke to me, but I didn't hear a word she said. Her voice was like the ocean, just background.

My heart raced in my head, pounding away. Thump. Thump. Thump. My face burned. My stomach swirled with acid, scorching my insides. I opened my mouth to speak and nearly vomited.

"August," the Devil said, "listen to me carefully. Maya is driving a Tesla, cruising Highway 1 southbound at a slow, catchable pace. Cambria is driving a Lexus, cruising Highway 1 northbound at a slow, catchable pace. In twenty minutes, they will put all their weight into the gas pedal and drive straight. Only straight. No matter what." A second of terrible silence. "Hurry."

The line went dead.

The Devil's Decision. Wednesday, May 3rd. O839hrs.

I STARED THROUGH MY car's dirty windshield, across the half-empty stall I half-parked in, and through the glistening windshield of the car parked across from me.

Thoughts often work like a stream. They flow continuously. Have you ever tried not thinking? It's difficult, if not bordering on impossible. In that moment, the river ran dry. My thoughts turned into puddles scattered across the barren ravine. The dried, cracked soil between each puddle represented complete erasure of conscious thought. Thoughts no longer played out like a movie, but appeared as a slow-motion slideshow.

Cambria and I on our first date. Cambria stepping out of the rideshare. Cambria and I on the beach. Cambria and I sitting on the back patio and watching the sunrise.

Maya laughing and smiling. Maya confident and so self-assured she believed she could tackle the world. Maya and I lounging by the pool. *Honda Civics aren't only more environmental and safe, they're more comfortable and enticing, especially for long drives.*

Daniel Quinn.

David Shaye.

Images. Names. Locations. Memories. They all jumped into my head, focused enough for me to notice them, and they sprinted away so the next could appear.

"I can't," I said, or maybe I thought it. I couldn't quite tell.

Nothing seemed tangible anymore. I existed as if in a dream—disassociated from reality. The world sort of moved around me, through me, and the laws of physics no longer existed. I floated away, phased through the roof of my car, drifted higher and higher into the sky, as if the angels had hooked me and reeled me in to them.

I zoomed out of the parking lot and saw the ocean laid endlessly before me—the stretch of Highway 1 curving along the shoreline. Cars lined the lanes like ants moving back and forth between their colony. Amongst them, Cambria drove one direction and Maya drove the other.

Who did I go after? Who did I save?

"August," Alina shouted, nearly ripping my arm from my shoulder as she shook me.

My suspended consciousness slammed back into my body, and I gasped.

"Did you hear me?" Alina asked.

"What?"

"Did you hear me?"

"What did you say?"

"Hypnotism."

The word came from so far out of play, I couldn't connect it to any dots. "What do you mean?"

"David Shaye is a hypnotist. There are videos on his Facebook page of him performing street shows."

"That explains the song," I said, catching up.

"It's a trigger. He uses it to trigger a hypnotic state in his victims."

I shifted into gear and burned out of the parking lot. "Call Detective Phillips."

"Why?" Alina asked.

"Tell him everything. Now!"

"Everything?"

"Everything." I shouted the word. "About David visiting Maya, Cambria, and Daphne by using Maxwell's name to enter their rooms. Ask if Maxwell owns Nick's apartment, and Johnny and Heather's place. Tell him about the song and the hypnotism. Everything. Phillips has to find David immediately."

Alina held her phone, but she stared at me. "If we're not going after David, where are we going?"

Highway 1 on-ramps quickly approached.

I had to decide. Left or right. North or south. Cambria or Maya.

I slammed on my brakes in the middle of the intersection and stared at my two options. The cars behind me slammed on their brakes, skidded around me, blared their horns.

"What are you doing?" Alina asked. She reached for the grab-bar.

"Call him!"

"August, what is going on?"

I closed my eyes and fought against a howling scream. Time was ticking. I had to decide. I had to choose one.

"Alina."

"What?"

"I have to choose between saving Maya or Cambria."

"What does that mean?"

"I can only save one."

Alina could have asked questions to clarify the situation. Upon reflection, I think most people might have. Why choose? Save them from what? How do you know they will die? Why can't we save them both? I don't know if the young woman saw something in my face, or if her natural intuition kicked in, but Alina offered me guidance without hesitation.

"Cambria," she said.

My heart skipped, fluttering and flying away. Why had she said Cambria? "What?"

"If you're forced to choose, save Cambria. Maya would tell you the same thing. Cambria doesn't die playing our game. Maya will gladly die playing the game—this game is her life."

Cars continued to honk as they passed around me. A whoop-whoop drew my eyes to the rearview mirror, and police sirens flashed behind me.

"You're sure?" I asked.

"This is an actual choice you face?"

"Yes."

"Save Cambria. Maya can look after herself if she has to."

At that point, I did scream. The police cruiser stopped behind me. The driver's door opened, and a shiny boot stepped onto the asphalt.

I slammed my palms against the steering wheel, and I dropped a leaden foot onto the gas pedal. The Honda Civic Hybrid fishtailed and I directed it onto the northbound on-ramp.

I went after Cambria.

As I sped through traffic, the police cruiser hot on my tail, I called Fred. His phone went straight to voicemail. I'm not a man to curse, but I cursed then.

"Detective Phillips," Alina said. "This is Alina. I had the displeasure of meeting you earlier with August Watson. Yeah. Now listen to everything I say without interruption. David Shaye is our killer. He's responsible for the deaths of Christina Wyss and Nicholas Lane. No. Listen to me, you arrogant pig! Get your head out of your... yes. Exactly! Now, find him before he hurts someone else." Alina hung up the phone.

I reached into the pocket where I stashed the burner phone gifted to me by Daniel Quinn.

"August Watson," Quinn answered with a cheery tone.

He knew everything; he had said as much. Quinn had discovered the Devil's identity, had contacted David, and shared all my personal information with him. He had arranged for this to happen.

"Why?" I roared the question. "Why involve yourself?"

"Because it's so much... fun."

"Call it off."

"No."

"Call it off!"

"I can't do that. Things are already in motion. By the way, out of personal curiosity, who did you choose?"

I hung up the phone, rolled down the window, and threw the device as far as I could.

My car's odometer flirted with a hundred miles per hour, testing the limits of my hybrid vehicle. The police cruiser kept pace. The lights flashed. The siren wailed. The traffic, though, split to the shoulders—as if I were Moses, the officer God, and the other vehicles the Red Sea.

On the phone, the Devil (David) had mentioned Cambria would drive a Lexus.

"Look for Daphne's car," I said. "Cambria driving Daphne's car."

I called Fred again. Still no answer.

If David Shaye had reached Cambria, that meant he had visited the rental home. What had he done to Fred and Daphne? I could barely breathe, and my lack of oxygen messed with my perception. The entire world tunneled, blurry on the edges.

Five to ten more minutes whittled away in terrifying, deathly silence. In that time I called Cambria about a thousand times. I called Maya just as much. Neither of them answered their phone. Straight to voice-mail every single time.

"David must have done it while they were drunk," Alina said, her voice like a brick.

"What?"

"Hypnotized them. With a weakened mind more susceptible to hyp-notism, he must have introduced the trigger on that first night when everyone was drunk. The second night, when we celebrated Rachel and Jake's pregnancy, he reinforced his grasp and pushed a little more. That's why Maya, Cambria, and Daphne all recalled him."

"Can you hypnotize someone against their will?"

"I don't know. If I had to guess, I would say that's what he did, though. Hypnotized them against their will." Alina bounced forward and pointed out the windshield. "What's that?"

I scanned the road for something abnormal. I saw nothing beyond the traffic. "What?"

"That looks like Evan's Tesla."

"Who?"

"Evan," Alina said. "Maya's date. He drove that same color Tesla with that stupid bird decal on the rear window. See it?"

It took me a second, but I saw it.

My heart plummeted to my stomach and sat there like a stone. Simultaneously, relief flooded throughout my body like a dam breaking. I knew before I came level with the vehicle who sat behind the wheel. Her unmistakable frohawk gave her away.

I drove parallel to Maya, and Alina rolled down the window and tried every trick in the book to grab her aunt's attention. When Maya glanced over and saw us, she slowed the car and pulled over to the narrow shoulder.

I fell in behind her. The cop fell in behind me—two of them now. Probably more soon.

My gaze remained fixed through the windshield, though, through the rear window at Maya's hair. Not Cambria's hair. Not the Lexus. The Tesla, and Maya's hair.

What had happened to Cambria?

"Is that Maya?" Alina fumbled with her door handle. "I thought you went after Cambria. I told you to go after Cambria. Is that Maya?"

"Wait," I said, or maybe I thought. I couldn't tell the difference. "Don't get out of the car." It took a lot of effort, but I peered in the rearview. The police officers had their door butterflied open. They stood behind them, using them as shield, and they had their sidearms drawn, pointed at us. "Alina."

She either didn't hear me or she didn't care. Alina threw open the passenger door and sprinted toward the Tesla.

I preemptively tensed my body, waiting for the gunshots.

Nothing—nothing except for the officers shouting commands at Alina. Commands which she ignored. The teenager ripped open the Tesla's passenger door and climbed into the cab. Through my dirty windshield and the Tesla's rear window, I watched Alina dive onto her aunt.

"He lied to me," I muttered.

In the rearview mirror, the police still hadn't moved. A puddle thought—a photograph—of Todd Phillips filled my mind. Had he contacted them? It was hard to stay focused on that question, what with Maya parked in front of me, and Cambria nowhere in sight.

David had provided me with the wrong directions. Cambria went north. Maya went south. I didn't choose who to save. I chose who would die.

My phone buzzed in the cupholder. With little thought, I grabbed it with a trembling hand and accepted the call. I didn't verbally answer.

"Why did you turn off the burner phone?" Quinn asked.

"I threw it out the window."

"Well, I wanted to let you know that someone called 9-1-1 a few minutes ago."

"Don't," I said, or maybe I thought.

"They noticed a Lexus driving at speeds over a hundred miles per hour. It drove straight, not bothering to brake or swerve. It drove straight through the center guardrails and into oncoming traffic."

"Don't."

"A semi intercepted the Lexus head-on."

I coughed on a sob. My eyes stung. My ears rang. Everything hurt—far more than my physical wounds ever pained me.

"You will be happy to know, the truck driver survived the collision without a scratch."

I stared wide-eyed, unblinking at Maya and Alina.

Something tapped on the passenger window. I glanced over and saw a police officer tapping the glass with his gun.

"August, are you there?" Quinn asked.

I disconnected the call, afraid I might lose my mind if I heard his voice utter another syllable.

Aftermath. Wednesday, May 3rd. 1043hrs.

A HIGH-PITCHED WHINE RANG all around me, coming from within me. It muffled most external noise.

Fred spoke to me, but I'm not sure what he said. I saw his lips moving, and I saw him staring directly at me, but I watched him on mute for all I heard.

My mind replayed Quinn's call over and over.

... a Lexus driving at speeds over a hundred miles per hour. It drove straight, not bothering to brake or swerve. It drove straight through the center guardrails and into oncoming traffic. A semi intercepted the Lexus head-on. You will be happy to know, the truck driver survived the collision without a scratch.

A Lexus... into oncoming... a semi... happy to know...

Over and over and over.

Somewhere between Quinn's phone call and Fred now vying for my attention, I had spoken with the officers; I had moved from the shoulder of Highway 1 to my vacation home. I remember little of it. The last lucid moment I have was the gun tapping against my window. I had transferred from the driver's seat of my car to a chair at the dining room table. I no longer held the steering wheel, but a hot cup of coffee.

The rest returned like a heavy night of drinking. I had fragmented memories that floated around with no context or substance. They existed, separated from time and distance—as if from a dream.

At one point I had held Maya. I hugged her tightly and cried against her shaking shoulder as she sobbed.

I spoke with Detective Phillips at some point, too. I'm not sure where or when that happened, or who had contacted whom, but I recalled the conversation well enough.

"We found him," Phillips said.

"Who?" I asked. I had almost asked about Daniel Quinn. Had they found Quinn? How had they found him? My thoughts centered on that man, drilled into him.

Reached speeds over a hundred... not bothering to brake or swerve... the truck driver survived.

"David Shaye," Phillips said.

"You found him?"

"It wasn't too hard. I called Maxwell and asked where David was. He said he didn't know, but he could check. Apparently, David drives a company truck, and it has a tracker on it. You'll never believe where we found him."

I don't know if I guessed or remained silent and waited for Phillips to continue.

"On the job, mowing some lawn at some house. We approached him. He smiled, then he ran. We found a bloody sledgehammer in the truck's bed. A pressed suit hanging in the backseat. We found a mask of a man's face. Maxwell also cooperated, and he allowed us to map the travel history. The truck visited all the murder locations at the time of the murders. Your vacation home. Your friend's hotel room. It all checks out. Not only that, but David confessed to the murders. There's one thing. He won't tell us how or why he did it. How did he murder Nick with Johnny in the same room? I can't wrap my head around that."

I remember Phillips' debriefing as a chunk of dialogue. I don't think I interrupted him and asked questions. If I had, my voice disappeared into the void, like losing the threads of a dream after waking. I only recalled the information Phillips offered.

When he finished, that's when I remember speaking. "Can I talk to him?"

"He wants to talk to you. Only you. He said if we can arrange a meeting, he will share the why and how."

"When?"

"I know you've been through—"

"When? The sooner the better."

"Later this afternoon?"

The memory faded after that. Had we agreed on a time and place?

I had nothing for an answer but that constant ringing between my ears.

Fred stood and moved away from me, replaced by Maya. She arranged the chair to sit knees-to-knees with me. Her icy hands wrapped around mine, and she dropped her forehead, resting it on mine.

"August," she said.

My voice caught in my throat, but I choked out my question. "Is she dead?"

Maya's forehead subtly moved, sliding up and down against mine, silently confirming what Quinn had shared.

I was hot and cold at the same time. I thought I might vomit or faint.

Maya whispered, "You're hurting me."

I realized my entire body had clenched like a vice. I squeezed her hands as tight as possible in mine. I exhaled and loosened my grip. "What happened?"

"Head-on collision."

"The truck driver survived the collision without a scratch," I said.

"Yes."

"I asked her to come on this trip. I asked her to join me on a work-related, dangerous case. What was I thinking?" I cleared my throat.

"It's not your fault."

"Can I see her?"

Again, Maya answered by moving her head against mine. No, the back-and-forth motion suggested. "I'm sorry."

I leaned away from Maya and rubbed my face, wiping away the snot and tears. I inhaled and glanced around the room, knowing I had to pull my act together. I could break down later, in private. I had work to do at the moment. "What about Johnny?"

Alina answered from across the table. "I've kept in close contact with Detective Phillips. It's going to take a couple hours to process the paperwork, but they're releasing him."

"I spoke to him," Fred said. He now sat beside Alina like a mountain might sit beside an anthill. "Johnny will transfer the money owed as soon as he has access to his accounts."

"Hi, I'm Evan," said another voice from inside the kitchen. I glanced sideways and noticed who I guessed was the bird scientist leaning against the island. He pulled in his lips and grinned.

I returned my attention to Fred. Anger swelled, churned by Evan's presence, amplified by Fred's failure to do one simple task—protect Maya and Cambria from the Devil.

I breathed and forced myself to remain calm, and I asked, "What happened here?"

Fred's eyes never left mine, which told me one thing. He wasn't ashamed of his inability to protect Cambria. "Daphne made breakfast. I watched cartoons. Cambria sat right there." He nodded through the open window to the picnic table on the back patio. "I had my eyes on her the entire time."

"What about Maya?" I asked.

"I snuck out of the house," she said. "Fred doesn't control me. Neither do you. I left to pursue the bird story."

Fred peeled a banana. "I heard a song play over the speaker system. I lost control of myself."

"The same thing happened to me," Daphne said. She stood behind Evan, wiping the kitchen counters with a sponge. "I had the eggs on the stovetop, and I just... I heard the song, then I went upstairs and laid down."

"I joined her," Fred said. "We went to sleep."

"I received a phone call," Maya said. "I answered it, heard the song playing from the other end, and that was it. I lost control of everything.

You and Fred might not control what I do, but the Devil did. He told me exactly what to do, and I had no choice but to obey."

"I woke up at 0930hrs on the dot." Fred lowered his gaze and stared at the table. "Alina had called about a million times. I called her back, and she told me everything."

I nodded and faced Maya, considering what Fred had mentioned. *She told me everything.* "You need to know something."

Maya sneered, half-smiling. "Alina told me. You went after Cambria. That's exactly who you should have gone after. You didn't mess up, August. You did the right thing, and it's pivotal for you to understand that. You did the right thing. None of this is your fault."

"I could have figured it out sooner."

Maya shook her head. "There's one person responsible for all of this. It's not you. It's David Shaye. That's it. Only him."

"Two people," I said.

"You're not at fault."

"Maybe not, but there's still two people." I reached into my pocket, removed my cell phone, and navigated to the recent calls. The number appeared—not blocked, but there.

I needed an outlet for my anger, and Daniel Quinn would serve that purpose.

"August Watson," he said.

"You have my attention. What do you want?"

Quinn chuckled. I hated that smug, confident sound coming from his lips. It lit a fire within me—an inferno that would devour Quinn. I would stop at nothing to find that maniac and see that he paid for Cambria's death.

"I want this marriage between us to last into perpetuity," he said. "We will rewrite history, you and me. We will become greater than Hector and Achilles. Than Cain and Abel. The world will remember Daniel Quinn and August Watson."

"You're a delusional psychopath."

"Grandeur is fun."

"I'm coming after you with everything I have."

"I hope you do, August. I love a good chase."

"I'm ending you."

"As you ended Aaron Brooks?"

I bit my lip.

"Had you taken my advice," Quinn said, "Cambria would still be alive. I offered to share with you what I knew about the investigation, and you refused my help. So, don't let your friends convince you otherwise. This was all your fault."

"This was your fault," I said. "Yours and David's. You could have stopped him."

"Why would I have? As you said, I now have your attention. This number will no longer reach me." Quinn disconnected the line.

"Who was that?" Maya asked.

I shared everything I knew about Daniel Quinn and his relation to my past cases and this case. When I finished providing them with information, they sat without saying a word. What was there to say?

"Detective Phillips just texted me," Alina said.

I glanced at her. "When can I meet with David?"

"Now."

Twenty minutes later, I sat across from David Shay in the precinct's interrogation room. A few officers, Detective Phillips, and Alina stood behind the two-way mirror.

David had blood clotting in his blonde hair, stained beneath his fingernails. The man couldn't have looked any more different from his brother, Maxwell. He was handsome, broad, and tall, and wielded a steel confidence like a sharp, deadly sword. He smiled at me, and I nearly hopped across the metallic table and ripped out his throat.

"I'm going to speak," I said. "You're going to listen unless I ask a direct question. Then you only answer that question. Do you understand?"

"Yes."

"Monday night, everyone had a few too much to drink."

I recalled Cambria needing Daphne to help her shower and vomiting three separate times. I remembered Maya, also drunk, leaning her head on my shoulder and spilling her life's deepest secrets. *Honda Civic Hybrids are more comfortable, especially for long drives.*

"Maxwell forgot to hand over the spare keys. You collected them, providing yourself with a way into the house, and you entered late that night. Somehow, you hypnotized my friends while they slept. Maya. Fred. Daphne." I licked my lips, finding it difficult to say the next name. "Cambria. Did you hypnotize anyone else?"

"Jake."

I hated he knew my brother-in-law's name.

"No one else was drunk enough—mentally weak enough—for the charm to take."

I swallowed and cleared my throat. "We celebrated my sister's pregnancy last night. Again, many people drank. You reasserted your hold over their mind." I licked my teeth and shook my head, knowing that I had stepped too far ahead. "Let's backtrack. When did Quinn contact you?"

"Early Monday afternoon."

Fred had first shared the nightmare case with us on Sunday afternoon. Quinn had solved it that fast? How? Who was Daniel Quinn, and why had he dedicated his life to making mine miserable? What kind of enemy had I attracted?

"You never really appeared in anyone's dreams, did you?"

"No."

"You played your song. That triggered their hypnotic state, and whatever you described to them, they saw as a dream. Right?"

"Correct."

"It all began because you approached them while they slept. You forced them to believe they dreamed and saw you as a nightmare. When you broke Nick's hand, though he believed himself to be dreaming, you were right there, in his apartment. He never saw you because of his hypnosis, because you demanded he forget about your presence. When you killed Nick, you played the song and demanded Johnny to forget, or not to watch, or something of the sort… and you murdered Nick right in front of him."

David said nothing, but I hadn't asked a question.

"Why?"

"Why did I do it?"

"Why did you kill them?"

"Heather and her little group of friends used to berate my older brother without end. I was a few years younger than him, but skinny and shy. I wanted to protect him because of his condition, because he didn't deserve their abuse, but I physically couldn't. Johnny and Nick were big for their age. I couldn't have fought them. Do you know how frustrating that is? To watch someone you love get hurt, but you can't do anything about it?" His eyes flashed with amusement.

I thought of Cambria, and once again I had to harness my stampeding anger.

"Max came home one day and attempted suicide," David said. "I found him half-dead in a bathtub filled with blood. Can you imagine that? I wasn't any older than ten, and I found my brother bleeding out in the tub. I called 9-1-1. I sat with him while he sputtered and faded. Me, because of them." David leaned back, breathing through his nose. "Not too long after that, Max went missing for almost twenty-four hours. Your clients had left him naked and terrified to... to ridicule him, I guess. Why? Because they could. Because it made them feel better about their miserable lives. Well, you know what made me feel better about myself? Murdering each one of them."

"You always planned to kill them through hypnosis?"

David shook his head. "I always planned to kill them, but not through hypnosis. That happened naturally, as if predestined. I took to hypnosis easily, and I found it intriguing. As I dove into the more obscure avenues, I learned that through specific and careful techniques, you could hypnotize someone while they sleep. I learned I could control what they saw and did, as if I implanted dreams into their heads. If I wished for them to see a dragon chasing them across a rainbow, they would have. That's when I had the idea. I would avenge my brother for all that he endured. I would first make them suffer, as Max suffered. They lost sleep. They became depressed and suicidal. Ugly in appearance. Broke. I shattered them. Then, I picked them off one by one."

"Did he know about your plan?"

"He never had a clue. He's too busy enacting his revenge in his own way—success."

"Why Cambria, Daphne, and Maya? They had nothing to do with your brother or with you."

David yawned. "Excuse me," he said, covering his mouth. "Daniel Quinn called me on Monday, introduced himself, and revealed to me everything he knew. He knew how I haunted Heather's little clique. He knew what I planned. He threatened to turn me over to the police, unless I did for him one simple favor. Make you choose between the two women."

... a Lexus drove straight, not bothering to brake or swerve. A semi intercepted the Lexus head-on. You will be happy to know...

"It surprised Quinn when you chose Cambria."

"You gave me the wrong directions."

David smirked. "That was also Quinn's brilliant idea. He wanted it to hurt when you chose, but to hurt even more when you chose wrong." David frowned. "I'm sorry for what happened, by the way. Only four people were supposed to suffer my revenge." He narrowed his eyes and looked over my shoulder at the two-way mirror. "Well, it ended with poetic justice, I guess. Four people suffered my revenge. Johnny escaped, didn't he, replaced with Cambria?"

"He's free," I mumbled.

"That's too bad. Though, if I had to choose one of them to live, I would have chosen Johnny. For that miserable group, he wasn't half-bad."

"Why that specific mask?"

"It symbolized my brother. He always wanted, at least when he was younger, a normal face. So, I chose a mask of a normal man with a normal face."

I tapped my fingers on the metallic desk. With no other questions pressing my mind, just the cascading voice of Quinn crowding my thoughts (... *driving at speeds over a hundred miles per hour... drove straight, not bothering to brake or swerve... into oncoming traffic. You will be happy to know, the truck driver survived the collision without a scratch.*)

I stood and signaled that I was ready for this nightmare to end.

A Cry for Help.
Friday, May 5th.
1829hrs.

I SAT ON THE floor, propped against the wall in the house Glacia had gifted to me. Alina, Maya, Fred, and Evan (yes, Evan the bird man—he and Maya had made their relationship official) arranged themselves around the empty living room.

We had returned home from Santa Cruz on Wednesday, unable and unwilling to spend another night in the vacation home. Daphne's Lexus was a crushed can, the top completely shredded off the vehicle. Maya rode with Evan, though, in his Tesla. Fred, Daphne, and Alina drove back with me.

I slept at the office Wednesday night. On Thursday, I returned to my apartment and stood outside my apartment door with the key stuffed into the lock, but I could not turn it and unlock it and allow myself entry.

Too many memories of a previous life connected me to that apartment. My alcoholic life after killing Aaron Brooks. Glacia. Alina. Cambria. Glacia now lived a state away. Alina had moved in with Maya. And Cambria...

You will be happy to know...

If I ever meant to move on properly with my life, I had to get out of my apartment. I couldn't sleep another night there.

With the key shoved into the door handle, I called Glacia.

"Hey, you," she said, her voice low and controlled. She had heard the news. Of course, she had. She and Alina spoke nearly every day.

I closed my eyes and rested my head against the door. "Hi."

"You doing okay?"

"No."

"Do you want to talk?"

"Not really."

"We don't have to. We can have an open line of silence. That's okay with me."

"I need a favor."

"Anything. What can I do?"

"I can't stay at my apartment any longer. I know we're supposed to do this the legal way, going through title and escrow and..." I trailed off and squeezed my eyes to cut off tears. "But I can't sleep at my place anymore."

"Okay," Glacia said. "Of course. Do you have keys to Nana's—to your house?"

"No."

"They're in the lockbox, which my agent attached to the hose bib off the side of the front porch. The code is... it's my birthday. 0208. Keep the key. It's yours anyway. I'll call my agent tomorrow and have her collect the lockbox."

"You're sure about this?"

"August, it's your house."

"I miss you."

"I miss you, too."

We hung up, and I removed the key from the lock and drove straight to Glacia's house without bothering to step inside of my apartment. Apart from clothes, I had nothing in there that I needed. And I could always buy more clothes.

"You guys know what today is?" Alina asked. Her voice echoed in the empty, high-ceilinged room.

"What's that?" Fred snacked on beef jerky.

"Miette Verdin's birthday. The real Miette Verdin. May 5th. Remember when she first came into the office? She said the changeling had circled May 5th on her calendar."

"That's right," I said.

I grabbed my phone and scrolled to Miette's number. The real Miette. It's quite confusing all around. Miette Verdin was kidnapped as a child, and an imposter (a changeling) replaced her. Well, after Miette Verdin escaped her captor, she returned to her family, throwing a wrench into everyone's lives.

I shot her a quick text. *Happy birthday. Hope all is well. From, the Blue Moon Office.*

After sending the text, I noticed I had a missed call from another previous client. Vincent Dupree. I rolled my eyes, but called him back.

"August Watson," he answered. "How goes it?"

"How are you?" I asked. I avoided his question, not wanting to lie to him, but also not wanting to answer honestly and explain the past week.

"I'm amazing." Vincent said. "So good. Shelly and I are thriving. The sex... better than ever. I don't know what changed, but it's incredible."

What changed was Vincent's wife had died in a hiking accident, and her long-lost identical twin sister had haunted the widower and convinced him to off himself so she could inherit his fortune. When I exposed the truth, Vincent believed that Shannon, the twin, was actually

Shelly, his dead wife. To further complicate his twisted rationalization, Vincent had proposed to Shelly (Shannon). When she accepted, he asked me to be his best man at the wedding.

For some ungodly reason, I had agreed to it.

"Anyway," Vincent said after a few seconds of me not responding, "we set a wedding date. July 4th. Shelly wanted fireworks when we kissed as husband and wife. I was thinking we could have the bachelor party in June. Shelly said no strippers, but, well, I'm telling you no strippers with a wink."

"What?" I asked.

"You're the best man."

"Okay."

"It's the best man's job to plan the bachelor party."

"Alright."

"No strippers, partner. Wink-wink."

"Sure."

"That's it. I'm looking forward to see what you have planned. Oh, and no golf. I really mean that. No wink-wink. I hate golf."

"No golf. No strippers," I said, drawing everyone's attention.

"Wink-wink," Vincent said. "Talk soon."

"Who was that?" Maya asked. She rested her head on Evan's stomach and stared at me.

"Dr. Dupree. He wants me to throw him a bachelor party."

"You are the best man," Fred said. "It's your job. What did he say? No strippers?"

"Wink-wink," I said.

"Are you getting him strippers?" Alina asked. She wrinkled her nose. "Don't be that guy."

"I don't even want to plan his party."

"I'll do it," Maya said. She sat up, suddenly buzzing with excitement. "I'll plan everything, and you can take all the credit."

"Really?" I asked.

"Of course."

"I won't pay you."

"I wouldn't take your money, anyway."

"Okay. Yeah, please. Let's do that."

The doorbell rang. Alina jumped to her feet. "I'll get it." She hurried to the front door.

A handful of seconds later, Alina returned with Adam, Jake, and Rachel.

Maya had promised Adam a twenty-first celebration, and she always kept her promises. Dinner first, then the bars. "Besides," she had said, "it will be a good distraction from everything."

We had lounged around the living room, killing time while waiting for Adam, Rachel, and Jake to arrive. Now that they had, everyone stood, collected their belongings, and made their way to the cars. We needed two designated drivers, so Rachel and I had volunteered. Rachel would drive Jake and Adam. I would escort Maya, Evan, and Fred.

No Daphne. She opted to stay at home and take a long, hot bath to decompress and process the past few days. Also, no Alina, though she asked if she could spend the night at my new house and hang out with everyone after we returned. In the meantime, she would catch up on homework.

As we piled into my Honda and Rachels' Acura (she always one-upped me) and sorted out who called shotgun first, my phone buzzed in my pocket.

An unknown caller showed on my screen.

My heart sank into my groin, and my balls shriveled to hard, hot marbles. An acidic sensation filled my stomach. I didn't want to speak to Quinn. I couldn't. I wouldn't allow him to ruin the night.

If he knew about Adam's celebration, though, about Daphne and Alina staying home alone, and if he meant to interfere, I had to know.

"Hello," I said.

"August, it's Ted," Officer Ted Wilson said.

He and I had gone through the same police academy together, and we had stayed in touch throughout the years. He currently worked for Sacramento Police Department.

"Hey," I said. I walked away from the chaos ensuing around the vehicles.

"The Vampire of Sacramento claimed his fourth victim last night. We've gone back and forth on it as a department, but the higher-ups have come around. I hate to admit this, especially to you because it'll go straight to your already-inflated head, but we're in the dark here. No leads. No suspects. We have nothing beyond dead bodies."

I thought of Patricia, the older woman I had danced with in the dive bar—the vampire's third victim.

"We'll pay you as a consultant," Ted said.

"What?"

"The department, that is. We'll pay you to consult on this investigation. We need outside, expert help. Four people have died. We can't keep allowing him to kill. What do you say? The job is yours to lose."

I glanced over my shoulder at the group. They laughed and bickered, reverberating with energy. I had spent too much time avoiding life, whether through drinking to unconsciousness or exercising or working. I had isolated my family and friends, and I had missed out on so much living.

Cambria had ignited that spark within me—that spark to enjoy the world, to love and to be loved. She had taught me to forgive myself and to let go. After her death, I couldn't allow myself to devolve into a self-absorbed depression again. I could feel sad and angry and lost, but I didn't have to feel sad and angry and lost alone. Cambria showed me that truth, and I meant to act on that newfound knowledge.

I swallowed back my initial response—the knee-jerk reaction that couldn't say no to helping someone in need. I swallowed that and thought of Cambria. "I'm going through it right now," I said. "I need some time for myself—time to recharge, you know? I won't say no, but I can't say yes right now. I need a couple of weeks off."

"You okay?"

"Someone shot me, and someone else stabbed me... and yeah. I'm hurting. When I'm better, I'll call you." The refusal took a lot of effort, but I felt a tremendous sense of relief saying no. "If the job is still there for me when I'm ready, we can discuss my rates."

"People are dying," Ted said. "Two victims in the past week. You know that right?"

Quinn's voice played through my mind. *You will be happy to know.*

Well, Quinn, I was anything but happy to know.

"What do you say, August? You going to help us?"

Maya stood on the car's floorboard, leaned out of the vehicle, beckoned me over. "Let's go! The drinks won't drink themselves. You coming or what?"

I thought of Cambria. Of our first date. She had said something that stuck with me. *Maybe I'm wrong. But I would rather be wrong for loving others than be right for judging those who don't agree with me.*

Maybe I was wrong to reject Ted's offer. Maybe it was right to accept the case and help catch the serial killer. In that moment, with the weight of Cambria's death heavy on my heart, with Quinn plaguing my mind like an infection, I only thought of reconnecting with my family and friends. Not working. Not disappearing. But being present with them.

If that was wrong, well, I deserved to be wrong for a change.

The End

What's Next for August and Friends?

Undead Dread

Sacramento native, August Watson is angry. No, strike that. August in filled with the kind of incandescent rage only the righteous can possess.

Someone killed his girl. Not just any someone, but an enigma of a man called Daniel Quinn. Quinn wants to destroy August and is willing to target everyone in his life to achieve his aim.

Why?

No one knows. Not even August.

Until he can locate the object of his murderous intent, August focuses his fury on another – the so-called Vampire of Sacramento.

Hiding in the shadows, California's latest serial killer is stalking their next victim. It's not August's job to stop them, but he's going to do it anyway.

He needs someone to pound on. Someone he won't feel bad about hurting.

Whatever you do, don't get in his way.

Other books by Alex Gates

Dead Awake

Dorian Miller, a private detective specializing in the supernatural, investigates a blackmail conspiracy involving the daughter of one of Sacramento's elite families who partook in a satanic ritual.

But the simple assignment soon turns un-deadly.

Zombies and golems rise around the city. The corpses of vampires are found slaughtered in a horrific manner. And rumors warn that a Revenant—the spirit of a dead Necromancer summoned back to this world—stands behind all the mayhem.

How much longer can Dorian run from Death before it catc

Books by Steve Higgs

The paranormal? It's all nonsense but proving it might just get them all killed.

When a master vampire starts killing people in his hometown, paranormal investigator, Tempest Michaels, takes it personally ...... and soon a race against time turns into a battle for his life. He doesn't believe in the paranormal but has a steady stream of clients with cases too weird for the police to bother with.

Mostly it's all nonsense, but when a third victim turns up with bite marks in her lifeless throat, can he really dismiss the possibility that this time the monster is real?

Joined by an ex-army buddy, a disillusioned cop, his friends from the pub, his dogs, and his mother (why are there no grandchildren, Tempest), our paranormal investigator is going to stop the murders if it kills him ……

but when his probing draws the creature's attention, his family and friends become the hunted.

Today's tasks:

1.Escape from underground cell

2.Recruit snarky d-bag werewolf to help

3.Invade demon realm and rescue a girl

For wizard detective, Otto Schneider, magic has always kept him out of trouble. Now it's working in reverse …… and he's just started the fight of his life. There's an ancient secret buried in the Earth's past and he just uncovered it.

Magical beings once ruled over us until their betrayed leader made a death curse with his final breath. Banished from the realm of man for over four thousand years, the curse is weakening, and these beings, these ... demons, are coming back to rule the Earth once more.

They are powerful, immortal, and unstoppable, but they don't know everything.They left some of their magic behind and their return has sparked an awakening.

Heroes will rise ...

Free Books and More

https://www.facebook.com/groups/1151907108277718

<u>**More Books By Steve Higgs**</u>

Blue Moon Investigations
Paranormal Nonsense
The Phantom of Barker Mill
Amanda Harper Paranormal Detective
The Klowns of Kent
Dead Pirates of Cawsand
In the Doodoo With Voodoo
The Witches of East Malling
Crop Circles, Cows and Crazy Aliens
Whispers in the Rigging
Bloodlust Blonde – a short story
Paws of the Yeti
Under a Blue Moon – A Paranormal
Detective Origin Story
Night Work
Lord Hale's Monster
The Herne Bay Howlers
Undead Incorporated
The Ghoul of Christmas Past
The Sandman
Jailhouse Golem
Shadow in the Mine
Ghost Writer

Felicity Philips Investigates
To Love and to Perish
Tying the Noose
Aisle Kill Him
A Dress to Die For
Wedding Ceremony Woes

Patricia Fisher Cruise Mysteries
The Missing Sapphire of Zangrabar
The Kidnapped Bride
The Director's Cut
The Couple in Cabin 2124
Doctor Death
Murder on the Dancefloor
Mission for the Maharaja
A Sleuth and her Dachshund in Athens
The Maltese Parrot
No Place Like Home

Patricia Fisher Mystery Adventures
What Sam Knew
Solstice Goat
Recipe for Murder
A Banshee and a Bookshop
Diamonds, Dinner Jackets, and Death
Frozen Vengeance
Mug Shot
The Godmother
Murder is an Artform
Wonderful Weddings and Deadly
Divorces
Dangerous Creatures

Patricia Fisher: Ship's Detective Series
The Ship's Detective
Fitness Can Kill
Death by Pirates
First Dig Two Graves

Albert Smith Culinary Capers
Pork Pie Pandemonium
Bakewell Tart Bludgeoning
Stilton Slaughter
Bedfordshire Clanger Calamity
Death of a Yorkshire Pudding
Cumberland Sausage Shocker
Arbroath Smokie Slaying
Dundee Cake Dispatch
Lancashire Hotpot Peril
Blackpool Rock Bloodshed
Kent Coast Oyster Obliteration
Eton Mess Massacre
Cornish Pasty Conspiracy

Realm of False Gods
Untethered magic
Unleashed Magic
Early Shift
Damaged but Powerful
Demon Bound
Familiar Territory
The Armour of God
Live and Die by Magic
Terrible Secrets

About the Authors

Alex and Steve met online through their mutual love of urban fantasy. Both established writers with their own successful series, they chose to collaborate on a spin-off of Steve's Blue Moon Investigation stories.

They duo hope to meet in person one day when pandemics and other global dramas allow, but one of them will need to cross the Atlantic first. Until then, they will continue to churn out thrilling fantasy tales.

Read on and enjoy.